Jessica Blair grew up in Middlesbrough, trained as a teacher and now lives in Ampleforth. She became a full-time writer in 1977 and has written more than 50 books under various pseudonyms including *The Red Shawl*, *A Distant Harbour*, *Storm Bay*, *The Restless Spirit*, *The Other Side of the River*, *The Seaweed Gatherers*, *Portrait of Charlotte*, *The Locket*, *The Long Way Home*, *Time & Tide*, *Echoes of the Past*, *Secrets of the Sea*, *Yesterday's Dreams*, *Reach for Tomorrow*, *Dangerous Shores*, *Wings of Sorrow* and *Stay With Me*, all published by Piatkus.

The Restless Heart

Jessica Blair

PIATKUS

PIATKUS

First published in Great Britain in 2002 by Piatkus Books
This paperback edition published in 2002 by Piatkus Books
Reprinted 2009 (twice)

A CIP catalogue record for this book
is available from the British Library

ISBN 978-0-7499-3330-2

Printed and bound in Great Britain by
CPI Mackays, Chatham, ME5 8TD

Papers used by Piatkus are natural, renewable and recyclable
products sourced from well-managed forests and certified in
accordance with the rules of the Forest Stewardship Council.

Mixed Sources
Product group from well-managed
forests and other controlled sources
www.fsc.org Cert no. SGS-COC-004081
© 1996 Forest Stewardship Council
FSC

Piatkus
An imprint of
Little, Brown Book Group
100 Victoria Embankment
London EC4Y 0DY

An Hachette UK Company
www.hachette.co.uk

www.piatkus.co.uk

Acknowledgements

My thanks go to Geraldine and Judith for their constructive criticism and to Lynn Curtis for her advice, constant support and brilliant editing, and of course to my publishers for their continued faith in my work

Author's Note

The earlier lives of the Fernley family referred to in this book can be found in

The Red Shawl

and

A Distant Harbour

Chapter One

The early-morning light of an August day in 1812 streamed over Whitby's rooftops and penetrated the bedroom window of Bell House, on the west bank of the River Esk.

Olivia awoke slowly and then, with sleep banished, luxuriated in the soft feather bed which cocooned her in its comfort. She stretched, the movement sensuous, as she recalled her flirtations yesterday during a friend's party at Rigg Hall on the cliffs between her home town of Whitby and Robin Hood's Bay.

She smiled to herself, revelling in the thought of her reputation among the younger Whitby set. She was friendly with them all but knew that her many admirers had been warned of dire consequences should they fall completely under the spell of Olivia Coulson. Enjoying her company, they ignored these warnings and responded to her vivacious personality. She exuded charm all the more when she saw, and was amused by, the glares of hostility from other young women as her many beaux were drawn under her spell.

Nevertheless when guest lists were compiled her name always appeared for she brought life to any party. She would grace it with the finest clothes suitable for the occasion. Her manners would be impeccable, thanks to her upbringing by a firm mother, a tolerant father, and the indulgent lead of her two elder brothers. Many would describe her as pretty; others would cast a slight doubt on that assessment, but they would be looking at only one aspect of her features. Chin just a little too firm maybe, cheekbones a shade too high or mouth a bit too wide, but even her detractors had to admit that her lips were exquisite. When parted, in that engaging smile which was all Olivia's, they revealed a perfect row of dazzling white teeth. Perhaps her best feature, the one that gave her the greatest claim to beauty, was a pair of large wide-set eyes, hazel with just a touch of green.

She slid from the bed and stood at the window. From here she could see the shipbuilding yard of Coulson and Sons. It had been founded by her great-grandfather in 1725, taken over by her grandfather in turn and inherited by her father twenty-five years ago. Expansion had been made on his ancestors' solid foundation and now her father was the leading shipbuilder in Whitby. Her grandfather had built the house in which she now lived, choosing a position close to and overlooking the proud family achievement.

Already she could hear the ring of hammers as a new day in the life of this thriving Yorkshire port dawned. Her gaze passed over the glistening waters of the river which ran between surrounding cliffs to meet the sea beyond the piers built to protect the estuary from the ravages of the North Sea when it was whipped into anger by ferocious winds. Beyond, on the east bank, houses climbed the cliff, seeming to stand one on top of the other as if reaching for light and air while denying that right to those below.

But Olivia's thoughts were of other things. She was tired of the life she led: the parties, the picnics, the endless At Homes enlivened by the occasional ball. True, she always attracted the young men's attention, and flirtation was second nature to her now, but the suitors she met were almost interchangeable and none of them had the power to force her to relinquish her single state.

Was there no special man out there who could give her the sort of future she wanted? Her brothers were set for life through their participation in the family business but she, being a girl, was excluded from active participation. Her future could only be marriage, and she certainly was not going to marry beneath her.

She sighed, turned from the window and dressed for breakfast.

'Good morning, Mother. Good morning, Father,' she said with her usual brightness when she came into the dining-room.

'Good morning, my dear. Did you sleep well? No effects from the party?' asked her mother, Lavinia.

'None,' returned Olivia, and kissed her parents.

Edward Coulson beamed at his daughter 'Good morning to you.' He pressed her hand with affection, never ceasing to wonder how every morning she could be so bright. Olivia had brought a new dimension to breakfast-time ever since her two brothers had married. When they were at home that meal more often than not had turned into a discussion about the business to be transacted that day, but since their marriages commercial talk had disappeared from breakfast. Now Edward appreciated all the more the company of his wife and the daughter who could twist him round her little finger. He knew it but enjoyed it.

Her father and mother had already started their meal so Olivia went to the sideboard to make her choice of bacon and scrambled egg along with some bread freshly baked that morning by Mrs Wilson, the cook who had been with the family for ten years.

As she returned to her place at table there was a gentle tap on the door. It opened and Sommers, the head butler, who had served the tolerant and thoughtful family as long as Mrs Wilson, came into the room. He placed four envelopes on the table beside his employer.

'Some mail, sir. The coach was late in yesterday. Wheel trouble, I'm told.'

'Thank you, Sommers. Not an accident, I hope?'

'No, sir.' The butler inclined his head as he stepped back a pace. In those few moments his eyes had swept across the

3

table, checking that everything was in order. If it wasn't there would be the devil to pay as he meted out chastisement to his underlings, male and female.

Edward glanced quickly at the writing on the envelopes and tossed three of them back on the table, keeping the fourth in his hand.

'Only one of real interest, my dear?' asked Lavinia from the opposite end of the long table.

He gave a little smile. 'Ah, this one may well interest you both if it is what I think it is.' He picked up the paper-knife which was always placed with his breakfast cutlery in case any mail had come into Whitby on the previous evening's coach.

Olivia looked at him with undisguised curiosity. Her father's mail was generally connected to his business, but, judging by the twinkle in his eyes this was something different.

He slit the envelope open, laid down the paper-knife with deliberate precision and then extracted a card from the envelope. His perusal of it caused a broad smile to appear on his face. 'Thought so,' he said in satisfaction.

'Well?' Lavinia enquired sharply.

He glanced up to see his wife and daughter, their breakfast in abeyance, eyes fixed on him, awaiting with keen anticipation what he was about to say.

Without preamble he read: '"Mr and Mrs Richard Chilton-Brookes request the pleasure of Mr and Mrs Edward Coulson and their daughter for the weekend at Cropton Hall to celebrate the twenty-first birthday of their son George from 5 p.m. 20th August to 11 a.m. 23rd August".'

'Well, I never.' His wife was almost overcome by surprise.

'You'll accept, won't you? You must!' cried Olivia, eyes wide with the thought of a weekend spent amongst the county's well-to-do. New faces, new people her own age ... maybe this invitation was an omen, a step towards fulfilling those dreams which had filled her mind this morning. Like her mother she had never met the Chilton-

4

Brookes but knew her father had done business with the owner of the Cropton Estate.

'Of course,' replied her father, even those two words full of satisfaction and pride.

He knew his father and grandfather would have been proud of the hard work, determination and shrewd judgement which had enabled him to expand the firm and led to this invitation to mix with Yorkshire's landed gentry.

Coulson-built ships quartered the world: merchantmen trading with the Continent, colliers running coal from Newcastle to London, convict ships bound for Australia, transports taking troops to Canada, whalers for the expeditions to the Arctic. Wherever a ship was needed, there would be a Coulson ship. The firm had a reputation for solid construction, a workmanlike approach, and for supplementing Baltic wood with finest English oak. Edward had an eye for the best timber, reliable and tough, which would stand the rigours of any sea. Though he had trained his sons in what to look for, he always carried out this side of the business himself.

Three years ago he had been looking for a new source. This took him beyond the high moors which closed in on the town, creating a sense of isolation in Whitby minds and turning most people's eyes to the sea in the hunt for prosperity.

Early one day in April he had viewed the weather with a critical and assessing eye, honed by experience, and decided to set out to look for oak. He told Sommers to send someone to see that his horse, which he kept stabled at the White Horse hostelry and coaching house, be ready for him in half an hour and he ordered some sustenance from the kitchen to tide him through his ride. After fond farewells to his wife and daughter, telling them he might be away for three or four days, Edward rode out of Whitby.

The rough and lonely track he chose was mainly used by pedlars and carriers. It crossed the wild moorland landscape to Pickering on the southern edge, overlooking the fertile vale that gave the small market town its livelihood.

He guided his horse through the bustle of the town in late afternoon as trading for the day was drawing to a close. Sharp-tongued farmers drove the sheep and cows they had purchased out of their pens. Dogs snapped at the animals' hooves. Drovers yelled abuse when their herds did not obey. Amid the hustle and bustle urchins raced and housewives scurried to find last-minute bargains before hastening home.

Edward rode down the main street and espying the Black Bull soon verified that he could have a room there. Once his horse had been taken care of he set about putting his initial acquaintance with the landlord on to a more friendly footing.

Pleased with this gentleman's trade, and with having someone different from his usual Pickering customers to talk to, the landlord was forthcoming with information about the area.

Accordingly the next morning, after a breakfast which had tested even his hearty appetite, Edward was riding at a gentle pace towards the village of Cropton, about four miles away. He relaxed in the saddle, enjoying the feel of the sunshine which was unmarred by a few trails of high thin cloud. The day was calm, the weather settled, just as he had predicted in his own mind when he had viewed the sky in Whitby only yesterday morning. It seemed much longer ago and, as Edward pondered the reason, he came to the conclusion that it was because this was the first time in over a year that he had escaped Whitby and work. Not that he did not like his work, he loved it, but now, away from it, he recognised he had needed this change to get away even if only for a few days. He would enjoy them, and central to that enjoyment would be his quest for timber.

Following the landlord's directions he found himself in gently rolling countryside with well-tended fields stretching northwards before rising to meet the moorland. Cattle and

6

sheep grazed unhindered but Edward's eyes gave them only a passing glance for they were drawn to the woods he could see in the distance.

Nearing them he drew rein, soothing his horse with a gentle pat and low voice. The sight of the fine trees had drained any tension that was left from his body and he sat, utterly relaxed, letting his eyes wander over them. Larch, elm, chestnut, sycamore ... but not what he had hoped he would see. With a little grimace of disappointment, he sent his horse along the grassy lane. Half a mile further on it swung around the edge of the wood. Unprepared for what he saw, Edward jerked his mount to a halt and gasped at the sight of a fine stand of oaks which occupied the distant border of the adjacent field. Excited, he quickly looked along the hedge for a gateway. Seeing it, he put his horse to it, leaned from the saddle and pushed it open. Once inside the field he manoeuvred the animal so he could secure the gate again then galloped towards the oaks.

Edward swung from the saddle and in a matter of moments was among the trees, leaving his horse to champ contentedly at the grass. Edward was in a fever of excitement. These were some of the finest oaks he had ever seen, but he did not see them purely as majestic trees. Instead he saw strong timbers for the ships he would build, timbers which would sing a song in harmony with the sea.

He must have them. He must! He hurried back to his horse and within a few minutes was in Cropton enquiring as to whose land he had seen the oaks on and where he could find the owner.

The directions he received took him to a fine wrought-iron gateway set in a long stone wall which, because he could not see its ends, he assumed either formed the boundary for the whole estate or enclosed land private to Cropton Hall, the name carved on the stone gatepost.

The front door of the gatehouse stood open and this led Edward to believe there must be someone inside. He ran his riding crop across the iron gate to attract attention. His action was effective for in a matter of moments a buxom woman with a rosy complexion appeared in the doorway. She was plainly dressed in brown with a white collar at her neck. Her mobcap held her hair in check, though a few wisps revealed that it was dark brown. Her eyes were sharp, demanding identification from the stranger who had disturbed her at her cleaning.

'Good day, sir. What might you be wanting?'

'Mr Chilton-Brookes, if he is at home, and if you'll be kind enough to let me through this gate?'

Mr Chilton-Brookes usually informed her whenever he was expecting visitors. The admission of strangers he left to her judgement, and this rider was definitely a stranger. However she had summed him up quickly, a practice she had developed to a fine art over the ten years she had been gatekeeper while her husband worked on the estate. This visitor seemed gentlemanlike enough. His soft voice, round face and ruddy cheeks indicated a good-natured character, and there was no impatience or hostility in his eyes. He sat his horse well and held it gently under control.

'Certainly, sir,' she said. 'Just follow the drive for about half a mile or so and you'll come to the house.'

'Thank you kindly,' said Edward as he passed through the gate held open by the woman.

He kept his horse to a walking pace, enjoying the sight of the rhododendrons about him and imagining them in their full glory in about a month's time. They were backed on both sides of the track by thickets of firs and fringed by well-manicured lawns stretching almost to the house itself. The carriageway curved to the front of an elegant building and then swung back on itself in a large circle. The centre of the circle held a rose bed whose flowers, when in full bloom, would make a perfect adornment to the house.

The building had a solid, well-tended appearance. The windows in its four bays sparkled in the sunlight. The pots of flowers on the balustrade of an elegant terrace, running the full width of the house, had clearly been tended assiduously.

Several chairs arranged there were unoccupied except for one close to the front door. Here, sitting with a rug over his knees, was a man of medium build. His hair was grey and his gaunt features seemed to indicate that he had not been well. At the sound of the horse's hooves he sat up but when he saw a stranger leaned back again and watched him approach.

Edward eased his horse to a halt in front of the man. 'Good day, sir,' he called brightly. 'Might I be addressing Mr Richard Chilton-Brookes?'

He nodded. 'Aye, you are that, but you have the advantage of me.'

'Edward Coulson. May I step down and discuss some business with you?'

'Business? What sort of business brings you seeking me?' Chilton-Brookes was openly curious.

'Something which I believe will be to our mutual advantage,' returned Edward. He swung from the saddle and came up the four steps on to the terrace beneath the portico with its pediment supported by six classical columns. He held out his hand. Richard Chilton-Brookes took it and the two men eyed each other for a moment before he indicated a chair next to his. Edward sat down.

'Well?'

'I am a shipbuilder in Whitby,' Edward began.

Chilton-Brookes raised an eyebrow. 'So what brings you riding in the country?'

'Timber, sir, timber. I am looking for the best English oak. Can't beat it for strengthening my ships.'

From Edward's delivery of these words it was plain that he had a passionate love for wood and that shipbuilding was his life. Chilton-Brookes gave a small smile. 'And you've seen my oaks and want to know if I'll sell?'

'You come right to the heart of the matter, sir. I like a man who does not beat about the bush, so I'll do the same. Is there any point in our talking further? If not I'll ride away and leave you in peace.'

9

The landowner pursed his lips thoughtfully. He was interested but did not wish to appear too keen. Allow the Whitby man to see that and he might place himself at a disadvantage in getting the best price. 'I would have to know which trees have caught your eye. I presume you have assessed some on your way here?'

'I have, sir. And if I had not liked what I saw I would not be here now.'

'Very well. Give me a few moments to change and I will ride with you.' He rose from his chair as he was speaking.

'Are you sure?' There was concern in Edward's voice.

Richard gave a grunt. 'You mean, am I fit enough to do so? I've been mollycoddled too long. It'll be a relief to be back in the saddle and out in the countryside. My wife's away for the morning so she won't know. I'll get my son George to come with us too. He's but eighteen, but as heir to the estate should be kept informed. Stir their interest when they are young and keep it is what I say.'

Edward nodded. 'I look forward to meeting him.' He had started to move from his chair.

'Sit there until we are ready. I'll tell Bates to bring you a drink. Sack?'

'Thank you. That is most hospitable of you.'

Edward relaxed with his drink and viewed his immediate surroundings. There was clearly money here. It was a house of grand proportions and, if the outside was anything to go by, well-maintained, as were the immediate grounds. All this, he was sure, reflected a well-run estate, a fine inheritance for the young man he was about to meet.

When father and son appeared, Edward stood up and greeted the younger man whose handshake was firm and eager.

'I am pleased to meet you, sir,' said George Chilton-Brookes with the genuine pleasure of one who liked to meet people and had the ability to make strangers feel comfortable.

'And I you,' returned Edward. In this young man he sensed an assurance beyond his years, but it was an assurance

which was kept under strict control and not allowed to dominate others. He liked the open, handsome face, the eyes that
were bright yet had an attractively diffident expression which
he calculated hid a keen awareness of everything and everybody around him. His slim build revealed by well-fitting
clothes, George was slightly taller than his father. His dark
brown hair was neatly cut and brushed back around his ears.
His chin was firm but not over-prominent and was finely
proportioned to the rest of his face.

'You are interested in timber, sir?' he enquired.

'Aye,' replied Edward, and went on to explain about his
shipbuilding, making sure that these two men appreciated
they were dealing with the owner of the most prominent
yard in Whitby.

As they were speaking a groom appeared from around
the side of the house, leading two horses.

'Shall we go?' suggested Richard.

'Father, should you?' George raised his concern again,
just as he had when his father had first told him about their
visitor and what he proposed to do.

Richard brushed aside his son's query with a dismissive
wave.

As they rode away from the house, Edward reflected on
the information that no one had previously approached them
for timber. If he got them interested today and negotiated
favourable terms he might gain exclusive rights to timber
from the Cropton Estate.

As they moved across the countryside, viewing more
stands of trees than he had seen on his earlier ride, he
realised that George had been well schooled by his father.
His knowledge of trees and timber surprised even Edward
who considered himself something of an expert. He felt
renewed admiration for the young man, not only for his
knowledge but his modest demeanour. He never pushed
himself forward as the person with whom the visitor should
deal but clearly respected his father's authority. Some
people would say George was shy but Edward soon realised

that this impression was wrong. He was simply a young man who knew his place before his elders. That attitude influenced his whole approach to life. It was purely respect for others that made him seem reserved.

On returning to the Hall they rode straight into the stable yard. The sound of hooves brought the groom hurrying from the tack room followed by two young under-grooms.

'See to Mr Coulson's mount as well,' Richard ordered. 'He'll be staying for a meal and won't need the animal until late-afternoon.'

'That's very civil of you,' said Edward, 'but I can't impose.'

'Nonsense.' Richard dismissed his objection with a wave of his hand. 'You must be hungry and we cannot see you leave before you have had some sustenance. Besides, we have an agreement to sort out.' He had started to lead the way to a side door.

'You are interested in selling then?' Edward put the question with eager anticipation.

Richard cast a glance towards his son. 'We are, aren't we, George?'

'I think it would be a good idea. It would enable us to thin various stands before Nature intervenes for us, and we have continued the planting programme the previous owners instigated so there will always be new timber available.'

When Edward met Esther, Richard's wife, he could see from whom George had inherited his good looks, for she still retained the prettiness of her early-twenties, though she was almost double that age, and exuded a charm which was captivating.

Out of deference to her presence, the sale of timber was not discussed during the meal but once that was over, knowing there were business matters to be taken care of, Esther left the men. She told Edward she hoped he would have a pleasant ride and expressed the wish that if ever he was near Cropton he would call on them again.

'If our talk is successful, my dear, I am sure Mr Coulson will visit us soon,' said her husband.

'Then I look forward to seeing you, Mr Coulson.'

'And it will be my pleasure too, ma'am.'

The next hour was spent in discussion and negotiation until a satisfactory agreement had been struck. Edward was pleased to secure three-quarters of the trees he had picked out at a price which brought smiles and amicable handshakes from everyone. Responsibility for felling was assumed by the Chilton-Brookes, Edward being accountable for the cost of transporting the timber to Whitby, but as father and son knew the best local hauliers for such work Edward was pleased when George said he would organise the hiring of teams.

From that day a friendship had grown between Edward and the Chilton-Brookes. Though never close it was always amicable and Edward enjoyed his visits to negotiate for more timber at felling time. Now, three years later, the friendship had taken a step forward with this invitation to him and his family to join in the celebrations for George's twenty-first birthday.

'Well, there you are, something to look forward to,' said Edward, beaming at his wife and daughter.

'Oh, my goodness,' cried Lavinia. 'Cropton Hall no less.'

'Aye, lass, no less.'

'You've talked about your business with the Chilton-Brookes, but I didn't know you were on these terms,' said Lavinia. She herself had come from a well-to-do Whitby family whose interests had expanded, three generations ago, from alum production to ship owning, the latter taking precedence in the last fifteen years. It was through their common connection to ships that Edward had met Lavinia, and it had been love at first sight for him. From that moment he had been determined to wed her, and had painstakingly won her devotion and love. She had become a great support to him and was proud of his achievements.

13

Though they moved freely in Whitby society she had never imagined them being on intimate terms with the landed gentry of Yorkshire. But now – well, if this was something Edward wanted she would be delighted to play her part.

'I've cultivated them carefully,' replied Edward. 'Never in their pocket and they never in mine. We have developed a very friendly business relationship and a real understanding of each other. Richard saw that I knew timber and that pleased him. You may remember, he came to Whitby for a day. You and Olivia were away in Scarborough for the week so you didn't meet him. I wanted him to see how the timber from his estate was being used, and that delighted him. He saw I cared for it and used it in the best possible way for the most important parts of the ship. I showed him—'

'Father!' Olivia interrupted, knowing that if she didn't they would be subjected to a eulogy about the business that they had heard many times. 'Tell us something about the family and Cropton Hall, so that we know what to expect?'

'Richard, Esther and their son George are likeable, unassuming gentlefolk.'

'He's an only child?' queried Lavinia.

Her husband nodded. 'Aye. Seems Esther was told she shouldn't have any more after George was born.'

'I suppose they inherited from Mr Chilton-Brookes's father?' said Olivia.

'No, that wasn't the case. The previous owner, known as Squire Hardy, was a bit of a stickler – kept his workers and tenants firmly in their place, I hear. "I'm right, you shouldn't have an opinion, keep your place and do as you're told," was his attitude.'

'He had no family?' queried Lavinia.

'He had a son but he was killed in a fall from the cliffs not far from Rigg House, so that afterwards there was a search for his nearest living relative, a very distant connection, and that was Richard. Apparently the Chilton-Brookes were a branch of the family who had once owned considerable property in Lincolnshire, but an ancestor who was a

14

bad manager and a gambler to boot lost practically every-thing. The family moved to Hull, seeking work, and it was there that the gambler's descendant, Richard himself, was found working as a shipping clerk.'

'So they had a big surprise?' commented Olivia.

'Oh, aye, but there must have been hereditary traits of refinement and business acumen that served them well, and they were fortunate to find a competent manager already running the estate for them.'

'And Richard's wife?' prompted Lavinia, who wanted to know what to expect from the lady who would be their hostess.

'Charming,' replied Edward. 'Gentle but not at all over-powered by her menfolk. In fact, I would say she subtly organises their lives to a great extent, though of course not on the business side. She is wise enough not to invade that territory. You'll like her, I'm sure.'

'And the young man whose birthday we are celebrating?'

Olivia had been wanting to ask this question but had not wanted to put her interest and curiosity to the fore. She was glad her mother had made the enquiry.

'Not bad-looking. A quiet, retiring sort of man, but very competent where the estate is concerned.'

Olivia was exasperated. She could have stamped her foot in annoyance. She would have liked much more detail than that. Here was someone new. Someone outside her usual circle of friends. He might be just the person to step into her life and lift it out of the doldrums into which it was drifting.

'An only child,' Lavinia recalled. 'So is he spoilt?'

'Not at all,' replied Edward. 'I would say his parents have been careful not to do that. He has charm in a quiet way yet is very alert and attentive.'

'He'll be rich?' The words came automatically with Olivia's flying thoughts. She hadn't meant to speak them aloud but they were out, accompanying the memory of the advice her grandmother always used to give her: 'Marry for love, lass, but love where there's money.'

'What a question to ask!' admonished her mother with a look of disapproval.

'Oh, aye, he'll be rich. He'll inherit a vast estate,' replied her father.

Olivia's mind seized on these two facts. Was it fate that had brought her this invitation? She hoped her father would expand his description of this young man but he didn't and before she could discreetly prompt him, said, 'We should have an enjoyable time, but I hope you both understand that our visit is primarily to advance my prospects of further business with Richard Chilton-Brookes and his son. So don't go getting your hopes up, Olivia.'

Chapter Two

'Wrap up well,' warned Edward when Lavinia and Olivia left the breakfast table. 'There'll be a chill wind across the moors.'

He was proved to be right. Though the sky was cloud-covered without the threat of rain, the moderate wind had a sharp chill to it which made cheeks glow and caught the breath.

Olivia did not mind. As the weeks had passed and the day of their departure for Cropton Hall drew nearer her excitement had heightened. Outwardly adopting a calm atti-tude, her real feelings of delighted anticipation only surfaced in the privacy of her room. What should she wear? She had changed her mind time and time again as she snatched up her choice of the moment, held it against herself and viewed it with critical appraisal in the full-length mirror.

Now her choices were stored in the bags securely fastened to the carriage which Edward kept at the White Horse in Church Street, along with a sturdy horse. He had arranged for a coachman to drive them to Cropton and to return for them the following Monday. Once his passengers were comfortably seated inside the carriage, the coachman cracked his whip above the horse and the animal responded. The carriage lurched until the horse had tested the strain and settled into a steady stride.

The climb out of Whitby was slow but once they had reached the moorland heights the going was easier for most of the way. Nevertheless a sharp wind penetrated the shelter of the carriage and mother and daughter snuggled down into their coats. Their spirits were high, though, and Edward was pleased to hear them keep up a constant flow of chatter which reflected their expectations of an enjoyable weekend.

Reaching the main gate to Cropton Hall, Edward leaned out and called a cheerful 'Good day' to the gatekeeper who raised her hand in recognition as the carriage moved through the gateway.

Olivia strained to catch her first glimpse of the house and was not disappointed after the description her father had given them. In fact the Hall surpassed what she had imagined. This was indeed a captivating building, not only architecturally but in the atmosphere it exuded. It was a friendly house, enveloping them immediately in a warm welcome. Olivia knew that no such feeling could come about unless it was nurtured by the occupants. She just knew this was going to be a successful visit.

Mr and Mrs Chilton-Brookes and their son were on the terrace to greet them. Three maids and two manservants hovered in the background. Word of the approaching carriage had also reached the grooms, two of whom were ready to hold and soothe the horse.

Greetings were exchanged and introductions made in the friendliest of terms.

Olivia liked Esther Chilton-Brookes from the moment when, after being addressed as 'Ma'am' by her young visitor, she whispered with a engaging smile, 'No more formalities, my dear.'

But it was George who held her attention when he said, 'Welcome to Cropton Hall, Miss Olivia. Your presence will brighten my party.' The compliment was delivered in a soft voice which sent shivers down her spine.

'You are too kind, sir,' she replied with a modest inclination of her head.

'Please, Miss Coulson, just plain George.'

'And I'm Olivia,' she returned.

'Splendid,' cried Richard. 'I hope you will all enjoy the weekend. Now, come in, come in.'

He stood to one side as his wife accompanied Lavinia into the house, then followed with Edward.

George stepped over to Olivia and held out his arm. 'May I?' He smiled as he made the request, one which he hoped would break down any barriers of formality that were left.

'Thank you,' she replied quietly. Taking his arm, she walked into the house.

Olivia caught a glimpse of the manservants disappearing up the graceful curve of the staircase with the Coulsons' luggage. The hall with its marble floor was of medium size but well-proportioned, not so big as to intimidate yet not small enough to be claustrophobic. Two gilded console tables set against the walls with a pair of straight-backed chairs framing each of them was all the furniture that was needed. More would have distracted the eye from the delicate wrought iron of the curving banister.

The maids had followed them in and closed the doors, the window-like construction of which added more light to that streaming in at the large windows to either side.

Esther had stopped in the centre of the hall and turned back to the maids standing by the door. 'Rose, will you see that Mrs Coulson is settled comfortably?' She turned to Edward next. 'John will be there already with your luggage. He will see to your needs.'

The maid addressed as Rose came forward.

Esther called to the other, 'Jane, look after Miss Olivia.'

'Yes, ma'am.'

'When you have settled in and freshened up, please come down to the drawing-room for a cup of tea and to meet some of the other guests.'

The Coulsons made their thanks and followed the maids up the stairs.

Olivia followed Jane along the landing overlooking the hall. The girl opened a door and stood to one side while Olivia entered the room. She almost gasped but controlled her immediate reaction for fear of creating the impression that she was not used to such elegance. She was, if not on such a grand scale. This room was almost twice the size of hers at home. The bed was enormous and looked as if it would be comfortable. A dressing table was placed to the right of the window so that the natural light would fall on it from the left. Its three mirrors would enable her to view herself from every angle. The table was laid with trinket box, hand mirror, brush and comb, all ornamented with the most exquisite pattern in mother-of-pearl. A wardrobe in satinwood, to match the rest of the furniture in the room, stood against one wall. A wing easy chair was positioned to give a view from the second window and there were a pair of small tables, one on either side of the bed.

'You'll find water in the ewer, miss,' said Jane, indicating a marble-topped stand with basin and ewer and pristine white towels.

'Thank you, Jane.' Olivia started to slip her cloak from her shoulders.

The maid stepped forward to take it. Olivia unfastened her bonnet, handed it to Jane and then slid her fingers through her hair, thankful to be free of the constraint.

'Would you like me to unpack your bag, miss?'

'Please.'

Jane went about the task quickly, using the drawers in the chest first, while Olivia poured some water into the ewer and slipped out of her dress. Jane was quickly beside her to take it from her and then returned her attention to the bag. She was particularly careful as she took the dresses over to the wardrobe.

'Have you worked here long?' Olivia asked as she soaped her hands.

'Five years, miss.'

'So you must like it here?'

'Oh, yes, miss. Mr and Mrs Chilton-Brookes are kind, and everybody in the district likes Mr George.'

Olivia would have liked to have heard more but when Jane asked her which dress she wanted to wear the subject of George was abandoned.

'Would you like my help?'

'No, it's all right, Jane. Thank you for what you have done.' Olivia wanted a few minutes alone to marshal her thoughts.

'If you want me at any time, miss, ring that bell.' The girl indicated the pull beside the bed.

'Thank you.'

As the door closed behind her, Olivia crossed the room to the window. In a pensive mood, she looked out but was merely aware of the generality of the landscape, not its details.

Thoughts of George occupied her mind. Was she disappointed? Had she been over-zealous in her imagining of the young man she would meet? Had she painted an illusory picture of a handsome, outgoing young beau whose attraction would be irresistible from the moment she saw him; who would mark his authority by sweeping her off her feet, her knight in shining armour to banish forever the boredom which threatened her in Whitby. There, the too-familiar was threatening to swamp her. She could flirt outrageously and enjoy it, but the young men who encouraged her and enjoyed her company were shallow. There was no depth to them, no real spirit. They would drift into the pattern preordained for them, marry, settle down with wives expected to conform in every particular.

Olivia sighed. George did not give the impression of someone who would sweep her off her feet as she had imagined he might, but there was nevertheless something attractive about him and he was the heir to a large estate and all the wealth that went with it. She had seen more handsome young men but never any with such striking features, especially his eyes. They were pools of sapphire

21

blue, lazy, veiled in mystery. This sort of sensation was new to Olivia and she felt an intense desire to uncover that mystery.

She recalled her grandmother's advice – well, she could love where there was money. She was as free as the wind to marry where she chose. She was sure she could win George's love and become mistress of Cropton Hall.

She started. The landscape swam into focus and details suddenly became clearer to her.

She was looking out across a beautifully cut lawn at the side of the house. It was bordered by a low stone balustrade beyond which the land fell away to a small valley. The rise on the far side was covered in trees. The hill gave way again to fields where cattle grazed, and further still she could glimpse the edge of moorland. And this was only a small portion of the estate she was sure she could grow to love, just as she would grow to love its next master.

She dressed quickly, checked her appearance in the mirror and then, satisfied, went out on to the landing. She looked over the banister into the hall. There was no one there except a maid standing at the bottom of the staircase, but voices drifted through from the drawing-room by the open door.

Her footsteps on the stairs drew the attention of the maid who said, 'They are all in the drawing-room, miss.'

Olivia's fine silk gown rustled as she crossed the floor. She pushed the door open and was met by a hubbub of conversation.

There were five groups of people inside in the process of getting to know each other over a cup of tea. One side of the room was occupied by a long table behind which two maids stood ready to serve tea and offer cakes.

The movement of the door attracted Mrs Chilton-Brookes's attention. She broke off her conversation with two people who were strangers to Olivia and came to greet her.

'Hello, my dear, do come and have a cup of tea. I'm sure you will be ready for one after your journey?'

22

'Thank you. That would be most welcome.'

'And then meet our friends,' Esther added as she escorted Olivia to the table.

Olivia had caught sight of George talking to two young ladies beside an ornate fireplace when she entered the room. She felt a little tightening in her stomach. Jealousy? It couldn't be. She chided herself for such an emotion. And yet ...

'You are quite comfortable in your room, I hope?'

Olivia started, only half aware of Esther's polite enquiry.

'Oh, yes. Yes, thank you,' she stuttered, and was thankful when the maid handed her a cup of tea.

'Mother, you go back to Mr and Mrs Jepson, I'll introduce Olivia to everyone.' George spoke softly but here was an offer that couldn't be refused.

'Oh, would you? I was just discussing village affairs and would like to resume while the facts are clear in our minds.' Esther glanced at Olivia. 'I'm sure you won't mind?'

Olivia, whose heart had fluttered when George approached them, gathered her composure quickly and said, 'Of course not.'

She glanced at him and met a smile which was meant to put her at her ease. She took a sip of her tea.

'I suggest I tell you who's who from here then you'll have some idea before I take you round the room. The two people you see talking to your mother and father are Mr and Mrs Sleightholme. They give their name to, or get it from, I have never fathomed which, a very secluded dale in the direction of Helmsley. You know Helmsley?'

'No, but I have heard of it and have a rough idea where it is.'

'They are an extremely pleasant couple, about the same age as my parents. The girl on the left, to whom I was talking when you came in, is their daughter Imelda. The other girl is Honor Jepson, daughter of the two people to whom my mother is presently talking. They have land on the opposite side of Cropton. The two families are longstanding friends

23

which is why they are staying here rather than going home. The rest of the guests have further to travel so naturally they are staying too.'

'It's wonderful that you can accommodate them all.'

'It's a big house.' George smiled, and continued his explanations. 'The four young people you see by the window are all cousins of mine: Robert and Cecilia Metcalfe, and Ursula and Timothy Dugdale. Their mothers and mine are sisters.'

'No other Chilton-Brookes, or are they yet to come?'

'We are the only Chilton-Brookes. At present I am the last of the line.' Before she could comment he went on, 'Their parents are with my father.' He nodded in the direction of the group. 'And that leaves only the four people you see together by the other window. They are one family, Mr and Mrs Campion and their son Archie and daughter Sabina. They come from the Wolds, near Beverley. We were very good friends when we lived in Hull. And there you have it. Now, when you have finished your tea, I'll take you round the room and we'll end up with Honor and Imelda. I was about to tell them of the arrangements for the weekend so you may as well hear them too.'

Though she felt a little nervous at having to meet so many strangers, Olivia's apprehension soon disappeared with the confidence that George engendered in her. His manner was quiet and reassuring, and his form of introduction such that no one felt more important than any other. He knew just what to say, gauged what would be of general interest, and Olivia was surprised by what he already knew of her and her family. He must have gleaned his knowledge during her father's visits to buy timber. As they moved around the room she was struck by the quiet composure with which he went about everything.

She took her cue from him, adopting an air of reserve which she knew would not offend and might even attract. She was pleasant, with a ready reply or comment, but most of all she captivated with her smile and projection of a warm personality.

24

'And now, last but by no means least, Imelda Sleightholme and Honor Jepson. Imelda, Honor, it is my pleasure to introduce Olivia Coulson from Whitby.'

Pleasantries were passed between the three girls. Olivia was well aware that she was being assessed by two people who were already friends of George's and probably had been from childhood.

'I told Olivia I was about to enlighten you on my birthday celebrations so let me tell you all now. This evening we will sit down to a feast. Only Olivia does not know what that means.' He gave a knowing little smile at Imelda and Honor. They returned it with a chuckle. 'Oh don't worry, Olivia, all it means is that Mrs Dawson, our cook, loves these occasions and excels herself. I hope you have a gargantuan appetite?'

'I'm sure I will enjoy Mrs Dawson's skills and will do my best to eat my share so that she will not be offended.'

'It will be a leisurely meal, in fact we may not rise from the table until near bedtime, unless the gentlemen are going to partake of port and cigars,' explained Honor, doing her utmost to make it plain that she had participated previously in such meals at Cropton Hall.

'And I can verify that,' put in Imelda, not to be outdone by her friend. 'I know you will enjoy it – I always do.'

'That takes care of this evening,' George went on, his voice quiet but decisive enough to turn the flow of the conversation. 'There is nothing organised for the morning so feel free to do whatever you want – stroll around the gardens, engage in friendly conversation, play croquet on the lawn or whatever you will. There will be a buffet lunch served outside if the weather is fine, and there are signs that we are in a settled spell. Those who wish to can attend a cricket match on the village green, starting at two. You can spend a lazy day there watching what promises to be a worthwhile contest.'

'Who's playing?' asked Imelda.

'You know I play for the village team and that my father

has helped them to create and maintain a good pitch? Well, the club committee wanted to do something in return and had the idea of organising a match to celebrate my birthday. They've invited members of several local teams to make up a side to play the village.' He turned his eyes on Olivia. 'Do you know cricket?'

'I'm afraid not,' she replied.

'Then I will have to explain it to you.'

'I will look forward to learning something new,' she replied demurely.

'And after the game?' prompted Honor, with a sidelong glance of irritation at Olivia.

'I believe that celebrations will go on until dark. A big tent has been up in the next field and the whole village has been invited to an evening of entertainment. On Sunday there is naturally a church service in the village for those who wish to go, the afternoon to be spent doing whatever you want. In the evening a continuous buffet at which friends from around about will join us. And there will be dancing in the great chamber.'

'It all sounds very exciting,' commented Olivia, allowing her true feelings to show for a moment. This was more like it! How would she ever settle back into life in Whitby after a weekend such as this one promised to be?

Chapter Three

Olivia stirred. She felt comfortable and relaxed in the drowsy haze of slow awakening. The light of a new day alerted her to her unfamiliar surroundings and brought recollections of the pleasant time she had spent the previous evening.

As George had prophesied Mrs Dawson had seized her chance to show off her culinary skills and had excelled herself. As dishes appeared one after the other the guests had admired their presentation and lingered over every mouthful.

The dining-room, panelled in light oak, was lit by oil lamps placed in metal brackets around the walls, and by two huge candelabra hanging from a ceiling of pristine white which helped to reflect their light. The room was big yet in no way intimidating. Olivia had felt comfortable in it and that had helped her to settle into the company of people she had met only briefly earlier in the day.

She had dressed to create an impact, for she believed first impressions were of vital importance. She had made sure she looked appealing when she had first arrived at Cropton Hall, but knew she would come under closer scrutiny at the evening meal.

Her silk dress of celestial blue had a high waist and hung tube-like to the top of her fine leather shoes. The neck was V-shaped to both back and front with a Van Dyke trimming of fine white lawn trimmed with delicate lace. The puffed sleeves left her arms bare, allowing her two plain gold bracelets to be displayed to perfection. The delicate chain she wore around her neck held an oval locket finely etched with a design of a ship caught in ice. Her hair was curled back from her face and drawn up from her neck to be pinned on top with two blue bows matching her dress.

She had entered the drawing-room just before the meal, deliberately late so that hosts and guests would already be assembled. Her entrance had had the effect she desired for her appearance brought not only complimentary comments from the ladies but glances of admiration from the men. It also attracted what she had wanted most: the immediate attention of George Chilton-Brookes.

As she had come along the landing and down the stairs she had been saying 'George Chilton-Brookes' over and over again. It had a fine sound to it. It had gradually changed to 'Olivia Chilton-Brookes'. That had an even finer sound!

She smiled to herself as George detached himself from Honor and came to greet her.

'May I say how beautiful you look?' he said for her ears alone as he made her a little bow, his eyes never leaving her.

She read admiration there and was satisfied with her first step.

The evening had passed off very much to her liking. As well as the mouth-watering food and the best wines, she found the company convivial, the conversation both intellectual and light-hearted. Mr and Mrs Chilton-Brookes and their son were the perfect hosts, making sure everyone was involved and no one was left out.

Though she would have liked to have been sitting next to George, she was happy enough to be seated on the opposite side of the table. Though not directly opposite him, she knew that his eyes kept moving in her direction and dwelt on her with curiosity and interest.

28

Now, with a new day, she hoped to deepen that interest.

She had been disappointed that George had made no approach regarding the morning but maybe she could move their relationship forward at breakfast.

She viewed the weather from her bedroom window and judged that once the early-morning mist had been burnt away by the sun the day would remain fine and warm. She decided she would contrive a situation in which George could be persuaded to show her around the estate.

Accordingly she dressed for the outdoors, choosing a dark red muslin gown, narrow-skirted from its high waist and reaching to the top of her black half-boots. The neckline of the fitted bodice was high too. As she tied a white chiffon scarf around her throat, Olivia studied herself in the long mirror. Satisfied with her appearance, she picked up a crimson velvet pelisse, a present from her parents especially for this weekend. She chose a small bonnet which would sit on the back of her head and not screen her face.

She was halfway down the stairs when she heard gentle, intimate-sounding laughter in the hall. George and Honor came into her view as they headed for the front door. Whatever had amused them was clearly something which only two people on close terms can share. Jealousy tortured her as she realised she had slept too long.

Her movement on the stairs attracted the couple's attention.

'Ah, good morning, Olivia. I trust you slept well?' enquired George.

'I did, thank you,' she replied with a courteous inclination of her head.

Honor smiled pleasantly but Olivia did not see it as such. Instead she read the smile of a rival who had secured an advantage.

'You were planning a walk?' asked George with a glance at the pelisse and bonnet.

'I thought so,' returned Olivia in a non-committal voice.

'A pity George promised to show me the horse his mother

and father have bought him for his birthday or he could have shown you round,' said Honor. Olivia could not mistake the tone of satisfaction in her voice, particularly when she added, 'You'll find there's still some breakfast left.'

Olivia, smarting under what she took to be a dismissal, was determined not to be outdone. 'After the meal we had last night, I'm not sure I can face breakfast.' She turned her eyes on George. 'Could I see your present, too?'

'Of course,' he replied politely. 'It will be my pleasure to escort two such charming young ladies.' He reached for Olivia's pelisse and draped it round her shoulders.

She enjoyed the intimacy of the moment, especially when she noted a flash of annoyance cross Honor's face.

When they stepped outside, George paused. He drew the fresh morning air into his lungs and surveyed the prospect before him. 'A view I never tire of,' he explained. 'One of the first things I do every morning is to come out here. The weather imparts many moods to this scene and I enjoy them all.'

Shafts of sunlight pierced the clouds and picked out the contours of the land beneath, emphasising bold outcrops here, smoothing gentle contours there. A few wisps of early-morning mist remained, adding an air of mystery to the view.

Olivia imagined herself standing here beside George every morning. 'It's beautiful,' she agreed. 'And you are going to have a sunny day for your cricket match,' she prophesied, drawing on the weather lore her father had taught her, much of it gleaned from Whitby sailors.

'Then we'll all enjoy it, and the race afterwards,' commented George.

'Race?' Olivia was bemused.

'I made an announcement at breakfast for those who did not know. It has been local knowledge for some time but it was only certain to take place if the weather proved to be right, and it is. I've been challenged to a horse race – four times round the cricket field.'

'And you accepted?'

'Wouldn't do any other. There's a friendly rivalry between myself and Kit Fernley in any sport we take up. We refer to each other as "my enemy friend".'

'Another landowner?'

'Depends what you mean by landowner,' put in Honor, with a small smile which revealed she did not class Kit Fernley in the same category as the Chilton-Brookes.

'Well, I ...' Olivia hesitated to give her own description of a landowner.

'Kit owns land but not an estate such as ours,' explained George. 'His grandfather was a tenant farmer here in Cropton. Good tenant, knew how to work the land to the best advantage, apparently. There was a kindly squire at the time and he, as a reward for diligence and loyalty, gave Kit's grandfather the security of his cottage and a small parcel of land. To cut the story short, Kit, who was brought up by his grandparents and then by his uncle and aunt, his father's brother and sister, inherited from his uncle who had expanded in a small way. Kit worked hard, enlarged the farm by some shrewd buying, and finally bought Howdale Manor and left the family cottage, though he still owns it and uses it occasionally. He kept it on the advice of his aunt so that if he marries, she will have somewhere to live.'

'Sounds to be a very enterprising person.'

'He is, and still only twenty-four.'

'And he's done all that?' Olivia showed surprise.

'Yes. He must have inherited his ambition and the ability to seize an opportunity from his father. Kit works hard and plays hard.'

'And he'll be out to win this race,' put in Honor.

'Why the challenge? Any special reason?' asked Olivia.

'He beat George's Black Mist on Fair Maid a few weeks ago,' explained Honor, 'It was just by a nose and I think he's out to prove it was no fluke.'

'He's challenged me with a fifty-pound wager,' George put in.

Honor raised an eyebrow, startled at this revelation.

'We'd better make certain we pick you the right horse then,' she said forcefully, 'but I don't think you can do better than Black Mist. She'll win this time for sure.'

Leaving the terrace by the steps at the east end, they headed for the stables. A gateway in the adjoining wall led into a large cobbled space. Facing them was a run of single-storey store rooms, to their left the kitchen area of the main house, and to their right a building with no windows completed the square. George led them via an archway through to the stableyard, its cobbles swept clean by two stableboys who dare not let either of the grooms see one alien speck. The stone building which formed three sides of the yard not only held stabling for twelve horses but also housed three carriages, a tack room, store room and space for feed. One section was of two storeys, the upper area given over to rooms for the stableboys and the grooms if they did not live in the village.

Olivia was impressed with the layout as George gave her a quick description of what was what.

The grooms and stableboys straightened from their tasks when he appeared, but when he signalled that he did not want to interrupt them, continued with their work.

The top halves of the stable doors were held open and secured by iron hooks set into the walls. From ten of the stalls horses looked out. Seeing George, their eyes brightened and they exuded an air of nervous anticipation.

'Let's see the new one first,' said Honor with an enthusiasm Olivia interpreted as that of a horse lover.

'Over here,' said George, obviously delighted to show off his latest acquisition.

'Oh, my goodness, what a beauty!' Honor looked ecstatic as she gazed at the young horse inside the far stall. The animal turned its head, gazed at them for a moment, then arched its neck to be petted. 'You're a little darling,' enthused Honor, reaching over to stroke it. 'A thoroughbred without a doubt.'

'Darley Arabian crossed with a leading Yorkshire mare,' George informed them proudly.

'A fine birthday present,' commented Olivia. 'You'll have many happy hours astride her.'

'No doubt I shall,' he agreed. 'Now let's find the one I'm going to ride later today.'

Olivia held back as they left the first stall so that she could observe the other two more carefully. As they moved from horse to horse it was obvious they shared a common interest, and their affection for horses was returned by the animals. As they became more and more engrossed in their deliberations, Olivia lingered behind and focused her attention on each horse in turn.

She stayed longer with the seventh, stroking its neck and talking to it in soft cajoling tones. The horse responded and the ferocity that had glinted in its eyes when she had first reached it disappeared. It was only then she realised George and Honor had bypassed this stall and wondered why. She shrugged her shoulders. It was no concern of hers.

'You're a beauty, aren't you?' Her voice was quiet, gentle. She slipped the bolt from the lower half of the door and started to step inside.

'Don't!' George's cry, ringing with alarm, startled her. She looked round to see him running towards her, his face alive with concern.

Olivia, sensing a change in the animal, rebolted the door.

'Why not?' she asked with a touch of belligerence, not liking the way he had spoken to her.

'Redwings can be rough.'

'What? Not him!' She gave a half laugh.

'I've been kicked by him. The stableboys won't go near him. Even the grooms who can handle him are wary. Redwings always plays up.'

'You've ridden him?'

'Yes, but it's not easy. I keep trying but he's awkward, and there's always the danger he'll kick out or bite.'

'I don't believe it!' Amusement curved her mouth and there was an expression of disbelief in her eyes. She turned to the horse. 'You wouldn't hurt me, would you?' She reached out to the animal which was quivering with nervous tension. Its eyes had a hint of fire in them now.

She was aware that George was keenly alert to any possible danger. She also sensed his suppressed anger at someone taking a liberty of which he did not approve, and knew it was just barely kept in check by his unfailing politeness – she was his guest and good manners should prevail. For her part she did not want to offend her host so, as much as she wanted to stay with the horse, she merely gave it another caressing stroke with her hand and turned away.

In the few moments she had had with the animal she had assessed it critically. She made no comment on her conclusions but merely said, 'I'm sorry, George. I did not know of your wariness of Redwings.'

'I know what he can do. I was only concerned for your welfare.'

'I am grateful.'

'Come, let's hear which one Honor thinks I should ride in the race.'

'She is familiar with them all?'

George smiled, 'Oh, yes. Our families became friendly when we moved here and she offered advice when father and I expressed a desire to expand the stables. She was invaluable. We ride a lot together.'

Olivia felt a pang of jealousy and she imagined the days spent in each other's company. 'So her word will count for a lot?'

'Of course.' George pursed his lips. 'But I do have my own opinion.'

And no doubt it will be the same as Honor's, Olivia thought irritably.

'Well?' he asked when they reached Honor who had been so wrapped up in a horse called Raven that she had not noticed George leave her as he saw Olivia approaching Redwings' stall.

Startled, Honor swung round. 'Oh . . . yes. Black Mist, of course.'

George smiled. 'I thought it would be. My choice too. Let's take another look at her.'

They strolled back to stall number ten.

'She's in excellent condition,' observed Honor, 'and she responds to you better than any of them.'

'She does handle well,' George agreed.

Olivia's lips tightened in annoyance at this show of accord. She held back her own opinion. For now.

As they strolled from the stableyard and passed under the archway, George said, 'Honor and I are going for a short walk, would you care to join us?'

As much as she wanted to say yes, Olivia declined with a polite, 'I'll take a stroll on the terrace and then write up my diary.'

'Ah, a diarist in our midst,' commented Honor, a slight tone of mockery in her voice. 'I wonder what she will write about us, George?'

'I don't write about people. Sometimes there can be disillusionment when you reread what you originally thought. I merely like to keep a record of events – looking back can be very enlightening.'

'I don't care to look back. The future is all that matters to me,' returned Honor. 'Look ahead, don't wallow in what has been. That's history as soon as the moment has passed.'

Olivia did not comment but merely said, 'Enjoy your walk.'

She kept an eye on George and Honor while pretending to admire the flowers along the balustrade or pass a brief word with some of the other guests who had chosen to take the morning air. As soon as the pair were out of sight Olivia hurried back to the stables.

The grooms and stableboys were still engrossed in their work but she knew she had not escaped their notice when she received a warning from the head groom. 'Careful, miss,' he called as she approached Redwings' stall.

'Thanks, I'll be all right,' she replied.

Redwings snickered nervously at her approach.

'Quiet, laddie, quiet. I'm your friend.' She made her tone soothing and stopped at the door. 'You are beautiful.' She looked the horse in the eyes and saw the fire in them subsiding, though she knew it could easily flare again. 'You're a nice fellow. Easy to get on with, aren't you?' She reached out slowly but the horse was still wary. It snorted and turned its head away. 'Oh, come now, don't be like that. Remember me? I was here a short time ago. We were getting on well then.' Her soft caressing tones drove the tension away. Redwings relaxed and turned his head to her. She reached out and stroked his forehead. They stayed like that for a few minutes, each building up their trust in the other.

Judging what she thought would be the right moment, Olivia reached down, unbolted the door and stepped into the stall. Redwings shuffled and stamped the ground.

'Good boy,' she continued, her voice assuming a soft soothing lilt. She let her hand slide over Redwings' neck. 'You're my favourite. You're not as bad as they make out, are you? They just haven't realised what you need.' She gave Redwings an extra hug, putting as much affection into it as she could, and was delighted when the horse nuzzled her in response. 'I'll see you later today.' She stepped outside, closing the door gently behind her.

When she turned round, she saw that the grooms and stableboys had been watching her in astonishment.

'I wouldn't have believed it, miss.' The head groom spoke for them all. 'We have trouble with him every time. You must have a way with horses.'

Olivia smiled. 'Speak gently to him.'

'We've all tried that, miss.'

'Maybe you haven't used the right tone. Try mine some time.'

'Yes, miss.'

She started to turn away, then stopped and looked at them again, putting a tone of earnest request into her voice. 'Not a word to anyone, not even Mr George, about this. At least, not until I say so.'

'Very well, miss.'

Feeling a great deal of satisfaction, Olivia left the stable-yard and took a thoughtful walk across the lawns before returning to her room. But she did not linger there for long.

George had said they were only going for a short walk. She hoped her surmise was right for it was imperative that she should see him as soon as possible.

Accordingly she returned to the terrace and was thankful to find it deserted. She took a seat close to one end and opened a book of Wordsworth's poems, but her concentration on the text was frequently disturbed as she kept an eye open for George's return.

A quarter of an hour later her patience was rewarded. George and Honor came in sight, walking briskly. Seeing Olivia, they came on to the terrace.

'Did you get your diary written?' asked Honor.

'A few words, but it was such a fine day it seemed a pity to be inside so I thought I'd come out here and read.'

'Where is everyone else?' asked George.

'I don't know. Some were out here when I returned from the stables but now ...' She gave a little shrug of her shoulders.

'Shall we sit awhile, Honor?' asked George.

Olivia stiffened, awaiting the reply, hoping it would be what she wanted. Relief came with Honor's answer.

'I think I'll go and change, if you don't mind?'

'Not at all,' said George. He too felt thankful, not that he didn't enjoy Honor's company but here was a chance to get to know Olivia better. He had been intrigued by her ever since her arrival, but had not had much of an opportunity to speak with her on her own. He had observed her throughout yesterday evening and liked what he had observed so far. He saw in her a person who could bring liveliness to any gathering if warranted. But apart from her personality he was taken by her looks. He had seen prettier girls but none who combined an attractive appearance with such an intriguing personality. He wondered what her accomplishments and interests were, and meant to find out.

'What are you reading?' he asked now.

'Wordsworth.'

'You read a lot?'

'I love to.'

'Then you must not neglect our library. Would you like to see it now?'

'I would rather look at the horses again.'

Surprise crossed his face. 'Again?'

'If you don't mind?'

'Not at all.' He rose from his seat and held out his hand to assist her. 'I didn't realise you were so interested in them?'

Olivia gave a teasing smile, as if she knew what he was really thinking. 'You thought I was only being polite showing an interest in your present, and that a girl from the town would not have the same interest as one from the country?'

'Well ...' George was embarrassed by her accurate assessment.

A trill of laughter escaped her and her eyes sparkled. 'I have two horses, stabled and cared for at a farm just outside Whitby, and a third stabled at one of the coaching inns so that I can ride out to the farm.'

'I didn't know.'

'How could you?'

George tightened his lips and shrugged his shoulders, acknowledging her premise. 'So that's why you were interested in Redwings?'

'Yes. I think you should ride him in the race. No, I don't think, I know you definitely should.'

They had reached the archway into the stableyard. George was brought to a halt by the conviction in her voice. He stared at her in surprise. 'Ridiculous! You've seen what he's like. Kit Fernley would be halfway round the course before I got my mount fully under control.'

Olivia shook her head. 'I'm sorry to contradict but I believe you'll win on Redwings. He could easily outrun Black Mist.'

'I'll grant you he's strong, but he's difficult to handle and that will lose me the race.'

'He'll not be difficult if you treat him correctly.' She saw the protests coming to his lips and anger flash in his eyes at what he believed she was implying, and added quickly, 'I have no doubt you have been kind to him, but what I suspect is lacking is the way you speak to him. He's a very sensitive animal. I don't know his history but I believe that whoever you bought him from treated him harshly at some time. Come on, I'll show you what I mean.'

Olivia started off and George followed, amazed by this girl's keen perception and knowledge of horses. She had obviously assessed Redwings' strength in the few minutes she had seen him and, unknown to him, compared it favourably with that of Black Mist.

As they reached the stables, the horse snorted defiantly at their approach.

Hearing the noise, grooms and stableboys appeared from various points around the yard. They watched with interest.

'Speak to him,' commanded Olivia.

'Come on, fella, don't be skittish,' George began.

The horse did not look any calmer. In fact its eyes kindled and it kicked out with its back legs, hitting the wooden panelling with a resounding crash.

'Stop that and come here!' Though George tried to keep harshness from his voice, it was nevertheless detectable beneath the surface. The horse sensed it and gave a truculent snort.

George turned to Olivia. 'See? He would be impossible in the race.'

'Because you aren't using the right tone of voice. I'll show you.' Olivia spoke to Redwings again in that soft lilting tone.

He came to the door and poked his head out. 'There's a good fellow. We're friends, aren't we? No one is going to harm you, not ever again. We all love you. Now, do you want to come out?' She reached for the bolt in the door and swung it open slowly. 'Come on then.' Redwings stepped forward and paused. Olivia stroked his forehead and rubbed his neck gently. 'Come on.'

George watched in disbelief. The horse seemed completely calm. He stayed meekly beside Olivia as she walked round the yard.

'Now you talk to him, George,' she suggested.

He did as he was told, using Olivia's tone. The horse cocked its head as if paying attention to this new voice. It turned its head to George and stepped over to him. He kept on talking quietly.

Olivia felt herself tensing. This had to go right! The special bond between George and Redwings must be forged now. She forced herself to relax. None of her anxiety must be transferred to the horse.

Redwings gave a low whinny as if approving this new treatment by George. He tossed his head then nuzzled at his master.

Olivia breathed a sigh of relief. 'Now I think he'll let you ride him to his full ability. Give him a run against Black Mist now and you'll see I'm right to pit him against Kit Fernley's mount.'

George turned to his groom. 'What do you think to Miss Coulson's suggestion?'

'Let's see, shall we, sir?'

The head groom rapped out instructions to the stableboys who dashed away to bring the saddles.

'Now remember, keep talking to him in the tone you've been using until you have him at a full gallop then give him his head. You'll see, he'll do you proud,' promised Olivia.

The two horses were soon ready.

'You want me to ride one, sir?' asked the groom.

Olivia regretted that she had no riding dress with her. She would have loved to take up the challenge and ride against George, but doubted if he would have let her ride Redwings. Besides it would be better if he did then he would see the horse's true potential and assess its prospects for the race.

40

'You ride Black Mist.'

'Right, sir.'

'And, remember, no holding back.'

'Yes, sir.'

They reached a large open field and, as the riders made last-minute adjustments, George kept speaking quietly to his mount. Redwings showed no hostility when he swung into the saddle. He twitched a little but was calm, unlike any other time George had ridden him when he'd protested, taking all his rider's skill to bring him under control.

'Twice round the field, Fred,' called George when he saw the groom was in the saddle. 'Miss Coulson will signal the off.'

'Very good, sir.'

Olivia, standing to one side with the under-groom and stableboys, waited until the two horses were lined up.

'Off!' she yelled at the top of her voice.

The two mounts, answering their riders, sprang away, Black Mist a head in the lead. They stayed that way to the first turning point after which Black Mist lengthened her stride and drew her lead to half a length. Hooves drummed thunderously on the turf, seeming to add to the watchers' tension. The positions had not altered when the horses had completed one circuit of the field.

George, low on Redwings' back, had kept up his smooth stream of praise and held the horse in check when he'd sensed he wanted to really run. Go too soon and the distance might prove too long at this pace. Judge it right and who knew what this horse was capable of? He sensed the racing tension that had come over Redwings. It was as if nothing else mattered but to speed across the ground as fast as he could. Taking the second turn, George saw Fred urge Black Mist a little more. The horse responded and her lead became almost a length.

It was now or never.

'Fly, Redwings, fly! You're the best!'

George had no need of further words of praise; sugary

41

tones were no longer necessary. Redwings knew he had been given his head and answered the challenge eagerly. His pace quickened, his stride lengthened, and the ground flew beneath his hooves.

George revelled in the new power that had come to the animal. One moment it seemed that Black Mist was almost a length ahead; the next the positions had been reversed. Redwings was flying. Every muscle in his body was honed to perfection, striving with one object in mind, to be the fastest.

Olivia, gripped by the tension of the race and fearing that Black Mist had got too far ahead, was suddenly jumping up and down with excitement. She was entranced by the power she saw, a power she had visualised in the stable but now saw in all its majesty.

The horses thundered past the little group of spectators, Redwings the winner by three lengths.

Olivia swung round and in her excitement flung her arms round the under-groom's neck. 'I knew it! I knew it!' Instantly realising what she had done, she stopped. An alarmed expression flashed across her face and she released her hold. 'Oh, I'm sorry. I forgot myself.'

The under-groom gave a little laugh. 'Don't be, miss, I felt like doing it myself.'

She laughed with him and their chatter and that of the stableboys buzzed with excitement as they waited the return of the two riders.

George's face was wreathed in a broad smile of satisfaction and delight at the way Redwings had run. 'Wasn't it marvellous the way he responded when I gave him his head! And the way he covered the ground! I never thought to win by three lengths.'

'Sir, there's only one horse for the race this evening.'

'You're right, Fred.' The two men slid from the saddles. 'Take good care of them both,' George went on. 'And when you come to the field for the race, keep Redwings back until Mr Fernley's horse has appeared. Then we'll

give him something to think about. Here's a couple of
sovereigns between you. You know where to place a bet?'

'Yes, sir. Thank you, sir!'

They handed their reins to the stableboys. 'Go with
them, Redwings,' George said soothingly. 'They'll look
after you.'

He gave a glance at George who patted his neck. 'You
did well, and we'll do it again later.' The animal gave a nod
of its head as if agreeing.

The two boys led the animals away, talking smoothly to
Redwings. The grooms followed.

George turned to Olivia. 'Thanks to you I'll be riding the
winner.' His eyes held hers, glinting with triumph. Then
there was affection in them as he took her hand and raised it
to his lips.

Chapter Four

Olivia felt satisfied with her day's work as she strolled on to the terrace half an hour before lunch. Some guests, among them her mother and father, were already there with their host and hostess, enjoying a glass of wine and pleasant conversation. Others, invited for the day, were just arriving. Their chatter added to the general buzz as they crossed the lawn to extend birthday wishes to George who was standing at the foot of the steps to greet them.

Olivia stopped for a few minutes to greet George's cousin, Cecilia Metcalfe, with whom the evening before she had exchanged opinions about Mr Walter Scott's *Marmion*, published four years previously.

Timothy Dugdale approached them then and engaged Olivia in animated conversation about the game of cricket when he discovered this would be the first time she had seen the game played. Puzzled by some of the terminology and his lengthy explanations, she was pleased when his sister Ursula broke up the conversation.

'I'm going to steal Olivia from you, dear brother, I want a word with her.'

'And after that try and explain cricket to her.' He pulled an expression of mock disgust. 'Do you know, she's never seen a cricket match!'

As they moved away Ursula whispered, 'I thought you needed rescuing. I know Timothy can be a bore when he talks about his beloved cricket.'

Olivia smiled. 'Thank you. From his obvious enthusiasm, I expect your brother will be playing?'

Ursula raised her eyebrows. 'He wouldn't miss a game for the world. He'd ride any distance to play. If a match is rained off it puts him in a foul mood. When that happens Mother and Father and I steer clear of him for the rest of the day.' She glanced skywards. 'Thank goodness it's fair weather today. It looks as if we'll have plenty of sunshine for the game and for the race afterwards. There'll be plenty of wagers placed, I'm sure.' She lowered her voice and, with the expression of a conspirator wanting to keep a secret, added, 'If you are going to place one, put it on Kit Fernley.'

'What?' Olivia was astonished at this suggestion. 'Be disloyal to our host?'

Ursula gave a little laugh. 'Disloyal? My dear, a wager is a wager and you make it in the hope of making money. Forget loyalty in these circumstances. You put some money on Kit to win.'

'You sound as though you know something other people don't?'

Ursula gave a knowing smile and leaned a little closer to Olivia. 'Kit Fernley told me in confidence that he will ride a horse he has just acquired, Fleet of Foot. He says it's the best he's ever handled and will leave George's Black Mist far behind. And Kit's not given to to idle predictions when it comes to horses.'

Olivia made no comment but she was troubled. George had expected Kit to ride Fair Maid and had judged Redwings' potential accordingly.

Laughter came from a group of young men who appeared to be chaffing their young host.

'That's Kit Fernley there, talking to George. The tall one,' Ursula pointed out.

Olivia turned her eyes on the group and her attention was immediately drawn by a man who stood a head taller than the others. Even from this distance she could sense a physical power to him honed by hard work, but more than that she felt the strength of his personality. It commanded attention even out here in the open. She wondered what it would be like when he walked into a room. He gave the impression of someone who enjoyed life, whether at work or leisure. His smile was enticing, his laughter infectious, eyes always alert, making him seem aware of everything and everyone around him without ever causing him to deviate his concentration from the particular person who happened to command his attention at that moment.

As he moved up the steps and fell into conversation with other people, Olivia saw that his features were clean-cut, his jaw square, his hair dark with just the hint of a natural wave to it. It imparted a happy-go-lucky touch to a man whose bearing was otherwise supremely confident. But more than anything she felt drawn by those dark, deep-set eyes which seemed to extend a challenge to the opposite sex to try to discover the real Kit Fernley.

Ursula had already embarked on Kit's life story and Olivia made no attempt to stop her. It refreshed her memories of what George and Honor had already told her about the charismatic young man.

'If his grandparents and then his uncle and aunt raised him, what happened to his parents?' asked Olivia when Ursula had finished.

'I'm told his mother was supposedly drowned in a shipwreck just south of Whitby, though there were rumours at the time that she survived and died later in America. His father was a whaling captain – you may have heard of him, Captain David Fernley?'

Olivia was surprised at this information. 'He's certainly well known in Whitby through his partnership in the firm of Fernley and Thoresby, though he spends most of his time in London running Hartley Shipping. I didn't know he had a son.'

'Well, that's him. It seems, as Captain Fernley was away

46

from home so much, Kit was given over to his grandparents here in Cropton.'

'I see.'

Before Olivia could glean any more, an announcement was made informing the guests that they could partake of the buffet which had been arranged on the lawn before the terrace.

Still holding conversations or exchanging greetings, renewing acquaintances or reviving friendships, guests moved towards the tables. The atmosphere was relaxed and good-humoured.

Succulent dishes of every kind to tempt even the most obstinate of appetites were arranged for everyone's delectation. Maids and manservants stood by to assist when guests had made their choices.

As they turned from the buffet tables with full plates, Ursula said, 'Will you excuse me? There's an old friend I haven't seen for some time.'

'Of course,' returned Olivia.

'I'll see you later at the game.'

Olivia looked around. Where was George? Even though Ursula had imparted the news of Kit's horse in confidence, Olivia felt she could not keep it from George. It was imperative that she should warn him. She moved back along the terrace and as she manoeuvred round a group of people, came face to face with George who had just broken off a conversation in order to continue circulating among his guests.

'Thank goodness I've found you.' The relief in her voice was immediately apparent.

He looked concerned as he asked, 'Is something the matter?'

She took his arm and led him to a place beside the balustrade. 'I've just heard some disturbing news – Kit Fernley won't be riding Fair Maid.'

'What?' George gasped. 'How do you know?'

'I was told in confidence that he will be riding a new horse, Fleet of Foot.'

'Never heard of it.'

'If its name is anything to go by then you'd better watch out. I'm told he says it's the best he's ever had and will show Black Mist how to run.'

'Aye, but Fleet of Foot won't be running against Black Mist. Maybe Kit Fernley's in for a surprise.'

'I hope you're right.'

He detected nervousness in her voice. 'Don't worry, I'm sure your judgement will prove correct.'

'I hope so,' Olivia said nervously. She was pinning all her hopes on Redwings and there was far more at stake than a simple wager.

'Have a glass of wine. It will take your mind off the race.' George stopped a maid who was passing with a tray of glasses.

'Thank you.'

He selected a glass of hock for her and placed it on the balustrade. 'You'll be at the cricket match, of course. That will stop you worrying about whether Redwings is good enough to beat this new miracle horse.'

'Timothy's been trying to enlighten me about cricket.'

George laughed. 'He's so enthusiastic and will prattle on so quickly you'll be more confused than if he'd said nothing, I'll be bound.

'His sister has offered to clarify things during the match.'

'Ah, now, there you will be in good hands. Ursula is very knowledgeable. She has to be, with a brother so keen and a father who is equally so. But I'll be around when we're batting, if you remain confused.'

'I look forward to that, but I should not take you away from your other guests and I expect there will be many people seeking your attention at the match.'

'I assure you no one will be neglected, but I must of course give special attention to our first-time guests – especially one as charming as you,' he went on. His voice was soft with a particular intonation that indicated the words would not have been spoken had they not been meant.

48

'You flatter me again.' Olivia blushed.

He shook his head. 'I do not.'

'Ah, George, you must introduce me to this charming and, may I add, beautiful young lady.' Kit Fernley broke into their conversation without a word of apology, as if it was the most natural thing in the world to do. A broad smile lent added animation to his face, while his dark eyes danced with delight at being in the presence of such an attractive girl.

For the briefest of moments Olivia noticed annoyance in George's eyes but then it was gone and in its place remained the genuine consideration he displayed towards all his guests.

'Kit, this is Olivia Coulson. Olivia, this is Kit Fernley.'

'The pleasure is mine, Miss Coulson.' Kit Fernley bowed but his eyes never left hers.

'I am pleased to meet you, Mr Fernley,' Olivia returned, without any outward sign that she was intrigued by this man. 'George's challenger later in the day, I'm told?'

His eyes shone with laughter. 'You refer to the race, no doubt, but we are opponents before that. I'll master him on the cricket field as well.' Kit gave his host a playful dig with his fist. 'Won't I, George?'

'As well, Mr Fernley?' Olivia raised her eyebrows in shocked disbelief. 'I think not.'

'Oh, you have a trusting guest, George.' He leaned towards Olivia and said with utter conviction, 'If you want to win a fortune, place a large amount of money on me to win that race.'

'Mr Fernley, I do not wish to lose my stake.'

Kit gave a hearty laugh. 'Suit yourself, little lady. George, you must tell me more about this fascinating guest of yours.' He paused but before George could speak, added, 'Better still, let her tell me herself. I'm sure you want to chat to some of your other guests?'

Olivia stiffened at the effrontery of the man dismissing his host in such a blatant manner, though so skilfully that

George could not take offence. Before she could respond, Kit had placed his hand on her elbow and guided her to a more open space where two chairs had just been vacated.

His easy confidence broke down the barrier with which she tried to shield herself. But it had been a half-hearted attempt only because secretly she was drawn by the spell this man was spinning. She wanted to know about him and he knew it.

'Well, Miss Coulson?' He paused. 'Oh, that sounds so formal, doesn't it, and I'm sure we are going to see more of each other, so may we use Christian names? May I call you Olivia?'

She found herself in a situation where she could not refuse. 'As you wish,' she consented with just a hint of ice in her tone.

He ignored it, knowing it would not be there for long. 'Good. You are not from around these parts, Olivia. If you were, even if newly settled, I would have known for your charm would have been immediately evident to the entire neighbourhood.'

'You have a glib tongue, Mr Fernley.'

He raised his hands in horror. 'I thought we were on Christian name terms, Olivia?'

She was compelled by the prompting of those dark eyes which seemed to plead with her not to make things difficult between them.

She nodded reluctantly.

'Well, where are you from, Olivia?'

'Whitby. My father has the biggest shipbuilding firm in the town.'

He raised his eyebrows. 'A man of talent and business acumen.' Though there was no direct question he looked to her for more information, and Olivia automatically gave it.

'The firm was founded by my great-grandfather. Grandfather expanded it and Father has built on the foundations they laid.'

Kit nodded his approval of men who had worked hard

50

and shrewdly. 'Coming from Whitby, you must know the whaling firm of Fernley and Thoresby?'

'I do indeed.'

'My father is a partner in it,' he put in quickly, before she had time to say that she had already been given this information.

'Yet you are farming near Cropton, I'm told.'

'Yes.' A wistful smile crossed his lips.

Did she detect regret? 'Strange. Seafaring generally runs in families.'

He shrugged his shoulders. 'Maybe it does, but my particular family circumstances took me into farming. It's a long story. You're going to ask if I have any regrets?' He gave a small shake of his head. She wondered if there was doubt in it nevertheless. 'No, I like farming and I've done well from it, though I say it myself. Besides I like it around Cropton and I've made good friends here.'

'Among them George?'

He laughed. 'Of course.'

'In spite of your rivalry?'

'It's a friendly rivalry, confined purely to our sporting activities. It's never strayed beyond that. You'll see there'll be no quarter given later today. Put a wager on Kit Fernley, he'll win handsomely. Do you ride?'

'Yes.'

'Then you must allow me to escort you through some of our lovely countryside.

'Thank you, but alas this is only a short stay for George's birthday. I brought no appropriate clothing. I did not expect an opportunity to go riding.'

'Maybe you will give me permission to call on you next time I am in Whitby? Then we could take a ride along the cliffs. Unless you have a beau who would object?'

'There is no one special.'

'A charming girl like you, and there is no one?'

'Oh, there are many friends but no one who would object.' Olivia smiled to herself as she thought of the young

51

men of Whitby with whom she was getting bored. This weekend had turned out far better than she had expected. Here were two attractive new prospects each very different from her Whitby admirers. They couldn't have appeared at a better time.

'Then I shall call on you,' Kit promised.

Though this left some confusion in her mind as to whether she would have preferred that suggestion to have come from George, she certainly wasn't going to turn it down.

Before she could make any comment, however, a voice broke into their conversation. 'Ah, my dear Kit, are you trying to persuade Olivia to place a bet on you? I have already done that.'

'Ursula, I thank you for your loyalty, though of course you know you are only recommending a certainty.' He glanced at Olivia. 'Take heed of her, she's very knowledgeable about my horses.'

Olivia could sense a spark between these two, and had noticed that Ursula had put undue emphasis on the word 'dear'.

Kit glanced around the rest of the guests, acknowledged a wave here, a gesture there, and said, 'Ladies, though it breaks my heart to tear myself away, I must have a word with Johnny Saggers before the game. Have to find out how he thinks the pitch will play.' He gave a quick wink at Olivia. 'Got to have all the information to make sure I put one over on our host, just as I will later in the race.' With a teasing gleam in his eye, he bowed to them both and was gone.

Olivia watched him weave his way amongst the people on the terrace with a natural athletic grace. He carried himself proudly, as if knowing she was watching him and wanting to impress.

'Thinks a lot of himself,' observed Olivia, using the comment to gauge Ursula's reactions.

'He does,' she agreed, 'but with reason. He's done well

for himself, though he doesn't often flaunt it. No need, really. He impresses with whatever he does. He probably just put it on a bit because you were a stranger.'

'And female,' added Olivia.

'Ah, now there you have it. You have to agree, he's handsome and attractive? Girls do fuss over him and there's no denying he likes it.'

The two girls spent the rest of the time together, chatting with other guests, exchanging views about Cropton, Whitby, the coming cricket match, and of course speculating on the outcome of the horse race.

By quarter to two, the buzz of anticipation that accompanies any exciting contest came from the large crowd of people gathered around the cricket field.

The wooded pavilion for the players, a generous gift to the village from the Chilton-Brookes, stood at one corner of the field. Next to it a large tent had been erected for the occasion. Inside was a hive of activity, for the ladies of the village, who generally provided good but modest teas for ordinary matches, intended to excel themselves on this occasion. It was not every day that the son of the gentleman and his lady at the Hall turned twenty-one.

Seats had been reserved in front of the pavilion for the house guests, and Ursula and Olivia chose two at the left-hand side. They had been settled only a few moments when Kit came over to them.

Olivia's heart gave a little flutter at the sight of him. Kit Fernley looked even more handsome in his cricket whites. He wore flannel trousers narrowing at the ankles towards highly polished black leather shoes. A white shirt was adorned at the neck by a green cravat, tied flamboyantly at the throat and held in place by a silver pin. A green waist-length jacket was worn closely buttoned and the sleeves cut tight at the wrist. He carried a tall black hat which had been carefully brushed until it was spotless.

'Good afternoon, ladies,' he said as he bowed in acknowledgement of their presence.

'Hello, Kit,' returned Ursula, while Olivia gave him a smile which confirmed that she thought he looked very elegant. 'You've chosen green for your side today, I see.'

'As you know, Ursula, green is my lucky colour.' He glanced at Olivia. 'And signifies a victory on the cricket field as well as in the race.'

She smiled. 'Confidence sometimes comes unstuck,' she reminded him.

'Ah, not with me, dear girl.'

'Did you and Johnny work out your strategy?' asked Ursula.

'Oh, yes. It makes us even more certain to win.'

'Nonsense!' cried George, who had overheard the last remark as he joined them. 'You'd be better thinking about the game than trying to commandeer the attention of these two charming girls.'

Olivia had been taking in George's appearance. He was similarly dressed to Kit with the exception that his short jacket was white and the cravat too. The whole effect was calming and added to the impression that George was never ruffled. It also seemed to enhance his fine features. Cricket clothes certainly suited him.

'Ah, but you have the wrong angle, George. The presence of these beautiful girls makes me all the more determined to succeed.'

'To show off more like,' replied George, a mischievous twinkle in his eyes. 'And that will be your downfall.'

Kit spread his hands protestingly. 'When do I ever show off?' He turned to Ursula. 'My dear, do I?'

'No,' she agreed fervently. 'It's just your natural and endearing way.'

'There speaks a wise one,' he laughed.

'What about you, Olivia? What do you think?' asked George.

'How can I have an opinion on such a serious and important

54

matter?' Her eyes were twinkling as she chose her words. 'I've known you both but a short time, Kit even shorter than you, George. So I must stay neutral and reserve my judgement until I see how he behaves both on the cricket field and then on the back of a horse.'

'Spoken like a true diplomat,' said George. 'Kit, you'll have to mind how you behave if you want Olivia's approval. Now we'd better make a start.'

A few minutes later she saw two men in frock-coats and grey trousers and wearing top hats emerge from the pavilion and start to walk towards the centre of the field.

'Who are they?' she asked. 'And why are they dressed differently?'

'They are the umpires,' replied Ursula.

George came from the pavilion followed by ten other men. As they moved on to the field they started throwing a ball to each other.

'Ah, here comes Johnny Saggers,' Olivia pointed out when she saw him, accompanied by another man, come from the pavilion with brisk, determined steps, eager to get to the middle and show their skill with the bats they were carrying.

'Johnny's a good batsman,' replied Ursula. 'Always opens the innings for the club Kit plays for. That's why Kit would want his opinion about the state of the pitch and whether they should bat first.'

Olivia nodded, not really understanding the deeper significance behind this explanation. But as the afternoon proceeded, Ursula kept her comments short and uncomplicated so that the terminology, so significant to cricket, seemed less confusing. Olivia began to appreciate the game and settled down to enjoy the contest.

At the fall of the first wicket Kit came out of the pavilion. He caught their eye, smiled his warmest smiles and raised his bat as if to say, 'Watch what I do with this.'

Olivia admired his flowing stride and strong step. Clapping broke out among the spectators as he appeared and, when he reached the wicket, a sense of expectancy settled over them. But the immediate entertainment came from Johnny who smote the next four balls to the boundary.

Ursula applauded each stroke, as did the rest of the spectators, with growing excitement. Playing defensively at the final two balls, Johnny left Kit to face the bowling.

Runs came steadily for half an hour during which time Ursula explained the difference between the two batsmen's technique and tactics. 'There's brawn behind Johnny's shots, grace in Kit's.'

Olivia saw exactly what she meant. Runs came from Johnny with hard but calculated strikes. From Kit they came with seemingly little effort, stroked away through the gaps between the fielders with perfect timing. There was poise and balance in his movement which held her attention, so much so that she began to wonder what it would be like to be whirled around the dance floor by this man who was so light on his feet. Maybe she would find out later.

'Ah, George is going to bowl.' Ursula's comment broke into Olivia's reverie. 'He's desperate to break up this partnership. They're getting too many runs for his liking.'

A new tension had gripped the spectators who knew of the friendly rivalry between the two men.

Olivia admired George's economy of movement. Legs, arms and body all moved in rhythmic unison that was a delight to behold. Kit scored no runs off George's first over.

'He's being cautious, waiting to adjust himself to the different pace,' commented Ursula. 'Oh, my goodness, George is bringing brother Timothy on!'

'You sound surprised. Isn't he a good bowler?'

'Not bad. He's medium-paced but can be awkward to play.'

His first ball was not a good one and Johnny, seeing runs for the taking, struck hard. He connected. The ball flew through the air towards the boundary.

'That'll be a six!' cried Ursula, expressing everyone's

opinion, but they reckoned without the agility of the fielder who was racing round the boundary. His eyes never left the ball. He must get it or it would be a six. The ball was dropping fast. He flung himself forward, right arm outstretched, fingers splayed. The ball hit his hand. His fingers closed. He crashed to the ground and rolled over. A great cry of astonishment rang round the field. Clapping resounded in the air. Johnny Saggers, shocked by this unexpected turn of events, stared in astonishment, hardly able to believe he was out to the wonder catch. Then he turned and walked dispiritedly towards the pavilion while the jubilant fielders congratulated their team-mate.

'That was marvellous,' said Olivia.

'Timothy's tail will be up now.'

And so it was. He took two wickets in his next over without conceding a run. Then Kit found another partner for a while and began to dominate the bowling.

'He's such an elegant batsman,' observed Ursula. 'George will want him out, otherwise the score is going to mount. He's going to have to do something about it.'

George clearly had similar thoughts now the score was on 120 for 4. He changed ends with Timothy and was immediately rewarded with a wicket. He knew that they were now among the less competent batsmen. Another dismissal would put them in a strong position to curtail the run making, but he still had Kit to contend with.

Kit took sixteen runs off the next four overs. Every spectator now expected him to take command, he was batting so well. But George had other ideas and two balls later deceived him with the flight and bowled him. A broad smile crossed George's face, and it grew even broader when he saw Kit, livid at himself, glare at the broken wicket as all his pent-up annoyance came to the surface. Then he took command of his feelings. He looked at his opponent and nodded. 'Good ball, George,' he called.

He acknowledged the compliment with an inclination of his head.

The innings disintegrated after that, George taking three of the remaining wickets with his slow bowling.

Watching the cricketers troop off the field, Ursula informed Olivia that they would now take tea.

A table set for the teams to help themselves had been positioned at one end of the tent so that there would be no delay in the match restarting. The remaining area of the tent was occupied by tables from which the spectators could get their teas.

The tent buzzed with comment and opinions on the game and its possible outcome.

Overhearing some of these conversations, Olivia asked Ursula, 'Who do you think will win?'

She pursed her lips thoughtfully. 'Well, a score of 190 is good and I think it will make for a tight game. It could go either way. Like the innings we have just seen, I think a lot will depend on what form Kit is in as bowler and George as batsman.'

Any further speculation was muted when Kit approached them. 'I hope you kept Olivia up with what was going on out there?'

'Of course,' Ursula replied. 'I think she'll be able to appreciate the next round of play all the better.'

'Did you enjoy that?' he asked Olivia.

'Very much,' she replied. 'I'm looking forward to the next innings.'

'And to seeing how we demolish that total with ease.' George took up her sentence as he joined them.

Kit gave a loud contemptuous laugh. 'Your team outscore us? Never! 190 is more than enough.'

'Well, we'll see.'

'Hadn't you better get ready?'

'No. My opening batsmen will be waiting for you to lead out your team.'

Kit eyed him with astonishment and suspicion. 'You aren't opening as usual?

George grinned. 'No. Now *there's* something for you

to think about. You'd better be off to re-study your tactics.'

'Maybe I should.' Then Kit brushed aside the remark with a nonchalant, 'Your change of batting order will make no difference to the outcome. In fact, it may well help us to win. I'd better be off. Keep your eyes on the game, ladies.' He bowed, tipped his hat and was gone.

'Will it make any difference, your not batting first?' asked Olivia.

'I'm hoping so. I'm going to go in at number four. My first three batsmen are all solid, no flamboyant moves except for the fellow batting number three who can cut loose if the state of the game warrants it.' George paused, glanced around then said, 'Should we resume our seats?'

He escorted them to the chairs they had occupied during the first innings, sought one for himself and came to sit with them.

Olivia enjoyed his company, kept in the flow of the general conversation between the three of them, and absorbed his comments on the game as it unfolded.

The score stood at fifty when the first wicket fell.

George jumped from his seat. 'Excuse me, ladies, I must get ready.'

When he had done so he rejoined them and they watched the score rattle along to 120.

'You're in a strong position now,' said Ursula. 'You should win from here.'

'It's a funny game,' he replied. 'It can soon change.'

Ten more runs went into the scorebooks. Then disaster struck. The last ball of the over clean bowled the opening batsman. George went in and watched the first ball of the next over go for a catch off the edge of the bat to the wicket keeper.

A keyed-up Timothy Dugdale came to the wicket.

Kit was repositioning his men. As he passed George he said in a low voice, 'Not working out, is it? Two batsmen in who haven't faced a ball.'

George ignored the remark which was meant to undermine his confidence and stood as if he hadn't a care in the world.

The field was set. The bowler ready. He ambled in at a steady run. His arm came over. The ball flew from his hand. Timothy narrowed his eyes, struck hard, and almost before anyone realised it the ball was over the boundary. Six. Timothy played out the over without scoring another run.

Kit now changed the bowling, bringing himself on bowl at George who, so far, hadn't faced a ball. During the next eight overs Kit and his fellow bowler tried all they could to get another wicket, but in vain. Both batsmen seemed at ease with the bowling in their different ways. Timothy fidgeted, shuffling as the bowler ran in, and was flamboyant with his stroke. George stood still, his stance relaxed, almost languid. His stroke came with the minimum of flair and yet it met the ball perfectly. His timing was impeccable, sending the ball to the boundary with little effort.

The contrasting styles took the score to 160 before the fourth wicket fell, that of Timothy. Although the ascendancy remained with the batting side, 31 wanted and still six wickets to fall, Kit was not one to concede defeat.

In the next over he took three wickets in three balls and changed the whole complexion of the game. Cheers and compliments rang round the field at this hat-trick so rarely seen. George had had to stand at the other end and watch his batsmen come and go. Three wickets remaining and still 31 runs wanted.

Olivia was thrilled at Kit's performance, gleaning the full impact it was having on the match from Ursula. She also felt the tension which had come over the spectators. This game could still go either way.

Ten more runs came without a wicket falling, but then the new batsman misjudged the trajectory of the last ball of the over, snicked it and was caught by the wicket-keeper.

George faced Kit. He still wore a casual air, as if he hadn't a care in the world and was unaware that he was batting in a tense situation.

He played the first five balls without scoring but took a quick single off the last one so that he faced the bowling again, bringing relief to the new batsman.

Tension deepened round the ground. There wasn't a sound to be heard from the spectators who were all gripped by the situation.

Four came off that over with George once again scoring off the last ball to face Kit again. He played the first three balls cautiously. The fourth was on its way when George took two quick steps down the wicket and met the ball on the full with the meat of the bat. His movement was swift yet seemed casual, his timing perfect. Kit hadn't fooled him with a slower ball. A roar went up from the spectators as the ball cleared the boundary. Six. Ten more wanted. Two wickets to fall. George's attempt to take a run off the last ball was thwarted by Kit's delivery.

The less experienced batsman faced the bowling then. He took three off the first ball but, ambitious to do the same again, lost his wicket in the next over.

'What's the position now?' asked Olivia. 'I'm lost in all the excitement.

'The last man is coming in. George's team need seven more. Kit's team needs one more wicket.'

Olivia nodded, her lips tight with anxiety, not knowing who she wanted to win. Both men were performing brilliantly and she had a feeling, vain though it sounded, that they were doing so because she was there.

George had a word with the new batsman. He nodded and then took up his position. He played at four balls without hitting them. The fielding side threw up their arms in despair, for each one had just missed the wicket.

George faced Kit again. He spent some time rearranging his fielders, hoping that the delay would upset George's concentration. But it did not work. George adopted his easy-going attitude. The first ball was despatched for two. Five wanted. No score came from the next four balls. Before Kit bowled the last ball he called his fielders to him.

George waited patiently while Kit delivered quiet words of advice to his men.

George took his stance. Kit ran in to bowl. George was caught by surprise by an unexpectedly poor delivery, but recovered his composure just in time to whack it. Three was what he wanted so that he would have to face the bowling at the other end and two needed to win. The batsman ran quickly. A fielder raced round the boundary. George kept his eye on the ball. It was slowing. He did not want it to go over the boundary. He had put just sufficient strength behind the shot so that it would not. It had almost stopped. The batsman had completed their third run and George called to his partner to wait. He had got what he wanted. The fielder, in his haste stumbled, half recovered but in doing so kicked the ball. A shout went up from the nearby spectators. 'Boundary! Four!'

Kit smiled to himself. He had guessed George would want three and not four so that he could face the bowling. Now the new batsman would have to do so. His ruse had worked perfectly. George tightened his lips but kept emotions under control. As he went to the other end of the wicket he had a word with his partner.

The tension around the ground was almost unbearable. The scores were level. Could the last batsman, who hadn't met ball with bat, yet sneak a run? Kit held up play, resetting his field, bringing men in as if menacing the batsman. That tactic made him all the more nervous. It clouded his judgement, causing him to forget George's instructions. He hit out at the first ball, felt wood hit leather and was off for a run. But he had not connected properly. The ball only went a few yards. A fielder pounced, grabbed the ball and flicked it to the wicket-keeper who broke the stumps with a resounding shout of triumph as the batsman unsuccessfully tried to regain the crease.

The game was tied.

Kit grinned as he shook hands with George. 'Fooled you there!'

He knew he hadn't really when George replied, 'When did you teach yon fellow on the boundary to play football?'

Kit laughed. 'A great match – a tie. That certainly won't happen with the horses. Want to double the wager?'

Chapter Five

The air was charged with observation, opinion and discussion as the spectators released their pent-up emotions after a game which had kept them all on tenterhooks. But all were agreed that it had been a most enjoyable entertainment splendidly befitting the occasion.

The players were applauded from the field and no one was more enthusiastic than Olivia and Ursula. Olivia knew she would never forget her introduction to cricket.

When they reached the pavilion, George and Kit came over to them, still discussing the adept footwork of the player who had 'accidentally on purpose', as George put it, kicked the ball over the boundary.

'Enjoy that?' he asked Ursula with a smile.

'You were both splendid.' She smiled her approval.

'Plenty of excitement,' commented Olivia.

'A splendid game for your first cricket match,' said Kit. 'You must watch more.'

'Indeed I must, but it will not be the same without you two playing.'

'Ah, a fair damsel speaking flattery,' acknowledged Kit, his lips parting in a bewitching smile.

Further conversation between them was prevented then. 'Well played, both of you!' called Edward, as he and Lavinia joined them.

'Thank you, sir,' replied George.

'Father, Mother, I don't expect you have met Kit Fernley,' put in Olivia. She glanced at him. 'Kit, this is my mother and father.'

'Pleased to meet you, my boy.' Edward felt his hand taken in a firm grip, the type he admired in a man, indicating friendliness and strength.

'It is my pleasure too,' Kit replied. His eyes swept to Lavinia. 'Ma'am, I can see from whom your charming daughter gets her beauty.'

'You are a flatterer, young man, and know how to please a woman old enough to be your mother.' Her eyes were warm with appreciation, however.

'Age cannot dull beauty, ma'am.'

'And you have a way with words.'

'But will he have a way with a horse?' put in Edward.

'Sir, there will be only one winner, and that will be …'

'Me,' George finished for him.

'Confusion, confusion,' bemoaned Edward. 'I was hoping to glean some inside information about the winner.'

'Ah, a man wanting to place a wager, no doubt,' said Kit.

'Right, young man.'

'Then place it on me,' put in George quickly.

'Take no notice of him,' rejoined Kit. 'He won't stand a chance.'

'Sir, take my advice,' said George with unmistakable sincerity. 'Now, if you will excuse me, I must go and change for the race and see that my horse is cared for when it arrives.'

'A signal for me to do the same,' said Kit. 'Please excuse me.' He bowed to the ladies and when he straightened up met Edward's eye. 'On me, sir, I'm a certainty. Tim Healy yonder will give you a good price.' He turned to Ursula. 'Be a love, introduce Mr Coulson to Tim and tell him he's to do right by him.'

'Of course I will,' replied Ursula, caught up in the exciting atmosphere.

The two young men headed for the pavilion. Olivia, wanting a quiet word with her father, manoeuvred him so that they were walking a few paces behind her mother who had taken up a conversation with Ursula about the village of Cropton.

'Put your money on George,' Olivia whispered.

'But Kit sounded so confident that he's riding a certainty.'

'Never mind what he said, his horse won't win.'

'But I understand his horse, Fair Maid, beat George's Black Mist last time they met? And there is a rumour going round that he's found a better horse now.'

'Even so, it won't win.'

'How do you know?' her father asked suspiciously. 'Have you seen it?'

'No. But I know what George is riding, and it won't be Black Mist. Keep that to yourself,' she said warningly.

'If you haven't seen Kit's horse, how can you compare them?'

'I can't, but I've seen George's horse run and I know what it is capable of.'

'What?' Edward was surprise. 'How could you?'

'Never mind, it's a long story. I'll enlighten you later. Just do as I say.'

They had nearly reached the man taking bets.

'What am I going to say to Ursula? She'll expect me to put my money on Kit.'

'Oh . . . just say that you can't be disloyal to your host.'

Ursula made the introductions. The red-faced, beaming Tim Healy said that he was only too pleased to take their bets.

'Mr Coulson, don't throw your money away,' gasped Ursula when Edward placed ten pounds on George to win.

'I must show loyalty to my host.'

Ursula shook her head. 'I tried to persuade Olivia earlier that she should wager on Kit but, like you, she has this notion of loyalty. A bet should not be made out of sentiment but to make money.'

'You are right, my dear, but nevertheless I'll put my money on George.' Edward turned to his wife. 'You too, my dear?'

'Well, I suppose the family must show a united front.'

Edward produced thirty pounds and handed them over to Tim who in his mind was already spending the profit he was making.

During the next half-hour people enjoyed the sunshine as they walked around the field or lazed on the grass. The convivial atmosphere was encouraged by the availability of a wide variety of home-made wines supplied by the ladies of the village and what seemed a never-ending supply of sandwiches, cakes and biscuits.

What began as a ripple of excitement at one edge of the field soon swept through the whole gathering. The first horse was arriving and it was Kit's. Soon the information that it was not the expected Fair Maid was on everyone's lips.

Olivia excused herself from her parents. She must see this horse. She caught Ursula's eye, smiled and nodded. The two girls headed across the field. The horse had been brought by two of Kit's stable workers who awaited his arrival to take charge.

'She's a beauty!' Olivia could not hide her admiration.

The animal was in first-class condition. She was sleek, yet Olivia recognised the power in her limbs. She started to have doubts about her own judgement of Redwings.

She stiffened herself. No need to be thinking this way. She had made a judgement and should not let anything mar the confidence she had in Redwings. And under no circumstances should the horse himself become aware of any lack of faith in him.

'She'll be a mover,' commented Ursula.

'She will,' Olivia agreed.

'Wishing you had put your money on Kit?'

Olivia gave a wry smile and shook her head. She had spotted George's two grooms approaching the field with Redwings. Ursula followed her gaze.

'That's not Black Mist,' she gasped. 'It's Redwings.'

'You know him?'

'Oh, yes. He's a rebel. What on earth is George thinking

of? He's ridden Redwings, of course, but never gets a real response from him.'

'He must have his reasons.'

'Let's find out.' Ursula started towards the group which now included George.

The horse was calm, though George feared that when he came nearer the spectators, many of whom were bound to crowd him to pass judgement, this might change. He rubbed his mount's neck gently and spoke softly to him. The horse nuzzled him with affection. Unexpectedly he tossed his head and snickered, fire beginning to glint in his eyes.

Ursula, still a few paces away, spoke to Olivia with disbelief. 'There, I told you, that animal will rebel. George must have taken leave of his senses.'

But he spoke quietly to Redwings again and the animal settled.

'I think he will manage,' commented Olivia and went to join him.

He smiled at her. 'So that's Fleet of Foot.' He nodded in the direction of his opponent.

'Yes, she's strong, will run hard, and I think Kit will let her do so at the start and try and establish a lead which he will hope you'll never close. But don't worry, Redwings will do you proud on the last circuit.' She patted him. 'You will, won't you?' The horse nuzzled her.

George climbed into the saddle.

'Good luck,' called Olivia, and turned to see a wide-eyed, disbelieving Ursula staring at her.

'You knew what George was up to, and you knew that horse. He responded to you. I've been near him a few times but I would never have dared touch him as you did. You must know horses?'

Olivia smiled. 'Yes, I do. Come on, let's get a place near the finish.'

Crowds had lined the course set out for the race but Olivia and Ursula managed to get a good position from which they could see every furlong and deduce the winner should the outcome be close.

Start and finish were to be at the same point. As the riders came on to the course and set their mounts at a walking pace towards the starter, Olivia could see George's lips moving quietly and knew he was talking to Redwings. She was thankful he was ignoring Kit's comments which she could clearly hear.

'Thought you'd spring a surprise on me too? Can't understand why you chose that rebel, but be it on your own head. I'll wait at the finish for you.'

They were nearing the starter who, at Kit's suggestion, was George's father since this was his special day. Olivia had been pleased by Kit's gesture, and felt new admiration when he stopped talking. She realised he wanted nothing to mar the start though a less sporting man might have connived at this.

A hush had descended over the whole field.

The horses were moving side by side. Through the skill of their riders they reached Richard Chilton-Brookes perfectly abreast. The green flag he had raised high, so that there would be no mistaking its movement, fell.

The horses leaped forward. The crowd shattered the expectant silence with shouts of, 'They're off!'

For a hundred yards they were neck and neck, then Fleet of Foot drew ahead. Hooves thundered and split the turf. The crowd yelled encouragement, hoping to urge their respective favourites to victory and enable themselves to celebrate with their winnings. Kit's followers were cock-a-hoop when, at the end of the first circuit, he had increased his lead by a length.

Olivia was gripped by anxiety. Had she misjudged Redwings' capabilities? Doubt crept in. In her mind, she was urging George to stay up. Oh, don't let Kit get any further ahead! But her silent pleas seemed in vain as, with another half circuit gone, Fleet of Foot drew a length and a half ahead. Olivia's lips tightened in despair. Her clenched fists drove her fingernails into the palms of her hands. The strain was unbearable but she could not tear her eyes away from the sight of the galloping horses.

They stormed past again, and the only comfort she could draw was that Redwings had not fallen any further behind. Her eyes were fixed on George who appeared to be in perfect control. Let him run now, she urged silently. Give him his head. Beside her Ursula was jumping up and down with excitement, urging Kit to win.

Olivia saw the power start to course through Redwings' body. His stride lengthened and the ground moved faster beneath his pounding hooves. It seemed an age before he made any impression on Fleet of Foot, but it was only a matter of seconds.

When they rounded the second bend Redwings had reduced the lead to a length. The back straight was a blur of horse flesh. Kit asked his horse for more effort but the immediate response quickly faded to the fast gallop he had maintained from the start.

'You've got him!' Olivia yelled.

The horses came off the fourth bend into the home straight neck and neck. Once again Redwings produced more power. The crowd gasped in amazement at the way the gap opened in that final run to bring George victory by a length.

His first thought was for Redwings as he let the horse gradually slow down. When they had pulled up, both panting and shaking from their exertions he heaped praise on Redwings. Kit came alongside and held out his hand.

'Congratulations! A fine race. I thought I had you at first. When did you find that Redwings could run and handle that well?'

George, basking in his victory, smiled widely. 'Olivia told me to run him against Black Mist this morning. That run, her persuasive powers and a little tip from her on handling him – well, you've just seen the result for yourself.'

'Shrewd girl.'

They had turned back and were moving through the

70

waiting throng of people. Congratulations were effusive, especially from those who had made a wager on George. Tonight they would be celebrating and helping the losers to drown their sorrows.

Olivia and Ursula pushed through the onlookers to greet them.

'Well done,' Olivia cried, her smile broad with delight. She caressed Redwings who rubbed his nose affectionately against her shoulder, obviously delighted with his win.

George slid from the saddle and came to her. There was a deep-felt appreciation in his eyes as he said for her ears alone, 'Thanks for your judgement. The victory was all the sweeter because of your involvement.'

She lowered her eyes and said softly, 'It was just a little advice.'

'It was more than that. You showed me how to handle Redwings and you had faith in me as a rider and in him as a runner.'

The horses were led away and Kit and Ursula joined them.

'I hear you were behind George's choice?' said Kit, his eyes on Olivia.

'And you didn't confide in me,' pouted Ursula.

Olivia smiled. 'You knew Redwings before today. Would you have believed me if I had told you he would win?'

'I suppose not,' came the grudging reply.

Honor came hurrying over to them. 'That was a wonderful ride,' she said admiringly. 'A good job you took no notice of me and made your own choice of horse.'

'It was Olivia's suggestion,' George admitted.

'Olivia's?' Honor looked puzzled.

'She assessed Redwings' potential when we were at the stables this morning. Persuaded me to run him, and she was right.'

'I'm surprised to hear you know horses that well, living in Whitby,' said Honor haughtily.

'You live and learn,' replied Olivia, with a little smile of triumph.

71

'Kit, let's get changed and then join the young ladies in the tent,' George suggested to defuse the tension. 'I believe that there are still refreshments to be had and I have been asked to be there for a while.'

'Somebody planning something?' asked Honor.

'Well, who knows?'

As they started to move away a smartly dressed middle-aged lady confronted them.

'Excuse me, all of you,' she said with a pleasing smile, and then let her eyes rest on Kit.

Olivia saw pride in that look.

'Kit, you let me down,' There was a teasing note in her voice.

'Not I, Aunt. This little lady outsmarted me. Aunt Betsy, meet Olivia Coulson, the rest you know. Olivia, my Aunt Betsy.'

'I am pleased to know you, ma'am.' Even in these few moments she had detected love and respect between aunt and nephew.

'And I you, my dear.' A twinkle of pleasure gleamed in Betsy's eyes. 'It gladdens me to hear that my Kit has been outsmarted by a girl. Good to have his high opinion of himself dinted for once.' She laughed and raised a hand to stop Kit's protests. 'I know you can handle it.'

He grinned and said, 'Aunt, no doubt you'll be interested to hear that Olivia comes from Whitby.'

Betsy raised her eyebrows. 'Does she now? Coulson . . .' She glanced at Olivia. 'Edward Coulson, shipbuilder. Any relation?'

'My father,' returned Olivia,

'Well, I never. He's here?' She glanced round as if she might see him.

'Yes.'

'Then I must renew old acquaintance. I met him on several occasions when I visited my brother.'

'Captain Fernley of the firm of Fernley and Thoresby, I'm told?'

72

'The same.'

'Come with us, ma'am. I've just seen my father going into the tent.'

Edward and Lavinia were delighted to meet Betsy again and were soon reminiscing. When she saw they were absorbed in talk of the past and exchanging news of mutual friends, Olivia chose the moment to excuse herself and slip away. George had just come into the tent.

He saw her threading her way towards him and, though people would have detained him, accepted their congratulations politely without stopping.

'Olivia, I'm glad I've caught you on your own. This is the first real opportunity I've had to give you my most sincere thanks for your expert judgement and advice.'

'It was nothing.' She tried to brush his praise aside.

'Oh, but it was. Although there was nothing tangible at stake, it was important to me to win on this occasion. Kit, a most likeable fellow, can be a bit full of his own importance and needs pulling down a rung or two. This defeat, though he wouldn't admit it, will have done him good. Our friendship will be all the stronger for it.'

'Then I'm pleased I was of some help.'

'Indeed you were. I never expected an expert on horses to arrive on my doorstep this weekend.'

Though flattered by the praise, Olivia felt bound to say, 'I'm no expert, George, but sometimes the attributes of a horse strike me as they did forcefully with Redwings. I just could not let it pass without telling you how I felt.'

'I'm glad and grateful that you did.'

'I was having butterflies in my stomach when I saw the lead Kit had taken. I thought he had fooled us with his new horse.'

'There was one point when I thought the same. Just before I gave Redwings his head. Then, when I did and felt the way he responded, I knew he would do it.'

At that point three musicians from the village, who had come quietly to one corner of the tent, started to play a waltz.

'Oh, there's obviously to be some dancing.' His eyes had widened in surprise. 'I didn't know about this.' People were spreading out around the extremities of the tent to leave the centre space vacant. A gentle clapping started and rippled round the tent. 'My goodness, they're expecting us to start the dancing.'

'Then let us do so,' Olivia smiled. 'The host should lead off, especially on his special day.'

'Then it will be my pleasure to have you as my partner.'

His eyes met hers and she felt they were searching for a deeper response but were hesitant to do so for fear of rejection. She made her smile encouraging and let her eyes dance with pleasure, hoping he would realise he had become important to her in a way she had never felt about anyone else.

They moved in time to the music, their steps in perfect unison as if this was a coming together of two kindred spirits. Olivia felt elated. This was more than she had dreamed of before leaving Whitby for the birthday celebrations at Cropton Hall.

'The grass is not conducive to dancing,' commented George, 'but everyone will manage and enjoy themselves. It's nice of the village to do this and it is keeping the party going for them, which I'm glad of.'

They whirled around the tent, with outbursts of clapping breaking out as they passed. They had been round twice before there was any move to join them. The first to do so were Kit and Ursula, and before long the space was nearly full.

So it continued until nearly dark, the only interruption coming when the dancing was stopped so that a representative from the village could present George with a new cricket bat and make a short speech, wishing him a happy future.

His words of acceptance were few but to the point and full of heartfelt thanks. They were greeted with loud applause and many cries wishing him well.

Olivia did not know when she had enjoyed an event so

much. She danced with Kit and felt as if she was floating on air, her feet did not seem to touch the ground. Timothy apologised every time he stood on her feet, which was often, but she only laughed with amusement at his embarrassment and his comment, 'Oh, I'm no good at this sort of thing but put me on a cricket field – that's different.' She always enjoyed dancing with her father who, in the spirited atmosphere, seemed to have shed ten years. He whirled her mother into a mazurka and she was pleased to see him taking Betsy through a gentle waltz, too.

Everyone danced with everyone, or so it seemed. Strangers became friends even if only for one dance after which they may never meet again, and all were sad when the last tune was played. Pleasurable moments had passed, never to be recaptured.

Villagers drifted back to their homes. Guests for the day made their thanks and farewells to their host and his parents and sought their carriages. Those who were staying at the Hall wandered across the fields in chattering groups, the young ones in pairs, still high-spirited from the jollification that had brought them together.

The evening in the Hall drifted lazily by in conversations, cards and piano playing. Eventually the excitements of the day took their toll and guests and hosts sought the comfort of their beds.

As she sank into the feather bed, Olivia sighed with contentment and in her mind was whirled away once more in the arms of George – only for him to be replaced soon after by tall, handsome Kit. The men drifted in and out of her mind as she tried to sort out the confusion of who should really be there. No, not who should be there, but who she wanted to be there.

Both had been attentive, charming and considerate. Both were good-looking in their different ways. George had a serenity about him which matched his gentleness. He would cope with life in a competent but unobtrusive way. He may stand out, be noticed occasionally, but would not seek the public eye. Life with him would be secure, calm and luxurious, for he, an only child, would one day inherit the estate and considerable wealth. His wife would be the lady of Cropton Hall.

Then Kit swept into her mind, just as he had done at various times throughout the day and just as he would do in real life. Caught up in his effervescent gaiety, she would be whirled along on a neverending stream of fun and excitement. Kit would live his whirlwind life to the full and take her with him, if she were willing and able to keep up. Olivia shuffled in her bed at the thought. Yes, life would be exciting with Kit but it would have its risks, too, for he was a person to revel in them. She had learned that he had done just that while expanding the farm and moving to his present dwelling. His gamble had worked but, from what she had gathered it could so easily have gone the other way. But wasn't the fact that he was prepared to take risks part of his attraction? She had thought that there would be no risk to his enterprises as he could always turn to his father, if he was in financial trouble, but had been told that that was not Kit's nature. He was his own man and would stand or fall by his decisions.

Olivia smiled to herself. Here she was comparing two men with an eye to the future when neither might be interested in her. But she didn't believe that. At heart she was convinced of her ability to take either man for herself. But which should it be?

Drowsily, she saw in her mind's eye a young man, handsome, contented and serene, quietly gazing out across the Cropton landscape from the steps of a big house which very much resembled the one in which she was falling asleep.

Chapter Six

Olivia woke the next morning determined to make the most of the day for tomorrow she would be returning to Whitby. Would that shut the door on her closeness to George? Not if she could help it!

Though under no obligation to do so, decorum required that the guests at Cropton Hall accompany their hosts to church. This was no hardship to Olivia who regularly attended services with her parents at the parish church on the cliff top at Whitby. The walk to Cropton church gave her the opportunity to study George further, admiring his bearing, his easygoing manner and rapport with his cousins and the rest of the guests.

As they left the church, he fell into step beside her. 'My cousins and I are planning a walk for this afternoon, would you like to come?'

'I would love to.'

'Good. We meet at half-past one on the terrace.' He paused, then added, 'What did you think to the sermon?'

Olivia pulled a face.

George laughed. 'My opinion too. The vicar always draws them out. Makes the same point over and over again.'

'And a bit too much hellfire and thunder, as if we were all bound for the pit below. Oh, maybe I shouldn't be critical?'

'Why not? If you have an opinion, express it. I think you are forthright enough to do that.'

Olivia smiled. 'If I weren't you wouldn't have ridden Redwings.'

'True enough. I hope you are enjoying your stay?'

'Oh, yes. Every minute of it.'

'Good.'

'And it's so beautiful around here.'

'I'll show you more of it this afternoon. Come, I must invite Sabina and Archie.'

They joined the young pair who were walking with their mother and father but broke away when George asked for them to be excused so that he could have a word with them.

They too were pleased with the suggestion of a walk which would allow them to escape a lazy afternoon spent on the terrace with their elders.

The ten young folk set off in a lighthearted mood. Couples paired off, broke up, and prepared to share each other's company, changing companions to no prearranged pattern. Conversation flowed, there was no shyness nor inability to join in, and George was the perfect host, seeing no one was left out. Topics ranged far and wide, were serious or lighthearted, raised out of curiosity or following from an expressed opinion. And all enjoyed the sunshine and fresh air.

George called a halt when they reached open ground after they had passed through a stand of young trees.

'See the ridges?' He indicated them, pointing out how they enclosed two large areas of the open ground in which they were now standing. 'It's said these were Roman training camps for the garrison stationed at what is now Malton.'

As the group split up to wander around the ridges and marvel at the fact that they were standing where Roman soldiers had stood eighteen hundred years ago, George laid his hand on Olivia's arm.

'Come, I'd like to show you something. Take my arm. We don't want you falling on this rough ground.'

They left the others exploring the ridged area and walked until George stopped on the edge of a steep drop looking down into a small grassy valley, stretching to left and right.

78

Opposite, the land rose to their level and rolled away in hedged fields and wooded areas. Sunshine and shadow drew out the character of the peaceful landscape.

'It's beautiful,' Olivia whispered, feeling that to speak in her normal tones would shatter the peace around them.

George made no comment.

The world stilled around them.

Reluctant to break the mood, he said, 'I ride up the valley coming from the left and continuing right round this rise we are on. It is a wonderful circular tour.'

'It must be.'

'Would you like to try it?'

'But I go home tomorrow, besides I have no . . .'

'You could come back.'

They had both continued to look across the landscape. Now she turned to him.

'Is that an invitation to visit again?'

'Yes. I would very much like you to ride with me.'

'Then I would love to.' Her heart was racing. This must mean he was interested in her. She had to rein in the feelings of joy that urged her to throw her arms round his neck. Propriety demanded she should add, 'If our parents agree.'

'Then we shall ask them when they are in a favourable frame of mind.' His eyes twinkled. 'Maybe when they've dined well tonight and the atmosphere engendered by music and wine has made them more receptive to the suggestion?'

She laughed then added gravely, 'I thank you for kindness this weekend and for your renewed invitation.'

'You shall ride Redwings when you come.'

'Oh, may I? I would love that.'

'Then you can look forward to it.'

'I will.'

Their conversation was broken by a shout of, 'George, do we go any further?'

'Coming!' he called.

They returned to Cropton Hall in high spirits. On reflection, Olivia thought that she had never been with such a

79

pleasant and friendly group of people of her own age. There were times when she'd suspected Honor was jealous of the attention George had paid to Olivia, but there was nothing to suggest outright hostility.

They slumped into chairs on the terrace and recounted their walk to their elders while they enjoyed tea and cakes. Gradually guests drifted away to their own rooms to prepare for the evening.

The house guests were joined by twenty local people invited to the final celebration of George's birthday, among them Kit and his aunt. Nothing had been spared and Mrs Dawson excelled herself with a buffet which catered for all tastes and which was continually replenished throughout the evening.

George persuaded Honor to play the piano before the musicians from the village arrived to provide music for the dancing. Olivia quickly realised that Honor was an accomplished pianist, and envied the expressive quality of her playing. She wished she herself had taken more seriously the lessons for which her father had paid. Then she could have persuaded George to turn the sheets of music for her as he was doing for Honor.

She determined to make the most of the dancing, but was disappointed when George chose Honor for the opening dance when the floor was left vacant for him to lead off. She glanced around, hoping that Kit would approach her, but he was in conversation with Ursula and Olivia knew that, once George and Honor had circled the room twice, Ursula would be in Kit's arms.

'May I have the pleasure of this dance, Olivia?'

She was startled out of her jealousy by Archie Campion. 'Er . . . thank you.'

She had not had a lot of talk with Archie but he had always been in the general conversation. He was likeable, friendly, but did not set her pulse racing. His eyes were continually wary as if he was frightened of doing the wrong thing, while his request held an intonation of apology for even daring to put the question. Olivia took his demeanour as a shield for shyness. But once they moved in time with the music, she realised he was an accomplished dancer with an acute sense of rhythm.

'You dance well, Olivia.' The words came tentatively as if he hardly dare voice a compliment.

'Archie, it is so kind of you to say so. I like dancing but have never been paid that compliment before.'

'Then it is very remiss of the young men of Whitby.'

Inevitably their talk turned to their host for the weekend.

'You've known George long?' Olivia probed.

'Oh, yes. When his family lived in Hull and we lived in Beverley. Times weren't easy for them compared to now. They were comfortable but with little to spare. George was a great comfort to his parents, particularly when his father was not well.'

'And then they came here.'

'That was fortunate for them. We knew that the family had originally been landed gentry but the connection was remote. It came as quite a surprise when they were told they had inherited the Cropton Estate.'

'They are charming people. I would guess that their good fortune hasn't changed them.'

'You're right. They are just the same people we used to know. They haven't forgotten old friends even though they readily made new ones when they moved here. They are highly thought of in this area.'

'And George?'

'The same. Coming into such wealth could have turned a young man's head, but not George's. He keeps a steady outlook on life, has used his advantages here to the best of his ability and adapted to country ways and country life better than any of us expected. A good, solid person. Oh, he enjoys life in his own way. What you have seen this weekend is genuine, nothing has been put on for the occasion. He respects the family's good luck and does not abuse it as some would have done. It is a privilege to know him and be his friend.'

81

The music finished, Archie bowed to her. 'That was a great pleasure, Olivia. May I book another dance later?'

'Indeed you may. I enjoyed it too.'

That was the theme of her evening – enjoyment. There was delight in her eyes, laughter on her lips, and quips on her tongue as she was whirled by one partner to another, from one dance to the next.

Kit transferred his lightness of step to her and swept her into a land of make believe where the joy of being with him alone pushed everything else aside. Their love would grow into an all-binding ecstasy which no one else would share.

George guided her on the dance floor as adroitly as she imagined he would through life. His dancing was perfection, something to which she responded by never putting a foot wrong. That was the way life would be with him. His love would never falter and would draw hers to match his forever.

She was flattered when he came to her for the final dance. As they moved in perfect unison, Olivia's mind drifted into a world where there was only her and George, here at Cropton Hall. As the last notes died, she made a resolve, one which she would do all in her power to keep. She wanted the love of this man.

He bowed. She curtsied. Their eyes met. Their expressions conveyed their feelings for each other. She sensed he would like to take their relationship further but was cautious. She thought this could be his reaction to any eligible female because he was the heir to such a vast estate. That was understandable, but she would see their relationship went further. She would cultivate his love and let him see that she was worthy of becoming the lady of Cropton Hall.

It was mid-morning when the guests started to leave the next day. Activity filled the terrace and drive in front of the hall. Carriages arrived, grooms steadied the horses, calming them in the hubbub of conversation between hosts and guests who were effusive in their thanks and farewells. Last-minute exchanges and final comments were made. Everyone seemed to be everywhere. Olivia had just said goodbye to Archie and then Ursula when she heard a familiar voice at her shoulder.

'I said you would brighten up my party and indeed you did.'

With a smile she accepted the compliment. 'That is kind of you. And thank you for a wonderful weekend. I will have a lot to think about. Many memories.'

'All pleasant, I hope?'

'Could they be anything else, especially in your company?'

Before George could reply Mrs Chilton-Brookes joined them. 'Goodbye, my dear. I hope you have enjoyed this weekend?'

'Indeed I have, ma'am. I thank you for inviting me.'

'Our pleasure. Now, George expressed a desire to have you visit us again. I considered the matter . . .'

Olivia's heart was racing. Her mind was willing his mother to approve.

'. . . and agreed, provided your parents gave their consent. I have seen your mother and father and they did so.'

Olivia had to keep tight rein on her desire to scream with delight and fling her arms round Mrs Chilton-Brookes. Instead she said decorously, 'Thank you, ma'am,' and flashed a glance at George, seeing pleasure in his face and eyes.

'He told me about you and Redwings and that you are a keen rider. Bring your riding habit.'

'I will.'

'Good. I have arranged for you and your parents to visit in three weeks' time.'

'Thank you, ma'am.'

Esther Chilton-Brookes glanced round. 'I believe your carriage is here and that your parents are ready to leave. I will say goodbye now for there is my sister about to go.'

'Goodbye, and thank you again.'

When his mother had gone, George's face broke into a

broad smile. 'So you will brighten up another weekend for me?'

Olivia's eyes danced. 'I will look forward to it. In fact, I wish it was now.'

George laughed. 'Come on. I must say goodbye to your parents.'

He escorted her to the carriage where her mother and father were waiting, made his goodbyes and saw them all comfortably seated.

As the coach drew away, Olivia raised her hand in farewell but it was her eyes which conveyed her true feelings. She wished she was not having to return to Whitby and hoped she would read the same feeling in George's eyes but he had turned away and, as behoved a good host, had directed his attention to the remaining guests.

'You seem to have made an impression this weekend, my girl.' There was satisfaction in Edward's voice as he leaned back in the carriage. 'I am pleased about that. It will do no harm to our negotiations for timber in the future.'

'An invitation to return in three weeks' time!' cried his wife, the euphoria in her voice unmistakable. 'I so liked the house. And to come again so soon is beyond expectation. What delightful people they are!' She eyed her daughter. 'It's thanks to you that we are coming again. George seems to have taken a liking to you.' Her expression became grave. 'Mind you do nothing to mar that.'

'Oh, Mother, is that likely?'

'I hope not.'

Olivia settled down to a quiet journey, wishing that she was still with George, sowing the seeds for a proposal that would make his vast estate her domain.

The next three weeks could not go fast enough for her. She woke every morning wishing the day was already over so that the time to return to Cropton was nearer. Her Whitby life resumed its normal pattern but there was no spark in it after Cropton Hall. The two parties to which she accepted invitations were, in her eyes, dull affairs compared to the one which still filled her mind.

She started to prepare for her second visit a week before their departure date. Her father acceded to her wishes and bought her a new riding habit. She chose and re-chose the dresses she would take, and decided on three that would be new in George's eyes.

As they neared Cropton Hall, Olivia calmed herself so that she should dismount from the carriage with an air of self-assurance.

The Chilton-Brookes came out to greet them as the carriage rolled to a stop. In no time at all their luggage had been taken out by the manservants and the carriage driven to the stables where their coachman would be accommodated for the weekend.

'I have put you in the same rooms as you had before. I thought you would feel more at home there,' explained Esther.

'That is very thoughtful of you,' returned Lavinia. 'We appreciate it.'

The two ladies fell to chattering as they led the way into the house while Richard informed Edward that he had a stand of timber in which he might be interested.

'It is good to see you again,' said George as he and Olivia followed.

'I am pleased to be here,' she replied. 'How is Redwings?'

'In fine condition. I'll take you to see him after you've settled in and we have had some tea. Tomorrow you shall ride him.'

'That's something to look forward to.' Pleasure shone in her eyes.

'And only that?' he teased.

'Of course not,' she replied indignantly.

Familiar with the house, they soon settled in. Relaxing with a refreshing cup of tea, they exchanged news and enquired after people they had met during the birthday celebrations. Though he courteously engaged in this talk, Olivia sensed George's attention fixed on her, but whenever she met his gaze she could not truly fathom what his feelings for her were. It was as if he was wary of letting them out. There and then she made a resolve to break down the barrier this weekend.

It was, therefore, with suppressed eagerness that she accepted the suggestion, made not only to her but to their parents, that he should show her Redwings.

'I am sure you would like to see him,' he concluded, 'and I am keen to know if he remembers you.'

When they reached the stable yard, Olivia asked him to allow her to approach Redwings alone. 'That way we will really know if he has a good memory.'

George held back, positioning himself so that Redwings could not be aware of his presence.

Olivia approached the stall sedately but in such a way that Redwings would know someone was there. She heard a movement and a moment later, with her only a few yards away, Redwings poked his head over the lower half of the door.

'Hello, old fellow. Remember me?' Her voice was low and gentle.

Redwings cocked his ears. He caught the familiar tone and his eyes softened.

'I'm sure you do.'

The horse gave a cautious snicker but that was replaced immediately with one of friendly recognition. He tossed his head and there was pleasure in his eyes.

Olivia reached out and stroked his forehead. 'You're a grand chap. You'll let me ride you tomorrow, won't you?'

George, who had witnessed the friendly reception, came to Olivia with a bright smile. 'I thought he would know you. There is something between you two which is a pleasure to behold.'

'And I hope that closeness grows this weekend, as others might.'

86

'I'm sure you're right,' replied George.

She thought her hint had not been lost on him when she saw his eyes narrow for a moment as if he was weighing up the full meaning of her words.

After dinner, when their parents decided to play cards, George suggested that Olivia might like to watch the sun go down from the terrace. The sky was clear with only a smattering of clouds visible far in the west.

'We could have a fine day tomorrow,' he surmised.

'That sky augurs well,' she agreed. 'I do hope so. I've been looking forward to riding in that valley you showed me when I was here last. Do we ride in the morning?'

'Oh, yes. Immediately after breakfast. I suggest you and I have that at seven-thirty.' He glanced at her. 'Unless that's too soon for you?'

'No, I'm used to early rising.'

'Good. Then we'll be away by eight. The grooms will have Redwings ready for you and Black Mist for me.' With that settled George added, 'Let's go to the west end of the terrace, we'll see the sunset better from there. I'm sure tonight's will be a good one unless those clouds thicken.'

They strolled along in a shared silence, one which Olivia felt brought her closer to him. Words were not needed in the empathy she felt certain was developing between them. A slight frown creased her brow. But could she be wrong? Was she imagining what she wanted to happen? She drove the doubt away. She could not be. George must sense the growing bond between them. If he hadn't wanted her company she would not have been invited this weekend.

She cast aside her doubts. They were intruding on the present, marring the pleasure of being with him.

The air was warm, the landscape still. No breeze touched the trees. Only the distant lowing of a cow broke the silence and, the moment it stopped, the feeling of the countryside settling in for the night intensified.

The sun slid towards the west, lighting the sky above

87

them for a final minute before allowing darker shades to take over. It lit the clouds from behind with a glow that painted their edges gold before turning its palette to pinks and reds which harmonised towards darkness.

'It's beautiful,' whispered Olivia, hardly daring to break the silence.

They watched the sun sink lower, weaving its magic in an ever-changing colourscape. It dropped from sight but left a glow on the horizon to let them know it was not lost forever. Gradually that light faded and took with it any nimbus it had thrown across the heavens, to leave only darkness and the moon.

An owl hooted. A rustle came from a nearby wood. The night was coming alive with the unseen but the two figures on the terrace were only aware of each other's presence.

They remained close, a slight tension between them as if both were afraid to take the initiative. Or was it that, if they broke the spell which the night had cast on them, they would lose these precious moments that would bring them closer?

Olivia longed for him to take her hand in his, to feel their fingers entwine. If she made the first move would he think her forward? Would it raise a barrier which would then have to be broken down? She wanted nothing of her doing to mar the way to a marriage that she was determined to achieve.

'Do you feel the chill?' George broke the silence but Olivia did not regret it for he took her hand as if to check the query he had posed.

'No,' she answered, her heart racing. The magic of the night was gone but in its place had come the wonder of his touch. Where there had been respect there was now affection and a bonding in which he desired to know more about her.

'Maybe we should go in, I don't want the responsibility of your catching cold. And,' he added with a chuckle, 'I suppose we should socialise with our elders.'

She smiled. 'I suppose we should or they'll be wondering what we are up to.' Her eyes glinted encouragingly.

'Thank you for being here.' He kissed her lightly on the cheek.

That kiss – the affection of a friend . . . or?

Maybe tomorrow she would find out.

Chapter Seven

Olivia was awake early. Excitement had interrupted her night's sleep but had not marred a feeling of exhilaration as she dressed and made her preparations to look her best.

Her new riding habit in bottle green fitted her to perfection and caught George's eye, as it was meant to do, when she walked into the dining-room.

'Most elegant and becoming,' he commented, rising from his chair. 'But then, why wouldn't it be, when you enhance any clothes you wear?'

She smiled. 'You are most kind,' she said with a slight inclination of her head.

He was attentive to her needs at breakfast but, eager to be off, she ate very little.

When they reached the stables they found Redwings and Black Mist saddled and waiting under the care of the grooms. A few minutes later, comfortable on their mounts, they rode from the stableyard.

'We've got the weather we wanted,' observed George.

'We're so lucky,' Olivia enthused.

They kept the animals to a walking pace, enjoying the morning air from which the sun had driven the early sharpness. They rode along the drive towards the main gate. Hearing the clop of the hooves, the gatekeeper came from her lodge. She returned their greeting politely and wished them a pleasant ride.

They took the trackway to the left and, as it turned away from the wall, Olivia asked, 'Are we still on your estate?'

'Oh, yes,' replied George. 'We will never be off it. This wall is to afford some privacy to the house, though, as you know, the grounds surrounding it are extensive.'

They moved into a small wood where the sunlight was shafted into rays by the branches and left patterns of light on the dry ground.

They left the trackway for a path which after about a hundred yards dipped into a small glade where a stream gurgled over stones and hissed alongside grass-covered banks.

Black Mist stepped towards the water and lowered her head to drink. Olivia allowed Redwings to do the same.

'This glade swings round into the valley I showed you when you were here last. We'll be able to let the horses run there, so let's give them a rest now.' George swung from his saddle, his movements smooth and athletic. He came to Redwings and held out his arms to help Olivia to the ground. She slid from the saddle. His hands took her round the waist and lowered her gently. Their eyes met and held. Olivia was sure he must be experiencing the same intense desire as she. Not a word was spoken. His lips met hers cautiously.

She was eager for his kiss to carry more than just that gentle touch, but her judgement warned her not to take the initiative. His lips brushed hers sensuously and then, all caution gone, he swept her into a passionate embrace which she was not slow to return.

He broke away. Disappointed, she let her arms slip to her sides, but, when he took her hand in his the touch regenerated the feelings she had discovered when he had kissed her. He led her to a large boulder. They sat, holding hands, not speaking while they watched the stream swirl past their feet.

'You have some beautiful places on your estate.' She broke the silence that had fallen between them.

91

'Yes. I don't think I will ever tire of this part of the country, even though it becomes more and more familiar.'

'I'm the same about Whitby, I love the people and the place, all the activity of a thriving port.'

'Then you must feel bored in this quieter part of Yorkshire?'

'Oh, no,' she added quickly, not wanting him to think she could never settle away from Whitby nor come to love the countryside as he did. 'It is people who make or mar places.'

'And do they mar Whitby for you?'

'The young people with whom I associate have begun to bore me.'

'That could be just a passing phase.'

She pursed her lips to show her doubt.

'And there are no young men who ...?' He left the rest of the question unspoken but his inference was clear.

She gave a little laugh. 'No. Oh, I've had my beaux but none I could take seriously.'

'I see.' He got to his feet, putting an end to this conversation, whereas she, seeing it as a means of finding out where his feelings lay, would have liked it to go on. He held out his hand to help her to her feet. 'We'll give the horses a run.'

She did not speak but held his hand until they reached Redwings. He helped her into the saddle and then climbed on to Black Mist. They kept to a gentle walk for another quarter of a mile at which point the glade turned into the valley Olivia remembered and they halted their horses again.

'Beautiful,' she commented, letting her eyes rove across the lush grass which gave way to gorse bushes close to the top of the hills that held the valley like a precious jewel.

He smiled. 'I like it.'

'I think you love it.'

He nodded. 'I do.'

'And that's why you ride here often?'

'Yes. The grass goes on beyond the turn.'

'Then we'll have a good run,' she cried.

'Not yet.' His words sounded like a warning.

She was puzzled but held Redwings back and when George let Black Mist walk forward followed suit. She soon saw the reason for his caution. A small stream, invisible from where they had been standing, cut across the valley. They let the horses walk across it then George put his mount into a trot and Olivia matched his pace as she drew alongside. The quicker movement sent excitement coursing through her in anticipation of what was to come.

George glanced admiringly at her, saw she was ready and yelled, 'Let's ride!'

Black Mist responded immediately and was into a gallop. Though she was expecting George's shout she was still caught unawares, so that Redwings started at a slight disadvantage. Hooves tore at the turf. The pace was fast but both riders held something in reserve. Olivia held her position, half a length behind George. From here she could watch the movements he used to command his horse. She would not surrender any further advantage to him.

George quickened the pace. Hooves beat a thunderous tattoo. Pheasants broke from their grassy cover, rabbits scurried for the safety of their burrows, and birds in the trees took flight. He glanced over his shoulder and saw laughter on Olivia's lips and excitement in her eyes. Beneath her the muscular animal surged with power and grace. She knew Redwings was enjoying this as much as she.

They came to the turn and when they rounded it Olivia saw the green swathe widen as the hills to either side retreated. Ahead a gentle slope rose to meet the juncture of the hills.

The sight jolted her into action. She did not know Redwings' aptitude on rising land, while Black Mist was a strong horse. Could Redwings match her when the going got harder?

She called gently to her mount. The horse heard and responded by lengthening his stride. His hoofbeats became faster. Olivia's intoxication at the increased speed infected Redwings. They became one and the ground flew away beneath them.

George saw Olivia's move and called to Black Mist. Olivia's lips tightened. Black Mist had drawn a little further ahead. She must not allow her to widen the gap.

'Come on, Redwings, you're not going to lose!'

The horse sensed the urgency in her voice. Turf flew behind his cutting hooves. He gained on Black Mist. Olivia yelled in triumph. They were alongside. She saw the determination on George's face and drew ahead, letting her laughter trail mockingly behind her as Redwings hit the slope and kept his pace without hesitation. A quick glance over her shoulder told her George was falling behind. Black Mist could respond no more.

She topped the rise three lengths ahead and allowed Redwings to slow down gradually as she guided him in a circle.

Both horses were panting heavily as they came alongside each other. George was drawing air deep into his lungs but there was pleasure in his eyes.

'You ride well,' he panted.

Olivia, pleased by his admiration, let laughter trill off her lips. 'That was a wonderful ride!' She shook back her hair. It had come unfastened when she lost her hat and now streamed down her back. The movement stirred George. He edged his horse close to hers, leaned across and kissed her.

'For the winner,' he said.

'Thank you, kind sir,' she replied, and then with a twinkle in her eye, 'I thought I would deserve better than that.'

'Then get down and you shall have it.'

She slid to the ground, came to him and no other word was spoken as he swept her into his arms and their lips met passionately.

94

Their ride back to the Hall was gentle, allowing the horses and riders to recover and bask in the enjoyment of an intoxicating morning and the kisses they had shared.

That night Olivia went to bed elated. She thought George was in love with her and the more she considered it, in the softness of her feather bed, with the moonlight streaming through the window, the more certain she became that she was right.

Doubt never entered her mind throughout Sunday even though they had little time to themselves. There was church in the morning. The Sleightholmes came for lunch and stayed until after tea. But their visit at least brought some satisfaction to Olivia.

When the conversation turned to shipbuilding and timber, Roger Sleightholme hinted that Edward might be interested in a stand of oaks he was prepared to sell. Immediately Richard extended an invitation to the Coulsons to stay an extra day.

'It will give you the opportunity to go to Sleightholme Dale tomorrow to inspect the oaks,' he concluded.

'That is very generous of you,' replied Edward. He glanced at his wife and read approval in her eyes. 'If it is no trouble?'

'That won't inconvenience us, will it, my dear?' Richard looked at his wife seated at the opposite end of the dining table.

'Of course not,' she returned. 'It will be most agreeable to have Lavinia's company for an extra day.'

'Good, then that is settled.' He turned to Roger. 'Edward, George and I will be over in the morning.'

Disappointment welled in Olivia. At the start of the announcement she had visualised an extra day with George, but now ...

That evening, as their parents became engrossed in their card game, George played the piano: soft, gentle music. She interpreted the smiles he kept bestowing on her as

95

expressions of love for her which stirred her into examining her own feelings. She liked him a lot but was she in love with him? When she questioned the doubt in her mind she recalled her grandmother's advice: marry for love but love where there's money. George would inherit the estate, and she was sure she could grow to love the man who could make her mistress of all this. She sat there basking in happy anticipation of her triumph to come.

The final note faded away. The silence was almost startling. She looked up and was aware of George coming to sit beside her.

'I'm sorry I have to go to Sleightholme Dale tomorrow but I really can't refuse.'

She read genuine disappointment in his voice.

'I'm sorry too, but at least we should get an extra evening together.'

He smiled. 'You always seem to look on the bright side. I admire that in you. What will you do while I'm away?' He gave a little grin. 'I don't suppose you'll want to spend the day listening to our mothers chattering?'

She laughed. 'I will certainly try to avoid that.'

'Then why not go for a ride. I'll tell the grooms to have Redwings ready for you.'

'May I?' Her eyes lit up with the thought. It would be a good way to use some of the time while George was away.

'Of course. Why not?'

So it was that Olivia rode out of the stableyard the following morning at ten o'clock. She kept Redwings to a walking pace. There was no hurry. Later she might let him run. She followed the same route which George had taken, wanting to relive the memories which were sweet.

She stopped at the edge of the trees and sat in the saddle surveying the glade where George had first kissed her. Silence absorbed the sound of the stream and the song of the birds and filled her mind with its magic. This was a place which would live forever in her memory.

She sent Redwings forward until she was near the stream and the boulder on which she and George had sat. She slid from the saddle, went to the boulder and sat down. She drew her knees up and leaned forward to rest her chin on them, watching the running stream.

The water broke the light into ever-changing angles, creating sparkling diamonds of sunlight. She imagined plucking them to form a shimmering necklace which George would slip round her throat, allowing his fingers to brush her skin gently. Foam formed around protruding rocks before it was sucked away to disappear and leave the water gurgling in its clarity.

How long she sat entranced she never knew. Her preoccupation was shattered when a voice caused her to jump and drove all her daydreaming away.

'A penny for them.'

She looked round, eyes wide with curiosity and a little alarm. She was relieved to recognise the new arrival. 'You!'

'Yes, me, fair lady.' Kit's smile was filled with pleasure as he bowed and then came up to the boulder.

'How long have you been watching me?' she demanded with a touch of indignation. She did not like being spied on.

'That is my secret. You made such a pretty picture I was reluctant to spoil it.'

'You have a glib tongue, Kit Fernley.'

'And you don't mind,' he said as he sat down beside her.

'You presume too much.'

'But I think I am right.'

Olivia would not admit to it but could not deny that she was intrigued by his unselfconscious charm.

'You were deep in your thoughts. I offered you a penny for them.'

'They are not for sale.'

'Ah, I am disappointed. I was hoping I might hear they were about me. Alas, if you will not sell I shall never know, and that is a grievous loss.'

'You will have to bear it.'

He raised his hands in horror. 'Oh, you have a cruel streak as well.'

'I think you will take no harm.'

'Maybe so, but you can ease what pain I suffer.'

Olivia was wary. What was he going to ask of her? She turned her gaze on him enquiringly, shifting slightly away from him at the same time so as to raise a barrier against too great an intimacy.

Kit was fascinated. Resistance. That he liked, for it challenged him to break it down.

'You ride alone, that surprises me. I wonder what George can be thinking of not to be in the company of such bewitching beauty?'

'A glib tongue again, even when you are asking questions.'

He inclined his head in acceptance of her assessment, and waited for her to continue.

'George has accompanied his father and mine to Sleightholme Dale to look at some timber in which my father might be interested.'

'How boring for him when he could be in your company!' Kit laughed. 'But that is my good fortune. And, I hope, yours.'

Wariness crept into Olivia's gaze again. 'You have not told me how . . .'

He held up his hand, stopping her words. 'That time has come.' He paused, letting the moment intensify her curiosity. 'I am attending a family party in Whitby a week on Friday. Would you allow me to call on you on Thursday and do me the honour of accompanying me to the party the next day?' His voice was serious now. His face had taken on a grave expression which added plausibility to his suggestion and indicated there was depth behind the light-hearted exterior he so often displayed. There was hope there too.

Could she refuse? She could, but did she want to? Would

she feel she was betraying George by accepting this invitation? But she was not committed to him, though she hoped that one day she would be. Would she mar that if she accepted Kit's invitation? This man intrigued her. His dash, his verve, his appearance of living life to the full, were all attributes she wanted to emulate.

'But I have not had an official invitation to the party. You said it was a family affair so I would be an intruder.' She made the objections as she felt she should while hoping he would brush them aside.

He did just that but with words she'd never expected. 'Family, yes, but they will not object to my bringing a guest. Besides it will give you the opportunity to get to know them, or at least those in Whitby, and that would be a wise thing to do.'

'Wise?'

'Well, the sooner the better, because one day you will be related to them.'

'What on earth do you mean? You talk in riddles.' Indignation sharpened her tone.

'One day you will be mine.'

Olivia was shaken by the certainty in his voice. She stood up and turned to face him and was immediately disarmed by the bright smile on his face. Nevertheless she displayed her annoyance at his assumption.

'You presume too much, Kit Fernley. I'll be tied to no man. Not yet!'

He laughed. 'You are even more tempting when you are annoyed. Come, sit down. We have time on our hands. I was going to see George but if he's away I may as well spend my time in your charming company.'

She hesitated a moment and sat down slowly.

'I am a happy man again, and will be happier when you give me permission to call on you in Whitby?'

'Granted.' The words came without undue consideration, but she had no doubt it would have been the same reply if she had taken time to contemplate his proposal.

'Maybe we could go riding on the Saturday?'

'I will look forward to that.'

'Do you know my Aunt Jessica and her husband Ruben Thoresby?'

'Not personally, though I know of them, but who wouldn't in Whitby?'

'Considering they, along with Ruben's sister-in-law, Jenny Thoresby, run the most important whaling firm in Whitby, I agree, who wouldn't? Do you know Jenny?'

Again Olivia shook her head. 'No. Though, like everyone else in Whitby, I know the story of the tragic loss of her husband Adam in the Arctic.'

'My father's best friend. I'm told he was devastated, especially as he lost my mother Ruth about the same time.'

'You never knew her?'

'No, I was only a baby. I wish I had, and I wish I knew what part of her I have inherited. Some of my wildness, I expect, seeing my father is more steady-going.'

'You've never asked him?'

'All I know is that she was drowned when the London packet foundered off Saltwick Nab in heavy weather after leaving Whitby. There were no survivors.'

The rumour that Ruth Fernley had died later in America, mentioned by Ursula, sprang to mind but Olivia thought it better not to mention it. She need have had no such qualms as Kit went on to say, 'Her body was never found, so naturally there were rumours that she had survived which led to preposterous stories that she had gone to America and died there. If that had been the case she could have been traced. Besides, why would she want to do that?'

'You've never asked your father?'

'Oh, yes, and like everyone else he says no one could have survived the storm that night.'

'And you accept that?'

'Yes.' Kit paused, frowning. 'But I never hear any real detail about her. Father praises her. Other members of the family say she was lovely to look at and a strong woman

100

then quickly get off the subject. Eventually I gave up trying to find out more about her. After her death I was given over to my grandparents and my Uncle John and Aunt Betsy because my father was going to be away at sea so much. He lives in London now, coming to Whitby only occasionally if business demands it.'

'You would still like to know about your mother?'

'Yes. I feel as if part of my life is missing, that there's something in the past I should know about.'

Olivia was pleased with the intimacy of this conversation. It seemed as if Kit was placing their relationship, short though it had been, on more personal terms, as if he trusted her with this very private information. Though she had nothing as dramatic in her family she wanted to return his confidence, to place their association on level terms.

'Thank goodness I have no such problems to bother me.'

'Your life's been straightforward?'

'Oh, yes, a good father, a loving mother.' She gave a little smile. 'The only blot was two elder brothers.'

He laughed. 'I'll bet they doted on you, a younger sister?'

'I suppose so. They are out of my hair now, both married.'

'So you have more time with your parents?'

'Yes, and that is very pleasant. But don't misunderstand me, I always got on well with my brothers and still do.'

'I sometimes wish my brother and sister were nearer – half-brother and half-sister really. You see, my father has been married three times. I do get on well with them when I see them but it isn't all that often seeing that they live in London.'

'What are their names?'

'Dominic is my brother. He was Lydia's child. My father met her in London, the daughter of a ship owner there. She died when Dominic was born.'

'And your sister?'

'Ailsa's a grand lass, I get on extremely well with her. She's the daughter of Father's present wife, Beth, a Shetlander.'

Olivia was surprised by this information. 'I suppose he met her when he was sailing to the Arctic?'

'Yes, but there's a lot more to her story. Some day I'll tell you. There's a lot of her mother in Ailsa.'

Though she would have liked to have heard more, it was obvious that Kit did not want to enlarge on the topic now. Olivia merely made one other query.

'Would you have liked to be a sailor like your father? Is the sea not in your blood even though you have been brought up a countryman?'

For a moment Kit did not answer. Olivia surmised what it would be before he spoke. She had seen a wistful faraway look come to his eyes and it was not the gaze of a countryman looking to the distant hills but of someone who saw horizons of greater distance and immensity.

He gave a reluctant nod. 'Yes, I suppose, born of a man who loved the sea and still does, it was inevitable that I should have the same urge, but that was sublimated by my upbringing. Who knows what would have become of me if my mother had lived and I had been brought up among the seafarers of Whitby?'

He lapsed into silence. For a few moments Olivia left him with his thoughts. Then she said, 'I think I should be getting back.'

He made no protest but asked, 'May I ride with you?'

'It will be my pleasure,' she consented, eradicating any show of hostility she had made earlier.

He helped her on to her horse and once he was in the saddle they left the glade which now held further memories for Olivia.

They kept to a walking pace, neither showing any desire to hurry. Their conversation and the feeling of companionship between them had brought their friendship to a new level.

Nearing the gates to Cropton Hall, Kit drew his horse to a halt.

'Will you not come all the way?' asked Olivia.

'I would be grateful if you would allow me to decline. Time presses me.'

She inclined her head in agreement to his request. 'Very well. I must not detain you.'

'Thank you, kind lady.' He doffed his hat, bowed his head and then met her gaze with a look which revealed his enjoyment of their meeting. 'You have brought pleasure to my day. I will remember it 'til we meet in Whitby.'

Before she could reply, he turned his horse and put it into a gallop.

She sat for a few moments watching his departure. The thunder of the hooves seemed to beat his name into her mind, forcing her to consider the attraction he held for her as she rode along the drive to the house.

There was a dash to him, a liveliness which would sweep her along but always on the edge of uncertainty. Was that what she wanted? It held an undeniable appeal for a girl who was finding life among her set in Whitby something of a bore. But wasn't that just a short-term phase? What of the future? What would that hold with Kit? Didn't she want the future to be on much safer ground? At Cropton Hall for instance? George represented security, financial and moral. And he was attractive, too, with a fine straight bearing and his own quiet magnetism. Hadn't she been thrilled by his kisses? Weren't they a sign that he loved her, even after so short a time? She felt sure of it. She knew she could love him, but now there was Kit Fernley . . .

George held her attention on his return from Sleightholme Dale. He enthused about his day, pleased that her father had taken his advice about the purchase of timber. But more than that he wanted to know about her day, regretting that he had not been able to be with her. He was pleased to know she had visited the glade where they had shared their first kiss, reading it as a sign that the place would always be special to her. She did not mention meeting Kit. There was an innate desire in her to keep that a secret.

Her sadness at leaving next day was alleviated somewhat by Kit's promise to see her when he came to Whitby for his family's party, and she was curious about his prediction for the future though by now she believed she could only live at Cropton Hall as George's wife.

At breakfast her father extended an invitation to the Chilton-Brookes to visit Whitby in three weeks' time.

'I thank you for the offer,' replied Richard, 'but Esther and I will be visiting relatives in Somerset at that time. We will be away for a further month after that. Maybe we can arrange a visit after we return.'

'Most certainly,' agreed Edward.

'I regret having to be away for so long,' he explained, 'but we have to clear up some family matters, and while we are in Somerset we thought we would spend some time with relatives we don't see as often as we would like. However, George is staying here to look after the estate so may I suggest that he accepts your invitation? It will give him the opportunity of seeing your shipbuilding yards without me hampering him.'

'You don't do that, Father,' put in George quickly.

Richard brushed away the statement with a sweep of his hand. 'My illness accounts for the fact that I'm not as agile as I should be at my age, let's not gloss over the fact.' He turned his attention back to Edward. 'What do you say to my suggestion?'

Olivia's heart was racing. Her wish could come true without any prompting on her part. If he accepted, his visit would not coincide with Kit's. Her mind was willing him to say yes.

'Very well,' replied Edward. 'We would be delighted to have George, if he would like to come?'

All eyes were on George. He smiled. 'Nothing would please me more. I thank you, sir.' He glanced at Lavinia. 'And you, ma'am.'

Later, as they strolled on the terrace, George and Olivia both expressed their delight at the arrangements, and sealed the promise of what they could mean with a kiss.

Olivia made no mention that before George's visit, Kit would in Whitby.

Chapter Eight

'Mr Kit Fernley to see Miss Olivia Coulson.'

The servant girl's eyes widened at the sight of the tall handsome stranger standing at the front door, smiling brightly at her.

Kit wore his clothes well and they were of good quality if not maybe the best. His coat with knee-length tails was cut away at the waist at the front. Its dark brown colour complemented that of his beige trousers. His black shoes were highly polished and his cravat neatly tied at the neck of a yellow shirt with a low collar.

'Er ...' The girl stumbled over her answer, then finding the words let them rush out. 'I'll see if Miss Coulson is receiving visitors, sir. Please step inside.'

She stood to one side, her eyes downcast, wondering who Miss Olivia's visitor might be? Then she was aware that he had moved past her and was waiting. She blushed, closed the door and started across the hall.

'Don't forget ...' His words halted her. She turned to see a teasing twinkle in the stranger's eyes. 'Mr Kit Fernley.'

'Oh, yes, sir. I won't,' she spluttered and blushed even more. Then she turned and hurried on her way, his amused but uncritical smile in her mind.

She knocked on the door of the drawing-room, opened it and disappeared inside. A few moments later she came out to say, 'Will you come this way, sir? Miss Olivia Coulson will be pleased to see you.'

Kit crossed the hall quickly, pausing only to hand his hat to the girl.

'Kit, I'm so pleased you kept your promise.' Olivia had risen to her feet to greet him. Her smile as she held out her hand to him expressed her pleasure.

He returned that smile with one of equal delight, took her hand and raised it towards his lips as he bowed. 'I always keep my promises, Miss Olivia. And I promise you a splendid evening tomorrow at our family party at the Angel.'

'Do I take that as a firm invitation?' she asked coyly as she indicated a chair to him.

'Did I not make that clear when you were in Cropton? I apologise if I did not.' He sat down on a red moquette-covered armchair opposite to her.

'Well, I wasn't quite sure, the party being a family affair. I thought you would have to mention it to other people.'

'I have.'

'Won't I be intruding?'

Before he could reply, the door opened and the servant girl reappeared carrying a tray of tea.

'I took the liberty of ordering some for you when I knew who was calling,' Olivia explained.

'Delightful,' he returned, and when another girl appeared with a tray on which there was a plate of scones, added, 'My favourite. They look very appetising.' He leaned slightly forward, eyes fixed on Olivia. 'To answer your question, I mentioned to Aunt Jessica that I would like to bring a guest to the party. Naturally she wanted to know who, and was even more curious when I said it was a young lady.' His infectious laughter rang out – when he added, 'My aunts are always saying I should find someone with whom to settle down. Well, when I told them who it was Aunt Jessica approved straight away and my request needed no backing from Aunt

Betsy. So, you see, you are known to the family.'

Olivia blushed slightly. 'A good reputation, I hope?'

Kit smiled. 'If it wasn't Aunt Jessica certainly wouldn't have given her approval.'

Olivia had poured the tea and handed a cup to Kit who placed it on the small table beside his chair. On Olivia's suggestion he helped himself to a scone, then piled butter and jam on to it. Olivia watched his actions covertly and could not help wondering how George would have approached the task. Probably he would have spread things with more care.

Kit savoured his scone and leaned back in his chair with a contented sound.

'I am flattered by your aunt's kindness. Is there a special reason for the party? I don't think you ever said.'

'I don't believe I did. It's a party to celebrate the betrothal of Jessica and Ruben's daughter Kate to John Fowler.'

'Kate and John? I don't really know them though I have met them occasionally at parties. I didn't know they were taking this step?'

'The last four years have brought them close, ever since John's father was lost with his ship in the Arctic.'

'I was sixteen at the time, and remember how shocked Whitby was at the loss.' A thoughtful expression crossed her face. 'I think John would have been seventeen then.'

'That's right. From what I've been told he wanted to sail with his father but he prevailed upon John to stay at home.'

'And then he had to face a second tragedy.'

'The loss of his mother?'

'Yes. You know the story?'

'Vaguely. I was at Cropton then, not in Whitby.'

'The loss of her husband upset Mrs Fowler's mind. She would go out on to the west pier every night looking for her husband's ship. John was aware of this and would bring her home. But one night a storm was raging. He did not expect his mother to go out on such a wild night but, unknown to him, she did. When he realised she was not in the house he

108

knew where she would be and immediately went to the west pier. He saw his mother at its extremity. Heavy seas, driven by a ferocious wind, were breaking over it. He was battling to reach her when he saw an enormous wave sweep her away.'

Kit looked shocked. His face was sombre. 'I knew she was swept off the pier. I did not know that John had witnessed her end. No wonder Aunt Jessica and Uncle Ruben would not talk of it and forbade me to mention his mother in front of him. They took him in, you know. He was alone. No brothers or sisters. No uncles or aunts. No one.'

'But Kate was there.'

'Yes. They became close. She supported his desire to follow in his father's trade. Ruben tried to dissuade him but could not counteract the pull of the sea. After all, he too had been unable to resist it.'

'I hope they will be very happy. Now, if it is that sort of occasion, I must take them a suitable present.'

'There is no need. They won't expect it.'

'Maybe, but I insist. I shall shop tomorrow morning.'

'Then please let me accompany you?'

'I will be delighted, but you may be bored.'

'How could I be in such charming company? Besides it could be interesting, I will probably be visiting parts of Whitby I never would otherwise.'

They spent a couple of hours enjoying each other's company and engaging in conversation which at times was serious and stimulating, at others humorous and light-hearted.

When Kit left Olivia felt a keen desire to have kept him longer. She experienced sensations she had never felt before. Emotions crowded in so that the yearning to feel Kit's arms around her and his lips on hers was almost over-powering. She had to make a strong effort to bring some semblance of order to her racing mind. She must keep her feelings towards the two men who had recently entered her life in perspective.

She contemplated the prospects life with each offered. Mrs Fernley of Howdale Manor would not carry the same social position as Mrs Chilton-Brookes of Cropton Hall. What did she really want? She was sure both men loved her. Distant voices seemed to be trying to direct her mind but she could not make out what they were saying. She sighed and hoped her confusion would be resolved to her benefit.

She rose from her chair and walked slowly to her room. Maybe these next few days with Kit would help to firm her resolution to marry soon – and as well as she could. That meant to George so why did a part of her still dwell on thoughts of a bright unquenchable smile and bold laughing eyes?

The following morning Olivia revelled in Kit's attention as they visited several shops in Church Street and Flowergate before she settled on a china tea service decorated with a delicate rose motif. She asked for it to be suitably wrapped and delivered to the Angel addressed to Miss Kate Thoresby and Mr John Fowler.

Kit accompanied her to her home and on parting said, 'I have enjoyed being with you and look forward to this evening. I will call for you at six-thirty.'

He in fact arrived several minutes before that and was talking to Edward and Lavinia when Olivia entered the drawing-room.

Kit could not control a small gasp of appreciation as he sprang to his feet. 'You look exquisite.'

Olivia smiled, feeling rather pleased that she had caused him some confusion.

Her mother and father added their compliments, proud that their daughter looked so engaging in her high-waisted silk dress of pale green, a colour which enhanced that of her eyes. The square-cut bodice with cross pleatings ran into short puffed sleeves, leaving her arms bare. Around her neck hung a silver necklace from which hung a small finely fashioned representation of a ship. Her hair was drawn on to the top of her head and held by a small white bow. She carried a chiffon shawl embroidered with an ivy leaf pattern.

'Thank you all.' She accepted their compliments gracefully. 'Shall we go?'

Kit gave his agreement and Olivia kissed her mother and father who wished them both an enjoyable time.

The evening was pleasantly warm and the air still. The buzz of Whitby life rose and fell about them, quieter than in the day but full of the vibrant tenor of any busy port.

It was only a short walk to the Angel where they were greeted by a gushing landlord pleased to have his inn chosen as the venue for a party arranged by such a well-known and respected family of whaleship owners.

'This is a great occasion,' he said as he escorted them to the room set aside for their use. 'I'm sorry your father couldn't be here, Mr Kit.'

'I wish he were. Sadly his work keeps him in London.'

'A great pity. He is missed in Whitby.'

As they entered the room was filled with chatter. The betrothed couple stood close to the door to greet new arrivals.

'Olivia Coulson, welcome. It is so nice to have you join us.' Kate's greeting held unmistakable sincerity. It was as if Olivia had always been on her list of special guests for this family party. 'And Kit.' She turned to her cousin. 'Thank you for coming and bringing Olivia.'

'My pleasure.' He kissed her on the cheek and smiled warmly at this cousin two years his junior, one whom he admired for her thoughtfulness, resolution and unswerving devotion to the young man beside her, especially through the trying times he had faced.

'I'm grateful to you and your family for allowing Kit to bring me,' said Olivia. 'And may I wish you every happiness for the future?'

111

'Thank you.' Kate's glance held a teasing curiosity as it switched from one to the other. 'Maybe we will see more of you two in the future.'

'Indeed you may,' returned Kit, responding to her hidden query as to the depth of his relationship with Olivia.

They turned to John and offered him their congratulations, then he and Kate thanked Olivia for her present.

'I hope it will always remind you both of this special day,' she replied.

'It certainly will. Now enjoy yourselves. I'm sure Kit will introduce you to everyone.'

As the evening proceeded he made all the appropriate introductions to his family and friends, some of whom Olivia already knew or with whom she was acquainted. Conversation was brisk, light-hearted, gossipy, occasionally serious but always enjoyable.

A room had been set aside for a buffet which continued throughout the evening, enabling the company to enjoy a wide range of mouth-watering delights. Music for dancing was provided by a local trio. Olivia was forever in demand for her reputation as a good dancer was widely known in Whitby. She was soon caught up in the enjoyment, a lively asset to the party without ever overstepping decorum.

She knew her dances with Kit and the attention he paid her throughout the evening attracted attention. She guessed from the way heads drew together and from the glances cast in their direction that his family were speculating what were the chances he had found a girl with whom he might have a future.

'Did you enjoy yourself?' Kit asked her as he walked her home.

'I certainly did.' Olivia's voice was filled with contentment.

'And my family?'

'There is no one among them with whom I would ever fall out.'

He smiled. 'A compliment indeed.'

'They are all so friendly, so easygoing.'

'Ah, but you have only seen them at an enjoyable social occasion.'

'I don't think they would ever cause offence. I have heard no stories against them, though I suspect that when it comes to business they are shrewd and determined in their quest for success.'

'You're right,' agreed Kit. 'Behind Aunt Jenny's gentleness there is a very strong woman. There had to be in order for her to cope with the blows life dealt her.'

'She's not your real aunt, is she?'

'No. One of these close family friends whom children, in order to make relationships easier, call "Aunt". Her father was a whaler who married a girl from a very rich family with large estates outside Whitby. Class eventually drove a wedge between them. She was leaving with one of her own kind when their coach crashed and she was killed. Jenny's father was devastated. It was the first he'd known of his wife's unfaithfulness. He committed suicide.'

'Oh, poor Jenny. How old was she?'

'Ten. She would have been put in an orphanage as none of her mother's family would own her. But a sailor friend of her father's, who had left the sea and had taken the Black Bull, on the corner of the Market Square and Church Street, took her in and brought her up.'

'Life there certainly didn't destroy the natural refinement she must have inherited from her mother, you can still clearly see it.'

'You detected that even on such a brief meeting?'

'Oh, yes.'

'She became a close friend of my father when he first came to Whitby. I know he still has a deep respect for her.' Kit gave a little smile. 'I think he might have proposed to her but she was Adam Thoresby's girl and they married.'

'And then poor Jenny suffered the tragedy of losing her husband in the Arctic.'

'Yes.'

'His loss and that of his father are still talked about in Whitby. It could have devastated the Thorseby family.'

'But Adam's mother was a very strong woman. She knew what the sea could do and was prepared to face it. She and her son Ruben set about keeping the firm going with my father as their partner, and that's how Fernley and Thoresby came into being.'

Olivia looked pensive. 'I wouldn't want a husband or son of mine to go whaling.'

Kit lifted an eyebrow expressing doubt. 'If it was born in them I don't think you could stop them.'

'Love could break that desire.'

'I wonder. The pull of the sea is a formidable enemy, it is so strong.'

'And you would know?' Her tone cast doubts on the veracity of his statement.

'Maybe.' His voice was quiet, as if he had taken offence.

She laid a hand on his arm. 'I meant nothing personal,' she said as she stopped and looked up, hoping there was no hurt in his eyes.

In that moment, when gaze met gaze, desire sparked between them. His hands came to her shoulders and he drew her to him. His kiss engulfed her, softening any resistance she might have shown. She met kiss with kiss. Her lips trembled. Her mind raced. Then George's image confronted her. His kiss, so different, held passion in its gentleness and conveyed a yearning that would only be fulfilled at the right moment. Whereas Kit's . . .

She drew away. He held her. 'Olivia, I . . .'

She put her fingers to his lips. 'Don't say it, please, not now.'

Confusion, hurt and regret mingled in his mind and were expressed in his eyes which searched hers for an explanation. When it was not immediately forthcoming he said, 'Is there someone else?'

'No. Er . . .' Olivia's mind was awhirl. What should she say? She liked Kit. Was she even in love with him? But

114

there was George and that vast estate, and he was coming to Whitby soon. 'Maybe.'

'Maybe? What does that mean?'

'I don't know.' She tore herself away from him. 'I don't know!' she cried again over her shoulder. She spun round and faced him again. 'Kit, I like you a lot. If only . . .'

'What?' he cried as she hesitated again.

Her eyes were full of pleading as she said, 'Please don't ask me to explain. One day . . .'

'Maybe,' he broke in. 'In that word I see hope. I will respect your wish for now, but don't ask me to give up seeing you.'

'Very well, I won't.' She paused then added, 'What about Ursula?'

'What about her? She's just a friend.'

'She thinks she's more than that.'

'Oh, we have some good times together but it's you I want.'

'Kit, don't.' She gave a troubled cry. 'You haven't known me very long.'

'Long enough.'

'Maybe your view will be different after you have known me longer.'

'Never. And don't tell me there wasn't passion and desire in your kiss.'

She did not reply but bit her lip. Her eyes were damp. She did not want to hurt him. Best to say no more for now. 'Good night, Kit, and thank you for a lovely evening.' She turned to the gate. As she opened it, he reached out and his hand brushed hers.

She felt that touch all the way to the house and into the night as she lay in her bed, her mind torn between confused thoughts of two men.

When she awoke the next morning last night's exchanges with Kit flooded her memory. Try as she would she could not dismiss them. She was flattered that such a handsome man, one who attacked life with a devil-may-care attitude while still holding serious views, should play court to her. Should she have let him say what he had wanted to say? Did she really want to hear it? If she had allowed him to do so, what would her answer have been? In the heat of the moment would she have answered yes? Wasn't she still hoping George would pose a similar question?

That last thought startled her for it reminded her that Kit had not arranged another meeting. Surely he would call on her today? But doubt niggled at her. She must do something about it.

She swung out of bed, annoyed now that she had slept late. She dressed quickly, choosing a practical but attractive outdoor dress and suitable shoes for her walk to the east side of the river.

She went without breakfast and left the house without making her morning greetings to her mother and father.

Whitby was already alive with its daily business. Ships were being victualled for an afternoon's sailing, others being loaded with cargoes for London and the Baltic ports. The sounds of hammers and saws rose from her father's shipyard and other sites along the river. The air vibrated with a hundred conversations and was penetrated by the raucous calls of sailors. She crossed the bridge and turned along the lower reaches of Church Street, thankful that she had learned at the party that Kit was staying with 'Aunt' Jenny.

She knocked on the door of number thirteen, a three-storey brick building of two bays with the date 1760 over the front door. The window frames had been recently painted white and two of the sash windows on the second and third floors had been raised.

The oak door was opened by a plain-looking servant girl, neat in her black ankle-length frock, white apron and matching mobcap.

'Good day, miss,' she greeted the caller amiably, knowing Miss Olivia Coulson by sight.

'I would like to see Mrs Thoresby if she is at home,' said Olivia. Though it was Kit she really wanted to see she knew

116

it would not do to request to meet a guest before seeking the agreement of the host or hostess.

'Please come in, Miss Coulson,' replied the girl. 'I will tell Mrs Thoresby you are here. Please follow me.' She led the way across the hall to the drawing-room.

As she waited Olivia glanced around the room with an assessing eye. It was pleasantly furnished without being ornate or overcrowded. It reflected perfectly the person she had met the previous evening, someone of good breeding, gentle, with a sharp but uncluttered mind; someone whom Olivia judged gave her love to one man but could love others on a different level, which would not give offence but gain her much respect. The furniture was of good quality. The original paintings on the wall showed a taste for art work and a knowledge of what made a good painting. She was examining these when the door opened.

'Miss Coulson, how delightful to see you.' With the friendliest of smiles, Jenny crossed the room and extended her hand to Olivia.

She took it and in that touch sensed a genuine warmth and hospitality. She noted that Jenny's dress, like the furniture, reflected her personality perfectly. With no frills or flounces, it was exquisitely cut and its sand colour drew out the deep brown of her eyes.

'It's a pleasure to see you, Mrs Thoresby. I am sorry for intruding on your privacy but, with your permission, I would like to see Kit. I believe he is staying with you.'

'Was, Miss Coulson. He left early this morning, about an hour ago. I had expected him to stay longer, a few days in fact, but he said he had things to attend to and should be getting back to Cropton.'

Disbelief showed on Olivia's face. Why had he gone? He had never mentioned returning to Cropton so soon. Was it because of what she had said last night?

'You look surprised, Miss Coulson?'

The query penetrated Olivia's confusion, startling her. 'Oh, er, it's just that it was unexpected.'

117

'You had arranged to see him? That's why you are here?'

'Well ...' She hesitated. She did not want to appear forward, as if she was pursuing him. She saw Jenny waiting for an explanation. 'When I met him in Cropton he suggested that next time he was in Whitby we should go riding.'

'It's not like Kit to forget, especially when his companion would have been someone as charming as you. If he made a firm arrangement then it is very remiss of him not to keep it.'

'Oh, please, he's not to blame.' Olivia surprised even herself with the speed with which she sprang to his defence. 'I surmised that's what we would do when he came to Whitby but it was never mentioned last night. I must have misunderstood. I am sorry to have troubled you, Mrs Thoresby.' She took a step towards the door.

'Do stay and have a cup of hot chocolate,' Jenny offered.

'That is most kind of you, but if you'll excuse me, I must go.'

Jenny bowed to Olivia's wish and escorted her to the front door.

'I apologise again for disturbing you,' said the flustered girl.

'Think nothing of it, my dear,' returned Jenny. 'I'm only sorry Kit was not here.'

Olivia found herself thinking the same as she walked home in a pensive mood.

Why was she so hurt by his departure? There was no doubt that she was flattered by Kit's attention but wasn't George the person who really filled her mind? And hadn't she detected clear indications that he was in love with her? That love needed encouraging for it could lead her to the life of a county lady. If that was what she truly wanted.

Such thoughts entered her head often over the next two weeks. Kit receded in her mind as the time for George's visit grew nearer but that too threw up a doubt. Was it just her own wishful thinking that had persuaded her George loved her? Would his stay prove anything to her?

If the weather on the day of his arrival were anything to go by then their meeting would be a disaster. Olivia stamped her foot in irritation as she stood in the window watching the rain run down the panes. This was not what she'd wanted for George's first visit. Why didn't the sun shine and put everyone in a good mood? With the rain lashing down, driven by a north-east wind, he would have had a trying ride across the moors.

Olivia could not settle to anything. She read a few pages of *The Lady of the Lake*, sighed and put the book down, picked it up again, saw the words without really taking them in. She tried to put a few more stitches in the tapestry she had started the week before but gave up when her mind drifted and she pricked herself. She walked to the window so many times that Lavinia lost count. Her mother's attempts to divert her with conversation brought only monosyllabic replies. Her daughter's restlessness amused Lavinia but she kept that to herself. She recognised signs she herself had experienced as a girl, wondering if Edward was in love with her.

'He's here!' The cry came automatically when Olivia, at the window once more, saw a carriage draw up in front of the house. She swung round and hurried across the room.

Lavinia chuckled to herself as she rose sedately from her chair and moved in a similar manner to the door which Olivia had thrown open in her rush.

A bell rang in the depths of the house. The appearance of the servant girl jolted Olivia into realising that she was not behaving with the decorum she should be displaying. She steadied her step and stopped close to the stairs, allowing the girl to carry out her duty.

When she opened the door, wind-lashed rain drove her back. The figure on the step did not wait to be invited in. He stepped over the threshold with water streaming from his garrick. Seeing the girl battling to get the door closed again, he dropped his valise and added his own strength to her efforts.

'George! Welcome to Whitby. What a terrible ride you must have had.' Olivia came forward.

'Olivia.' He took her hand and raised it to his lips. 'Seeing you makes the weather pale into insignificance.'

'Mr Chilton-Brookes.' Lavinia appeared from the drawing-room. 'Welcome to our home.'

'Ma'am.' George bowed. 'It is a pleasure to be here.'

'I am sorry the weather is so atrocious. You must be soaked.' Lavinia took charge immediately. 'Mary,' she turned to the girl who was standing to one side waiting to be of service, 'take Mr Chilton-Brookes's coat and hat and see that they are thoroughly dried.' As she gave these instructions she crossed the hall to a bell pull. A moment later a manservant appeared. 'James, take Mr Chilton-Brookes's valise upstairs. You know the room he will be occupying.' She turned to their guest. 'James will look after you.'

'Thank you, ma'am.'

'When you are more comfortable, come to the drawing-room and have some warming tea.'

'That will be delightful, ma'am. What about my horse and carriage?'

'They will be taken care of. My husband made arrangements for them to be looked after at the White Horse. Mary, when you go to the kitchen tell William that Mr Chilton-Brookes is here. He will know what to do.'

'That is very good of you, ma'am.' George glanced at James and nodded his readiness to be shown his room. As he started for the stairs he glanced at Olivia and smiled.

Lavinia and her daughter waited a moment then walked back to the drawing-room.

'Feeling calmer now?' asked her mother as Olivia closed the door.

It was only then that Olivia realised how fidgety she had been. She saw a twinkle of amusement in her mother's eyes and knew how patently clear her feelings for George were

120

to the older and more experienced woman.

When George appeared ten minutes later he was followed almost immediately by Mary and another girl with the tea.

'I must say, this looks delicious,' he said, eyeing the scones, jam and cakes.

'I pride myself on having a cook who is an exceptional baker. Please do sit down.' Lavinia indicated a chair. 'I trust your room is comfortable.'

'Delightful, Mrs Coulson. I will be most happy there.' He took the proffered cup of tea and placed it on the small table beside his chair.

Olivia handed him a plate, a knife, and then held out the scones for him to choose one.

'I'm sorry Father isn't here to welcome you,' she said. 'He should be home about five.'

'I can't get him to work less,' explained Lavinia.

'I understand, Mrs Coulson. Running a successful business with the reputation of Coulson's is no small feat, and I am sure it requires all your husband's attention.'

'I have two brothers. He should give them more responsibility,' said Olivia.

'You know your father, Olivia, he wants to be involved in everything.'

'And I expect your sons make it appear so while keeping their own areas of control,' said George.

'That sounds like the voice of experience.' Lavinia smiled. 'I think you are right and believe Edward knows it too.'

'Then you have a shrewd family who know how to keep a ship afloat without undue trouble.' A twinkle came to his eyes. 'And can Miss Olivia be as subtle?'

'Ask no questions, hear no lies,' she put in quickly, and added in order to soften the challenge, 'Did your parents get away on time for their visit south?'

'Yes.'

'They were well, I trust?'

'I don't think Father was looking forward to the journey but Mother will soon calm him down.'

121

Olivia caught Lavinia's glance and saw a teasing light in her eyes. For one moment she thought her mother was going to refer to her agitation before George's arrival but fortunately she did not.

'I am hoping the weather is going to relent for your visit. I believe it is the first time you have been to Whitby.'

'Not the very first, ma'am. Apparently I was brought here as a child. I was too young to remember it and what the occasion was I don't know. But, yes, this can be considered my first proper visit.'

'Father will most certainly take you round his shipyard,' said Olivia.

'So I can see how our timber is used.'

'Is there anything special that you wish to do?'

George put down his cup and looked at Lavinia. 'With your permission, ma'am, I would like Olivia to show me round the town. I've heard it is a very interesting place.'

'Of course she may.'

'And maybe we could go riding on the cliffs?'

'Of course,' agreed Lavinia. 'Olivia likes nothing better.'

'Then let us hope this awful rain abates and we see the sun. But what does it matter? I have the pleasure of the company of two charming ladies and will soon have the pleasure of a genial host. What more could I want?'

When Edward arrived home he made a great fuss of George before excusing himself to change into his evening clothes.

'Terrible weather,' he apologised when he reappeared. 'But it will be fine tomorrow.'

'You sound certain, Father,' observed Olivia hopefully.

'Nothing more sure, my dear. This storm will blow itself out, and the wind will be reduced to a breeze from the west.'

'And that's a good quarter, sir?'

'Yes.'

George and Olivia traded glances of hope that he was right. In that exchange they both read a desire to be together.

122

'Tomorrow I'll show you the shipyard,' promised Edward.

'In the morning, Father,' put in Olivia before he could elaborate on any other plans. 'I'm taking George round Whitby in the afternoon.'

'Er . . . very good.' Edward knew better than to object. His wife would certainly have sanctioned this. Besides he was pleased that his daughter was going to spend some time with the heir to the Cropton Estate.

'And the following morning we are going riding,' added Olivia.

Her father nodded his agreement. 'Then maybe in the afternoon I could introduce you to some more shipbuilders. We generally gather in the Angel about four o'clock. Business talk, you know.' He gave George a surreptitious wink. 'It might give you the opportunity to sell more timber.'

'That's thoughtful of you, sir.' George gave a wry smile as he added, 'But no doubt you'll want me to keep the best for you.'

'That goes without saying, young man. You know me by now.'

The next morning Olivia's first thoughts were for the weather. She had prayed last night that today the sun would shine and the wind would drop, and that nothing would mar her walk with George. She slipped from her bed and tripped lightly to the window. Surveying the clear sky, she was thankful to see that the rain had stopped and the clouds had broken, leaving only remnants as a reminder of yesterday's lashing rain.

She glanced at the clock standing on the mantelpiece. She would be late. She was sure her father and George would be at breakfast already and she did want to see them – well, George – before they left for the yard.

She dressed quickly, but in spite of her haste made sure that she looked her best.

Her feet barely skimmed the stairs. She raced across the hall, paused at the dining-room door, drew a deep breath and then strolled in casually.

123

'Good morning, Mother, good morning, Father, and also to you, George,' she said as she closed the door and went to kiss her mother on the cheek. She went to her father next and did the same, wishing she dare go on to George.

He had risen from his chair and stood with napkin in hand. He bowed, extended his greetings to her and waited to resume his seat until she had taken hers.

Conversation never flagged throughout the meal even though it was not of any deep consequence. Olivia admired George's ability to enter into whatever course it took and that he always expressed a lively opinion of his own. She found herself wondering what it would be like to share such mornings with him, just the two of them, in a home of their own.

As soon as Edward saw that George had finished his meal he spoke to his wife. 'If you'll excuse us, my dear, we must away. There's a lot for George to see.' Receiving her nod of approval, he looked at Olivia. 'George will be back for that walk by half-past two.'

'Not before?' Her eyes flared with annoyance. She had expected to have him to herself before that. 'Won't you be home for your meal at twelve?'

'No. I'm taking George and your brothers to have something to eat at the Angel. It will give him an opportunity to get to know them.'

She did not reply. Edward went to his wife. As he kissed her, George caught Olivia's pout and raised his eyebrows as if to say, 'There's nothing we can do about it.'

Olivia spent most of the morning in her room. The meal she shared with her mother at midday was quiet and Lavinia knew it was best not to question her daughter about her reticence. She knew what caused it and found she was right when at twenty minutes past two George arrived at the house. Immediately there was a new spark of life in Olivia's demeanour.

'You look very elegant,' said George when he came down-

124

stairs after changing into more suitable clothes for the afternoon.

Olivia was waiting in the hall. Her pale green muslin frock came to her ankles revealing the black half boots she had chosen for the walk. Her crimson pelisse with its wide Van Dyke collar and long sleeves was tied lightly at the waist and she wore a becoming small bonnet.

'Thank you, kind sir,' she acknowledged. 'And may I return the compliment.'

His well-fitting fawn coat flared from the waist to knee-length and matched his trousers. He wore a waistcoat patterned in red and yellow complemented by the subtle hues of his silk neckcloth.

Her heart had missed a beat when he appeared at the top of the stairs. He looked so elegant and imposing.

'I'll just tell Mother we are going.' She turned to the drawing-room.

He followed her as she opened the door. They made their goodbyes and left the house.

Throughout the rest of the afternoon Olivia found George an interested and willing listener. She also encountered his alert and enquiring mind and noted his continual observation of everything around him, all of which made the tour of Whitby more meaningful and interesting to her. It gave her an added insight into George, one which helped to strengthen her admiration for him. But more than anything she found her pleasure in his company, which she had experienced at Cropton, deepening. It wouldn't have mattered if there had been no town to show him, just being with him was enough.

She drew delight from the attentions he paid her and pleasure from his admiration of her knowledge of the port, its activities, buildings and history.

On leaving her home she led him to the cliff top through the new town, expanding on the west side of the river.

'What a view!' he gasped when she stopped near the turn of the cliff overlooking the sea and the river. His gaze swept upstream towards the bridge, taking in the many activities on the river. Ships from distant ports were being unloaded while the holds of others were being filled with all manner of local produce for the ports of Europe. Small boats plied their way from bank to bank. Baskets of fish were being swung ashore from two vessels newly arrived from the nearby fishing grounds. Beyond the bridge more quays heaved with activity and new vessels were taking shape in the shipbuilding yards. The buzz which rose from the scene mingled with the plaintive cries of the seagulls as they flew lazily above it all.

His gaze swept across the river and soared over the red tiles of the houses precariously climbing the side of the east cliff towards the old parish church and ruined abbey.

'What a magnificent ruin, and what a wonderful site,' he exclaimed.

'It is,' Olivia agreed. 'The abbey is a landmark sailors look out for on their return to their home port, a symbol of Whitby.'

'This is a sight which will always spring to mind whenever I hear the town mentioned in future.'

'The abbey? Not me?' queried Olivia, putting on the air of one who is disappointed.

'Oh, no! I didn't mean you'd be forgotten. You, my dear Olivia, will always come to mind whenever Whitby enters the conversation.'

'Only then?' She held the hurt expression.

'Oh, dear, I'm really making a hash of this, getting deeper and deeper into the mire. Please don't be offended.'

She started to laugh. 'You should see the expression on your face! My dear George, I'm teasing. I take no offence.'

His serious expression continued for a moment, then, seeing the twinkle in her eyes and the laughter on her lips, he joined in the merriment.

He luxuriated in the sight of her smile which enhanced all her features, creating a beauty that had to be noticed. He had been drawn to her at that first meeting in Cropton but now he felt closer to her, for he had discovered unexpected depths in her character. He had realised her knowledge of and talents with horses when she was at Cropton, but now he saw that her education had produced a lively and retentive mind with an interest in everything with which she came into contact.

The laughter gradually faded from his lips and a more serious expression took over, though it still held lightness.

'You are a remarkable young woman and I love your ability to tease without giving offence. I admire the way you enjoy life, and yet I believe I detect a serious side that will be a great asset when someone marries you.'

Olivia's heart skipped a beat. What was this leading to? Was he going to propose? Her mind urged him to say four words – a question which could be a signpost to the Cropton Estate and to the rest of her life. The sense of expectancy almost overwhelmed her but it was deflated in an instant when he said, 'I should like to go and see the abbey.'

Her dream world tumbled around her yet her mind rose above the ruination of her hopes as it continually impressed on her, 'He loves you, he does, I know he does.' His voice penetrated her thoughts as he repeated his statement. She started.

'Oh, yes, I'm sorry, I was miles away.'

He smiled. 'You certainly were. A penny for your thoughts?'

'Oh, no. I couldn't.'

'As private as that, were they? I wonder what they were?'

Olivia was flustered. She must break the course of this conversation. 'The abbey? Yes, well, we'll pass it tomorrow during our ride. We can stop then to see it.'

'Admirable,' he returned. 'And what now?'

'We'll take the path down to the riverside, walk out on the pier, return to the bridge and cross to the east side.'

'You've thought this guided tour out most carefully, I'm grateful.'

They set off and, though she found it hard to dismiss the thoughts and disappointment she had just experienced, the tour of Whitby and their responses to each other resumed as if they had never been interrupted.

The air was bracing, their walk on the west pier invigorating. George enjoyed every moment. When they left the pier he took an interest in the ships berthed at the quays beside the roadway along which they walked. He exchanged brief words with some of the crews, learning something about their trade. The flow of people about their daily lives increased as they neared the bridge. Halfway across he paused to survey the scene upstream and then followed her into Church Street. He remarked on the cramped living conditions in the snickets running down to the river and in the number of yards leading off the opposite side of Church Street and crowding each other as they climbed the cliff face. He commented on the squalor of some, contrasting them with the cared-for appearance of others.

They reached the end of Church Street and were faced with the one hundred and ninety-nine steps to the churchyard.

'We'll not climb those today,' she said.

Though he was tempted by them George kept his own counsel. After all she was the guide and was doing a splendid job.

'Let's go along Henrietta Street.'

This was narrow, its houses reflecting the care of people who took a proper pride in their property. The houses on one side were built close to the cliff face and he expressed his view that they could be a dangerous place to live.

'True,' agreed Olivia, 'but home is home and people believe it won't happen to them. Some of the houses were swept away in a cliff fall in 1787 but still it remains a fashionable area.'

Beyond the end of Henrietta Street they paused before returning, for it gave them another wonderful view, this time across the river to the west cliff and of a broad sweep

128

of sand towards Sandsend and the towering cliffs beyond the tiny hamlet.

'Wherever you take me there are magnificent views or prospects of much interest. This is a memorable day for me. As we came along Church Street I noticed some jet workshops. I know little about jet, but I'm sure you do. You must enlighten me as we walk back.'

Olivia was able to grant his request, and when she had finished her story he remarked, 'I can tell that you have a great liking for jet. You must let me buy you something in remembrance of my visit and this particular day together.'

'There is no need,' she protested.

'Maybe, but I would like to do it. In fact, I won't allow you to say no.'

She saw insistence in his eyes and knew he would be hurt if she refused. Was this another sign of his love for her? Should she read it as that?

She took him to a workshop where she knew the craftsmen were exceptionally skilled. The foreman was pleased to meet a gentleman so genuinely interested in the skill of his workers and produced an array of necklaces, bangles and bracelets for Olivia to make her choice.

After careful consideration she chose a bracelet of broad links each delicately etched with spouting whales.

'But isn't this really one of a pair?' enquired George, having noted that a second one, etched with whaleships, was similar in size and shape.

'You're right, sir,' said the foreman. 'But the young lady can have just one if she wishes.'

'It would be a pity to split them up,' declared George. 'She shall have them both.'

The protests which sprang to her lips were halted by George's glance. She knew he would be hurt if she said anything.

'And what about this for your mother?' He fingered a finely worked necklace with a central drop bead.

129

'I'm sure she would love it,' replied Olivia.

'We'll take it then.'

The foreman thanked him and moved away to wrap the items in soft paper and place them carefully in two small boxes.

'You are most generous,' whispered Olivia.

'It is my pleasure,' returned George.

When they reached the gate of the Coulsons' house, he stopped. 'This has been a wonderful afternoon. I thank you for making it such a pleasure for me.' He leaned forward and kissed her lightly on the cheek. 'I look forward to tomorrow. I know that our ride will be just as pleasurable.'

Olivia made no comment but her mind spoke for her: 'I certainly intend to make it so.'

Chapter Nine

Olivia cast a glance at the sky, thankful that the wind had driven the threatening clouds away to leave the ruined abbey bathed in sunshine.

She and George had kept their horses to a walking pace as they climbed Green Lane to Abbey Lane near the cliff top. Now they swung from their saddles, tethered the horses and walked to the ruins.

George was fascinated to be walking where monks had walked seven hundred years before and became absorbed in the information Olivia imparted on the abbey's history and that of the earlier foundation established in the seventh century by St Hilda and destroyed by the Danes.

When they rode on they were satisfied with a gentle pace so that they could enjoy the coastal scenery, something unfamiliar to George.

After an hour Olivia suggested they turn back and when they reached a sheltered dip in the land proposed that they should sit here a while. They allowed the horses freedom to champ the grass at their will, knowing that they would not stray far, and found a comfortable place for themselves near the cliff edge which afforded them a view across Saltwick Bay to the nab.

'That's a huge forbidding lump of rock,' George commented, eyeing the mass which projected across the bay like a massive whale.

'It is,' Olivia agreed. 'It's been the graveyard of many a ship.' She held back from telling him that this was the place where Kit had lost his mother when she was on board the London packet. It was not a day for such morbid stories. She changed the subject.

'I hope that meeting the other shipbuilders with Father this afternoon will not be too boring for you?'

He smiled. 'Well, it is only courteous I accept his invitation, though I must say I would rather be spending time with you than listening to talk about ships, shipbuilding and timber.'

'It's sweet of you to say so. And I would rather have your company than be left to my own devices.'

He reached out and took her hand. 'We must meet once more before too long. You will have to come to Cropton again, but that will have to wait until Mother and Father return from the south.'

'Then I wish they were returning tomorrow.'

'You must have enjoyed your visit to Cropton?'

'You know I did. Some things happened there which will always be in my heart.'

'Our kiss in the glade?'

'You remember it too?'

'How could I forget the sweetness of your lips?'

'Then you shall recall them again in the setting of the cliffs and sea.' She leaned closer to him and her lips met his. Her kiss was soft, like the brush of velvet. She felt him tense, but it was not the tension of resistance, rather that of absorbing a new sensation. She let her lips linger enticingly. His arms came around her shoulders and let her feel the power of her attraction.

The rest of the morning was a song of joy in her heart. There were no confused thoughts, no turbulent emotions. She was sure now that he loved her, saw today as a significant step on her way to becoming the wife of the heir to the vast Cropton Estate.

As she changed from her riding habit on returning home

she dwelt on the morning's events. It was only then that she realised George had never once said he loved her. But she was certain he did. His kisses spoke of a deep feeling for her, but she did want the certainty of those three words.

The chance never came. Her father commandeered George's attention in the afternoon and the social meeting in the Angel lasted longer than expected. She could not engineer an encounter that evening. Her mother, in return for their generosity to Olivia, had invited Jessica and Ruben Thoresby along with Kit's Aunt Jenny to dinner. She had thought it an ideal time to invite them, for they could meet someone who was friendly with their nephew.

The evening passed off pleasantly enough but Olivia wished she had George to herself again. She did not even have an opportunity the next morning before he returned to Cropton, but she knew she would treasure the final brush of his lips on her cheek and the light in his eyes as he'd said goodbye. After he had gone she clung hopefully to his words: 'You must visit Cropton again.'

George was thankful the weather was better for his drive home than it was for his journey to Whitby. His thoughts were not distracted by the constant beat of the rain and howl of the wind, and that suited George who wanted to contemplate his visit to Olivia.

Did his future lie with the girl he had left behind in Whitby? In the tenderness she had shown him, was there the love he wanted from a wife? Was she the person with whom he would spend the rest of his life? There was much at stake here. His inheritance was massive. Was she choosing to love where there was an assured future, the prospect of money? He chided himself for having such thoughts, and yet ... hadn't previous experiences taught him to be cautious?

And what of his own feelings? He liked Olivia. He found her attractive, pleasant company, someone who could move him passionately ... but love? He still held a question mark over the word.

Chapter Ten

He was no nearer finding peace of mind three weeks later. There were times when his thoughts were in turmoil. A vision of Olivia beckoning with arms outstretched to him constantly forced itself into his mind. Then she would vanish suddenly only to appear again, riding fast across his land, her hair streaming out behind her. Though he reached out to her, in his dreams she was always tantalisingly out of reach. He would wake puzzling over the visions that tormented him.

One day, with his recurring dream unresolved, he ordered Redwings to be saddled. Maybe a gentle ride in the countryside he loved would help settle his mind and his future.

George relaxed in the saddle. The sun was warm on his back, and the gentle breeze caressed him. Did he feel Olivia's fingers on his cheeks, the tender brush of her lips? Was his destiny in that touch?

He rode without any thought for where he was going. After a while he started and drove his idling thoughts away when he realised he was nearing the glade he had once shared with Olivia. Was this a sign? Memories of those moments with her flooded back, but with them came renewed doubts about the strength of her love for him. He stopped and swung lightly from the saddle, tying his horse to a tree. He would walk the rest of the way through the copse to the glade so that nothing would impede on his attempt to fathom these doubts about their relationship.

He walked slowly, his mind on other things. He came to the edge of the trees and stopped, not because the terrain, sloping to the stream, needed more care but because the atmosphere over the whole place had a magical quality. It was as if time did not exist here. He had found a perfect moment and he held on to it. It would be with him forever. His mind was clear. Everything and everybody else, even Olivia, had been driven from it. He knew immediately that this moment had altered his life for all time.

He held back in the shadow of the trees, standing silently, hardly daring to breathe for fear of destroying the picture that held him entranced. A stranger was sitting on the rock beside the stream. There was an aura about her that said she was of this place and that it needed her. George felt as if he had been taken into a new world, one which held the destiny for which he had been searching.

In profile she held herself proudly but with no self-consciousness; her serenity would not allow that. She looked at peace with the world and gave the impression she was absorbing the beauty of the glade so that she would carry it with her wherever she went. Her plain riding habit was of impeccable quality and emphasised her slim build. She had discarded a small cap which lay on the rock beside her and allowed her long dark hair to tumble around her, shimmering in the sunlight like the water of the stream at her feet.

George did not move. He watched, taking in the loveliness that outshone the beauty of the landscape he loved so much. Whoever this person was she was already special to him. Who was she to have moved him so much in such a brief passage of time? He needed to know. He stepped forward, regretful to disturb such enchantment but knowing from this moment on the vision before him would be engraved on his heart.

The noise of his steps disturbed her. She turned, without

135

haste or anxiety. Their eyes met. Time did not exist. Only this instant mattered. There was no past, no future. This was the moment of their real existence.

Now he could see her more clearly. Her face was smoothly moulded over high cheekbones and a round chin. The corners of her full lips held an enchanting smile for him, one which seemed as if it would always be there. Her eyes of deep blue were perfectly set and brought symmetry to her features. They drew George deep into pools of mystery where the light danced, bold and unexpected, with the wildness of distant places. He could sense in them restless urges which she kept under control, except maybe in her thoughts and dreams. But nothing else about her was secretive. Her face was open and frank.

'Hello,' he said easily, instinctively knowing that she would want no undue formality.

'Hello,' she returned. Her soft voice held a lilt which George placed from the far north. He was intrigued. Who was this girl who had already changed the course of his life?

Only two words spoken. There was no need for any more. Two people whose destinies had been entwined in the mists of time and would be as long as the wind blew.

He sat down beside her. Their hands met and touched on the rock, a natural coming together, a physical contact that brought unity to the love each had immediately felt for the other. They sat for a few moments without speaking, the silence broken only by the rippling water and the song of the birds. It drew them closer.

The wind played with her hair and sent strands curling across her face. Her long fingers smoothed them away. The graceful action brought him back to reality.

'I'm George Chilton-Brookes.' His smile was warm and, as she had expected, held more than friendliness.

She was taken by his handsome features, sensing the gentleness in him. He was slim and athletic. She had noted his lithe movements when he had walked to the rock, seen the confident way in which he held himself. This was a man who could handle himself in any situation, worthy of respect. She was drawn by his sapphire-blue eyes which tempted her to think he was easygoing but behind which she read a keen determination and an ability to sum up other people quickly. She realised that although they might give the impression of being casual there was an awareness in them of everyone and everything around him.

'Oh, my goodness, I'm trespassing on your land!' she responded with a little alarm.

He chuckled, eyes dancing with merriment. 'You expect me to warn you off?'

'Would you?'

'After what has sparked between us?'

A little colour came to her cheeks.

'Come to this place whenever you like.'

'That is kind of you. But, alas, I cannot.'

'Why?' There was despondency in his tone.

'I live in London.'

'London?' He frowned, not liking what he was hearing. Not wanting such distance to be between them.

'I'm afraid so.'

'Who are you, and why are you here?'

'I am Ailsa Fernley, Kit's half-sister.'

'What? Where has he kept you hidden all this time?'

She laughed at his astounded expression. 'It's not Kit's fault, I only come to visit him occasionally. London is a long way off.'

'And how long have you been here this time?'

'A week.'

'And why hasn't he brought you to see me?'

She shrugged her shoulders and gave a small smile. 'Maybe we were destined to meet this way.'

'You are right. This place, this moment in time, are ours. I felt a moment of magic when I first saw you. My heart would not allow me any other feeling but love for you. I knew you were my destiny.'

137

'And am I still, even though there will be distance between us?'

'No matter how far, I know that one day we will be together.' He frowned, troubled by a thought that had instantly sprung to mind. 'You have no one else?'

'No.' She shook her head, but her eyes still held his as she asked, 'Have you?'

'No.'

'We'll meet tomorrow?'

She shook her head.

Alarm crossed his face. 'Why not? We are both free.'

'I return to London tomorrow.'

'You can't! You mustn't.' His pleading cry was like that of a wounded bird.

'I must. My passage is fixed. My parents will be expecting me.'

'When will you be back?'

'I don't know.'

'Arrange it soon.'

'I'll try.'

'I will not rest until I see you again.' He reached up and stroked her face as if he wanted to remember the feel of it forever.

'Nor I you. Something special happened to me today. Now I know what love truly is.'

'Can I walk you back to Kit's?'

'Please don't be hurt if I refuse,' she said as she stood up and faced him. 'I want to remember you here, in this glade, a place which will always be special in my heart. I want to picture you here until we meet again.' Her lips brushed his with all the love that was in her heart.

He slid from the rock and swept her into his arms. His kiss was one she would hold dear for it spoke of a love which had been hers since the beginning of time and would last for eternity.

When she turned to go their fingers lingered together as if to bind the love they had just expressed.

138

'Goodbye, George. My love is yours.'

'You will be in my heart until we meet again.'

He watched her leave the glade and pause at the edge of the wood where she turned and raised a hand in a gesture of farewell which expressed regret at leaving but also held a promise to return in the future. Then she was lost among the trees.

George sank back on to the rock, his mind awhirl. His future held dazzling promise for now there was someone with whom he must share it.

He glanced round the glade, wanting to imprint it on his mind, as it was today, the day he truly fell in love.

As he did so he was reminded of another occasion, not so long ago, when he had sat on this very stone with another girl whom he had found attractive, whose kisses had sent the blood coursing through his veins. But the two experiences were different. Both had their attractions, both promised much, but only one really drew from him something he had never experienced before. Already he was longing for Ailsa to be back. He had never felt such an intense longing for Olivia. He had looked forward to seeing her again, true, but now there was Ailsa and she had brought a different and exciting dimension to his feelings.

There was only one thing he could do. His lips tightened. He sensed Olivia was in love with him. He knew a rebuff would hurt her and regretted that. Should he wait until Ailsa returned and confirmed her love for him? But why? He knew with certainty that she loved him just as he loved her. To prolong the parting from Olivia would only make it harder and more hurtful. Far better to make the split as soon as possible. When and where? Whitby? He remembered he had suggested that she should visit Cropton again. Maybe that would be better. He would consider carefully.

Ailsa decided to keep her meeting with George to herself. Neither Kit nor Aunt Betsy would understand how she could fall in love at a first meeting, but she knew in her heart of hearts that she had met the man with whom she wanted to share her future.

The following afternoon Kit put Ailsa's valise in his carriage as she was saying goodbye to Aunt Betsy.

'Come again soon, love. We don't see enough of you,' said Betsy as she gave her niece a big hug.

'I will, Aunt,' she promised, but Betsy had no inkling of the real reason behind that vow.

'Safe journey. Give my love to your father and mother and Dominic.'

Kit helped her into the carriage and when he saw she was comfortable, climbed beside her and took the reins. As they moved off Ailsa waved to her aunt and settled down, her mind on the countryside she loved but which now had a deeper and special meaning for her.

'Enjoy your stay?' asked Kit.

'Of course. I always do.'

'And we love having you. Do try and come more often.'

'Yes, I mean to.'

The ride to Whitby passed pleasantly and after they had left the carriage and horse at the White Horse Inn they went to Aunt Jenny's where they were to stay the night.

The London packet left the following morning at ten and Kit and Jenny were on the quayside to see her sail. Ailsa remained at the rail until she could no longer see them then moved to a position which gave her a more advantageous view of Whitby as the ship left the harbour and settled on a course for London.

Most of her life had been spent in London, though she did have some recollections of her early childhood in New Bedford on the east coast of America. But the capital had never really won her heart. It was where she lived happily with her mother and father, it was home, but her heart had always held a longing for open spaces, something she thought must come from her mother's upbringing in Shetland. On the occasions when she had been brought north she'd felt an affinity with Whitby and the open country beyond. But those visits had been few. This was the first time she had been allowed to come alone. She hoped she could arrange more frequent visits for now there was an added reason to sail north.

As they left the quay Jenny said, 'Kit, I have something I must say to you, something to which I should draw your attention, a failure which I believe you should rectify.'

'This sounds serious, Aunt,' he returned, trying to inject some lightness into the moment.

'I think it is, and don't try to turn your flippant charm on me nor brush this easily aside. You can call me an interfering old fool but I feel I must say what I have to say.'

'You are never a fool, you aren't old, and you never interfere, though you do say what's on your mind. I'm listening.'

'When you were in Whitby for the party you left early the next morning. A little later the young lady you'd brought to the party, Olivia Coulson, came to my house to see you.'

'She did?' Kit raised an eyebrow.

'It seems she thought you had promised to go riding with her. Said you had suggested it when you met in Cropton. Her surprise that you had gone was marked and gave me the impression that what she said was the truth. Was it?'

Kit looked somewhat embarrassed. 'Yes, it was,' he admitted.

'Then it was very remiss of you not to have told her that you had to return home without fulfilling your prior arrangement. I think you should call on her and offer her an explanation.'

Kit knew there was no way that he was going to get out of this. He had a great affection for his Aunt Jenny, an affinity which stemmed from his father's deep respect for her.

He nodded. 'Very well, Aunt, I'll do that. It might mean I stay another night with you?'

141

'If it makes things right between you then by all means stay as long as you like, but what about Betsy?'

'She'll be all right. I told her to expect me when she saw me and only send out a search party if I wasn't back within a week.'

'Then you have the perfect opportunity to put things right with this young lady. She was genuinely upset that you had left.'

He smiled. 'I believe you are matchmaking?'

'Away with you! I'm doing no such thing, Kit Fernley,' Jenny replied, annoyed that her usual calm demeanour was becoming ruffled. 'You're one to follow your own course in affairs of the heart.'

Chapter Eleven

Kit was thankful that he found Olivia at home alone when he called later that morning. He was only sorry that her greeting held some coldness which led him to plunge straight in with his apology.

'I am sorry that I left Whitby so abruptly after the party. I have not been here since but have taken the opportunity of this visit to beg your forgiveness. My Aunt Jenny told me you called on her and asked to see me only to find that I had gone. I did not mean to offend you and hope I am forgiven?'

Olivia listened to him, her face expressionless. She was giving nothing away but inwardly she was touched by his downcast manner.

'It hurt at the time. I thought we were to go riding?'

'So we were. I had not forgotten the suggestion I made in Cropton.'

'So why did you leave? It must have been something I said the night you walked me home after the party? You took umbrage and ran away. Not what I would have expected of the Kit Fernley I saw at the cricket match, nor the man I saw on the back of a horse.'

He shrugged his shoulders. 'I softened under your beguiling charms, and when what I wanted to say was thwarted I was hurt. All right, I ran because I was rebuffed. I was afraid I might say hurtful things to you.'

'And now?'

'I ask if we can take up where we left off?'

Her nod was friendly, her smile of forgiveness warm. 'I see no reason why not.'

'May I see you again before I return to Cropton?'

'Certainly.'

'This afternoon? A walk on the pier?'

'I look forward to it.'

She escorted him to the front door. Before she opened it she placed a hand on his arm and kissed him on the cheek. 'You are a good friend, Kit Fernley,' she whispered.

'Some day I hope to be more than that. Until this afternoon. I'll call at half-past two.' With that he opened the door and was gone.

Olivia strolled back to the drawing-room deep in thought. As she sat down she was examining her heart. Where did it lie? Kit had almost swept her off her feet with his apology, for she was definitely attracted to the man. But there was George who still held a strong place in her heart although that promise of another visit to Cropton had not materialised as soon as she had hoped. Could she be wrong in her supposition that she had his love? There had surely been signs or had she read them wrongly? Maybe she should take the initiative and find out.

Kit was as good as his word and clocks were striking half-past two when he was admitted to the Coulson house.

'Good day, ma'am,' he said gracefully when he was admitted to the drawing-room and found Lavinia there.

'Welcome,' she returned. 'It is a pleasure to see you again. I'm sure Olivia is ready, but you know what girls are, always a last-minute something.'

Before he could answer the door opened and Olivia walked in.

'Hello, Kit,' she said brightly.

The expression in his eyes showed his approval of her high-waisted linen dress of deep yellow, with its high neckline and long sleeves coming tight at the wrists. The dress was plain, without flounce or frill, which helped to set off the only piece of decoration; a delicately crafted marcasite ship which she had pinned above her left breast. Her hair was drawn up from the back and pinned on top so that nothing would look out of place if she decided to wear the small bonnet she was holding. Over her right arm she carried a finely woven woollen shawl. She knew that even on such a warm day the breeze on the pier could be cooling.

Her mother wished them a pleasant walk and they left the house.

As they strolled towards the west pier their conversation ranged around their personal interests and the activities around them.

As they moved out on to the pier beyond the shelter of the cliffs, Kit helped to drape her shawl around her shoulders. His hand brushed her chin. She felt a spark of emotion at his touch, sensed that he longed for more than such casual contact. She looked up at him over her shoulder and gave a gentle smile. He knew she sensed what he was feeling. For a moment he was puzzled by his own reticence to express his feelings. Once he would have swept her into his arms there and then and expressed his love for her with all the ardour he felt. He would have pounded down the barrier he sensed she had set up against any deepening of affection. But he knew if he did that now he could ruin his chances forever. In this case patience could pay off.

But he was not going to allow the moment to pass without letting her know something of his feelings. He kissed her lightly on the cheek. 'For a very dear friend who one day I hope may be more.'

Olivia met his gaze. He saw a momentary hurt in her eyes as if she regretted the fact he had not declared himself fully. She turned away and he fell thoughtfully into step beside her along the pier.

Olivia's thoughts were in turmoil. She was convinced that two men loved her but still had her mind on the one whose inheritance was the Cropton Estate.

145

Chapter Twelve

'Ailsa seems to have enjoyed herself. She chattered all the way home about her time with Kit,' remarked David Fernley to his wife Beth as they got into bed.

'Did she mention anyone else?'

'Only Betsy. She doesn't appear to have seen anyone else. She enjoyed being with them and exploring the countryside.'

'She's in love. She *must* have met someone else.'

David sat up and twisted round so that he could see his wife. She smiled at the shock on her husband's face.

'Don't tell me you didn't know?'

'How could I? She didn't tell me.'

'You've forgotten the signs.' Beth's smile broadened with the teasing lilt in her voice.

'Signs? What signs? Did she tell you?' The questions poured out indignantly as David thought he had been left out.

'No, she didn't. But she's so radiant, so happy, so full of life.'

'But that's Ailsa, she loves life.'

'I know, but there's a different spark to her somehow.'

'Love? How could she fall in love? She's only been away a week. That's no time at all to meet someone and fall in love.'

Beth looked hard into her husband's eyes with an affection

that knew no limits. 'Have you forgotten a tiny remote bay in Shetland?' There was a caressing lilt to her question.

'How could I? So much happiness sprang from there.'

'I walked out of the sea and what happened?'

'I fell in love.'

'There and then?'

'You know I did. And so did you.'

'Yes, I did. So why can't love at first sight have happened to Ailsa?'

'Well ... she ...' David's spluttering stopped. He knew Beth was right. 'I'll go and ask her.' He started to get out of bed.

'David Fernley, you'll do no such thing!' The sharpness in her voice stopped him. David knew better than to defy her; besides he always trusted her judgement. He lay back on his pillow.

She turned over to face him. 'She'll tell us in her own good time.'

He nodded. 'She's come home so they've obviously parted,' he mused, then added with deep feeling, 'I hope that parting didn't hold the traumas ours did.' His arms came round her shoulders. He felt her shudder with expectancy, looked into her eyes and saw the vision he always saw, one the passing years could not mar: a young woman walking barefoot along the strand of sand with the white-flecked fingers of water swirling round her toes. Her thin blouse is clinging to her small firm breasts and her skirt falling gracefully from the narrow waist of her sylph-like body. Her every movement is slow, as if she is drifting in another world. She tosses her head, sending her dark hair cascading down her back, causing it to shimmer in the sunlight like some cascading waterfall.

'Why should it?' Beth answered him. 'Times and circumstances are different now.'

'But if he's a whaleman?'

'If he is they'll survive. We did. Didn't the danger draw us closer? Love born in danger makes living all the more joyous. But Ailsa spent no time in Whitby so I rather think whoever she has fallen in love with is of the country.'

He tried again. 'We'll ask her in the morning.'

'We won't! Let her tell us when she is ready. You were remembering Shetland a moment ago, I could see it in your eyes. Take your mind back there again.' A huskiness had come to her voice. Her eyes shone with temptation. She leaned slowly towards him. Her kisses came slowly before they quickened in the passion that had first overtaken them on that isolated shore in Shetland.

'Tomorrow I will be going to Cropton, to the Chilton-Brookes,' Edward Coulson announced.' Richard will be back from Somerset and I want to strike a bargain now for next year's timber.'

Olivia grasped at this information. It was ten days since Kit had returned to Cropton and she still had not heard from George. The expected invitation to visit the Hall again had not come. Was she wanting too much, too soon? But if he loved her ... She stiffened herself. She would take the initiative.

'Are you going to stay?' she asked.

'No. I'm going to make an early start and return as soon as I've completed my business,' her father said.

'Could I come with you? I'll be company for you. I may as well ride with you instead of alone on the cliffs.'

Edward pursed his lips, hesitating to approve this suggestion.

'Olivia's right,' put in Lavinia. 'She'll be company for you.'

'Very well,' he agreed. 'I'll tell James to see that there are two horses ready by seven.' He glanced at his daughter. 'Too early for you? It won't have to be. I'll not wait if you aren't ready.'

But Olivia was ready.

Their ride on a day which was clear but cloudy was

uneventful. Edward was glad to have his daughter with him; she took the tedium out of the journey, made the moors seem less wild and the horizons less distant.

The sound of their horses brought George from the stable where he had been discussing the health of one of his horses.

His heart turned over when he saw Olivia. He had not expected her to come like this without an invitation. He quickly concealed his surprise.

'Good day, sir. Good day, Miss Olivia.' His greeting was amiable; his expression, once the initial surprise had gone, revealing nothing.

She was instantly perturbed.

'I've ridden over on the chance of seeing your father,' Edward explained. 'I hope it won't inconvenience him?'

'Not at all, sir. As a matter of fact he was saying only yesterday that we should be inviting you to visit again.'

Olivia picked on this statement. Had she anticipated too soon? Well, she was here now and there was no time like the present to affirm their feelings for each other.

George led the way into the house. His conversation was made chiefly with Edward, only the odd polite word to Olivia. He never offered any expression of delight at seeing her again.

She was a little hurt and began to think that her presence was an embarrassment to him. Then she chided herself for thinking that way. She had too vivid an imagination. Or was the back of her mind making suppositions and comparisons? Would Kit have been more enthusiastic in his greeting?

They were welcomed by Richard and Esther and after they had partaken of some refreshments, Olivia enquired if she could see Redwings.

George was cornered. He could not refuse but would have to be with Olivia alone then. He must face the promptings of his heart. Since Ailsa's departure his mind had been filled with nothing but that vision of her first seen in the glade. He had felt an intense longing to be with her. He could recall her touch, hear her voice and feel the warmth of her smile in his heart. She cast aside any other images he had once treasured, even strong ones of this girl here with him now. He would have to tell her that he did not love her.

When they went on to the terrace he did not turn to the steps which would take them to the stables. Instead he turned the other way. 'Do you mind if we walk first?'

'No,' Olivia answered, puzzled and surprised by the seriousness of his tone.

He said no more until they had left the terrace and were walking across the lawn.

'Olivia, the last time we parted in Whitby I suggested that you should visit Cropton Hall again. I have not in fact extended that invitation because I have since found someone with whom I want to spend the rest of my life.'

The bold statement, straight to the point, hit Olivia's heart like a striking harpoon. She stopped and stared at him with disbelief. 'You've done what?' Her cry was filled with astonishment but there was no mistaking from his expression that what he'd said was true. 'You can't!' Her voice came like the cry of a stricken bird. 'You love me!'

He shook his head. 'No. I'm sorry, Olivia.'

'But what we meant to each other . . . does that not count for anything?'

'Of course it does, and always will.'

'I knew it! You *do* love me. You can't love someone else. Somehow she's trapped you.' Olivia was shaking with emotion, her eyes on fire. The placid girl he had previously known was no longer there. He had roused a volcano deep within her, one which was very rarely seen.

'I've not been trapped, except by my own love.'

'But that was mine.'

'Not in the way I feel now.'

She grasped his arms and stared at him wildly. She could

150

see the Cropton Estate and all it meant to her dreams vanishing. 'George, you love me. Don't destroy what there is between us on this whim.'

He pushed her hands away. 'This is no whim, Olivia. I love someone else in a way I never loved, nor could ever love you.'

'What? Does that glade, our glade, mean nothing to you? Did our kisses there mean nothing? I don't believe it.' Desperation had come into her voice.

'Yes, they do, but . . .'

'There you are. I'm right, you love me,' she cried. There was wildness in her eyes and an assertive yet pleading tone to her voice.

'But,' he went on to finish, 'I met someone else there.'

'What? In our glade?' Anger turned to fury.

'It's true. When I saw her I knew she had my heart.'

'And I was banished?'

'Banished? No. You will always be special to me. You brought a new zest to my life, and for that I am thankful. I thought that maybe one day our relationship would develop into the love I sought, but I found another . . .'

'When?' she snapped.

'Eleven days ago.'

She turned away, biting her lip, tears welling in her eyes as a variety of emotions churned within her.

He reached out and laid a hand on her arm. She shook it off.

'I'm sorry,' he said quietly.

'Sorry?' Her eyes blazed with the fury of a woman scorned. 'One day you will be truly so. No good will come of this love you say you've found. Then you'll know it was me you loved.' He shook his head. 'It is! It is!' Her voice rose. 'It's me you love! You'll realise it one day but by then it will be too late.' She turned and ran.

He watched her go, sadness in his heart that he had hurt her and that she could not comprehend that he had never loved her in the way he now loved Ailsa.

It was only with this thought that he realised Olivia had not asked the name of his new love.

Olivia raced across the grass, her mind reeling under the enormity of what had just happened to her. Her world was shattered. Mistress of Cropton Hall, wife of the master . . . her expectations were destroyed. But more than anything she was deeply wounded by his rejection. Overwhelmed by misery, she moved like a wounded animal, heading she knew not where, only knowing she had to escape from her immediate surroundings in a bid to find security and peace.

She reached her horse, climbed into the saddle and set the animal to an earth-pounding gallop. Her eyes were misted by tears. She did not care. The wind was sharp on her cheeks. Her hair came loose and streamed behind her.

'Why?' Her cry to the heavens was torn away. 'Why?' The cruelty of George's disclosure pierced her mind. 'Curses on you, George Chilton-Brookes!' The words were filled with anger and hatred as she struggled to comprehend the blow she had been dealt. 'Some day you'll regret what you have done to me.'

Still seething with anger she let the horse run without knowing where she was going. Gradually the first fury faded. Her mind cleared. She must control her feelings, compose herself for her return to Cropton Hall. There was no way to avoid that. She must give no outward indication that she was distressed. She wiped her eyes with her silk handkerchief, sniffed back any more tears and began to take a grip on her feelings. With the horse under her control, she slowed it to a walk though still let it take its own course. She straightened herself in the saddle and took on a more determined attitude. She had plans to make.

After another ten minutes without being aware of her surroundings she pulled the horse to a halt on the edge of a slight dip in the land. Beyond it the fields rose to a ridge on which stood a house, not big but substantial, with buildings of the same stone forming a rectangular yard to one side. She stared at it for a few moments, then as she started to turn away her eyes drifted to the bottom of the dip and a man leaning on a gate watching her.

She was startled. She had not been aware of him when she had arrived at this point for all her attention had been on the house. Her eyes narrowed. There was something familiar about his figure. Then he straightened and she knew. Kit Fernley! Her thoughts raced again. Was this fate? After George's shocking announcement, had providence drawn her to this meeting?

Kit had opened the gate and was walking in her direction. Her immediate instinct was to avoid him but she could not turn away. Something compelled her to stay. Was her destiny being forged in these moments?

'Good day, fair lady,' he called from a few yards away. Olivia felt comforted by his tone. 'It is a pleasure to find such charming company so close to my home.'

'Your home?' Her eyes went from him to the house.

'Yes, mine.' He was beside the horse, stroking its neck and looking up at her. 'You did not know?'

She shook her head.

'Then fate has brought you here. Welcome. Walk with me to the house?' He raised his hand to help her to the ground.

After only a moment's hesitation she slid from the saddle. He took her weight and lowered her gently. A moment in time held their gaze upon each other. Then he turned, took the reins in his right hand and supported her elbow with his left.

'I think fate had more in mind than guiding you in this direction, I believe it told me to forget about riding into Pickering as I had planned and then directed me to be at that gate at the precise moment you arrived.'

She made no comment for her mind was toying with the same ideas. This meeting was more than luck. Was it showing her where her fate truly lay?

'And I believe,' he went on, 'that you are here because of that one word you once uttered in indecision – maybe.'

Denial sprang to her lips but she suppressed it.

He stopped and turned her to him. 'Am I right?' he asked.

She met the hopeful look in his eyes, eyes which searched for the answer he wanted her to give.

She nodded.

'And the answer?'

'If the question you were going to ask that day I stopped you was "Will you marry me?" the answer is yes.'

She saw his doubtful expression vanish in a flash to be replaced by one of excited joy. He let the reins go and swept her into his arms. He looked deep into her eyes.

'I love you, Olivia Coulson. Have done since the first day I saw you. I feared George might see what I saw, but thank goodness he didn't. I'm the lucky one.' His lips met hers with an ardour that spoke of his love.

Olivia responded. She must. Kit must be left with no suspicions that his fear had almost materialised. Her mind spun, barely able to grasp what had happened to her and how her future must have been preordained in her request to accompany her father to Cropton Hall.

With their arms around each other's waist they walked slowly towards the gate.

'What brought you to Cropton apart from the fact that you were destined to meet me?' he asked.

'Father was coming to see Mr Chilton-Brookes and I rode along as company for him.' She certainly wasn't going to disclose her real reason for doing so.

'If your father's here then I will take this opportunity to ask him for your hand in marriage.'

She stopped. 'No, not now, not here in Cropton.' Her face had taken on a grave expression.

'Why not?' he asked, troubled that she should not agree. 'This is a golden opportunity.'

'Kit, please, I'd rather you didn't. I'd like you to do that in Whitby in more appropriate surroundings.'

154

'Your home, with your mother close by?'

'Yes. Then we can all celebrate together.'

'All right, maybe that's the best thing to do.'

'I'm sure it is. And, Kit, I would like you to tell no one about this until after you come to Whitby and have spoken to my father.'

'But I must . . .'

She guessed what he was going to say and stopped him with, 'No one! Please, not until my father gives permission.'

'All right. If that is your wish.' He did not want to spoil things between them.

'It is. Just be patient a little while longer.' She kissed him and the touch of her lips promised much for the future.

'When shall I come to Whitby?'

'The day after tomorrow?'

'Not sooner?' He frowned mischievously.

She laughed and was glad that she could bring lightness to the sound after the shock she had received only an hour ago.

'I know Father has a busy day tomorrow.'

'The day after it shall be.'

'You will come to Whitby tomorrow. Call on us casually and invite me out. Then the next day see Father, having supposedly proposed to me the evening before.'

'And that will make it appear we are following the rules of decorum?'

'Right.' She smiled. 'Then the world can know.'

Her eyes strayed from the gate where they had stopped and took in the house at the top of the rise.

He saw the direction of her gaze. 'Your future home,' he whispered close to her ear. 'Come, let me show it to you.'

'Not yet. Let me remember what I see now, for the memory of this view will always be with me, a reminder of the day I said yes.'

'Very well.'

When she rode away she paused to look back. He was

155

still standing by the gate. She raised her arm and saw him respond. She gazed upon the house again. Not Cropton Hall as she had expected but, who knew? One day she may be in a dwelling to rival it. Kit had ambition and she would see that it always burned bright. With her help he should go far. Maybe she hadn't followed her grandmother's advice but its substance might not be so far away. As she rode back to the hall Olivia took an iron grip on herself so that she was composed and outwardly calm by the time she reached the house.

In a matter of an hour or two she had been plunged into the shattering depths of despair and had risen to the heights of euphoria. Seeing Kit had brought her to make a conscious decision to rise above her disappointment and meet life head on with all the resolve she could muster. She was reminded of those thoughts when she saw George on the terrace.

She made no attempt to turn away but rode up to the steps and dismounted there. She knew his eyes were on her, trying to assess her feelings.

'I'm sorry I rushed off like that, George,' she said firmly as she strolled up the steps. 'It was ill-mannered of me. I regret my reaction to your announcement and apologise if it caused you any hurt.'

She was on the terrace beside him, her eyes meeting his. He felt embarrassed by the frank way she referred to their last painful meeting and at the same time puzzled by her attitude after the deep feelings she had revealed. He had not expected this about face. Had a period of reflection made her realise his feelings for her were no stronger than deep friendship, or had something else happened to make her see reason? He was on the point of asking her but realised he could not. Unless she offered an explanation it would not be in order for him to try to enquire further.

'It is I who should be apologising for any upset I have caused. Believe me, Olivia, it was the last thing I wanted.'

156

She saw remorse on his face but her mind cried out, Why did you do it then? She wanted to express her feelings but restrained herself, knowing that another scene would do no good. She would accept what had happened but would use the future for her own ends.

These thoughts were stifled as he went on, 'I hope you understand? Please do. I don't want to lose your friendship.'

'Nor I yours,' she answered quietly. 'I hope you will visit us again in Whitby?'

'Thank you, I should like that,' he replied, accepting the olive branch.

'Has anyone missed me?'

'No. I have been out here all the time awaiting your return, hoping to speak to you before you faced the others.'

'Good.' She forced relief into her expression. 'Then no one will know about the foolish scene I made. Forgive me again, George.' She laid a hand on his arm with an appealing touch.

'There's nothing to forgive.' She started towards the house but he stopped her. 'I would like to say one thing more. I thought a lot of you, Olivia, and still do. There was a time I believed I was in love with you, as you imagined, but then . . .'

'Someone else came along and took your heart from me?' she completed his sentence. Outwardly she was graceful in defeat; inwardly she was seething and with it came a ruthless determination that she would make the future go her way. Some day he would dearly wish he hadn't rejected her.

'Should we go in?' she added calmly.

He nodded. When they joined their parents she was once again the Olivia he admired. It was as if she had never been devastated by his announcement. He was glad she had not ridden straight back to the Hall. The ride had obviously calmed her. Or if not the ride itself, something had happened to change her view and make her accept that he loved someone else. But what? It was not until five days later that he was able to make a guess.

Chapter Thirteen

'Mary, run and tell Miss Olivia that there is someone to see her,' Lavinia instructed when the girl had shown Kit into the drawing-room.

'Yes, ma'am.' The servant girl scurried away.

'It is so kind of you to call,' Lavinia said to Kit. 'Do sit down. Are you in Whitby for long?'

He sat down opposite her. 'It is a pleasure to see you too, ma'am. I am not sure how long I shall be in Whitby. It really was a spur of the moment visit, though I did want to see a couple of merchants here. I thought I would pay my compliments to you and Mr Coulson while I was here and seek your permission to walk with Olivia – that is, if she would like to accompany me?'

'I'm sure she would. Ah, here she is.' The door opened and a smiling Olivia appeared. 'You can ask her yourself.'

'Kit Fernley,' she cried as if surprised, and added, 'We are delighted to see you, aren't we, Mother?'

'Of course.'

'What was it you wanted to ask me?' she said, turning again to Kit.

'I was suggesting to your mother that you might like to take a walk with me?'

'It will be my pleasure,' she returned. 'I'll get my pelisse and bonnet and be with you in a minute.' She hurried from the room, giving the door a flick so that it shut behind her.

'Oh, to be young and full of energy,' sighed her mother.

'I'm sure you could match her,' Kit teased.

'In my day maybe.' She gave him a wistful little look as if her mind was latching on to some treasured memory.

'But I think there must be compensations in all ages?'

'True, young man, true. As, God willing, you will find out for yourself.'

'Here I am.' Olivia breezed back into the room.

Kit jumped to his feet. 'You look very smart.'

'Isn't it wonderful having a young man saying such nice things to you?' Lavinia smiled.

'And you look equally attractive in that beautiful blue dress, ma'am.'

'Away with you,' she returned with a dismissive wave of her hand, though secretly she revelled in his words. 'Young man, for that compliment I shall invite you to dinner this evening.'

Kit bowed. 'I thank you, ma'am, and accept. It will be a great pleasure.'

As they set off down the street Olivia and Kit laughed together. 'It couldn't have worked better, you flatterer! And you've given her every cause to like you.'

'That was my intention. I realised the last time I was here that your mother has a great deal of influence on your father's thinking, especially away from his work.'

'So you believe that if you win her you'll win my father?'

'Most certainly.'

'How right you are – as no doubt you will see this evening.'

Throughout their walk the empathy between them grew and they experienced the joy of being together. Olivia sensed he loved her and it made her examine her feelings for him. Was he the one she had truly loved all the time? Had she been blinded by a craving for wealth and position which had marred her judgement? Yet thoughts of Cropton

Hall still loomed in her mind. Could she fire Kit with an ambition to rival it?

'Come, Olivia, let us leave the gentlemen to their port and cigars,' said her mother, rising from her chair at the dining-room table.

'There is no need for that, my dear,' Edward demurred.

Lavinia gave him a nod. 'You don't often get the chance of man-talk after an excellent meal so you enjoy it now when you have Kit here.'

'Well, all right, if you don't mind,' replied her husband, pleased to have the opportunity to relax this way.

Olivia said nothing but exchanged a knowing look with Kit and followed her mother from the room.

As they crossed the hall to the drawing-room Lavinia said, 'I think that young man wants to ask your father something.'

Olivia saw the slight twitch at the corners of her mother's mouth, a sign that she was delighted she had engineered something to her own satisfaction.

'What do you mean?' asked Olivia in pretend innocence as she opened the door to the room.

'Don't tell me you don't know that Kit is going to ask your father for your hand in marriage?'

Olivia looked aghast and then let her expression slide into a smile. 'So that's why you suggested we should leave the room?'

'Of course.'

'How did you know?'

'Well, my dear,' went on Lavinia as she sat down and arranged her dress to her liking, 'I recognised the symptoms throughout the meal. Though you both enjoyed the food and took part in the conversation, I realised that other thoughts were in your minds. You both showed anxiety and nervousness, though you probably weren't aware of it. In Kit I could see your father when he was about to ask mine if he could marry me. In you I saw myself at the same point

160

in time.' She paused and eyed her daughter with a searching look then said, 'Do you love him?'

'Yes, Mother,' Olivia answered firmly and without hesitation. She wanted no doubt to be sown in her astute mother's mind. She knew that when her father came to join them he would not have given Kit a firm answer but would have suggested they confer with his wife, so Olivia wanted her on her side. Marriage to Kit would take her to Cropton and all the possibilities for revenge that held.

'Very well. That's all I want to know. There was a time when we thought George Chilton-Brookes might be the one, but if it's Kit Fernley who has captured your heart then so be it.'

Olivia made no comment.

Twenty minutes later the door opened and Edward strolled in followed by Kit who closed the door behind them. Edward had the aspect not only of a man who had dined and supped well but also of one who was about to break some news he thought no one else knew.

He strolled to the fireplace and turned to face them. 'Olivia, this young man has just asked me if I would give you in marriage to him.' He turned to his wife and said with not a little pomp, 'What do you think of that, Lavinia?'

She countered his question with another one. 'What did you say?'

'Well, I said ... er ... that we would have to have your opinion.'

'What would you have said if I hadn't been here?' Behind the seriousness of this question lay light-hearted pleasure in getting him into a corner.

'Well, I ... er ...' He turned his eyes on his daughter. 'Well, Olivia, do you want to marry him?'

'Yes, Father, I do.' She sprang from her chair and went to Kit's side, linking her arm with his. She smiled at him. 'Of course I do.'

Edward beamed. 'Then so be it.' He came to his daughter,

kissed her and shook Kit by the hand. 'Look after her, young man.'

There was delight in Kit's eyes and his grip on Edward's hand was firm and reassuring. 'Of course I will, sir.'

Lavinia had risen from her seat and come to the couple. She hugged her daughter and whispered in her ear, 'Be happy.' Then she turned to Kit. They kissed and, after she had hugged him with motherly affection, she leaned back and looked up at him, then glanced at her daughter. 'You'll make a handsome couple.' As they all sat down, she asked, 'You'll no doubt be living in your present house at Cropton?'

'Yes, ma'am, but I do have ideas of expansion, gaining more land – and then, who knows? A bigger, finer house, one such as Olivia deserves.'

'Like Cropton Hall?' She could not help but put the question.

Kit smiled. 'Nothing is impossible in this life.'

'Well said, my boy, well said.' Edward showed his approval with a smile. 'If my family hadn't adopted the same attitude we would probably have remained no more than skilful carpenters. Instead they took risks, and what came from them? The best shipbuilding yard in Whitby.'

'And when would you propose to get married?' asked Lavinia, thinking of the practicalities.

'Next spring,' put in Olivia quickly.

'So soon?' Her father looked astonished.

'Why not?' she returned. 'We love each other, why spend time in a long engagement?' She saw that she had caught Kit unawares but he was quick to hide his reaction and agreed with her. 'Let's fix a firm date now – March the first.' She glanced at her mother, seeking approval. Lavinia gave a nod of consent. When Olivia looked at her father she saw he wore a pensive expression. 'Well, Father, that will give you plenty of time to practise your speech,' she teased him.

Jerked out of his thoughts he spluttered, grunted and nodded. 'If that's what you want, lass, then it shall be the first of March.'

Celebratory drinks were taken and the rest of the evening passed pleasantly with Edward and Lavinia getting to know more about Kit, his ability and ambitions.

When he was taking his leave he put a request to them. 'May I take Olivia to break the news to my relatives in Whitby tomorrow morning? And in the afternoon may she accompany me to Cropton so that she is there when I tell my Aunt Betsy? I should of course be glad if one or both of you would accompany us to Cropton. Aunt Betsy has been like a mother to me, and I think would be very interested to meet you again.'

'That is thoughtful of you,' said Edward. 'Work will hold me here, but I'm sure Lavinia would be pleased to see your aunt.'

'Thank you, Edward.' She smiled at Kit. 'I will be delighted to come with you to Cropton.'

Pleased by her mother's agreement, Olivia hugged her.

'I am so happy for you,' said Lavinia, linking arms with her daughter when the door had closed behind Kit.

'So am I,' said Edward as he followed them across the hall to the drawing-room. 'I thought it might be George Chilton-Brookes you were sweet on.'

'Now, Edward, don't start sowing the seeds of doubt. Kit's an exceptional young man.'

'There are no doubts in my mind, Father,' said Olivia quietly, and turned the conversation to another subject.

But she could not deny that doubts crept into her mind later as she lay in bed with bright moonlight streaming through her window. She tried to cast them aside as would any girl who had just committed herself to marriage. She loved Kit, of course she did, but she still felt bitter about George's rejection of her and about losing a future at Cropton Hall when she had been certain that he loved her. But Kit had ambitions and she was determined to foster them. One day she would see that they fulfilled her own dreams and made her a rival to the estate she had lost.

*

163

The following morning Kit took Olivia first to see Jessica and Ruben. They were delighted that he was to marry Olivia, having seen that he was in love with her when he had brought her to the party. With the excitement of their announcement dying down Kit glanced at Olivia and received a slight nod in return.

'Cousin Kate, we'd like you to be one of the bridesmaids.' He smiled when he saw her excitement over the wedding intensify at this invitation.

She hugged and kissed him then turned to Olivia. 'Thank you so much for thinking of me. I hope you'll both be very happy. Who else will be a bridesmaid?'

'We are going to ask Anne. She and Aunt Jenny have always been special to our family. I know that will please Father. And, of course, Ailsa,' said Kit.

Olivia was pleased that she and Kit had discussed this aspect of the wedding on their walk across Whitby that morning. She had immediately agreed to his suggestions. She had no sisters and there were no really close friends she felt she must have as a bridesmaid.

Jenny was equally pleased at their news, and felt sure she could speak for her daughter and accept the invitation for her to be a matron of honour. 'I know Anne will be absolutely delighted. I appreciate you asking her, our families have always been close. And who is to be your best man?'

'I haven't decided yet. Maybe I should ask Dominic.'

As Kit drew the carriage to a halt outside his home late that afternoon his Aunt Betsy came out of the front door.

'I've brought visitors, Aunt,' he called as he jumped to the ground and lifted her off her feet as he hugged her. From his exuberance she recognised that he had something important to tell her but knew that would have to wait until he had attended to his passengers.

He turned and helped Lavinia from the carriage.

'Welcome to my home. It's so nice to see you both

164

again.' Betsy kissed her visitor on both cheeks.

'And you, Betsy, returned Lavinia. 'We are sorry to arrive without notice but ...'

'Think nothing of it,' cut in Betsy, wanting to turn her attention to the lovely young girl Kit had just swung to the ground.

He still had one arm round her when he said, 'And, of course, Olivia.'

'It is a pleasure to see you again,' said Betsy, and received a kiss from her.

'And for me to see you,' replied Olivia.

'I can hold back no longer,' cried Kit. 'Aunt Betsy, Olivia and I are to be married.'

Betsy held up her hands in astonishment. Though she had guessed that this was the reason Kit had brought Lavinia and her daughter, it was still a surprise to hear his words. 'Come here.' She held out her arms to Olivia and Kit and hugged them. 'I am so pleased for you both. I know my Kit has got a grand lass.' She gave Olivia an extra squeeze. Tears welled in her eyes but she held them back.

Lavinia smiled warmly as Betsy released her hold and turned from the couple. The two older women fell into each other's arms and shed a few tears of joy.

'Come, let's not get sentimental,' said Betsy at last, dabbing her eyes with a handkerchief. 'You must be tired after your journey and here I am keeping you outside.' She ushered them through the door and was soon the competent mistress again, organising the two servant girls to prepare bedrooms for the new arrivals and informing the cook that there would be two more for the evening meal.

It was soon arranged that Lavinia and Olivia would stay three nights and then Kit would drive them back to Whitby.

The following morning after breakfast Kit announced that he and Olivia would go riding for he wanted to show her the extent of his land. Once they were in the saddle and had left the vicinity of the house he announced that before he did that they would surprise George by asking him to be his best man.

It cost Olivia a great deal of effort to keep her composure. 'But don't you think you ought to ask Dominic or even your father first? And there's Ruben ...'

'I gave it a lot of thought last night. I know I should really have a relation, but I've seen a lot more of George than of my family so I've decided to ask him – and there's no time like the present. Besides I would like him to hear of our engagement from us before he learns of it from someone else.'

From the insistence in Kit's voice Olivia knew it was no use trying to dissuade him. Besides it might look odd if she protested too much. All she could do was brace herself not only for the immediate meeting with George but also for having him so closely involved in her wedding.

When they reached Cropton Hall they found him at the stables.

'This is a pleasant surprise, Olivia.' He did not hide his astonishment at seeing her. 'I didn't know you were back in the area again?'

'How could you, George?' laughed Kit. 'She only came yesterday. I brought her from Whitby. I went there to ask her to marry me and she accepted.'

'You ...' George's eyes widened in shock, his gaze moving from one to the other, and then he embraced them both. 'You're going to be married?'

'Yes. So congratulate us, George.'

'I do.' He still looked astonished and saw that Olivia enjoyed seeing him so taken aback by the news. 'I didn't know you two were so close.'

Olivia knew he must be wondering how this had come about after her shocked reaction to his announcement the last time she had visited Cropton Hall with her father.

'I've admired Olivia from the moment I met her during

166

your birthday weekend,' Kit enthused.

'And when he realised he was in love with me he wasted no time in coming to Whitby,' she put in, wanting to take over the explanation.

George's thoughts were racing at the news that the girl he had once thought might be his was to be married to another. Had he been a fool to turn away from her when he knew she would have said yes to him? But the picture of Ailsa still burned bright in his mind. He now knew what love really was. But did she love him? Did she think of him? He had not heard from her since that first meeting. Was there someone else, maybe in London, just as he had told Olivia his heart was elsewhere? Would Kit know? But this was not the time to ask. Instead he must offer his congratulations.

He nodded at Olivia's explanation. 'Kit Fernley was always a fast mover. I hope you will both be very happy.' He held out his hand and took Kit's in a warm grip. 'Well done. Take care of her, you've got a charming girl.' He slapped his friend on the arm and turned to Olivia. 'Congratulations to you, too. I know Kit will make you happy.' He hoped she would read the clear inference that she should do nothing to upset the delicate balance between the three of them.

'I'm sure he will,' she replied dutifully, glancing at Kit. 'A little different, I know, but am I allowed to kiss our best man-to-be?'

Kit laughed at the astonished expression that had come over George's face.

'Best man? Me?'

'Yes, why not?'

George shrugged his shoulders. 'Well, indeed, why not?'

'Then seal it with a kiss, Olivia.' Kit beamed at her proudly.

Olivia's eyes met George's as she leaned closer to kiss him on the cheek. Her lips lingered tantalisingly close for a moment as she whispered in his ear, 'Beside me at my wedding ... maybe on the wrong side.'

These words brought a sense of unease to him and almost made him miss what Kit was saying but he did catch, '. . . and you'll be escorting the chief bridesmaid, my sister Ailsa.'

Chapter Fourteen

'Ailsa, are you sure you've packed everything you want?'
Beth put the question to her daughter for maybe the seventh
time that morning. It was only a mother's natural concern
with an important family event, in which Ailsa would be a
prominent participant. Kit's wedding was little over a week
away. Nothing should be left to chance. Nothing should be
forgotten. Whitby was too far away to rectify errors.

'Yes, Mother. I am nineteen, you know,' replied Ailsa, a
touch of exasperation in her voice.

Beth's smile begged her daughter's forgiveness. 'I know,
love. I'm sorry to fuss, but it's an anxious time. I do want
everything to be right for your brother's wedding, especially as you're the only one to have seen him in the last
five years. We don't know the bride-to-be. I hope he has
made a good choice.'

Ailsa gave her mother a loving, understanding smile as
she came over to her and hugged her. 'I'm sure he has.
Aunt Betsy's letters have been reassuring, as have Aunt
Jessica's and Aunt Jenny's. They all seem to like her.'

'I hope we do.'

'Don't worry so, Mother. Everything will be all right, I
know it will.'

As she stood back Beth saw so much of her husband in their
daughter. Confidence, optimism, an ability to cope whatever
the circumstances. She knew that while these attributes had

been born in David they had been honed even more sharply on the Arctic whaleships sailing out of Whitby and on those leaving London for the long voyage to the Pacific through the vicious storms around Cape Horn.

There was a knock on the door of the bedroom, it opened and her husband looked in. 'You two ready?' he asked. 'We'll have to be getting to the dock, Dominic's in the hall waiting.' He stepped into the room and smiled proudly at them both. 'My two best girls look smart.' He came to them, holding out his arms, and they felt safe and protected by the love which was expressed in his embrace.

Ailsa was so much like her mother, the same fine features touched by the untamed beauty of Shetland. At times a look would come to her eyes that reminded him so much of Beth as she had stared out beyond the horizon from the cliffs far to the north. Shetland would always be in their blood.

As she tripped down the stairs excitement surged in Ailsa. This was the moment she had longed for, ever since the letter had come from Kit announcing his wedding and asking her to be chief bridesmaid. In that letter he had named the other bridesmaids but it was the name of the best man which had brought elation to her. Not only would she be seeing George Chilton-Brookes again, she would be walking down the aisle beside him as they left the church.

She hoped the feelings he had expressed when they had met still burned in him. Throughout these past months she had thought often of those moments in that beautiful glade when she had fallen in love. Now they were to meet again and this time she would be in the north longer, for her parents had decided to stay in Whitby until Kit and his bride had returned from their honeymoon. Maybe she could even scheme to stay on some days with Aunt Betsy at Cropton and seize the opportunity to see more of George.

The dressmaker Mrs Coulson had employed to make not only her daughter's wedding dress but the bridesmaids' stood outside the church to make any last-minute adjustments. She was casting a critical eye over her work as they awaited the arrival of the bride.

Ailsa was impatient. Since her arrival in Whitby there had been no opportunity to see George. Now he was waiting in the church and soon she would know whether he still had strong feelings for her. She hoped she would be attractive to him in her embroidered muslin dress which flared from her waist around which she wore a belt of silk ribbon in red and blue. The circular neckline was interlaced by a thin mauve band of silk matching the broader ones on the lower half of the skirt. The sleeves puffed from the shoulders and came in tight to frilled wrists. She wore a small deep blue velvet hat and carried a posy of spring flowers.

The bridesmaids fidgeted with their sleeves and readjusted their flowers, all wishing these last few anxious moments away, wanting the bride to arrive, knowing that once they took those first steps towards the church door some semblance of calmness would return to them. They were thankful that March winds were not blowing and there was only a gentle breeze warmed by the sun from a sky flecked by white clouds.

Last-minute arrivals hurried past with a quick word or glance of admiration.

The seconds seemed endless. Then they heard the clip-clop of hooves. A few minutes later a smiling Edward was helping his daughter from the carriage.

The dressmaker hurried forward to make the final adjustments to Olivia's dress of white embroidered net patterned in large motifs of leaves and flowers. It was worn over a white satin underdress and came from the waist less fully than in the bridesmaids' gowns. The sleeves, puffed to the elbows and tight at the wrists, were also patterned with small flowers and leaves. The neckline was close to the throat, partially hidden by the large white bow of the ribbon which held her brimmed white hat in place.

She smiled at the bridesmaids, and they exchanged a few quick words. Olivia's arrival had been announced in church and they heard the organ strike up. The procession arranged itself with Kate and Anne leading side by side. Ailsa came next, walking alone, followed by the bride and her father.

Olivia caught quiet gasps of admiration and comments of approval as she walked down the aisle. She knew her dress and those of the bridesmaids had captivated the congregation. After a few glances to the right and left, offering smiles to friends, she concentrated on the two men in the front pew, eager to see their reactions when they saw her. George might regret he had chosen someone else. For a moment she wondered who it was? Who had taken her place and would now become mistress of Cropton Hall?

Kit and George turned to watch her proceed the last few steps towards them. Kit's face was wreathed in an adoring smile. His eyes sparkled and there was no mistaking the fact he thought himself the luckiest man in the world. All this Olivia took in with one sweep of her eyes. She met Kit's, smiled, and allowed her gaze to move to George.

For one fleeting moment their eyes met. She read approbation of her appearance there but that was all. There was no regret that he was not in Kit's place. She saw his eyes pass her by and linger on Ailsa, and read there an unmistakable adoration mingled with deep love. The shock hit her. It was Ailsa who held his heart.

Jealousy cut deep even as she walked down the aisle to another man and a future which would tie her to Ailsa, Kit's sister, the girl who had stolen George's love.

An overwhelming desire to turn and run swept over Olivia then at that moment she felt her father squeeze her hand. His touch was filled with comfort, reassurance and love. She knew he would always be there for her if ever the need arose, and it brought her back to the immediacy of the moment and gave her strength to go forward to her new life, one which she was determined to shape to her own liking.

172

The parson was standing at the front of the sanctuary, holding a prayer book. He smiled benignly at them as Kit stepped close beside her. When the small group were all in position the organ stopped playing and silence filled the church. Then Olivia heard words.

'"Dearly beloved brethren, we are gathered here today ..."' The parson's voice gave way to Kit's then words were being directed at her. She repeated them.

'"I now pronounce you man and wife."'

When exactly she had half turned towards Kit she could not remember. His hands came to her shoulders and he kissed her. A buzz of happy and excited observations broke out among the congregation. She felt George's lips on her cheek and heard him say, 'Be happy.' Then Ailsa's face was close to hers. The cheek-to-cheek contact was gentle and there was genuine feeling in Ailsa's voice. 'I'm so glad to have you as a sister-in-law.' Her eyes were bright with the joy of the occasion but there was more, there was the happiness of a girl deeply in love. For when her eyes had met George's as she walked down the aisle behind the bride, she knew that the love between them, born in that secluded glade, was still there.

'Mrs Kit Fernley, Mrs Kit Fernley ...' Olivia kept repeating it to herself. She savoured the words and as she did so determined to fill the role of Kit's wife to the best of her ability for who knew what other opportunities may come in its wake?

People were saying how lucky she was, what a handsome couple they made, and she realised that there was truth in that. Kit certainly was handsome. His tall, erect, athletic figure would catch any eye and his smile, enhanced by the happiness he had found, showed a zest and love of life, an ability to get the best out of it. No doubt there were girls who envied her and would cry into their pillows tonight at losing him.

*

After the bride and groom had been given a rapturous send off the party continued at the Angel where the wedding feast had been held. Gradually other guests began to drift away, but David and Beth found this not only a great opportunity to become better acquainted with Mr and Mrs Coulson, their sons and their families, but also to enjoy the contact with their own relatives after so many years.

David sought out Jenny and led her to a quiet corner. 'It's good to see you again and looking so well,' he said by way of opening the conversation as they sat down.

'You should come to Whitby more often.'

He smiled, his thoughts dwelling on the past. 'Maybe.'

'You've been happy?'

He nodded. 'Yes, though sometimes I've wondered what might have been. We could have been happy together, Jenny.'

'I don't doubt that, David.' She laid a hand gently on his arm. 'But there would always have been Adam, you know that. He had my heart and still has. He's so close even after all these years.' Her voice cracked a little.

'I'm sorry, Jenny, I shouldn't have said that. To return to your question, yes, I've found happiness. With hind-sight, I think going to London was for the best.'

'I was sad for you when you lost Lydia.'

David nodded as bitter memories came flooding back. 'But then I refound Beth and Ailsa. They've brought me so much happiness, as have Dominic and Kit in their different ways. And, of course, there have always been special friends.' He patted her hand. They looked at each other and the years fell away. They were young again, standing on the cliffs beyond Whitby's ruined abbey. The silence between them was filled with poignant memories.

Jenny started and gave a little laugh. 'We'll be melancholy in a minute and shedding tears, and that's not you or me. David, I've something to ask you. When I knew you were coming to this wedding I thought it would be a perfect opportunity for those with a financial stake in Fernley and

174

Thoresby to meet. I have a special reason for asking if we can arrange that?'

'Of course. We are staying until Kit and Olivia return, so whenever it's convenient for you.'

'Then it may as well be as soon as possible. Shall we say tomorrow?'

'Yes, if that is convenient for Jessica and Ruben.'

'Shall we find them and ask?'

They stood up but Jenny made one more remark. 'Bring Beth. She has no direct stake in the company but of course she has one through you.'

After they had found Jessica and Ruben, informed them of the meeting and agreed a time, David had a few words with Dominic then asked him if he had seen Ailsa.

'Yes,' he replied. 'After the bridesmaids had changed I saw her leave the inn with the best man. She said they were going for a walk.'

Only comments about the wedding passed between Ailsa and George until they reached the top of the west cliff and had left behind the hubbub of the port and its people.

'I've thought a lot about you since you visited Cropton last year,' he said. 'I often wondered when you would return.'

'I wondered about you too,' returned Ailsa. 'I questioned whether the love we experienced then was still felt by you.'

'It never left me. And you?'

'Sometimes I thought that day was only a dream but when our eyes met as I walked down the aisle today, I knew it wasn't. I hope you saw my love for you?'

'The light in your eyes at that moment told me all I wanted to know.' He turned her to him. 'I love you, Ailsa, and always will.' His lips met hers and sealed his promise.

'And I love you, George.'

They kissed again, their lips lingering over the blissful sensation.

When their kiss ended they turned and strolled hand in

hand, lost in their lovers' world, until George broke the silence. 'When do you return to London? Soon?'

'We are staying until Kit and Olivia return two weeks today.'

'Then we can ...'

She laughed at the enthusiastic note that had come in to his voice. 'See each other again,' she finished for him. 'Yes, I've got it all planned.'

He looked at her hopefully.

'Aunt Betsy will have to return to Cropton because there'll be things to see to there with Kit away. I'll ask Mother if I can go and keep her company. If she says yes Father will be bound to agree. I think I heard Aunt Betsy saying she was going home the day after tomorrow.'

George laughed. 'You're a crafty vixen!' He grasped her in his arms and whirled her round. 'But how I love you for it. To have you with me for ten days!' She laughed with him and matched the passion in his kiss.

They parted once they were inside the Angel and Ailsa sought out her mother.

'I enjoyed my visit to Aunt Betsy last year. If I went to Cropton with her now I would be company for her while Kit is away.'

Beth looked thoughtful. 'Yes, you would. It could be a good idea and will help her get settled in her new cottage.'

'New cottage?'

'Yes, didn't you know? Aunt Betsy said she would move out of the manor house when Kit brought his bride home. He didn't want her to but she insisted, so only a fortnight ago he bought a cottage for her nearby.'

'Then I can help her get straight.'

'We'd better ask her.'

They found Betsy who seemed delighted at the prospect of having her niece with her for a few days.

'I must go and find your father, please excuse me.' Beth left Ailsa and Betsy talking about the new cottage.

When she found David talking to Ruben she quickly made

an excuse and drew him away. 'I wanted you to know that I have just given Ailsa permission to go to Cropton with Betsy for a while. It will help her settle into her new home.'

David looked thoughtful. 'I suspect going to Betsy is only a cover so she can see George Chilton-Brookes.'

'What? The best man?' exclaimed Beth.

'Yes.'

'How do you know?'

'They've been out for a walk together just now.'

'And how do you know that?'

'I was looking for her and asked Dominic if he had seen her. He told me he'd seen them leaving the Angel together. Remember, I wanted to question her when she returned to London the last time she visited Cropton but you wouldn't let me. Now we know, I think we'd better put a stop to the visit,' said David, annoyed that his daughter had used her aunt as a cover.

'Why?' asked Beth with a disarming smile. 'She was in love then and still is if I'm not mistaken. We agreed to let her tell us about it in her own good time. That still holds good. And remember I reminded you then that we fell in love at our first meeting.'

'But ...'

'No buts, David Fernley. Make no stipulations, let the girl go. Show her you trust her as you always have and she'll love you all the more.'

He nodded. 'You're right, of course,' he admitted.

'Then don't worry about Ailsa. If she's capable of rebuffing the attentions of the young beaux of London she's certainly capable of looking after herself in Cropton. Besides Chilton-Brookes is a good young man. I'm sure he'll take care of her. And no word of this to Betsy. Let her think she's the reason for Ailsa's visit. It flatters her and does her good to think she's the focus of attention. She'll find out in her own good time about Ailsa and George if their feelings for each other blossom as I rather think they might.'

*

177

The following morning, as arranged, David and Beth arrived at Jenny's at ten o'clock. They found Jessica and Ruben already there. Their hostess saw they were all comfortably seated.

'You don't mind if Anne attends this meeting?' she said as her daughter walked in. 'What I have to say is important to her. She has some idea of what it is because I have discussed with her my reasons for calling this meeting. I am also taking this opportunity to acquaint David with the financial position and workings of the company. He does not come north as much as we would like.'

'I know everything is in good hands, and as far as I am concerned you and Jessica and Ruben are doing a grand job,' he said. 'I appreciate your inviting Beth, too. She has always shown interest in all our enterprises though she plays no direct part.'

'Nor do I want to,' she put in. 'I leave that to the experts, but nevertheless what interests David interests me and I thank you for allowing me to be here.'

'You are very much one of the family,' replied Jessica.

Conversation was interrupted when a maid brought in a tray of cups and saucers followed by another girl carrying two jugs of steaming hot chocolate.

Anne was quickly on her feet and pouring the first cup. When Jenny was satisfied that everyone had something to their liking she took up the proceedings.

'First of all, David, the financial position of the company is strong. I have the figures here for your perusal and approval. I will not waste time going through them in detail. They are here whenever you want to look at them.'

'Your word is good enough for me.'

'Jessica and I can vouch for them,' put in Ruben.

'I have every faith in you all.' David cast his eyes over each one in turn.

'We have three ships leaving for the Arctic before the end of the month,' Jenny went on. 'Captain Marriot will take the *Ruth* in two days' time, Captain Wells will be in charge of the *Lonely Wind*, sailing five days later, and Captain Timms will be master of the *Mary Jane* about a week after that.'

'Any reason why they aren't all sailing together?' asked David.

'Repairs,' Ruben offered the explanation. 'The *Mary Jane* suffered some damage winter trading in the Baltic.'

David nodded, already thinking of the pangs he would feel when he watched them sail. He could spare himself by not being on the cliffs, but knew nothing would keep him away. The pull of watching the whaleships sail would be strong. He knew he would choose the east cliff rather than the staithes for there he would recall the girl with the red shawl who'd waved to the ship whenever he and Adam Thoresby sailed from Whitby.

'Now to the reason for which I called this meeting.' Jenny broke into David's reverie and focused his mind on what she was saying. 'I have had what I am about to say in my mind for a while so have had time to consider the matter from all angles. When I knew that David and Beth would be coming to Kit's wedding I realised it presented an opportunity for this meeting. I wish to announce that I propose to resign from playing an active part in the company.'

This was met with silent disbelief.

Jenny had played an important role in the firm ever since her husband had been lost in the Arctic. Not only had her work provided a source of income for her, it had also brought her the feeling of still being close to Adam.

'Why?' Jessica was the first to break the silence. 'You and I have worked so well together.'

'We have,' Jenny agreed. 'Never a wrong word with you, nor with Ruben. It has been a most harmonious partnership which I have valued highly. But I will still be around to offer advice if ever it is needed, and will retain some shares, but I want to hand over the bulk of them to Anne and her husband, Phelan. I wish to make their future assured.'

179

'Does that mean Phelan is giving up the sea?' asked Ruben.

'No,' replied Anne. 'As you know he has been loyal to Simpson and Bond ever since they gave him the opportunity to advance with them, but now with the break-up of that firm he is hoping he might take over the *Mary Jane* when Captain Timms retires after this voyage. Phelan would have been here today but Mr Simpson wanted his ship away to the Arctic last week.'

'Phelan has a good reputation, David,' explained Ruben. 'I know neither Anne nor Jenny will sing his praises in these circumstances but I for one would be more than happy for him to take command of the *Mary Jane*.'

'Your judgement is good enough for me,' replied David.

'Thank you,' said Anne, relieved that her husband's appointment had been accepted without question.

'What about your position, Jenny?' asked David.

'I would like Anne to take over that. She is keen and wants the challenge. She has already learned everything I can teach her about the running of Fernley and Thoresby.' She looked directly at Jessica. 'I'm sure you two will work well together just as we have.'

'I'm sure we shall.' Jessica smiled reassuringly.

'Ruben?' Anne looked quizzically at him.

'I can't visualise any discord between us.'

'It only needs your approval, David?' said Jenny.

'You have it.'

'Thank you, all of you. I am pleased to have my daughter's future settled.'

'And may I express my gratitude?' said Anne, her eyes a little damp as she looked round them all.

'Good.' Jenny gave a nod of satisfaction. 'I think a glass of wine is called for to toast a new era in the firm of Fernley and Thoresby.'

Chapter Fifteen

'Well, Ailsa, here we are.' Betsy peered out of the window of the carriage which had brought them from Whitby. 'I'm glad you're seeing my new home in the sunshine.'

The girl leaned forward to look out of the window. The coachman was bringing the horse to a halt outside a single-storey cottage built of stone. The window frames were fresh with paint and the garden well cared for. Daffodils filled the borders along the front of the cottage and livened the trimmed hedges with their yellow.

'It's lovely,' commented Ailsa. 'I hope you'll be very happy here.'

'I'm sure I shall. Kit wanted me to stay at the manor, but it was no place for me. Newlyweds need to be on their own.'

The coachman opened the door and helped them to the ground. He took charge of the luggage and followed them to the front door. It was opened before they reached it and a girl of about sixteen, neat in a plain brown dress with a white apron tied at the waist, smiled a greeting.

'Welcome home, Miss Thoresby,' she said brightly.

'Thank you, Alice. This is my niece, Ailsa. She'll be with us for a few days.'

Alice bobbed a curtsey at Ailsa and said, 'Welcome, miss. I hope you'll like it here.'

'Thank you. I'm sure I shall.' Ailsa gave her a friendly smile.

Alice took charge of the luggage.

When she was out of earshot Betsy said, 'I only got her ten days before I left for Whitby. Thank goodness I did! She's a quick learner and a hard worker. Did wonders in this place before I left so I had no qualms about leaving her.'

They had been taking off their coats as she spoke and now she started a conducted tour of the cottage for her niece.

Ailsa was charmed by it, so cosy and friendly, an atmosphere enhanced when they returned to the dining-room and found a meal awaiting them. The oak table had been neatly laid and a spread of cold meats with an accompaniment of home-made bread, pickles and hard-boiled eggs awaited them.

'Is this your work, Alice?' queried Betsy. There was doubt in her voice. Since the start of her employment Alice had shown no inclination to cook.

'I laid the table, miss, just as Ma showed me.'

'Well done, but what about the food?'

'Ma cooked the meats, miss, and that's some of her home-made pickle and bread. I hope it will be all right?' A worried note had come in to the girl's voice.

'I'm sure it will be excellent,' said Betsy. 'When you visit your mother tomorrow afternoon bring her to see me.'

'Yes, miss.'

'And don't look so worried. I only want to thank her.'

'Yes, miss.' Alice looked relieved. 'Shall I make some tea, miss?'

'Yes. Remember the way I showed you?'

'I do, miss.'

The girl scurried away and aunt and niece sat down.

'Alice seems to have been a lucky find,' commented Ailsa.

'She certainly has. This is more than I expected.' Betsy took a sliver of ham and tasted it. 'Mmm, delicious. If this is her mother's cooking I might be able to make use of her.

I have an income from the farm so I may as well make use of it and let Alice's mother cook for me. It will help her. She's a widow and won't have much to live on.'

'That's a kind thought, Aunt. It's just like you to be so considerate.'

'Away with you, lass. What are you buttering me up for?' A twinkle had come to Betsy's eyes as she looked directly at her niece. 'Though it will be nice for me to have you for a few days, and you'll help me settle in my new home, I think you had an ulterior motive in coming to Cropton.'

Ailsa blushed but smiled, knowing it was no good trying to fool her aunt. 'Was it so obvious?'

Betsy chuckled. 'To me it was. I think George Chilton-Brookes has taken your fancy and I believe he's smitten with you. He paid you a lot of attention at the wedding and you were pleased to receive it.'

'Well, I do like him, Aunt.'

'Then it will be no surprise if I see him come calling tomorrow, as I'm certain he will, for I'm sure you planned it between you.'

Ailsa looked concerned. 'You aren't annoyed, are you, Aunt?'

Betsy laughed. 'Who could be annoyed at love?'

'And you approve?'

'He's a fine young man. If your heart's set on him then of course I do. Have you told your mother and father?'

'No.'

'I think maybe you should as soon as you return to Whitby.'

Betsy smiled to herself when she heard the sound of hooves approaching her cottage the next morning. She glanced out of the window and saw, as she'd surmised she would, George Chilton-Brookes in the saddle.

'He's here,' she called out, but Ailsa was already hurrying to the front door.

183

George was swinging down from the saddle when she came out of the cottage. He turned to the gate and stood still when he saw her. Their eyes met in mutual admiration. But there was more than that. The love they felt crossed not only the distance between them but the bonds of time. They never doubted that their love had always been and had only needed them to meet.

He opened the gate and came up the path, his eyes never leaving hers. He held out his hands and she took them willingly in hers. Not a word was spoken, but each knew the other's thoughts. They kissed, lips trembling at the touch that sealed their love forever.

As their lips parted Olivia said quietly, 'Come and see Aunt Betsy.'

He nodded and followed her into the cottage.

Betsy heard their footsteps and called from the back room, 'I'm in here. A cup of hot chocolate for you. I'll bring it through.'

Ailsa started for the room on the right but George grabbed her arm, shook his head and pointed to the back room. He knew the layout of these cottages and that there would be a cheery fire crackling in the grate. He was right. As they came through the door Aunt Betsy was just turning from the fire with a pan of hot milk.

'Oh!' She gave a little gasp. 'I said I would bring it through.' She looked a little embarrassed that Ailsa should have brought George into what served as her kitchen.

'I know, Miss Thoresby, but I also knew it would be cosy in here.'

'Quite so,' said Betsy, taking the pan to the cups which were on the oak table set in the centre of the room. 'Do sit down. We won't be disturbed, Alice has gone to the village.'

George pulled the chairs from under the table and saw that Betsy and Ailsa were seated before he took his place.

Over their chocolate Betsy observed George more closely. She knew him from afar. It was only at Kit's

wedding that she had come into close contact with him and
that for only for a short time. Now in the more intimate
atmosphere of her kitchen she was able to contemplate him
more closely. She liked what she saw, a young man who
was comfortable here, one who had no airs and graces
though they would have been easy to adopt when the family
had come into unexpected wealth. His conversation was
pleasant, not opinionated, and showed consideration for
others. Betsy was impressed and had no doubt he would
make a good husband for Ailsa.

'Miss Thoresby, may I have your permission to visit
your niece every day? Her time here is so short and . . .'

'Of course you may if that is what Ailsa would like.'
Betsy saw relief in his eyes. 'Did you think I would be a
stuffy old maid? I have known love though alas it was not
to blossom. Make sure yours never lose the bloom I see in
you now.'

Throughout the next ten days George escaped his daily
duties as quickly as he could so that he could share as much
time as possible with the girl he loved. She was always
ready when he called. They walked, they rode, she came to
know the Cropton Estate and saw how deeply it was
engraved in George's heart. She knew how much he loved
this land and was determined that she would grow to love it
just as much. They talked of the future and she sensed that
he was exploring her feelings about London where she had
spent most of her life. She made sure that he had no doubt
that she could settle in and love the countryside as much as
he did. So it was no surprise when on the day before she
was to return to Whitby and thence accompany her parents
and Dominic to London he proposed marriage.

There was joy in both their hearts when she accepted but
she dissuaded him from going to Whitby with her to ask for
her hand in marriage.

'I would rather we keep this to ourselves until I return
again. Mother and I have always been close, drawn

185

together by the circumstances of my birth and childhood in Nova Scotia and America. I would like to tell her myself and let her get used to the idea that we will be parting. Then when I come north again we will break the news to your parents and everyone else.'

'Very well, if that is what you want. But come back soon, I'll miss you so.'

'And I'll miss you. Love me always.'

'Always, no matter what lies ahead.'

'I don't want this to end.' Olivia stretched in the luxury of their feather bed in a hotel on the south cliff of Scarborough.

'We can love wherever we are,' murmured Kit. 'Always and forever.' He twisted over and raised himself on his elbows to look down at her, then kissed her tenderly. 'I have something to tell you about Howdale Manor.'

He saw her expression become serious and was pleased, for what he had to tell her was important to him and he wanted her to be part of it.

'I've moved on from what was my grandfather's and my Uncle John's. Getting more land and the manor house was but a step in what I plan to achieve. Now, having you makes me even more ambitious, Olivia. I want only the best for you – a big house, a fine estate and a fortune to rival George's.'

This announcement came as a surprise to her but its impact was undeniable. She saw the fiery light of ambition in his eyes and knew that success meant everything to him. In that moment she realised all her dreams of becoming mistress of Cropton Hall had been a mistake. She was with the man she loved and, knowing his aims, would do all she could to help him rival George. Losing Cropton Hall and what went with it was not the end of the world. Kit had opened a new door and she would go through it with him.

Her arms came around his neck. 'Whatever you plan, I'll be beside you, helping in any way I can,' she whispered.

'You want that?'

'More than anything in the world except your love.'

'You've got that no matter what.' His lips met hers and she shuddered with the passion that surged through her. 'You and I were meant for each other. We'll show everyone what a wonderful couple we are and make them jealous of our achievements. With you to work for everything is possible.' He pulled her to him and kissed her passionately as if that would imprint the vow on their minds so that it would always be there to spur them on.

'I love you, Kit Fernley, for what you are, for making me feel special, for giving me your love and for the ambitions you have stored in that mind of yours.'

'Ambitions that will be fulfilled for you,' he said with an intensity that left her in no doubt of his determination.

'You'll have me to help,' she confirmed. 'Don't expect me to sit around looking pretty, I want to be there with you.'

'So you shall, my love. This will be our joint enterprise.'

'And what might the first step be?'

'Land, that's what we want. More land. I have none to inherit like George but, by God, I'll work for it.'

'Have you some in mind?'

'Aye. There's a small farm coming up for sale on the south side of my . . .' he pulled his words up short and then continued '. . . our land. If I can get that it will enhance my present holding. It's good grazing land on which I could run prime cattle. I'd rear them and then sell on.'

'Are there buildings?' Olivia's interest was roused. She was down to specifics, wanting to know all the details.

'Oh, aye, a small house and cottage.'

'What would you do with them?'

'Sell them if I could. If not I'd let them.'

'When are they being sold?'

'At auction in Pickering, two weeks after we get back.'

'Won't the owner sell privately?'

'No. The sale has come up because of the death of the

owner. The land and buildings have been left to two sons who have never seen eye to eye. Neither will sell his share to the other so they've decided to sell the lot. And even then they couldn't agree. One wanted to sell privately to me but the other would not so it has to be at auction where I can make my bid with my rivals.'

'Right, then we'll be there,' said Olivia, and added with fire in her eyes, 'And we'll get it.'

'Don't be so sure,' he cautioned. 'There's the question of cost. I have a limit I can go to.'

'And that is?'

'Two thousand pounds.'

'And if the property looks like going for more?'

He shrugged his shoulders. 'Then we'll miss out and have to wait until something else turns up.'

Olivia tightened her hold on his neck and let her eyes emphasise her resolve. 'We won't do that. If we need more money then I'll sweetheart my father.'

'I don't want charity,' protested Kit, seeing it as undermining any achievement on his own merits.

'It won't be. It will be a loan. Father will be only too glad to help on a business basis.' She gave a little smile when she saw his frown. 'Don't look so doubtful, my love. We'll make things work in our favour.' She pursed her lips enticingly as she drew him closer. 'Forget business for the time being, I'm going to.' Her lips met his with a passion which urged him on.

188

Chapter Sixteen

Olivia felt very much a part of the Fernley family when she sat down with them for an evening meal at Jessica's house. She and Kit had arrived in Whitby in the early-afternoon and after visiting her mother and father had gone to Jessica's as had been arranged at the wedding.

The atmosphere was relaxed, the meal excellent. When they settled in the drawing-room afterwards Olivia took the opportunity to speak with Ailsa.

'Did you have a pleasant time in Cropton?'

'Most enjoyable.'

'Aunt Betsy would like having you for company.'

'Yes, she's so kind. And thinks a lot of Kit.'

'As he does of her.'

'I do hope you and she get on when you are settled in Cropton.'

'I'm sure we shall. It was most considerate of her to move out of the manor house.'

'That's Aunt Betsy.'

'Did you see anything of George Chilton-Brookes while you were there?' Olivia watched Ailsa intently and gained the impression that she had the look of someone who was pleased with the attention she had gained from a man and that must be George.

'Yes.'

'He was well?'

'Yes.'

'Busy with the estate?'

'Yes.'

Olivia sensed Ailsa was going to give nothing away so let the matter drop, but took the girl's avoidance of the subject as an indication that there was something she did not want to disclose. She would make sure she learned more about it.

Any further conversation between them was halted when David took up a position in front of the fireplace and addressed the family.

'Now that we are all here I want to take this opportunity to put to you some thoughts I have been turning over in my mind these last few days. I want to do it before Kit and Olivia and Betsy leave for Cropton tomorrow, and we for London the next day.'

His serious expression caught their attention and they fell silent to listen carefully to him.

'Everyone here except Olivia and Kit knows that Jenny recently called a meeting of the shareholders in Fernley and Thoresby. For Olivia's and Kit's benefit I will summarise the measures she is implementing. She is ceasing to play an active part in the firm though she will still be available to give advice. She is keeping a few shares but will be transferring the bulk of them to Anne and her husband. Anne will take over her mother's role and Phelan will take over the *Mary Jane* when Captain Timms retires after the present voyage.

'Jenny's action set me thinking that maybe I should do the same as regards my holding in the firm.' This unexpected announcement shocked them all. Bewildered looks were exchanged. He went on, 'This is what I propose: I will retain a few shares but, as I am rarely in Whitby and am more involved in London with Hartley Shipping, it seems only right that I relinquish the bulk of my holding here. My son Dominic has shown a great interest in Hartley Shipping, which is only natural because of his association with it through his mother and grandfather. Its only link

190

with Fernley and Thoresby is through me. I propose, therefore, to split Hartley Shipping from Fernley and Thoresby as it will become Dominic's one day, though I will also make provision for Ailsa to hold shares in it. Neither she nor Dominic will have any shares in the Whitby company.

'Which leaves the disposal of my shares in Fernley and Thoresby. As I said, I will retain a few. Because of the way in which Jessica and Ruben, along with Jenny, have worked to keep the company successful while having little personal stake in it, I am going to hand over the bulk of my shares to them. There will also be a few for Kit so that the name of Fernley is still associated with the company even after I am gone. Kit has the farm at Cropton which has also been Betsy's life. By past arrangement she has an income from it and will enjoy one for the rest of her life. I know Kit and now Olivia as she is part of the family will look after my sister. I hope my decisions are agreeable to everyone?'

There were no comments. An uneasy silence hung in the room, everyone taken by surprise by David's announcement and needing time to digest it.

Jessica was the first to speak. 'I am overwhelmed by the generosity of my brother and I thank him on behalf of myself and Ruben. It is of real comfort to know that our future and Kate's is secure – depending of course on the effort that we put into running Fernley and Thoresby along with Anne. I assure the other shareholders they can depend on us to keep their interests at heart, and I hope that if they have any comments, suggestions or criticisms of what we do, they will not hesitate to voice them.'

After a moment's pause during which no one else spoke, Ruben said, 'I too must thank David. I think this is something of a new beginning for all of us, and that, together with the fact that the newlyweds are back with us, calls for a celebratory drink. Give me a hand, Kate.' Father and daughter left the room to enlist the help of the maid in preparing a tray of glasses while they chose the wine.

'Is that to your liking?' Olivia asked her husband quietly as the others began conversations of their own.

He raised an eyebrow. 'I want time to think about it. I had no idea Father was going to do this.'

'I don't think it's fair,' whispered Olivia. It was apparent that she had made her own quick assessment.

Realising this Kit said, 'We'll discuss this later. Not here.'

'You are going to have more to say and do helping to run Hartley Shipping,' commented Ailsa to Dominic. 'Does that please you?'

'Of course it does,' he replied, eyes bright with enthusiasm. 'I know some people will say I'm too young to take on such responsibility, but as you know I've been brought up to it and am well schooled by Father.'

'And he'll be there with advice.'

'Do you want to play any part in the business? After all, Father said the company would be yours and mine?'

Ailsa shook her head. 'No. I trust you to do a good job.'

'I can't wait to get back to London now.' There was burning enthusiasm in Dominic's tone.

'You haven't enjoyed Whitby?'

He shook his head. 'No. Life's not the same here. It's a busy port, but it hasn't any of the other attractions of a big city. I'll be glad when we leave tomorrow, won't you?'

'No. I like it here.'

'But you've scarcely spent any time in Whitby.'

'I enjoyed it at Aunt Betsy's, and wish I was going back with her.'

'Do Mother and Father know this?'

'No, and don't you tell them.' Her words, though whispered, were spoken with a force which left Dominic in no doubt that there was more behind them than she had revealed.

He gave a knowing smile. 'I think you and I are close enough to read each other's mind. You've met someone, haven't you?'

She gave a little nod. 'Don't tell anyone, please. I will do

192

so in my own good time.'

'We've shared secrets before. This one's safe with me.'

David and Beth had fallen into conversation with Jessica and he was soon enquiring about the sailings of their three whaleships. Beth saw the wistful expression come into his eyes and knew he was remembering the days when he'd left Whitby on the deck of a ship bound for the Arctic whaling grounds. She had seen that look often over the years at this time of the year. That faraway quality would come into his gaze and she would realise he was seeing the distant horizons that held the magic of the Arctic. The call of the north was here again and this year he would feel it all the more when he watched the *Ruth* leave the tranquillity of the river to meet the broad ocean and set sail for the north.

The first moment of privacy for Kit and Olivia came when they went upstairs to bed.

She drew a deep breath as she sat down on the side of the mattress. 'I'm not happy with your father's disposal of his shares in the company. I think you should have had more, don't you?'

'I can understand his reasoning but I agree with you.'

'You are the eldest and you are getting the least. Dominic and Ailsa are going to get all of Hartley Shipping between them, while Jessica is getting the bulk of the Whitby company. I know you have the farm but from what you tell me it was only small when you took it over, so really all the additional land you have now and the manor house are from your own efforts, not an inheritance like the others enjoy. You are getting nothing from your father except the initial farm and now a few shares in Fernley and Thoresby.'

'But what can we do about it?'

'See him, talk to him, put your case, let him see that you think you have not been dealt with fairly. He won't have had the papers drawn up yet because he wanted the

193

approval of all the family. You'll have to do it before he leaves for London. He'll probably have everything made legal when he gets there.'

Olivia's words had come fast, sharpened by a desire to further Kit's prospects and thus procure more land and subsequently a house and property to rival that of George Chilton-Brookes.

Kit felt the urgency in her voice, and rose to its challenge. Be ambitious, go for all you can get.

He came to her, took her hands and pulled her gently to her feet. He gazed down into the eyes of the girl he loved. He was drawn into the spell she cast, spurred by a desire to do everything in his power to make her happy. She wanted him to take up the matter with his father and be dealt with fairly. The look on her face, encouraging him to do this, filled his mind. Do it he must! Do it he would!

His hands came to her waist and slid around it as he drew her close. 'For you anything, my love.' His lips met hers, the promise in them giving way to passion until all thoughts were submerged in their need for each other.

David was awake early. He kissed his wife. 'You sleep on, I'm going to see the *Ruth* sail on the morning tide.'

Beth nodded sleepily. It was what she had expected. Let him have these moments alone while in his heart he was sailing north.

David dressed quickly and went downstairs where the landlord of the Angel, who had been forewarned, had some breakfast ready for him.

He hurried to the bridge as early-morning Whitby came to life, breathing deeply of the salt air and realising how much he missed it in London. He glanced along the river as he crossed to the east side and the activity on the *Mary Jane* held his attention. He paused. His mind flew back over the years to his first sailing on the ship, a raw young lad who knew nothing about whaling but was drawn to the sea. On board that vessel the friendship he had struck up with Adam

Thoresby was strengthened when he saved Adam's life, only to see him lose it later to the unrelenting Arctic. In their years together Jenny had always watched them sail. He wondered if she still watched the whaleships leave. The thought automatically turned his footsteps in the direction of her house. He was twenty yards from it when he saw her come out of the front door. He stood and watched her approach. A plain woollen coat covered her dress, protection against the cool wind that was blowing this morning. Around her head and covering her shoulders was the red shawl he remembered so well.

Intent on her walk, her thoughts miles away, she only looked up when she neared him and was aware that someone stood in her way. 'David!'

'I wondered if you still watched the whaleships sail?' he said quietly, though it was obvious to him where she was going.

'I never miss. It brings Adam close.' Her voice faltered a little then she added quickly, 'And you, of course.'

He turned with her and they fell into step. 'In Whitby, I could not but be on the east cliff when the *Ruth* sailed this morning.'

'And you were coming to fetch me?'

'I hoped to.'

Her hand slid into his with the warmth of something deeper than friendship, of the love between them that did not impinge on hers for Adam. 'We have a lot of memories, David. I have always been grateful that you and I shared so much.'

'And I have never forgotten you and all you meant to me when I first came to Whitby.'

'Memories? I sometimes wonder if they are easy to live with?'

'We could not live without them. No, there's nothing wrong in remembering. In fact they give us strength in times of need.'

'You've found that too?'

195

'Yes. At those times I have walked these cliffs with you in my mind and found peace and courage to go on. This is no reflection on Lydia and Beth, life would have been hell without them, but there are special times when memories of Whitby and you return with such vividness I could almost reach out and touch you.' He glanced at her and smiled, squeezing her hand affectionately.

She returned his touch but said nothing. They shared a silence which said so much.

It was only broken when they started up the one hundred and ninety-nine steps leading to the parish church and the cliff top.

'Your announcement that you were relinquishing the majority of your shares to Anne set me thinking that I should do the same,' David told her. 'I have done just that. I believe you have a right to know as it affects the composition of the shareholdings.' He went on to explain to her what he had proposed at the family meeting.

She listened carefully and when he had finished said, 'The disposition of your share of the company is entirely a private matter and really I have no right to comment on or influence your decision.'

'But you know I would value your opinion.'

'Yes, I do. And I know you will take no offence at anything I have to say. Really it's but one thing: are you being fair to Kit? After all, his mother helped you build your company.'

'He knows nothing of that. Knows very little about Ruth, in fact. He does not know her background or of the life she led in Whitby. He believes she was drowned when the London packet broke up off Saltwick Nab. He was brought up on the farm, as you know, and farming is his life.'

'All the same, I think he might be entitled to a few more shares.'

David lapsed into a thoughtful silence.

Jenny said no more until they reached the top of the steps and were walking through the graveyard. 'You asked for my opinion, I've given it. Take it for what it's worth and act as you think best. Now, let's see the *Ruth* sail.'

The ship took to the sea. Jenny waved her red shawl. Memories which only these two people could know were shared in silence.

When David reached the Angel he found Kit and Olivia waiting for him.

'I'm sorry,' he apologised. 'Am I holding you up from returning home?'

'No,' replied Kit. 'We have decided not to go until tomorrow. Aunt Jessica says it is all right to stay with her another night and I have informed Aunt Betsy.'

'Good. It will be grand to have you for another day.'

Kit's reply of, 'You may not think so,' brought a startled look to his father's face. 'I would like to have a word with you in private,' he added.

'Very well,' said David. 'There's a little room along there I'm sure we can use.'

Kit turned to Olivia. 'See you later, my love.' He kissed her on the cheek.

The two men went into a parlour. It was sparsely furnished with four chairs set around a table in the centre and a small table against one wall. They sat down.

David thought his son looked a little embarrassed so he broke the silence. 'Well?'

Kit dampened his lips and said, 'Father, I'm not happy you are only giving me a very small proportion of the shares you hold in Fernley and Thoresby. I don't want you to think I'm greedy or grabbing but I don't think you have been entirely fair to me.' He paused as if gathering his thoughts.

'Why is that?' prompted David.

'I am the eldest but I get the least.'

'You have the farm.'

'Yes, but if you go back to your original gift to me it is small in comparison with what the others get.'

197

'Why go to the original?'

'Because that is the basis I think you should work from. After all, the expansion of the farm and the purchase of the present house was all my own doing.'

'You have a point. That might be rectified in due course. But remember, you never showed any interest in whaling so I thought . . .'

'I never had the chance!'

'Naturally. You were raised in the country.'

'And whose fault was that?'

David frowned. 'What do you mean?' A harsh tone had entered his voice.

'You dumped me on my grandparents and Aunt Betsy and Uncle John after Mother was drowned. I never had a chance to get to know you properly or what your trade was like.'

David's lips tightened. 'I put you with your grandparents – not dumped – because it was the best thing to do. I was away at sea most of the year.'

'You were only whaling for six months of it.'

'True, but we had to make money by using the vessels in winter trading, and when I wasn't sailing there was the company to see to.'

'I know all this. But I still think you could have found some more time for me.'

'I came to visit you at the farm.'

Kit gave a little laugh of derision. 'How often was that? You were a stranger to me. Oh, I knew you as my father but beyond that what did you do for me? You never even took me to Whitby. Never took me on board a whaleship.'

'You wouldn't have liked it.'

'How do you know?' There was a snap in Kit's voice. 'Don't you think there's something of you in me? Didn't you think I might have had a yearning for the sea. They say it runs in families.'

'We can easily find out,' returned his father coldly. 'I can hold up the *Mary Jane*'s sailing and we can both be ready to depart with her. You can have a taste of the whaling life and I'll be there to see how you like it.'

'I want no special privileges,' rapped Kit, rising to the challenge.

'You won't get any! I'll see to that. Then we'll find out if there's a real man inside you.' David jumped to his feet, flung open the door and stormed up the stairs to the room he and Beth shared.

She, Olivia, Ailsa and Dominic were enjoying a cup of hot chocolate there when their pleasant conversation was interrupted by the arrival of David with Kit following close behind. The anger that clouded their faces told the onlookers there had been trouble.

'Kit is sailing on the *Mary Jane* and I'm going with him!' David's forceful announcement left everybody thunderstruck.

Beth was the first to recover. 'You can't,' she gasped as she was struck by what this meant. She had dreaded the day that David would be drawn back to the Arctic and its dangers. She knew he'd always dreamed of returning at least one more time. What had happened between father and son that had given him the impetus to fulfil his desire?

'I can and I am! This whippersnapper says I deserted him, never gave him the chance to follow in my footsteps. Well, he can now. Let's see how he likes the life of a whaleman. See if he really is entitled to more shares as he says he is.'

Olivia had at first been struck dumb by the sight of her angry father-in-law. Then she took in the significance of his words and exclaimed, 'Kit, we've only just got back from our honeymoon. You can't desert me now. Please don't go.'

'I'm not deserting you, love, just postponing our being together.'

'But what am I to do?'

'Go to your parents until I return.'

'I was looking forward to us being together in our own

199

home. Please think again, give up this foolish idea?'

'If it means getting what I think is my fair share, I'm going.'

'But we've the farm to run. All the plans we made will be ruined.'

'They needn't be.' He grabbed her by the shoulders and met her pleading gaze. 'I've an idea. There'll be time to discuss it later.'

'I'm going to see Captain Timms.' His father headed for the door.

'Wait!' cried Beth, but he was gone. There were tears in her eyes as she turned to Kit. 'Please stop this. You don't know what the Arctic can do.'

'I can't.'

'Please?' Olivia repeated.

'There's danger,' Beth warned. Her voice faltered but she drew on her strength to try to change what she considered to be a hotheaded decision. 'Even if you survive there's the possibility of serious injury. I've seen men return from the Arctic scarred for life, broken in mind as well as body. And even if you come through all that unscathed there is the mysterious call of the north. It can grip a man so that it becomes irresistible, forever calling him to return.'

She looked at Olivia. 'If that gets into Kit's soul you'll have a battle on your hands. You might have to forget the farm and all the plans you had for it.' She turned back to Kit. 'I triumphed over that call, or thought I had. I knew that every year about this time your father's heart was in Whitby, sailing with the whalers, but he had made a promise to me when we were married that he would never return to the Arctic. He kept that promise though it was hard for him to do. Now he has seized on an excuse to break it and sail north. You can prevent it, Kit.'

'I can't.' There was regret in his voice that he could not oblige his stepmother. He would have done so if he could, for he thought a lot of her and was grateful for the happiness she had brought to his father. 'A challenge was thrown down and I had to accept. If I don't I will always wonder if my father was right – that I couldn't cope with a whale-man's life. I need to prove myself to him and must go for my own peace of mind, too.'

'Kit, please reconsider.' Olivia's voice broke.

'I've got to go, my love. I'm sorry. It pains me to leave you so soon after our wedding. But please try and see it from my point of view. It will only be for five months, I'll soon be back.'

'Five months too long.'

'Come, my love, let us make plans for you.' He slid his arm around her shoulders and started for the door. There he paused and looked back at his stepmother with sorrow in his eyes. 'I'm sorry. Please try to understand.'

Tears streamed down her face as she sat down on the sofa between Ailsa and Dominic, also cast down by seeing their mother cry.

She took them into her arms and hugged them tight, saying, 'And we shall have to make plans too.'

By the time David returned, Beth had composed herself. She washed the tearstains from her cheeks and hid the red rims round her eyes with a dusting of powder.

She had been angered by what had happened and at the fact that David had broken his promise to her. She had felt an urge to lash him with her tongue, make him feel so guilty he would reverse his decision. But by the time of his return she had come to accept it, knowing that this was the best way to keep harmony and strength in the love that burned between them. In her heart of hearts she had known that one day the call of the north would triumph, but when the moment had come it had not been any easier to accept. Still, accept it she must and with it give David all the love she could so that he would have something to remember and cling to in the harshness of the long Arctic days.

When he walked in she knew immediately that his mood was so different. Tranquillity reigned instead of anger and a readiness to ride roughshod over anyone prepared to oppose him.

He came straight to his wife and held her in his arms. 'I'm sorry,' he whispered close to her ear. 'Please try and understand and give me your blessing?'

'I do,' she replied, a catch in her voice.

He looked into her eyes with such adoration she knew he appreciated the fact that she had not raised a barrier between them because of his decision. His kiss was full of love and she returned it.

At that moment Ailsa and Dominic walked in.

'Oh, sorry,' they gasped together.

Beth and David smiled as they turned to face them. They held out their arms.

'Don't be embarrassed, we aren't,' said Beth. 'Are we, David?'

He shook his head.

'Nor are we, Mother,' replied Ailsa as she and Dominic come over to them. 'Don't think we don't notice things. Holding hands, kisses when you think we aren't looking, glances exchanged that mean something special to you both. We know these are indications of how much you love each other, and that makes us feel safe. It shows the strength of your marriage and brings security to the whole family.'

Beth's eyes were damp as she said, 'I hope you will take that to your own marriage one day.'

It was on Ailsa's lips to tell her parents about George then but Dominic started to speak and she decided to withhold the news. Maybe with all the trauma of the last few hours it was better not to add to it.

'If you are going on this whaling voyage, Father, does that mean we will have to stay in Whitby until you return?' Dominic asked.

'Let's sit down and decide what is going to happen. I think you would rather be in London?'

'Yes, Father, I would.'

'Then you shall be.'

'But he'll be on his own unless Ailsa goes with him,' pointed out Beth. 'I'm certainly going to stay here until you return.'

Ailsa took in every word. She did not want to go to London. At least there would be a chance of seeing George if she was in Whitby with her mother.

'I think Dominic is capable of standing on his own feet. Cook and the maids will look after him at home. And I don't mean him to be idle while he's there. He has shown great interest in Hartley Shipping, and as I said it will be his and Ailsa's one day. He knows the running of the company. He can take it up now.'

'Thanks, Father. I'll not let you down.' Dominic's excitement was obvious.

'I know you won't, son.'

'But it is such a responsibility,' protested Beth.

'I can handle it, Mother, and I'll have Mr Sproats to help me.'

'And what that man doesn't know about Hartley Shipping and the way we do things isn't worth knowing,' David pointed out. 'I'll write him a letter of explanation. You can write one for Cook.'

Beth resigned herself to the decision. The men had their heads set.

'Do I take the sailing we were all going to take?' asked Dominic.

'There's no reason why not,' replied his father. 'Now, there's your mother and Ailsa to settle. I have an idea for them.'

Ailsa's heart sank. What had her father in mind?

'Beth, I know you've always had a yearning to see Shetland again in spite of some unhappy memories, so why not sail that far with us? I'll arrange for a voyage from there back to Whitby.'

'Oh, I don't know.' She looked doubtful.

'You go, Mother,' put in Ailsa quickly. 'You and Father can revive old memories if I'm not there. I'll go to Aunt

Betsy's. I'd rather. I'll be company for her and I might be of some help to Olivia in settling on her own if that's what she decides to do.'

David pursed his lips. 'I think Olivia is determined to go to Cropton, and I admire that decision rather than staying with her parents. Maybe it's not a bad idea for you to go there, too, if you are sure you don't want to come to Shetland?'

'I'd rather go to Cropton and I'd be of more use there.'

'Very well, if your mother agrees then you can go. I'm sure Betsy will be delighted to have you.'

Ailsa, hoping that her mother was not going to object, looked enquiringly at her.

'All right,' said Beth quietly, knowing full well that she was pleasing her daughter.

'You could still change your mind.' Olivia put the suggestion quietly as she lay in Kit's arms in the depths of their feather bed.

'I can't, love. Surely you can see that after the way things turned out?'

'I can understand it but that doesn't mean I like it. We've just come back from our honeymoon. We've been married a little over two weeks, and now I'm going to lose you.'

He rolled over to face her, saw that her eyes were damp. 'Don't cry, love.' He kissed the tears away. 'I'll miss you too.' He kissed her on the mouth. 'I can't ignore what my father implied.'

'He wouldn't mean anything by it. It would only be said in the heat of the moment.'

'Maybe, but it was said, and that means the thought was there. Darling, I've got to go, to prove him wrong, to prove that I could have taken to the whaling life just as he did, and that I'm worthy of stepping into his shoes as far as the business is concerned.'

'But the farm, your ambitions to make it bigger and become a landowner on a par with George? All the things we talked about on our honeymoon.'

'I still mean them. The farm is my first love. It must be. I was brought up on the land.'

'If you go, you won't be able to close a deal on this farm you want to buy.'

'No, I won't, but you can.'

'Me? But I don't know anything about it, where it is, what it's worth, or . . .'

He stifled her objections with his fingertips. 'I'll give you all the information tomorrow. You can do it, love. I know you can. I'll give you a note for Jeremy Halstead. You met him at the cricket match though you may not remember him, he was one of a crowd, but you saw more of him at the wedding. Burly man, about my age, looks more like a farmer than an attorney. He'll see you follow the right procedure to buy that land.' Kit gave a little chuckle. 'I think with your capabilities you might even get a taste for handling such things and help us to fulfil our dreams.'

'You have such faith in me?'

'Who better to have it in?'

'Stay with me and we'll work together.'

'I can't.'

'This voyage means so much to you?' Her searching gaze demanded an honest answer.

'Yes, my love, it does. I must prove I could have followed my father's calling.'

Her arms came around his neck and she pulled him gently to her. 'Then go, my love.'

Their lips sealed the pact and their loving would give them much to remember during their parting.

Chapter Seventeen

'Let go fore and aft!'

The mooring lines were let go.

'Bend y' backs.'

Oars dipped into the water and the boats, in position to tow the *Mary Jane* to midstream, took the strain. Slowly the ship eased away from the quay.

Kit hauled in the line quickly and went to the rail. Olivia was there with Aunt Jessica, Uncle Ruben, Aunt Betsy and Ailsa. At that moment he felt a touch of self-doubt but drew on his strength of character to dismiss it, though he also wished he could jump ship and sweep Olivia into his arms, tell her how much he would miss her and that his love would always be hers. Across the distance their eyes met and held. Her right hand was raised in goodbye, her left brushed tears from her eyes. His heart ached, wanting to kiss them away as he had done the previous night.

He glanced along the ship. His father was standing at the rail with Beth. They held hands, waving farewell to those on the quay. Kit could sense the excitement in them. They were sharing something special. They had never sailed to Shetland together, and now were returning to the islands that meant so much to them. In spite of the harsh life that Beth had experienced there, those memories of outrage and eviction, leading to a voyage of horror on an emigrant ship to Nova Scotia, were outshone by the recollection of the love she had found there with David.

Once she had accepted the fact that this voyage had to take place Beth put any fears to the back of her mind and allowed the excitement of seeing her homeland again to grip her.

As she stood beside her husband and sensed the yearning he had suppressed for so long coming to fruition, she knew that after this their love would only know greater depths, if that was possible. Beth thanked God for David, blessed the day he had come into her life on that lonely shore, and prayed that he would return safely from this voyage.

Wives and sweethearts yelled last farewells from the quay. The crowds called their good wishes. Orders rang out. The oarsmen were cajoled to greater effort. She glanced in the direction of the drawbridge. The opening looked so narrow that she wondered if the ship would pass through, though she knew there was no doubt that it would.

People crammed the riversides, crowded the staithes and the piers and lined the cliff tops. This was a whaleship that was leaving and it merited a special send off from Whitby folk. Whalemen were special. They risked their lives in the cold Far North where they hunted creatures, some of them sixty feet long, from tiny boats with hand-held harpoons, all this to add to the fortunes of Whitby and its people. They were men apart and recognised as such. Whitby folk gave them a hero's send off and would wait anxiously for their return.

The *Mary Jane* passed through the drawbridge and in the lower reaches of the river began to feel the breeze.

'Get singled up!'

'Loosen fore tops'l!'

'Hoist it!'

The mate's commands rang clear, demanding instant obedience.

Kit had finished coiling and was now pulling with the rest. He had been told his duties when leaving port and knew that he would be given no privileges even though he was the owner's son. Not that he wanted any. He had been given a bunk in the fo'c'sle with the ordinary members of the crew and was thankful that he was not going to be under his father's eye all the time.

David had insisted to Captain Timms that Kit be treated as any other member of the crew. He himself had refused to take over command of the ship. 'This is your ship, Captain,' he had said. 'Whatever other position you want me to take, I will do so. I want no privileges for myself.'

Captain Timms placed him on the ship's roll as second mate and offered him his own cabin.

David refused. 'If I am a mate, then I'll use the mates' quarters.'

Captain Timms bowed to David's wishes but insisted that David and Beth occupy his cabin at least as far as Shetland, where she would leave the ship.

The breeze caught the sails. The rowing boats cast off and amidst cheers from the crowds the *Mary Jane* sailed sedately to meet the sea.

Beth was amazed by the send off. She had never experienced anything like it and began to realise something of what David had missed. Whaleship sailings from Whitby were something special. She glanced at her husband and followed his gaze, fixed intently on the crowds on top of the east cliff.

He had been open with her about his life before their marriage and she knew of the special relationship that existed between him and Jenny and how the waving of a red shawl held particular significance for him. She saw it waved now and felt his grip tighten on her hand.

'Jenny's there?' Though her intonation implied a question she knew it was really a statement.

'Aye. And Adam will be in her mind.'

She made no comment, leaving him to his own thoughts. She felt the ship heave, looked to the bow and saw that the *Mary Jane* was clearing the protection of the piers and meeting the first swell of the sea. She glanced over the side and saw the water, cut by the bow, sliding by as white foam, to slip beyond the ship and resume its calm undulations.

She straightened and breathed deep of the salt air, pulling her shawl more tightly round her shoulders.

'Cold, my love?' said David taking her arm. 'Want to go below?'

She shook her head. 'I love it here, especially when I have you beside me.' She removed her small bonnet, shook her hair loose and let the wind blow through it. It shimmered in the sunlight as the strands twisted and turned. David's heart swelled. This was as it had been the first time he had seen her. He looked at her with love in his heart and rejoiced that her beauty was unmarked by the passing years.

'Kit will be all right, won't he?' she broke into his thoughts.

'Of course he will.'

'You'll see he's all right?'

'Don't worry, Beth. He's not a boy, he's old enough to look after himself.'

'Will the crew give him a rough time because he's your son?'

'That will be up to him. They'll maybe have a go at him, but if he handles it right they'll respect him all the more.'

'But you won't let them be rough?'

'If I interfered that would really go against him. This is a different life from the one he's been used to but I think he can handle it, and if he does he'll be all the better for it.'

'I hope this separation so soon after their marriage doesn't spoil things between him and Olivia. Life will be different for her, too. On her own at the Manor after being used to being with her parents in Whitby.'

'She'll have Betsy and Ailsa nearby. That was one reason for Ailsa going to Cropton.'

Beth smiled. 'I rather think the real reason was a young man, and that can only mean George Chilton-Brookes.'

'Has she said anything about him yet?'

'No. But Betsy confirmed our suspicions that Ailsa might be losing her heart though she swore me to say nothing. After this visit to Cropton Ailsa might be ready to come to a decision, if she hasn't already done so.'

'You are sure you won't change your mind and stay with us?' Lavinia put the question anxiously to her daughter as Olivia was about to enter the carriage.

'Certain, Mother. I've got to get on with my new life.'

'Very well. Remember we are here if you want to come back to us for a while.' Lavinia kissed her daughter on both cheeks.

Olivia embraced her father. 'Thank you for being so understanding about the loan,' she said quietly, so that Ailsa and Betsy in the carriage would not hear.

'It's my pleasure to help my daughter. I hope you manage to get the land – but don't pay more than it's worth.'

'I shan't. I'll have Kit's friend Jeremy Halstead to guide me.'

'Good.'

'I'm determined to make a success of it and surprise Kit on his return.'

'An admirable idea.' Edward kissed his daughter. 'Let us know how you get on.'

'I will.'

She climbed into the carriage. As she settled, Betsy leaned forward and with a smile of gratitude said, 'It is most kind of you to arrange our means of transportation to Cropton, Mr Coulson, both Ailsa and I thank you.'

'Think nothing of it. Olivia had to get there so it was the obvious thing for you all to travel together. William will see you safely there.'

'I will that, sir,' said the Coulson coachman, who had been standing by the door. 'Now, ladies, are you comfortable?' Receiving their assent he closed the door and climbed on to his seat.

Farewells were called as the carriage was set in motion.

Betsy let the younger ones settle down before she asked, 'Olivia, would you like us to stay with you? You might be lonely on your own.'

'That is thoughtful of you, Aunt Betsy, but I must get used to it. It might help me settle in quicker if you'd tell me something about the servants?'

'Mrs Charlton is the cook-housekeeper. Very efficient, a good cook and a fine organiser. A friendly person and easy to get on with. She came with the Manor when Kit bought it. Liza is the maidservant, a girl of seventeen. She's been there two years and been well trained by Mrs Charlton. Leave her to her job, she knows what she has to do but is always willing to oblige with anything new. You should get on with them all right.'

'And the farm hands?'

'Kit employs two full-time and uses occasional workers when he need extra hands. Jack Hall is regarded as the senior of the two and will accept responsibility. He's in his early-thirties, knows all the running of the estate. Matthew Bell will be about four years younger. He's a hard worker and devoted to the family after Kit's Uncle John gave him a job and looked after him when his parents died.'

Olivia nodded. 'It sounds as if I am very fortunate.'

'The only tip I can give you is to treat them fairly. But you will have seen that from your parents' attitude to their own servants.'

Ailsa, her mind on the surprise she would give George when she told him she might be in Cropton all summer, had been sitting quietly, taking little notice of this conversation.

Her thoughts were interrupted when Olivia said, 'Ailsa, you must come over whenever you like. Maybe we could go riding together?'

'Thank you,' returned the girl. 'It will be an opportunity to get to know each other better and to explore the country-side.'

'I also think we should call on the Chilton-Brookes.

George will be interested to hear Kit has gone on a whaling voyage.' Olivia had come to realise that animosity to George would achieve nothing. She must regard him as a friendly rival, one whom she must help her husband to match. No doubt she would derive satisfaction in that after George's rebuff.

'Maybe tomorrow? It will be better if he hears it from you,' suggested Betsy. 'You'll have to explain to Jack and Matthew why Kit won't be home, and rumour has a way of soon getting around even in the country.'

'Right,' said Olivia. 'I'll get things in order in the morning and ride over to you about two o'clock. Will that suit?'

'Certainly,' returned Ailsa, embracing this opportunity to see George so soon after her arrival in Cropton.

The carriage took Betsy and Ailsa to the cottage on the way to Howdale Manor. Olivia quelled the apprehension which threatened to swamp her when she was alone and allowed a surge of excitement to take over instead. This was her land, her home. She would be mistress of the house and she had the man she loved, though once she would have sacrificed that love to have had the Cropton Estate and be the lady of Cropton Hall. Kit had ambitions and she would see that she fired them further. Everything must be channelled into that. There should be no domestic upheavals to get in the way. Accordingly on her arrival she greeted Mrs Charlton with dignified friendliness while retaining her air of authority.

After informing the housekeeper that Kit had sailed with his father to the Arctic, she added, 'I want you to carry on as you have always done. I know my husband would want that.'

'Very well, ma'am.' Mrs Charlton was pleased to reach an understanding at the outset. 'But if there is anything you'd like altering, please do tell me.'

'I shall, Mrs Charlton, but I'm sure the routine that you and Liza have established will be highly satisfactory. Tell me, what time do Jack and Matthew start in the morning?'

212

'They both live in the village, ma'am, but they will be at the stable by seven to see to the three horses first.'

A strange bed, country noises she was not used to and the creaks and groans of an old house did not lend themselves to early sleep but eventually the day's excitement and the strain of travel took their toll.

Olivia came awake in a daze, wondering where she was at first. When realisation struck her she was overwhelmed by a desire for Kit to be beside her. Five months of waking in a lonely bed faced her. She bit her lip to hold back the tears which threatened. Then, roundly chiding herself for weakening the resolve she had made the day before, she swung out of bed. She had a date with the two farm hands though they did not know it. Or so she thought.

She dressed quickly and when she appeared downstairs found that Mrs Charlton had her breakfast ready.

'That was very perceptive of you, Mrs Charlton,' Olivia praised her.

'I heard you moving about, ma'am, and thought you would rise early when you'd asked what time Jack and Matthew arrived. By the way, ma'am, I told them you would be seeing them at the stable. They always let me know they have arrived, then we know they are about and are not worried if we don't see them.'

'An admirable arrangement, Mrs Charlton. Give them a hot drink every morning when they arrive. It will be a good start to the day for them.'

'Thank you, ma'am. They'll appreciate that.'

Twenty minutes later, Olivia left the house by the back entrance, crossing two flagstoned areas to a long low stone building. A double door was partially open and from the sound coming from it Olivia knew she would find Jack and Matthew there.

'Good morning to you both,' she called pleasantly, seeing them mucking out one of the stalls.

213

They ceased working and straightened up. 'Good morning, ma'am,' they said together.

Though earlier Mrs Charlton had sung Olivia's praises to them, they were aware that the cook was judging the new mistress from her own viewpoint. Would she be just as amiable towards them?

'Mrs Charlton no doubt told you that Mr Fernley has sailed to the Arctic on a whaleship.' They nodded. 'He will not be back for five months. The farm still has to be worked and run properly. I know nothing about farming, though I do know about horses. I am therefore relying heavily on you two. Before he left, my husband told me that you both knew the way he likes things to be run and will know what has to be done and when. I would therefore like you to carry on as if he were here, but please let me know what is happening and why. I do want to learn as much as I can before he returns. If there is any need to employ extra labour at any time, please consult me first. I shall need to know so as to pay for it. Is all that agreeable to you?'

'Yes, ma'am.'

'You don't mind the additional responsibility?'

'No, ma'am.'

'I have no doubt that if all works out to his liking, my husband will reward you. Now, I would like to see the extent of the estate. I suppose you do ride, Jack?'

'Yes, ma'am.'

'Saddle two horses right away. I'll be back in a few minutes.'

When Olivia returned two saddled horses were held by Matthew. Hearing her arrive, Jack appeared from the stable. He helped her into the saddle and then climbed on to his own mount.

'You decide the best route to take,' directed Olivia.

He led the way north from the farm buildings, climbing steadily up the long gentle slope. At the top Olivia called a halt and turned her horse so that she could look back. From

214

here she could see that whoever had built the house had chosen the site with care. The hill they had climbed gave it shelter from the north, and a southern aspect with a view across open land. She studied the position of the outbuildings and judged that if the farm buildings were converted and joined by a new building to the house the whole complex would make a grandiose home. And there was room for new farm buildings to be erected a suitable distance from what would be the main block so as not to be intrusive. Olivia surprised even herself with the way she was thinking. But why not? Wasn't this the way to overcome her disappointment at not becoming mistress of Cropton Hall?

'It's a good position,' was all the comment she made to Jack who had sat silently on his horse awaiting her instruction to move on.

'Aye, it is that.' He went on to indicate the boundaries of the estate they could see from here.

By mid-morning Jack had completed his tour and Olivia was highly satisfied with the extent of the land Kit owned, though of course it could not match that of the Chilton-Brookes.

'Jack, did my husband ever tell you of some land in which he was interested that is coming up for sale at auction?'

'He did, ma'am. He thought it would be an asset and it has some good stands of timber on it.'

'Will you show it to me?'

'Certainly, ma'am.'

He took her to a slight rise on the western edge of Kit's land and pointed out the area that was for sale.

'To whom does it belong?'

'Gentleman farmer whose main property is in the valley east of Pickering. He died recently and his sons want to realise some money and concentrate on the main farm.'

He respected Olivia's silence while she studied the terrain.

215

'Is it good farmland?' she asked.

'Yes, ma'am, and the trees are an asset, mainly oak.'

She nodded thoughtfully.

'And joining our land would make it easy to work and look after from the Manor?'

'Yes. If Mr Fernley had been here I think he would have attended the auction even if he believed he had little chance of getting it.'

'Why should he think that?' she asked.

He sensed a touch of indignation in her voice. 'Ma'am, I was not implying he could not afford it. I know nothing of Mr Fernley's financial position. The reason for my observation was that the land is also next to the Cropton Estate.' He pointed in the appropriate direction. 'And if the Chilton-Brookes want anything, there's no one around here who can outbid them.'

'I see.' Olivia made no further comment but turned her horse for home.

When they reached the Manor she thanked Jack and asked him to have two horses saddled for two o'clock.

As arranged Ailsa arrived at the Manor shortly before then and within ten minutes they were riding to Cropton Hall.

'Are you settled in with Aunt Betsy?' Olivia queried.

'Oh, yes,' replied Ailsa. 'She is such an easy person to get on with. I always regret that I have not seen more of her.'

'You did not come north very often previously?'

'No. Father's time was occupied in London and he knew the Whitby company was in the capable hands of Aunt Jessica and Uncle Ruben. Besides, I think Whitby held some painful memories for him.'

'Oh?' Olivia was curious.

'He never spoke of them but always talked about the good times, his relationship with Adam and Jenny Thoresby and the companionship of the whalemen. Still, I know there was trouble here for him in the past.'

'Maybe it was because his first wife was drowned near Whitby?'

'It could be that. He never talked much about Ruth. Once I asked him but he turned the subject aside, saying there was little to say.'

'And Kit told me he knows almost nothing about his mother. Strange,' replied Olivia. Then, not wanting to appear too nosy, she changed the subject by saying, 'I asked Jack Hall to show me round the Manor estate this morning.'

'Kit has worked hard to make it pay and then expand it.'

'And he told me there is more land he would like – Jack pointed it out to me this morning. I think it would be an asset.'

'A pity Kit isn't here to make an offer then.'

Olivia did not reveal what was in her mind.

Informed of their arrival, George came hurrying into the room where Olivia and Ailsa had been shown by a maid.

'My dear ladies, this is a most pleasant surprise.' He bowed and smiled to each in turn, his eyes lingering for a moment longer on Ailsa. 'You have brought pleasure to my day.'

Olivia recalled similar words on her first meeting with him when she had come to Cropton Hall to attend his birthday celebrations. Memories flowed back, of how she had been charmed by him and the prospect of marrying into this family. Well, that had not come about and now she was visualising Howdale Manor expanding to rival the Hall. See how George liked that.

'I'm sorry my parents aren't here. They're visiting the Sleightholmes. You'll remember them from my party, Olivia?'

'Indeed I do.'

'You are both well, I trust?'

Olivia and then Ailsa assured him that they were.

'When did you return?'

'Yesterday,' replied Olivia.

'And Kit? Is he well?'

'As far as I know.'

George looked askance at her for this struck him as a curious answer.

'He sailed with his father on the whaleship *Mary Jane*.'

'He what?' gasped George, taken aback by this announcement. 'What on earth made him do that?'

'It is a long story. No need to bore you with it. Let's just say he's done it to prove a point.'

He accepted her obvious desire not to enlarge on the reason and turned to Ailsa. 'Is that why you have not returned to London?'

'Yes. I saw little point in doing so when I like it better in the north.' She was sure he would read the real reason behind her statement. 'Dominic has returned to London, his choice, and will help in Father's business there. Mother has sailed with Father to Shetland to see her homeland again and will return from there to stay with Aunt Jenny until Father comes back from the Arctic.'

'And you? Are you staying with Olivia?'

'No. With Aunt Betsy, probably until the beginning of August. I would like to be in Whitby to see the *Mary Jane* return.'

'Good. Then I must see that you are both kept suitably entertained while Kit is away. So let me start by offering you tea.' George crossed the room to the bellpull beside the fireplace.

'Olivia, what is going to happen about the farm?' he enquired as he returned to his seat.

She gave the ghost of a smile. 'I'm no farmer as you can guess, born and raised in Whitby, but Kit gave me instructions to pass on to Jack Hall and Matthew Bell. He has faith in them to carry on while he is away. From what I saw of Jack when he rode round the estate with me this morning, I'm sure Kit is right. And I'm a quick learner.'

'Well, if there is any advice you need, I'd be happy to oblige.'

'That is very kind of you, George, but I'm sure you will be very busy with your own affairs.'

These words, apparently innocently put, drew Ailsa into a trap. Olivia saw the sharp glance she gave George and gained from it confirmation of the opinion she had formed at her wedding. Ailsa was the girl for whom she herself had been rejected. If they married, her sister-in-law would fill the position Olivia had coveted. So be it. She had Howdale Manor and would see that it rivalled what would one day come to George and Ailsa.

The afternoon passed off pleasantly and as George was helping Ailsa on to her horse he managed to whisper, 'I'll call tomorrow afternoon, two o'clock.'

She gave the merest of nods in return.

'George seems to like you,' commented Olivia as they rode home. She glanced at Ailsa and before she could answer, added, 'Oh, don't deny it, you are blushing. But the important thing is, do you like him?'

'He's very pleasant.'

'More than that, I should say. Had you met him before the wedding?'

The question was slipped in so casually that Ailsa was caught unawares and answered automatically. 'Yes, the last time I stayed with Aunt Betsy.' She tightened her lips then, annoyed with herself for divulging so much.

'Ah, that's why he was so attentive at the wedding. It was more than merely a best man paying his respects to the chief bridesmaid. Maybe he's the reason you did not want to go back to London?'

Ailsa gave a small smile. 'I see I can keep no secrets from you. I will have to be more careful in the future.'

Olivia laughed. 'I hope that will not spoil our friendship.'

'I don't see why it should. I think it would have to be something momentous to do that.'

Olivia fought down the pang of jealousy that threatened at the thought of Ailsa becoming the lady of Cropton Hall.

She must concentrate on furthering Kit's ambitions and with them her own. They must not just match George, they must surpass him.

Chapter Eighteen

'Shetland!'

David, off duty, was standing at the rail beside Beth. He pointed to the larboard quarter.

She strained her eyes to see the smudge on the horizon. Her homeland. She felt a strange sensation in the pit of her stomach. When she had left it with her parents so long ago, driven out by a grasping laird who wanted the land cleared of its crofters, she had never expected to see it again. Then her future had seemed to consist of exile in Canada. Now she stood beside the Yorkshireman she had loved then and thought she had lost forever, watching her homeland draw nearer and nearer.

'How long will you be here?' she asked, a catch in her voice.

'I've asked Captain Timms for three days. Time for me to arrange your passage to Whitby and for us to pay a visit.'

'Doesn't he want to be away sooner?'

'Aye. Whaling captains like to leave Lerwick as soon as possible, same day if they can. Stay too long and a captain can lose many of his crew to drink and women. It's the last time they'll see either for nearly five months.'

'I hope I'm not causing trouble?'

'No, love, you're not. Captain Timms is an old hand at these calls, he knows how to handle his men. He'll give them fair warning and will stand no nonsense.'

'And Kit? Will he be all right?'

'Aye. He experienced opposition at first from some of the crew. They weren't too sure how to take the son of the owner being among them. Thought they were being spied on and that he would be seeking privileges. They soon saw that was not the case, and he was quick to show them he could work with the best of them and muck in with them all. I think it's doing him good to see an unfamiliar way of life and mix with a different set of people.'

'Sumburgh Head?' asked Beth, pointing to the cliffs which were becoming clearer.

'Aye,' David replied, his mind drifting back to his first whaling voyage and sight of these new horizons in the company of Adam Thoresby.

The *Mary Jane* anchored in Bressey Sound overnight among other whaleships making their last port of call for five months. The next morning, with many of them leaving, Captain Timms was able to find a berth at the quay. Before allowing the crew ashore he made it plain that they were all expected aboard again that night but that with a further day's stopover they would be allowed ashore again. He emphasised that he would not tolerate any behaviour which brought a bad name to his ship.

David was excused duties until sailing time the day after tomorrow, early-morning. He put first things first and found accommodation for himself and Beth for two nights, and then for Beth alone until she returned south. His enquiries about which vessels were leaving for England led him to the *Speedwell*, a merchantman trading out of London. He found it captained by an old friend, Bill Sharman, who readily agreed to give Beth a passage to Whitby when he left Shetland in five days' time.

'I'm glad we got that settled so easily,' he said as they left the *Speedwell*, and took Beth by the hand. 'Let's walk.'

They hurried through the streets with their grey stone

buildings which seemed to dispense an unforgiving atmosphere. They were pleased when they reached the outskirts of the town and started to climb the hill. At the top they paused and drank in the beauty of the scene. They breathed in the clear air, enjoying its sharpness in their lungs. They shared the silence, two minds entranced by Shetland's magic. The coastline was cut by voes, small and large, where the sea seemed reluctant to mar its own blue beauty by any movement but still managed to send sunlight shimmering across its water.

'Do you miss it, Beth?'

'Yes.'

'You've been away a long time.'

She gave a little nod. 'I have, but there has always been a part of me here. Once Shetland is in your blood it never leaves.'

'Even though there were bad times?'

'I remember only the good. And you?'

'Though I am no Shetlander it will always be carved on my heart. I found my love here.'

They had started down the hill.

'See, there it is, Dales Voe.' David pointed.

Beth stopped. He turned to her and saw that her eyes were damp and she was biting her lip as if trying to hold back tears.

'Do you want to go on?' he asked gently.

She nodded.

He took her along a path he had last trodden many years ago. It took them along the side of the slope which plunged to the voe. The steep side eased and then curved gently into a tiny bay. It was a magical scene as he recalled it with the sun casting diamonds in the sand and across the sea. The silence was almost overpowering and drew them both into a world apart. Neither wanted to mar the beauty by moving and yet David was compelled to go down the path towards the bay. His eyes were on the water running lazily up the sand.

He stopped. 'It was about here that I first saw you,' he

whispered, and felt her hand tighten on his. 'You came out of the sea, clothed only in a clinging skirt and blouse.'

'You remember?'

'It's an image I've carried with me ever since. You were a dazzling sight. Time stood still for me then.'

'And for me when I looked up and saw you only a few yards away watching me. You know, I never saw you come on to the beach.'

'It didn't matter, we were together.'

'And we are now.' She turned and looked up at him. 'I love you, David Fernley.'

He swept her into his arms and his lips met hers with a gentle love which was soon overtaken by passion. It tore back the curtain of the years and they loved as they had before in this tiny bay across the strands of time.

When they lay quietly in each other's arms she said, 'Thank you for bringing me home to Shetland.'

'I hope it won't make the return to Whitby and eventually London too upsetting for you?'

'My love, it won't. That's where life has taken us. That's where our destinies lay, and wherever they take us we will fulfil them together.'

'Thank you for being you.' He kissed her with tenderness.

They knew in those moments that no matter what their age their love would always burn with brightness for each other.

Later, when he said, 'We'd better get back,' and helped her to her feet, she paused and pointed along the spur of land running along the edge of the voe towards the sea. 'Remember Kebister Ness?'

'A landmark I could never forget.'

'I'll be out there when you sail just as I was so long ago.'

'Thanks, love.' David knew that an image of her there would be printed on his mind and kept with him throughout the long Arctic days.

When they reached the top of the hill Beth paused for one

224

more look at the place which had meant so much to her and now meant even more. 'There was magic in the air so I made a wish,' she explained to her husband. 'I wished that our three children will find the happiness we have known.'

At that moment Ailsa could not have been happier. She was in the arms of the man she loved, in the glade where they had first met – a place now special to them both.

'Fate played into our hands, my love,' said George.

She smiled. 'I could hardly believe my ears when Father said he and Kit were sailing to the Arctic on a whaling voyage. What a chance it gave us, and with my excuse of being company for Aunt Betsy and also available to Olivia if she felt lonely at the Manor, the situation was made for us.'

'You mustn't neglect either of them or they will suspect . . .'

Ailsa chuckled at these words of caution. 'Oh, Aunt Betsy already suspects there is something between us, but she won't say anything until we do and I want Mother and Father to know first, and be told together, so any announcement of our intentions will have to wait for Father's return.'

'If that's the way you want it, my love, then so it shall be.'

'I'll call on Olivia in the morning and you may call on me in the afternoon. And please bring Smoky again, he's a lovely horse.'

'I'll do better than that. It will be much more convenient if you keep him at Miss Thoresby's, then you can use him as you like.'

'But stabling?'

'I've noticed a small stone building behind the cottage. Is it used for anything?'

'No, it's empty, but it will need cleaning out.'

'I'll send two of my men over in the morning to do that.'

225

'That would be wonderful!'

'Can you manage to saddle a horse?'

'Of course. I was taught that when I first started riding in London.'

'Good. It will give you much more freedom. One of my men can come over each day and muck out for you. We'll ask Miss Thoresby if she is agreeable, of course.'

'I'm sure she'll raise no objections.'

The following morning two of the under-grooms from Cropton Hall arrived with Smoky and had soon prepared stabling for him.

Once she had seen the work underway, Ailsa walked to Howdale Manor to see Olivia, only to be told that she had gone into Pickering.

Olivia's first enquiry was the only one she had to make to find the office of Jeremy Halstead. It was situated at the top of the slope which formed Pickering's main street. A brisk morning trade was being enacted at the shops that climbed towards the tall-spired church that overlooked the market town like a sentinel. People bustled about their business or stood in idle gossip. Carts and wagons rattled on the dry earth which Olivia could easily imagine becoming a quagmire in wet weather. The air was filled with the babble of voices, the barking of dogs and neighing of horses.

Reaching her destination she slid from the saddle and tied her horse to a hitching post outside the building she sought. She stood for a moment viewing its façade. Two large windows were separated by a central door flanked with imposing columns. It was smartly painted and had the air of a successful business, giving Olivia a sense of assurance that all would be well.

The door let into a small hall in which a clerk was busy making entries in a ledger. He looked up when Olivia came in and was immediately all smiles and attention. It was not often that such a charming lady entered these premises. More commonly, he had to deal with gruff farmers and

226

bloated merchants who demanded immediate attention, or else landed gentry who thought he was beneath them.

'Good day, ma'am.' He beamed, rising courteously from his stool. 'Can I be of any help?'

Olivia used her most dazzling smile and was amused by the spell it cast on the clerk. 'I would like to see Mr Jeremy Halstead.' She kept her voice soft and pleasing.

'Certainly, ma'am. I'll just see if he is available,' spluttered the man as he turned and almost stumbled over his stool. He grabbed it before it clattered to the floor, made a little embarrassed sound and scuttled towards a door on Olivia's left. He was about to knock when he stopped and shuffled back to her. 'I'm sorry, ma'am, I forgot to ask your name?' He raised his eyebrows enquiringly. Olivia thought it made him look like a startled rabbit.

'Mrs Olivia Fernley.'

'Yes, ma'am.' He scuttled away again, saying her name to himself as he did so.

He knocked on the door and entered the room. A moment later he reappeared and said, 'This way, please, ma'am.' He stood beside the door and she gave him a sweet smile as she passed him. He blushed and fumbled with the knob as he closed the door.

Jeremy Halstead had risen from a chair behind his large oak desk and came to greet her. 'Mrs Fernley, it is a delight to meet you.' He took her hand and raised it to his lips. 'Please, do sit down.' He escorted her to a chair opposite his own. 'You seem to have flustered James.'

Olivia liked the merriment in his eyes. 'I hope it doesn't cause him to make mistakes in those ledgers he was intent on when I walked in?'

'I'm sure he'll make no more entries this day. He'll be thinking only of the vision who has entered our lives, his and mine.'

'You flatter me, Mr Halstead.'

'Indeed I do not.' He threw up his hands to dismiss her observation. 'And please, I think it should be Jeremy for I

227

have the feeling that your presence here means we will be seeing much more of each other. I am surprised Kit is not with you, though?'

'I am afraid that he is unable to be here. At this moment he is on a whaleship bound for the Arctic.'

'He's where?' Jeremy Halstead obviously couldn't believe what he had heard.

'He's gone on a whaling voyage to the Arctic.' Olivia's voice had a no-nonsense tone about it as she repeated the information.

His eyes widened even further in astonishment. He saw she was making no joke and toned down his disbelief that his friend should have taken such a course. 'I'm surprised he left his bride so soon after the honeymoon,' was all he said.'

Olivia gave a slight nod of her head. 'There were good reasons.'

'I have no doubt. But strong ones for him to leave you.'

'They were personal. Family matters.'

Jeremy raised a hand. 'Say no more, dear lady. Families can be trying at times.' When Olivia made no comment he added, 'You are at Howdale Manor?'

'The estate still needs seeing to, though his staff are capable.'

'Indeed they are,' agreed Jeremy. 'I know them through visiting Kit.'

'He told me that there is some land he is interested in purchasing.'

'That is so. I have looked into the legal aspects for him. Kit was trying to raise capital. I suppose you are here with instructions from him?'

'Not as such. He told me to deal with it and to contact you. Don't look so surprised, Mr Halstead, it's true.'

'Forgive me, Mrs Fernley, but it is very rare to see a young lady here on business matters. And if we are to be business associates I must insist you call me Jeremy, please.'

'Very well, Jeremy. I anticipate that there will be a number of things we will need to discuss while Kit is away so Christian names it shall be. Now, about this land. I made it my business to view it yesterday.'

'And?'

'I think it would be a most useful addition to Kit's estate.'

'Indeed you are right, it will be purely a question of price.'

'You discussed that with him?'

'Not in detail. Only what we estimated the land is worth, not what he was prepared to pay for it.'

'Could we not make an offer?'

'I looked into that but the owners want to go to auction. They believe they will get more for it that way, and I think they are right. I must warn you we'll meet opposition, especially from the Chilton-Brookes. It borders their land as well as Kit's.'

'Then we shall have to see what we can do. I understand that the auction will take place here in Pickering a week today. We should meet again before that. I suggest you come to the Manor on Friday. We shall dine at one and then we can go and view the land more carefully.'

'Very well, I'll look forward to that.'

As she rode home Olivia felt satisfied with her visit. She had established a good relationship with Jeremy Halstead. Maybe he could help her to learn more about Kit, the man she had married and parted from all too soon.

Betsy watched Ailsa's love blossom. She was pleased for her and hoped nothing would mar her happiness. Though she had never known George terribly well, only as a friendly rival of Kit and the son of the owner of the Cropton Estate, she now got to know him better and was taken by his kindness, gentleness, courtesy and the affection he showed her niece.

He visited the cottage every day, took Ailsa riding or walked with her in the countryside. They were happy in each other's company. They did not want this time to end and yet they did, for that would mean her father would be home and they could announce their intention to marry.

Olivia was not surprised that she did not receive as much of Ailsa's company as might have been expected. When she did so the girl was so radiant and full of life that one day Olivia could not help making a comment.

'I think you used your aunt and me as an excuse to come to Cropton,' she observed.

Ailsa could not evade telling the truth. 'Promise me you will tell no one? I want Mother and Father to be told before the news is made public.' She waited for Olivia's agreement and went on, 'George and I plan to marry.'

'I thought as much.' Olivia smiled and held out her arms. As they hugged each other she said, 'We shall be neighbours. We'll be able to see a lot of each other.'

'Of course we shall. Kit will be pleased.'

Outwardly Olivia showed delight but it was as if a cloud had entered her mind. Ailsa would one day become mistress of Cropton Hall, a position she had coveted for herself. The thought would darken her mind even further in the days to come.

Chapter Nineteen

'We now come to what I believe is the prime site of the day – but have no fear they are all important to me and will receive my undivided attention . . .'

'I should think so,' called a voice from the back of the crowded hall. 'They all mean commission for you.'

The comment provoked laughter and the auctioneer did not demur. Lightheartedness among buyers always made for a better sale.

'We all have a living to make,' he replied lightly.

'Aye, and auctioneers better than most.' Cries of agreement mingled with the laughter.

'Gentlemen, please.' The auctioneer's tone was one of mock reproof. 'How can you say that, you in your fine clothes and me in my rags?'

A roar of disagreement went up and then subsided quickly as a loud striking of the gavel on his desk called a halt to the banter.

'There is no need for me to describe the land on offer in this lot. You will all have read the schedule, I don't doubt, and anyone interested will have viewed said land in his own time. So will someone start the bidding?'

An air of expectancy descended on the hall.

'I thought George would have been here?' Olivia whispered to Jeremy.

'So did I,' he replied. 'And I can see no one who is

likely to bid on his behalf.'

'Then maybe we will be lucky and get it cheaper than we thought?'

'Possibly.'

The bidding had started with four local landowners contesting each other, with what Jeremy considered were low bids.

'Make ours,' prompted Olivia.

'No point in doing so yet. Let's see who's left at the end of their bidding.'

Olivia was on edge. She did not want to lose the land Kit desired. She let her gaze move to each bidder in turn and speculated who might be left to rival her. Again she was aware that she was the only woman in the room. On arrival she had received many glances of disapproval, and there had even been snorts of disgust that she was intruding into what was regarded as man's work. Well, these men would have to get used to her now she was in charge of Kit's estate.

One bidder shook his head.

'Come along, gentlemen, this land is worth much more. What say you?' There was no movement to increase the latest bid. 'Once.' The auctioneer hesitated.

Olivia glanced at Jeremy but only encountered a blank look.

'Twice!'

'Two thousand!' The call came firmly from the back of the hall.

A new bidder who had sent the price up by five hundred pounds. Everyone turned to see who it was.

George, breathing heavily, was standing just inside the doorway. 'I'm sorry I'm late, gentlemen, but thank goodness not too late.'

'Ah, the rival we expected,' whispered Jeremy, his tone charged with eager anticipation of the contest ahead.

'Mr George Chilton-Brookes bids two thousand.' The auctioneer was elated for he estimated from this opening bid that George was determined to kill off any opposition. Another bidder and his commission would be sent soaring. 'Now, gentlemen, what say you?'

His eyes rested on the three men who had been bidding previously. Two shook their heads but to his delight the third bid another two hundred. He looked to the back of the hall and saw George raise three fingers.

'Two thousand, five hundred.'

The other man shook his head.

'Two thousand, five hundred to Mr Chilton-Brookes. Have I another bid?'

The crowd fell silent.

Olivia was tense. What was Jeremy doing?

'Once,' called the auctioneer. 'Twice.' He raised his gavel.

'Three thousand!'

A ripple of surprise ran round the hall. A new bidder had entered the fray.

Olivia felt the tension drain from her.

'Three thousand to Mr Jeremy Halstead.'

George raised one finger.

So the contest went on rising by one hundred pounds each time, George raised one finger, or Jeremy gave the slightest of nods.

Finally George made no sign except to shake his head and tighten his lips in exasperation.

'I'm bid three thousand six hundred by Mr Jeremy Halstead. Any more bids, gentlemen?' When nothing was forthcoming the auctioneer cast one more glance around the hall. He came back to George with a query in his eyes but once again George shook his head. The auctioneer went through his usual patter and closed the bidding on this particular lot. 'We will break for ten minutes and then resume,' he announced.

The crowd started to disperse. George, disappointment evident on his face, stood still. He felt a word of congratulation to Jeremy was merited but also hoped his curiosity would be allayed for he knew that the lawyer must have been bidding for someone else.

His answer came as the crowd thinned and he saw Olivia rise from her seat. Her face was wreathed in a smile of satisfaction as she exchanged a word with Jeremy. They moved towards the door.

'You had the outbidding of me there, Jeremy, but I am surprised to see who was backing you.' George bowed slightly, his eyes on Olivia. 'I suppose I am right?'

'Indeed you are,' she returned, a touch of triumph in her voice.

'No doubt Kit told you of his interest in the land before he left?'

'He did. I was determined to secure it for him.'

'Do you know what you will do with it?'

'Not yet. Jack Hall will advise me. Kit has great faith in him.'

'A good man. But if you do need any advice, remember I'm not far away.'

'That is kind of you. Thank you for the offer.'

They made their goodbyes as they went outside and a highly satisfied Olivia accompanied Jeremy to his office. She had got what Kit wanted and she had triumphed over George.

'Well done, Jeremy,' she said as she sat down, 'but you had me on tenterhooks.'

He smiled. 'I've done this before.'

'And you seem to enjoy dashing hopes just when a rival bidder thinks he has made a purchase.'

'There is a certain pleasure in it.' He chuckled.

'Well, you may have more to do if we can find some further land or other assets to buy.'

'So this isn't the end of it?'

'No. I'd like to give Kit an even greater surprise when he returns, so keep your eyes and ears open.'

'I certainly will.'

'How long have you known my husband?'

'We went to school together. Lost touch for a while

234

when I was away getting my qualifications and then renewed our acquaintance when I returned.'

'Do you know anything about his mother?'

'Not really. She was drowned when he was a baby, so of course I too never knew her. As far as I was concerned, and indeed I suppose as far as he was, Miss Betsy Fernley was like a mother to him.'

'You don't even know who his mother was?'

'Well, Kit tried to find out about her from his aunt and I would imagine from his father but he told me he wasn't encouraged to learn more about her. It seemed as if none of the family wanted to discuss her, though I don't know why. He had me try to find out what I could. All I managed to find out was her maiden name.'

'And what was that?'

'Harwood. Ruth Harwood. You won't find any of her family around here, though. They left soon after she and David moved to Whitby. I could find no trace of where they went or why. Bit of a rough family from rumours I picked up from some of the old folk around Cropton. Some said that Ruth was her mother's daughter but not by the man she was married to.'

'So that makes her background difficult to trace?'

'Yes. Especially as Harwood was her mother's maiden name. You'd like to know more, obviously?'

'Apart from my own curiosity, I think it would help me find a better understanding of Kit and also his family with whom I get on very well so far. And I think he would like to know too.'

'I'm sure he would, though it is some while since he asked me to find out what I could.'

'It is surprising what may turn up unexpectedly, so if you do chance to come across anything . . .'

'I'll let you know,' broke in Jeremy. 'Now, a glass of wine to toast our triumph before you leave?'

'Why not?' agreed Olivia with a smile.

*

235

'Ma'am, I heard you got that land. Well done! I know Mr Fernley will be pleased when he gets back.' Jack expressed his opinion when Olivia walked into the stable the next morning.

'Thank you, Jack. I'm pleased to have your interest. My husband has a high opinion of you so I would be grateful for any advice you have.'

'I'll be pleased to give it for what it's worth, ma'am.'

'It will be worth a lot to me while my husband is away. When I first arrived we rode around the estate. I would like to do that again, but this time you must talk about it in more detail.'

'Very well, ma'am. When would you like that to be?'

'In half an hour.'

'I'll have the horses ready.'

They rode at a steady pace while Jack informed Olivia of the uses of the land and indicated some of the plans Kit had for it.

'How do you think he would want to use our new acquisition?' Olivia asked.

'I don't really know his intention.'

As the morning wore on they reached the western edge of Kit's holding. They had come to the edge of a slope from which they overlooked a river. It was not wide but had carved out a pretty sheltered valley between the hills.

'Who owns this land?' she asked.

'Almost all the river, the Seven, we can see and a field's width to either side for about a mile belongs to a man called Gurney. He lives in Helmsley, occasionally comes here fishing but not very much over the past year. I did hear tell that he has lost interest since his brother, who used to accompany him, died.'

'Would his land and stretch of river be of use to us?'

'I think it would. The fields could be useful, they're good pasture, and I know Mr Fernley would love to have his own stretch of water for fishing. And of course he could always let the fishing rights.'

'And that could bring in some income?'

'Yes. There's always someone looking for fishing rights.'

'Then we shall have to see what can be done.'

The following morning Olivia visited Jeremy Halstead again.

'I did not expect to see you again so soon, Mrs Fernley, but it is indeed a pleasure.'

'I thought we said it would be Christian names,' she returned.

'Indeed.' He inclined his head in apology.

'I want you to try to purchase some land and part of the River Seven. No, I don't want you to try, I want you to do it.'

'You don't waste much time, Olivia.'

'I don't intend to.'

'If you don't mind my saying so, you spent a lot of money purchasing that farm land. I know you told me everything was taken care of, but I must ask if this purchase will also be covered?'

'Of course,' replied Olivia with a snap in her voice. 'I wouldn't be asking you to do this if it weren't.'

Jeremy held up his hands in a gesture of apology. 'I'm sorry, but I had to exercise caution. After all, we do not want Kit returning to find himself in debt.'

'I'll see that doesn't happen.'

'Good. Now where is this land and water?'

'It borders Kit's land to the west stretching along the River Seven and is owned by a Mr Gurney whom I believe lives in Helmsley.'

'I know the man slightly. He is getting on in years and was distraught by his brother's death about a year ago. I think there might be every chance of a purchase.'

'Good. I will look forward to hearing from you.'

Three days later Jeremy appeared at Howdale Manor. He was shown to the drawing-room and a few moments later Olivia appeared.

'My dear Jeremy, this is a surprise. You have word for me so soon?'

'Maybe more than you expect.' He was obviously taking pleasure in the news he had for her.

'I can get the land and that section of the Seven for you. Mr Gurney had been thinking of selling and was more than pleased to have someone make him a good offer and save him the trouble of advertising it. He also told me that he owned a small parcel of land to the north side of yours. I thought you might be interested so I obtained more details from him. Apparently it has a find stand of oaks.' He saw her eyes brighten. 'I thought that might appeal to you.'

'Of course. Father will be most interested.'

'You would like me to make the purchase?'

'Yes,' replied Olivia firmly.

'I'll see to it tomorrow.'

'This deserves a celebratory drink.' She rose from her chair and crossed the room to pour two glasses of Madeira from a decanter on the oak sideboard.

As he took the glass Jeremy said, 'But that is not all.'

'No?' There was curiosity in Olivia's voice. She could see from the excited twinkle in Jeremy's eyes that he was enjoying this.

He settled himself more comfortably in his chair, raised his glass to Olivia and took a sip of the wine. 'Mr Gurney told me that included in the sale of the woodland was a dilapidated cottage which he thought might be done up and made suitable for one of your workers.'

'Is that going to increase the purchase price?'

'No. He was merely pointing out that it was there. But I learned something interesting about that cottage. I was curious to know more about it and he told me that he believed it was originally built as a woodman's cottage. Later it was used for various purposes as the land on which it stood passed through different hands. It fell into disuse about thirty years ago. The last tenants wrecked the place. He was a drunkard, she was a slut, and they had unruly children. When they left the owner was disheartened by the state of the cottage and did nothing about it. Besides he had no need for it.' He paused and took another sip of his wine, his eyes still on Olivia. He knew he had her undivided attention.

'So?' she prompted, expecting more.

'He knew the name of the last tenants.'

'Well? Get on with it, Jeremy. What has this to do with my interest in the land?'

'Nothing, but everything to do with what we talked of the other day.'

'Kit's mother?' Excitement gleamed in Olivia's eyes.

'Yes. The family's name was Cornforth.'

'That's no help.'

'But it might make tracing them easier. Gurney told me that there were seven children, three of them boys. They were notorious in the district apparently. Their mother's name was Rebecca. He also said that there was another child who was older than the rest and went by another surname, Harwood, though when I mentioned the Christian name Ruth it didn't jolt his memory. But he did say there was a bit of a mystery about her. She was not as rough as the others.'

Olivia's interest was truly aroused. 'Well done, Jeremy. I'm grateful for this, but please keep delving. This unexpected clue might be just what I'm looking for.'

'It's important to you, isn't it?'

'Well, I'm curious. It seems strange Kit does not know more about his mother and that no one in the family will talk to him about her.'

'Be careful, Olivia. You might uncover something unsavoury, something the family think better he does not know.'

'If I find that to be true, and believe it's best that he does not hear the story of his mother's life, then I will say nothing about what we have found out, and will expect you to stay silent too.'

239

'You have my word on it. So you want me to keep probing?'

'Certainly. I said something might turn up unexpectedly.'

'Just think, if you hadn't shown interest in that land and water when Jack showed it to you, we wouldn't have had this information.'

She raised her glass. 'To finding out more.'

Over the next two weeks Olivia heard nothing from Jeremy and began to think that the purchase of the land had come to nothing and he had made no progress regarding Kit's mother.

She was tempted to broach her investigation with Aunt Betsy, but remembering that Kit had told her the subject seemed to be taboo with the family, she deemed it best not to do so. She would have to wait for Jeremy to get back to her. In the meantime she busied herself getting to know more about the estate. In consultation with Jack she decided to run horses on the new land. Accordingly she bought three mares and took them to stud. During this time she saw Ailsa on a couple of occasions when she visited Aunt Betsy. On one of these she arranged to spend a day with her sister-in-law and visit the market in Pickering.

The weather was pleasant and, after leaving their horse and trap in the care of two young boys eager to make a penny, they mingled with the crowds thronging the main street and milling around the stalls. Shopkeepers and stall-holders vied with each other to attract custom, shouting their wares for all to hear. Bargains were struck, purchases were made amidst all the hubbub of trading and the whole town buzzed. Housewives sought to make the best use of their money. Farmers and cattle dealers argued over live-stock before shaking hands on a price. Urchins chased around the stalls to receive curses from stallholders. Groups stopped to gossip. Drunks lurched from hostelry to hostelry. Both girls were swept into the activity. Neither had had experience of a rural market day and revelled in

240

this encounter with a way of life that was new to them.

They were nearing Jeremy's office when he came out. He started off to the left but, spotting them, turned in their direction.

'Good day, ladies.' He raised his hat and gave them a warm smile.

'Good day, Jeremy,' returned Olivia. 'You may remember Ailsa, Kit's sister, from the wedding?'

'Indeed I do. You've decided to stay in the north while your brother is away?'

'Yes, and most pleasant it is.'

He gave a little smile. 'Well, you are seeing life today.' He cast his eyes over the market scene. 'You must forgive me, if I hurry away, I have an appointment, but it is fortuitous that I have met you.' He directed his gaze at Olivia. 'If it is convenient I will call on you tomorrow afternoon about two? I have some news about the enquiry you wanted me to make, and after my appointment this morning I think I will have news about the second purchase of land.'

'That would be convenient,' she replied. She had nothing planned but if she had would have put it off to hear Jeremy's news.

As he left them Ailsa said, 'So that's the person who outbid George?'

'He told you about it?'

'Yes, and I must say he was a little upset. I don't think it eased his feelings when he found out that Mr Halstead had been bidding for you.'

'I hope he doesn't bear me any grudge?'

'No, he's got over his disappointment. Besides, as I said to him, does he really need more land? He explained why he did but I didn't really understand all his reasons. Have you done right with Kit away?'

'Oh, yes. He told me he would like that land so I was determined to get it for him.'

'Then he will be pleased with your success.'

The rest of the day passed off pleasantly though much of

241

Olivia's thoughts were occupied with speculation on what it might be that Jeremy had to tell her.

The next day she waited impatiently for two o'clock. Jeremy was a good time-keeper and was shown immediately into the drawing-room.

'You've certainly had me wondering since we saw you in Pickering yesterday.' Olivia gestured for him to sit down.

'I thought you might,' he answered with a smile.

'Well?'

'First, the appointment I was going to when I saw you was to finalise the purchase of Mr Gurney's land. He had nominated someone in Pickering to act for him and I was going to conclude the sale.'

'All went well?'

'Yes. I drew a note on the bank as you had instructed me with no difficulty. The land, the river rights, plantation and the dilapidated cottage are now yours.'

'Splendid. And what about the other matter? You seemed to indicate yesterday that you might have some further news.'

'Yes, I have. I made some enquiries with a couple of old people who used to live in Cropton and now live in Pickering. Both remembered the Cornforth family. Terrors, they said, except for one, an older girl. Sadly they couldn't remember her name. I might say that both these people are over eighty and their memories are failing.'

Olivia looked disappointed.

'Don't look glum, there is a ray of hope. They were both certain that this girl was not known by the surname Cornforth. They also said she ran away from home, one that she might have gone to Whitby.'

'This certainly sounds as if it's Kit's mother. Maybe it's because of this connection with the Cornforths, knowing their reputation, that the Fernleys don't talk about her.'

'More likely because she was a bastard, if you'll pardon my language.'

Olivia frowned at this supposition. 'She carried her mother's surname so David Fernley must have known Ruth was illegitimate when he married her. Maybe her background on her father's side made up for the Cornforths.'

'So why keep it from Kit?'

'There must be something they did not want him to know about, or else something happened after Ruth married David. It becomes even more intriguing.'

'There is more.'

'More?' Anticipation gleamed in Olivia's eyes.

'One of the old people I talked to remembered that a Cornforth boy went to live in Scarborough. His name was Zack.'

'Unusual name.'

'Yes, thank goodness, because it made him easier to trace.'

'You've found him.'

'Yes. I took a chance and went to Scarborough hoping he was still there. After all it must be about forty years since he went.'

'And you found him among all those people?'

'I thought if he had taken a bad reputation with him and still lived up to it he might be known to the Watch. Sure enough he was. He had been in trouble with them from time to time, they kept track of him and were able to tell me where he lived.' Jeremy gave a little chuckle. 'He gave me short shrift at first but the sight of a little money soon made him change his mind. He became most cooperative, though there were times when he pretended his memory was failing him.'

'And what did you learn?' pressed Olivia.

'He remembered his half-sister. Didn't like her apparently – stuck up, he said. Thought a bit about herself. His father wouldn't tolerate that. Beat her for it. I could tell Zack had enjoyed seeing that. Pleasant fellow, isn't he? Yes, her name was Ruth and he said she'd run off with a Fernley lad. He doesn't know what happened to her after that and he doesn't care. Even her mother turned against her so then any connection was lost. But there was one other thing. When I asked him about the rest of the family he told me he knew nothing about them except that his father had died and the last he'd heard of his mother she was in Hull. That was about ten years ago.'

Olivia grimaced. 'He didn't know anything about Ruth's background? Who her father was?'

'No. His mother never spoke of it.'

'So what's next?'

'I'm going to Hull.'

'Do you think you can be lucky twice?'

'It's the only chance we have. The woman may be dead for all we know, but unless I try we can't be certain.'

'You know, I have a feeling about this ... I'm coming with you.'

'But it might be to no avail.'

'Then so be it. But if you find her, I want to be there.'

'Very well. How soon can you leave?'

'Any day to suit you. After all, you have your work.'

'Then we'll make it tomorrow. Coach to Malton and then another across the Wolds to Hull. We may have to stay the night in Lund, a small village on the Wolds.'

'Very well. What time does the coach leave?'

'Midday.'

'I'll be at your office half an hour before that. Now, a cup of tea before you leave?'

'That would be most kind.'

Olivia rose from her chair and tugged the bellpull beside the fireplace. A short while later a maid brought in a tray of tea. Over it Olivia and Jeremy discussed the forthcoming visit to Hull.

'I know an attorney there who may be able to help us,' he told her.

'Let us hope his suggestions bear fruit.'

The following morning Olivia told Jack to prepare the trap and that he was to drive her into Pickering. She walked into

Jeremy's office barely two minutes late. He brushed aside her apologies and, after checking that he had everything he needed and that she was ready, they left the office together and walked to the inn from which the coach would leave. He had booked seats inside and was solicitous over seeing Olivia comfortably seated. Four other people boarded the coach. Once the driver was satisfied that there were to be no more travellers he cracked his whip and urged the horses forward. Shouts of goodbye and well wishes filled the air as the coach got underway. Once clear of the town the coachman set the horses into a steady pace on the road to Malton.

They reached the old Roman town without incident. Here they parted company with three of the passengers, but two more had joined those travelling on to Hull before the coach left an hour later. Olivia and Jeremy had partaken of a meal at the Green Man and felt fortified for the journey across the Wolds.

'I checked with the coachman and we are having an overnight stop in Lund,' warned Jeremy.

Dark clouds, driven in from the east on a freshening wind, glowered over the rolling landscape and threatened rain. The coach rumbled along the lonely track. Olivia, never having been further than the environs of Whitby, was depressed by the area's sense of isolation. She would be glad when they reached the inn.

Heavy rain assailed the coach as the driver hauled his team to a halt. A thin man with a coat slung around his shoulders to shield him from the downpour dashed from the inn and hauled the coach door open. He helped the passengers from the coach. With heads bent against the rising storm, they scurried into the inn.

Because they were scheduled to stop overnight in Lund Olivia had expected it to be a town of similar size to Pickering and Malton. Instead she found they were staying in a small village with a single inn.

The landlord, a stout rosy-cheeked man with a beaming smile, welcomed them and called to two boys who were hanging about to take their luggage. They needed no second bidding for they knew that they would receive a penny or two from the landlord and might receive the same from the travellers. The landlord fussed over the newcomers as they shook off their outer coats and then ushered them to their rooms. Olivia found that though the furnishings were sparse there was all that she needed. In anticipation of the coach the landlord had seen that a fire burned cheerily in the grate, a haven from the howling of the wind.

'When you have refreshed yourselves there will be a meal downstairs for you,' he informed them.

A table had been set for the travellers at one end of a large room the real purpose of which was drinking, something which became obvious as the evening drew on and men from the village and neighbouring farms came to the inn in spite of the driving rain. By the time Olivia and Jeremy had finished their meal a group of men were becoming somewhat rowdy and their glances in the direction of the overnight visitors brought a nervous response from her.

'Don't worry,' Jeremy tried to reassure her. 'I don't think this landlord will stand for any nonsense. If you are concerned push a chair under the door knob, and if you have any cause for concern knock on the wall. I am only in the next room.'

Olivia settled down for the night uneasily but the journey had brought a desire to sleep she could not resist in spite of the noise that resounded from the room beneath.

She came awake with a start. The room was only dimly lit by the moonlight that filtered through the curtains. Flames in the fire, which had sent dancing light across the room when she had climbed into bed, had now dwindled. What had woken her? A low sound, a rattle. The wind on the casement window? No, it came from the door. Could it be the knob turning? Someone was trying it ... Maybe it was just her imagination. No. There it was again. Olivia shuddered. She slipped down the bed and drew the blankets up to her chin as if that would ward off danger. Her heart thumped. She was glad she had taken Jeremy's advice about the chair which had hindered someone. She was stiff with fright, unable to move. With all her concentration she tried to detect any further movement. Then she heard footsteps moving faintly to the stairs. She lay awake, fearful that they might come back, imagining some drunkard gaining entry and then . . . She shuddered at the thoughts that ran through her mind. If only Kit was here. Oh why had he gone? After a while she was aware that the wind had dropped and the rain no longer beat at the window. Silence descended on the room and sleep would not be denied.

She was awake early, thankful that it was daylight and that soon they would resume their journey to Hull. Deeming that it would delay their departure, she did not mention the incident in the night to either Jeremy or the landlord. As the coach moved away she glanced up at the creaking sign, something she had not noticed in her haste to get in out of the rain the previous evening. It depicted a dangling skeleton with black lettering informing the traveller that this inn was known as the Hanging Beam. An omen? Did something sinister await them at the end of their journey?

Jeremy saw Olivia shudder. 'I noticed the sign when we arrived but as it was gruesome I did not draw your attention to it. Were you disturbed last night?'

'Well, now you've asked, yes, I was. Someone tried my door.'

Jeremy looked serious.

'I asked the landlord whether there was any significance behind the name of his inn or if it was just someone's morbid idea. He told me that many years ago a young man hung himself in the room you occupied, and that his wife came looking for him.'

Olivia shuddered. 'I'm glad I didn't know that story before. And I hope we don't have to stay there on the way back.'

'I'll see that we don't,' he reassured her.

As she settled down to the rest of the journey she

wondered what Kit would have thought about this expedition she had instigated. Would he approve? She devoutly hoped so, and that something worthwhile would emerge from it.

On reaching Hull, Jeremy found them accommodation at the Neptune Inn in Whitefriargate. After the sparseness of the village inn at Lund Olivia found this one, in the heart of the more elegant quarter of Hull, far more to her liking. Here was luxury. Its rooms were large, handsome and comfortable; the mahogany furniture in her bedroom exquisitely crafted. The pattern of the moreen curtains matched that of the dimity hangings on the four-poster bed which looked inviting after the strain of the coach ride.

Jeremy informed her that he just had time to contact his attorney acquaintance and acquaint him with the facts while she settled in. Over their evening meal he told her of the outcome of his interview.

'Roger will do what he can to help but says it will be like looking for a needle in a haystack with so little to go on. Ruth's mother might be dead, might have married again or even moved from Hull. I don't want to sound despondent but I prefer not to raise your hopes.'

'Are there any other enquiries we can make or any other places we can look?' she pressed.

'Not at the moment. I think we just have to be patient. Roger tells me that he has several people he employs from time to time on investigations. Some of them aren't the most salubrious of characters but he finds them most useful if he needs information out of the more notorious parts of the city. He will ask them to make enquiries right away and, hopefully, will have some news before long.'

'Any idea how long that will be?'

'Not really, but he did say to visit him the day after tomorrow.'

Olivia looked a little crestfallen.

'You can't expect miracles,' Jeremy pointed out.

But that was what it seemed like two days later when they

248

visited Roger Stanton in his offices in Parliament Street at ten o'clock, the time arranged by Jeremy on his first visit.

Olivia took to the Hull man immediately on being introduced. She judged him to be younger than Jeremy but he oozed confidence. She felt she was in the hands of a young man who would do all that was humanly possible to help a client.

He saw them comfortably seated before he resumed his own chair behind the desk.

'Mrs Fernley, this may be an impossible task so I don't want you to have false hopes. The person I thought most likely to help was making enquiries all day yesterday and throughout last night. He called here this morning a few minutes ago but had had no success. In fifteen minutes I should be getting my second report so if you'd care to wait you can hear this one for yourself.'

'If you don't mind we shall do that. Is that all right, Jeremy?'

'Most certainly. We may as well get all the information we can as soon as possible even if it is negative.'

Twenty minutes had passed before there was a knock on the door and Roger's clerk announced that Frosty Duggan and companion were here.

'Show them in.' As the clerk retreated Roger whispered, 'If Frosty has someone with him it could be hopeful.'

A small stocky man entered the room clutching a dirty cap. His hair was white but Olivia judged that this was not the only reason for his nickname. There was no warmth in his deadpan expression. It seemed as if he had nothing to smile about nor ever had had. His clothes were ill-kempt, his jacket torn at the pockets and he had a dirty muffler tied at his throat.

'Good day, Mr Stanton, sorry we's late.' His voice was grave. He glanced at Olivia, touched his forehead with his right forefinger and said, 'Ma'am.'

She nodded.

'This 'ere's Lizzie Cartwright.' He introduced the woman

who had followed him into the room. She was no cleaner than Frosty but Olivia saw a pride below the shabby surface when Lizzie, taking in Olivia's appearance, brushed her matted hair from her face and adjusted the worn shawl to hang more elegantly round her shoulders.

'You have news for us, Frosty?' queried Roger.

'Maybe.' He was wary. Information meant money and he liked to be clear about that.

'You'll be paid the usual rates,' promised Roger.

'Ah, but there are two of us, Mr Stanton.'

'Then double the pay if the information is worth it. We won't know that until you tell us.'

'This is an unusual case, Mr Stanton.'

'Come now, Frosty, it can't be too different from our usual dealings.'

'Oh, I don't know. Dealing with strangers ...'

He cast a quick glance in the direction of Olivia and Jeremy.

Roger gave a half smile. Frosty was a wily old bird and Roger knew that if he was taking this attitude then he judged that the information he had obtained was significant.

'All right. An extra payment for you both.'

Even this did nothing to melt Frosty's expression but a smile of satisfaction crossed Lizzie's face. She had kept quiet throughout the bargaining just as Frosty had told her to. Now she knew why, and would be pleased of the extra money thanks to him.

'I had no knowledge of the person you are enquiring about and with her being female I thought I'd enlist the help of Lizzie straight away. I tell you what, Mr Stanton, it was a difficult task and it wasn't until late last night that Lizzie came up with a possible answer.'

'Save us all the details, Frosty, just give us the essentials.'

'Lizzie had better tell you.' He glanced at the woman who had been standing silently by, trying to smooth her worn skirt and blouse to look more respectable in front of these 'posh folk' as she assessed them in her mind.

250

'The names Cornforth and Harwood meant nothing to me but somehow they niggled at my mind. Try as I would I couldn't think why. If only I'd had my mother to ask, but she died five years ago. She had a good memory right up to her dying day and she was eighty. Then I thought maybe old "Granny" Hargreaves may know something. She and my mother were good friends and right old gossips together. From what Frosty had told me those two and this Cornforth woman would be about the same age, and if she was as rough as you had made out then it could be she came to the same part of Hull. Oh, I don't try to disguise the truth about my mother, God rest her soul.' Lizzie glanced upwards. 'It took some time to locate "Granny" Hargreaves 'cos she'd moved on twice since I last saw her and that was years ago . . .'

Olivia had to control impatience. She wanted Lizzie to get on but knew better than to interrupt the flow. She might lost vital facts if she did.

'It was difficult getting "Granny" to remember the past. Her mind is going and whenever she did remember something she became weepy. But eventually she recalled Ma telling her some lurid story about a woman who had come from somewhere up north. That jolted my memory. I hadn't taken much notice of my mother's story at the time 'cos she had a vivid imagination but once "Granny" had mentioned it I remembered that was why the name Cornforth had nagged at me. It was the name of the woman in my mother's story.'

'But did you find out where she is now?' asked Olivia eagerly when Lizzie paused for breath.

'Well, "Granny" told us where she used to live so we went there. Mrs Cornforth had moved long since but we did not give up. One sighting led to another and, as poor as some of our information was, eventually late last night we came to what was little better than a hovel in the poorest part of Hull.'

'You can take us there?' pressed Olivia.

'Aye.' Lizzie looked her up and down. 'But it ain't the place for the likes of you.'

'It sounds as if this might be the person we want to see so nothing will stop me going.'

Neither Jeremy nor Roger raised any objections. They had recognised the determination in Olivia's voice. There would be no turning her from her objective.

Though she had seen some sights on Whitby's poor east side she was not prepared for the poverty and filth she encountered as she followed Lizzie and Frosty into the slums of Hull.

'This is the street,' said Lizzie as they turned a final corner.

It was no worse than the last two they had passed through. Rubbish was strewn in front of dilapidated buildings which still tried to present themselves as dwelling places. Torn curtains hung at some windows; others had wood nailed up where the glass had broken. A woman in a dirty apron stood on a doorstep shouting curses at a neighbour who had upset her. Their argument ceased when the strangers appeared and the women eyed them suspiciously. What were 'posh people' doing nosing around here where they had no right? No good would come of it. Their eyes followed the little band of visitors, curious to know where they were going.

'This is it.' Lizzie stopped in front of a door devoid of paint except for a few traces which showed that somewhere in the distant past someone had lovingly cared for it.

Lizzie pushed open the door and stepped inside followed by Frosty. Olivia entered with Jeremy and Roger close behind. Their arrival disturbed someone in a room along the corridor. A head came around a door. 'What d' y' want?' a voice asked suspiciously.

'Nowt t' do with you,' snapped Frosty. 'Git back inside.'

'That old hag's supposed to look after Mrs Cornforth,' he informed them as he started to follow Lizzie up the rickety stairs. 'You'll see what a good job she's making of it.' He gave a derisive snort.

Lizzie knocked on a door on the landing above and then

252

pushed it open. It led into a room whose floor was covered in rubbish. The sagging table by one wall had remnants of some mouldy food on it. A bed was placed under the window which hardly let any light in because of the grime upon the glass.

Olivia took a handkerchief from her handbag and held it to her nose, thankful that she had sprinkled it with lavender water. When Lizzie moved to the bed Olivia was aware that what she'd first thought was a bundle of bedclothes was in fact a human being. She shuddered. Was this the person they'd come to see? Surely not, living in these conditions?

'Mrs Cornforth, it's Lizzie again.' The woman's voice was gentle. 'I've brought someone to see you.'

Olivia was standing beside Lizzie. The bundle in the bed stirred and half turned. A gaunt wizened face grimaced up at them. Deep-socketed eyes peered upwards, straining to make out who had interrupted her sleep.

For a moment there was silence. Olivia was trying to find the words to which this poor woman would respond. Before she could the frail figure on the bed shifted more eagerly. A semblance of joy came over the wizened face, a touch of brightness to the eyes fixed on Olivia.

'Ruth! I knew you'd come, Ruthie, my own little girl,' she croaked.

Olivia started with surprise but, quickly realising what was happening in the woman's clouded mind, deemed it best to keep up the illusion.

Sensing that someone was about to reveal the mistake, Olivia gesticulated with her hand to stop them. If Mrs Cornforth thought she was Ruth then she might learn more by keeping up the charade.

'Yes, Ma, I'm here.'

'I'm glad, Ruthie. It's time things were put right between you and me.' The words were interrupted by outbursts of fierce coughing. Mrs Cornforth held out one grimy hand and Olivia took it in hers, cringing at the feel of the bird-like bones.

253

'What is there to put right, Ma?'

'I should have stood up for you against your stepfather. No good bastard! Shouldn't have let him beat you ...'

'That's all right, Ma. But who was my real father?'

A chuckle rattled in Mrs Cornforth's throat. 'Ah, that's my secret.'

'But haven't I a right to know, Ma?'

'I promised I would never say. Signed a paper.'

'But what's it matter now? He must be dead.'

'Aye. Like I'll be soon.'

'Then all the more reason to tell me. If you don't the secret will die with you and I'll be left wondering for the rest of my life. Please tell me, Ma, please.'

Mrs Cornforth lay quietly pondering the request, then croaked, 'Maybe you're right, lass. He was a bastard too. Had his way with me and then left me to fend for myself.'

Olivia's mind was racing ahead. If Mrs Cornforth had had Ruth illegitimately and had had to swear her parentage to secrecy then the father who had no doubt forced her to sign such a paper must have been someone of authority and position in the community.

'Who was he, Ma?' Olivia insisted.

'Maybe you ought to know.' The voice was weak. 'It can do no harm now.' Mrs Cornforth lay back on her dirty pillow, breathing deeply.

'Tell me, Ma, please.' Olivia leaned closer.

Mrs Cornforth hesitated then, voice low, said, 'Squire Hardy.'

Olivia gasped. The implications of this statement raced through her mind. Ruth was the squire's daughter! But an old woman's word would not be enough. Kit could not be blamed if he refused to believe this. He could put it down simply to an old woman's rambling mind. Olivia needed signed testimony. But would Mrs Cornforth be strong enough to do that?

She glanced at Jeremy and saw equal astonishment reflected on his face. She turned back to Mrs Cornforth. 'Ma, will you sign a paper saying that this is true?'

'It'll do you no good, Ruthie. The squire has a legitimate son. They'll not own you. They're both hard men.'

'But it'll clear my name if ever I'm asked.'

Mrs Cornforth gripped Olivia's hand tighter as a bad coughing bout racked her frail body. 'All right, love, if it'll make you happy. You deserve that after all you went through.' She gave a little smile of recollection as she said, 'But we had happy times until I married that bull Cornforth. Didn't we, love?'

'Yes, we did, Ma,' Olivia soothed her. She glanced over her shoulder and saw that Jeremy was already writing on a sheet of paper and was thankful that he had had the foresight to bring paper and a portable ink well and pen with him.

He passed it to Roger who read it quickly and gave it his approval.

'Here we are, Ma,' said Olivia, taking the piece of paper. 'This says that I am the daughter of Squire Hardy of Cropton Hall. Can you manage to sign it?'

She supported the old woman while she took a careful grip on the pen that Jeremy handed her. The effort was almost too much for her but eventually she produced a scrawl that could be read as 'Rebecca Cornforth'.

'Thanks, Ma.' Olivia eased her back on to the pillow and leaned over to kiss her on the forehead. 'I love you.'

Tears came to the old woman's eyes. 'Look after yourself, Ruthie. Don't make my mistakes.'

There were tears in Olivia's eyes, too, and she heard Lizzie give a sniffle. She turned to her. 'Lizzie, if I leave you some money, will you see that she is better taken care of?'

The ragged woman nodded and brushed the tears from her eyes. 'I will, ma'am. I don't think she will be with us much longer but I'll see her last days are more comfortable.'

'Thanks, Lizzie, and to Frosty too for finding her.'

'We'll see she's all right, ma'am,' he said.

When they reached Roger Stanton's office, the document signed in the hovel was made official by the signatures of four witnesses, Roger, Jeremy, Lizzie and Frosty.

Over dinner that evening at the Neptune, Olivia thanked Jeremy and added, 'I would like you to keep what happened today strictly between ourselves. I must see to certain things before I break the news to Kit when he returns from the Arctic.'

Chapter Twenty

The following morning as she and Jeremy were preparing to leave the Neptune Roger arrived with news from Lizzie that Rebecca had died during the night.

Even as she expressed her regrets Olivia was thinking of the future and what the signed paper could lead to. If there was any chance that the Cropton Estate was Kit's by right then she meant to have it. She had dreamed of becoming the lady at Cropton Hall and now it might be within her grasp. It would all depend on Squire Hardy's will. Would he have recognised his illegitimate daughter in his will even though he had not done so in his life?

By the time she reached Cropton she had decided on her course of action and the following day left for Whitby ostensibly to visit her mother and father.

Over dinner on the day of her arrival she told them she would like to visit her father's solicitor to make a will.

'I'm sure Noah will be only too pleased to oblige. Would you like me to come with you?' her father offered.

'No, I'd like to do this myself, but thank you for the offer.'

Edward knew better than to press his daughter to allow him to be there as her adviser. He admired her stand. She had become an independent woman with the self-confidence to handle her own affairs. 'I have always found ten o'clock in the morning a good time to make a speculative visit. His appointments don't really start until eleven. Mind you, you might be unlucky and have to make an appointment for another day.'

The next morning at precisely ten o'clock Olivia was shown into the Flowergate office of Noah Smithson.

'Good day, Mrs Fernley.' A stocky man, immaculately dressed in grey, rose from his chair to greet her. It was rare that he had such a beautiful young woman call on him. He fussed as he took her hand and held it that fraction of a second longer than was normal. 'It is a pleasure to see you. Please do sit down.' He held a chair for her and then, satisfied that she was comfortable, returned to his own. 'How are your mother and father? Well, I trust?'

'They are indeed.'

'And it will be a great pleasure to them to have you at home. Now, my dear, is there something I can do for you?'

'I am not certain, but I hope so.'

'I'll do my best.'

'Before I say any more, I must ask you to keep what passes between us in the strictest confidence.'

Noah threw up his hands in horror. 'My dear Mrs Fernley, trustworthiness is one of the foundations of my profession. Nothing that passes between a client and myself is ever spoken of with a third party. My clerks see my papers but they are employed on the strict understanding that if they ever disclose anything they hear or see they will be instantly dismissed, and if called for charges will be laid against them. I hope that reassures you?'

Olivia smiled sweetly. 'Mr Smithson, I was not casting aspersions on your professional integrity. That was the furthest thing from my mind. I just wanted you to know that my enquiry is very important to me. Besides, in this case, nothing need be written down.'

He returned her smile, nodded and waited for her to go on.

'Some information has come into my possession regarding Squire Hardy who used to live at Cropton Hall. He died some years ago. I wondered if you handled his affairs, and if so whether you could tell me anything about him?'

'I'm afraid not. We certainly had no dealings with him.'

Olivia looked disappointed. 'Oh, dear.' She gave a little shrug of her shoulders. 'I will have to look elsewhere.'

'That won't be easy. Do you even know if he employed a Whitby solicitor?'

She shook her head. 'No, I don't.'

'That certainly makes it harder.' He looked thoughtful. 'Old Jason Bickerstaff of Bickerstaff and Whalley had some clients who lived outside Whitby, I know.'

'Then I shall go and see him,' said Olivia brightly, seizing on the chance before Smithson could go on.

He raised a cautionary hand. 'I'm afraid he is dead, Mrs Fernley.' He saw her enthusiasm wane. 'But wait, all is not lost. His place in the firm was taken by his nephew, Giles. A decent young man. If his uncle dealt with Squire Hardy Giles might be able to help you.'

'Where do I find his office?'

'In Skinner Street.'

'I am most grateful to you, Mr Smithson, and sorry to have taken up your time.' She rose from her chair.

'Not at all, Mrs Fernley. It has been a pleasure meeting you.'

Olivia left Flowergate for Skinner Street and was soon reading a brass plaque which announced that she had found the office of Bickerstaff and Whalley. Her request to see Mr Bickerstaff was granted in a matter of moments when she was shown into a pleasantly furnished room with a large oak desk set across one corner. A tall man rose to greet her. She judged him to be in his early-thirties and noted his sharp eyes which made a quick assessment of any stranger. The conclusions drawn would generally be right, Olivia guessed. She saw the judgemental expression disappear and knew he had made up his mind about her. She had put on her brightest and friendliest of smiles when she entered his office.

259

'It is so good of you to see me without an appointment, Mr Bickerstaff.'

He shook her hand and she felt a completely different handshake to that she had experienced from Mr Smithson. This one was firm, instilling confidence, and did not linger to feel more of a lady's touch. 'I always have time for casual callers, they may become the clients of the future on which my business will thrive. Please do sit down.' He indicated a comfortable armchair which had been placed conveniently to impart a feeling of confidentiality. He sat down in his chair, rested his hands on its arms and looked intently at her. 'What can I do for you, Mrs Fernley?'

'I have some information regarding the Cropton Estate and wondered if your firm might have handled Squire Hardy's affairs? I went to my father's solicitor but he knew nothing and suggested that, as your uncle had handled the affairs of some people who did not live in Whitby, you might know if he knew the squire.'

With a thoughtful look he nodded. 'Yes, Mrs Fernley, my uncle did have dealings with Squire Hardy. It was in my early days with the firm so I was not involved personally. It is some years ago since Squire Hardy died but I do remember a good-looking woman, maybe in her thirties, coming to see my uncle at the time of the squire's son's tragic death in a fall from the cliff. Curiously enough her name was Mrs Fernley too.'

'She would have been my mother-in-law had she lived.' Olivia saw no reason not to be open with him; after all she needed to gain his confidence if she was to elicit further information from him.

A frown creased his brow but disappeared as he realised the probable answer to his unvoiced question. 'Ah, yes, she was drowned when the London packet was lost with no survivors, I believe.'

'Yes.' Olivia decided this was her opportunity to come to the point of her visit. 'I now have evidence that Ruth Fernley was the illegitimate daughter of Squire Hardy, and that made me wonder if she had any rights in his estate?'

Giles tightened his lips thoughtfully. 'An illegitimate child is generally precluded from any automatic rights unless the person making the will expressly indicates that offspring born out of wedlock should benefit. I suppose you are wondering if there was any such provision in Squire Hardy's will? I would have thought that if so my uncle would have acted on it.'

'Would you still have the original will?'

'It is possible.' He gave a small smile. 'We are a firm that tends to let documents gather dust. You would have to give me time to delve into our archives, though.'

'I would be grateful if you would.'

'I presume your evidence that the late Mrs Fernley was the illegitimate daughter of Squire Hardy affects the present ownership of the estate?'

Olivia suppressed a tremor of excitement.

'It could well do so.'

'If you will be good enough to return at ten o'clock the day after tomorrow I will be able to tell you if we have Squire Hardy's original will.'

'That is most kind of you and I am sorry that I have taken up your time.' She rose from her chair.

'Not at all, Mrs Fernley. It is always a pleasure to have such a charming person as a potential client.' He bowed and saw her to the door, stopping as he was about to open it. 'It might be as well if you brought with you what evidence you have relating to the late Mrs Fernley.'

Olivia left the office in Skinner Street in a state of high elation. She walked towards the top of the west cliff. By the time she reached it she had calmed her mind. She should not raise her expectations too high. Squire Hardy's will might no longer be in the offices of Bickerstaff and Whalley, and even if it were the squire may not have made any provision for his illegitimate child.

*

261

Over the next two days she found it hard not to betray her impatience but, not wishing to provoke her parents into asking awkward questions, she passed her time quietly at their home since her reason for visiting the town was ostensibly to spend time with them.

She drew deeply on her self-control as she walked to Skinner Street at the appointed time.

'Good morning, Mrs Fernley. A good time-keeper, I see.' Giles Bickerstaff glanced at the wall-clock and smiled cordially at her.

'I believe in punctuality, Mr Bickerstaff. Time is valuable.'

'Indeed. Then we shall get down to your request straight away. I know you will be anxious to discover if I have found anything.'

'Yes.'

'I have.' He picked up a bundle of papers and deeds from his desk. 'We had to dig deep to find these but my clerk is a young man who won't be beaten. He has a highly retentive memory and remembered seeing something a year or two back when he was looking for some other papers.' Giles selected a number of sheets of foolscap and put them to one side. 'Those are irrelevant to the matter you raised, but these,' he patted the second pile, 'definitely are not. I took them home last night and made a thorough study of them.' He paused and drew breath, seeing that she was watching him with anxious curiosity. 'I don't know whether you are aware that Squire Hardy had a son, Jonathan? When the squire died the estate went to Jonathan. He left no heirs but interestingly there was a will made out by him benefitting any child of Mrs Fernley.'

This was a new twist to Olivia. So Kit should have inherited in any case! Her hopes were racing but were suddenly pulled up and shattered when she heard Giles say, 'But that will was rescinded by a second one made the day afterwards. It was in an envelope marked "To be opened in the case of my violent death". Apparently my uncle must have judged Jonathan's fall from the cliff to be so for the envelope was open and annotated in my uncle's writing, "Opened by me on ..." with the date. The will in that envelope cancelled the first made by Jonathan and left the estate and his monies to distant cousins on his mother's side by the name of Chilton-Brookes.'

Olivia's heart sank, seeing her dream of becoming mistress of Cropton Hall shattered once more. The piece of paper she possessed would not support a claim against Jonathan's expressly nominated heirs. Rebecca's testimony was worthless.

'That seemed the final conclusion but there were still some papers I hadn't read and as I had them with me I thought I may as well do so.' Giles's voice penetrated her disappointment. 'Squire Hardy's will and its attachments made interesting reading. He had altered it from time to time. There were alterations and additions to smaller bequests but in them all the bulk of his estate and monies went to his son Jonathan. However, there was a signed attachment to the last draft. This stated that if there should be any illegitimate children traceable to him, with sufficient proof of parentage, they should take their share of the estate along with his son. In other words the estate should be shared equally between his legitimate and illegitimate offspring. My uncle had written a note on this attachment to the effect that he had been unable to trace any and that, knowing Squire Hardy as he did, he believed there weren't any. So naturally the estate went to Jonathan and, as I have shown, on his violent death passed to the Chilton-Brookes.'

'What would be the position if it could be proved now that there was in fact an illegitimate child?'

'Which is what you say you can do?'

'Yes.'

'You have this proof with you?'

Olivia opened her handbag and withdrew an envelope. She passed it to Giles who laid it on his desk. 'I'll look at that in a moment. There is one other thing I must make

263

clear to you. If, as you told me, your mother-in-law is the illegitimate daughter of Squire Hardy then the estate would go to her. On her death it would normally pass to her husband.'

Olivia was shaken by this news and cursed herself for overlooking this possibility. Then she heard him continue.

'Or that was my belief until I read a codicil which had been made and signed by Squire Hardy. This stated that if there had been any illegitimate issue, the estate should continue to be passed on to their children so that there would always be Hardy blood at Cropton. That precluded it ever going to a spouse and therefore possibly passing out of Hardy control. Rather complicated,' he gave a little smile, 'but we do get wills even more complex than this.'

Olivia's heart had soared again. 'This means the estate should have gone to Squire Hardy's daughter Ruth, and on her death to her son Kit, my husband.'

'That would indeed seem to be the case provided what is in this envelope,' he tapped the envelope Olivia had given him, 'is proof that your mother-in-law was Squire Hardy's illegitimate daughter.' He opened the envelope, extracted the sheet of paper carefully and unfolded it.

He read it and then reread it, assessing every word with care. The signatures and date came under close scrutiny. Finally he looked up. 'Tell me why and how you came into possession of this?'

Olivia told him that she'd wanted to investigate Kit's mother's background because he had been unable to find out very much from his family. She explained how she had found Ruth's mother.

'So now, after what I have explained to you, you believe your husband to be the rightful owner of the Cropton Estate?'

'Yes.'

'Well, let us examine the facts carefully.' The attorney went through everything again, step by step. 'My uncle genuinely believed there were no illegitimate children so the

264

Chilton-Brookes were installed and established in Cropton Hall.'

'Yes.'

'Now we come to the piece of paper with which you have presented me. It seems genuine enough to pass careful scrutiny. Wisely you had witnesses, two of whom I do not know, and two of them reputable attorneys. Their reputations are sound. There can be no grounds for disputing that the signature is genuine and therefore the statement is true.'

'And my husband should by right have inherited Cropton Hall?'

'It would seem so. Everything will have to be verified, of course. Would you like me to do that?'

'If you would. What will it mean?'

'I will need to go through everything again with another solicitor so that there can be no evidence of misdemeanour.' He started to gather up the papers.

'I would like to keep the piece that is signed by Rebecca Cornforth,' said Olivia.

He hesitated.

'I really do need it,' she pressed.

'Very well.' His voice showed his reluctance. 'But I must point out that it is important evidence and I will need it again. If anything happened to it ...' He left the implication unspoken.

Olivia gave a wry smile. 'I am well aware of that. I assure you nothing will happen to it!'

'The Chilton-Brookes will have to be informed, naturally. I have no doubt that they will take it very hard – after all, they will be losing a big estate and considerable wealth. Would you like me to break the news to them?'

'No, I shall spare you the unpleasant task. I know them so I will do it.'

'May I suggest that if your husband can ease the trauma of their loss in some way it might be advisable. Could eliminate any desire to contest the issue on their part.'

'I will consider what should be done for them. My

husband is on a whaling voyage and I would rather have all this cleared up before his return.'

Giles nodded his understanding. 'He'll receive a big surprise. What a fortunate man to have a wife such as yourself, Mrs Fernley.'

'Your mother should be back in Whitby, don't you think you ought to visit her?' Aunt Betsy put the suggestion to Ailsa one morning at the breakfast table.

She agreed with a little reluctance in her voice.

Betsy smiled. 'I know it will be hard to leave him, love, but I think you ought to go. You can come back soon.'

'Very well. I'll see if Olivia would like to accompany me. Maybe she'd like to visit her mother and father.'

'A splendid idea,' agreed Betsy. 'You go to see her and then we can make arrangements.'

'We haven't seen much of each other recently,' commented Ailsa after greetings had been exchanged between the two girls when she called at Howdale Manor.

'I'm sorry about that,' replied Olivia. 'I've been busy looking after things while Kit is away and had some business to see to in Hull so I was there for a few days. But I suppose you have been seeing a lot of George?'

'Yes, I have. Oh, Olivia, I'm so in love with him! I'm wishing the time away so that Father will be back and I can tell him and Mother of our plans. And it will be so exciting living here with you and Kit so close to us . . . I am looking forward to it! I love it here, and to think I'll be sharing my life with George on a beautiful estate. I'm so lucky, Olivia.'

'You won't miss London?' Olivia kept the conversation ticking over and her outward demeanour unruffled despite the fact that, before long, Ailsa was in for a shock. She regretted what this would do to her. Although the desire for revenge on George had been tempered she knew that revealing Kit's right to the Cropton Estate to him would give her satisfaction.

'Not for one moment. I love the country.' Ailsa was feverish with excitement. 'I hope you'll be my matron of honour?'

'Of course.'

'But not a word to anyone about it yet.'

'Your secret is safe with me.'

And not the only one Olivia nursed in her bosom.

'I'm going to Whitby for a few days. Mother should be back from Shetland by now. If you are thinking of paying your parents a visit, why not come with me?'

Olivia's nimble mind immediately saw the opportunity Ailsa's absence would present. She could confront George and have the whole matter of the estate settled while Ailsa was away and before Kit returned.

'That's a nice thought but I do have a lot to see to. I've just visited Whitby, and I do want Kit to realise that I am interested in his estate.'

'I think he'll realise that well enough from the purchases you have made.'

'There are other things to see to. I have to consult Jeremy about the release of fishing rights on the new stretch of river I acquired, and I must decide what to do about the tumble-down cottage. So I really can't spare the time.'

'A pity. It would have been good to have had your company.'

'Won't Aunt Betsy be going with you?'

'She didn't say so but I might be able to persuade her.'

'When will you go?'

'Nothing has been decided yet, but I think it might be in a week's time.'

'When you know, tell me and I'll arrange for Jack to drive you to Whitby.'

'That's most kind. It's so good to have you as a friend.'

'How long will you be away?'

'I don't know. It will depend on Mother.'

A week later Jack drove Ailsa and Betsy into Whitby and saw

them safely to Jenny Thoresby's before he made arrangements for his own overnight stay at the White Horse in Church Street.

Greetings were enthusiastic but a mother's instinct told Beth that her daughter was not as effusive as she might have been. She seemed well in herself, was bright and seemed genuinely pleased to see Beth, but there was something which struck her mother as different about her. Ailsa denied that she was out of sorts, so when the opportunity arose Beth mentioned her observations to Betsy.

She gave a knowing smile as she said, 'Your daughter's in love.'

'I guessed as much. Who is it?'

'George Chilton-Brookes.'

'I thought it might be when she was so keen to come to you rather than go with me to Shetland.'

'I can tell you she anticipates returning with me.'

'Well, she isn't going to like it when I tell her we are going to London.'

'She certainly won't!'

'It might be for the best. It will be a test of how much she thinks of him and he of her.'

'She will be very upset if she can't return to Cropton, believe me.'

'Then I'm going to ask you to come to London with us.'

Betsy hesitated, looked doubtful about the suggestion. 'Do you think this is a good idea?'

'She'll not have you to go to at Cropton and will therefore take more readily to the idea of London. We'll be back in time for David's and Kit's return. By then Ailsa will really know if she is in love.'

'I think she knows that already,' replied Betsy. 'But if that is what you'd like me to do then I'll come.'

'Thank you.' Beth gave her a hug. 'I know that's what David would want.'

Betsy returned the affectionate hug. 'Besides, it will give me an opportunity to see London.'

'Then that is settled. I'll make arrangements sometime tomorrow for our passage next week.'

'You'd better break the news to Ailsa first.'

The girl was in good spirits later that afternoon when she returned to Aunt Jenny's after visiting her daughter Anne. She had enjoyed their chat and seeing the activity around the ships tied up at the quays, but her good humour was dealt a blow when her mother announced, 'We are returning to London for a few weeks.'

'Why, Mother? I thought we were staying here until Father returned.'

'I think I should go and see that Dominic is all right.'

'Of course he will be. Mrs Kenyon will look after him well,' replied Ailsa a little sharply, as if she hadn't patience with her mother's concern.

'I know, but it's the first time Dominic has been on his own. I think I should be there for a little while. So I'm arranging our passage for next week.'

'Must I come? Can't I return to Cropton with Aunt Betsy?'

'She is coming with us.'

Ailsa's lips tightened. She felt cornered and frustrated, finally shrugging her shoulders in resignation. 'I suppose I'll have to come then,' she muttered.

'We'll be back before the whaleships return.'

Ailsa knew there was no more to say. She went to her room and quickly penned a letter. When she had finished it she read it over. Satisfied, she sealed it in an envelope, addressed it and, grabbing her shawl and bonnet, left the house. She hurried along Church Street to the White Horse and made enquiries for Jack Hall, waiting impatiently until he was found.

'Thank goodness you weren't out.' Her relief was unmistakable. 'Please deliver this letter to Mr George at the Hall as soon as you return to Cropton.'

'Certainly, miss. It will be delivered tomorrow.'

'Thank you, Jack.'

*

It was mid-afternoon when Jack left the letter at Cropton Hall and evening when George saw it lying on a table in the hall on his return from Pickering. He took it to his room, slit it open and read:

My love,
It is with an aching heart that I write to tell you that I have to return to London with Mother. Aunt Betsy is coming too so I do not have her as an excuse to come back to Cropton, and to you, my love. Please bear our parting with fortitude as I shall. I was going to write that maybe our love will grow stronger for the parting but that would not be true. My love for you cannot grow any stronger than it is. It is all powerful and consumes me every moment of every day.

I long to see you again, to feel your arms around me and your lips on mine. Until that day be patient, my love.

We will be back for the return of the whaleships. Then you can speak to my father and I trust and pray that shortly after that we will be united forever.

My love is ever yours,
Ailsa

George sat for a few moments, almost overwhelmed by the thought of not seeing Ailsa for some time. He rose from his chair slowly and crossed to the window, looking out across lawns and fields to the fringes of the moors.

'I love you, Ailsa,' he whispered. 'One day you will share all this with me and we will walk this land and feel the wind blow free, binding our hearts for eternity. Hurry back, my love.'

*

Olivia took the piece of paper she had guarded so carefully from the drawer of her dressing table and sat contemplating it. Just a few words and a scrawled signature but they meant so much. A gross injustice would be put right. Kit would inherit his rightful due and she at last would become the lady of Cropton Hall, the role she was destined for all along. She allowed herself a smile of satisfaction. After replacing the paper she closed the drawer but sat on unseeingly, her mind occupied with her course of action. The more she thought about it the more she realised she must get her timing right. George must be off the estate before Kit returned, and preferably by the time Ailsa and Aunt Betsy resumed residence in the cottage. She must find out when that was likely to be. They had been gone a week and could return at any time.

'Jack, when you took Miss Betsy and her niece to Whitby, did they say when they were likely to return?' she enquired.

'No, ma'am. But Miss Ailsa gave me a letter to deliver to Mr George Chilton-Brookes. He might know.'

'Thanks, Jack. Saddle me a horse for one o'clock.'

It was a pleasant afternoon and as Olivia rode across the Cropton Estate she imagined herself in the company of Kit, viewing this land when it was theirs.

George rose from a chair on the terrace when he saw his visitor approaching. 'Good day to you, Olivia. If it's me you have come to see you are lucky. I was just about to go riding.'

'Then let us ride together, unless you have business to attend to?'

'There was nothing specific. I was just doing my regular check on various parts of the estate. I will be pleased of your company. Won't be a moment, my horse will be ready.'

They rode away at a gentle pace, both relaxed in the saddle.

Olivia dwelt on the thought that this was what it would have been like if George had not told her that someone else had won his affection. Then she would never have looked into Kit's mother's past and never have uncovered Kit's right to the Cropton Estate. So many futures turned on that single momentous decision made by George, and he did not even know it – yet.

'You've seen quite a lot of Ailsa since she came to her

aunt's – I believe Jack delivered a letter from her to you. I'm not prying, but I wondered if she indicated when she and her aunt would be returning to Cropton?'

'Apparently when she got to Whitby her mother informed her they were returning to London for a while, and Miss Betsy Fernley has gone with them.'

'Then they might be gone for a while?'

'Possibly. Ailsa said they would be back for the return of the whaleships.'

'And that will be in about two months' time.'

Not wanting to make her enquiries too noticeable Olivia changed the subject. 'How's Redwings?' she asked.

'Very well.' George smiled. 'I'll always be grateful to you for recognising his potential. That was a good day.' He smiled at the memory.

'It was,' she agreed.

George halted his horse and Olivia stopped beside him. He looked her in the eye. 'I hope you have no regrets about what happened between us?'

'Of course not. It was one of those things. I thought you loved me but then you met someone else for whom you found a stronger love.'

'You will always have a special place in my heart as I hope I have in yours?'

'Could it be otherwise? We came close. I could have loved you, George, and we would have made an impressive master and mistress of the Hall.'

'Was that where your affections truly lay?' he laughed, little knowing how near the truth he was. 'I trust none of this affects your love for Kit? I know he loves you very much.'

'And I him.' Their eyes locked for a brief moment. Then Olivia called, 'Race you!'

She urged her horse forward and turf flew as hooves gouged at the earth.

Reaching the Hall after an exhilarating ride, George invited Olivia to have some tea. As it was served his mother made an appearance.

'I am delighted to see you, my dear. We haven't seen much of you lately.'

'I have been busy with Kit being away.'

'Isn't it lonely for you?'

'I don't mind. There are people in the house.'

'Do come over any time you feel in need of company.'

'That is most kind of you.'

'And please excuse my husband's absence. He is unwell again.'

'I'm so sorry. I hope he will soon recover.'

As she rode home Olivia almost regretted that she would soon upset the lives of these kindly people but then she pulled herself up sharp. Kit should have what was his by right, and with his inheritance would come the reflected glory of her own role as mistress of a prominent house and estate. Olivia could hardly wait.

A month before the estimated time of arrival of the whale-ships in Whitby, Olivia sent James to Cropton Hall with a letter addressed to George requesting him to call on her the following day at two o'clock on a matter of some importance.

Curiosity brought him to Howdale Manor on the stroke of two. He was shown straight to the drawing-room by the maid as instructed by Olivia.

When she turned from the window where she had been standing awaiting his arrival, George saw that her face was grave.

'Is there something wrong?' he asked. 'Can I help?'

A reply was not immediately forthcoming. Olivia had rehearsed this moment over and over again, trying to deduce the best way to break the information to him, but everything had paled beside the direct approach.

'Sit down, George. I'm afraid you are not going to like what I have to say.'

He sat down, feeling unaccountably disturbed at finding her so serious. Olivia remained standing. It seemed to give her an additional authority, warning him that what she was about to say should not be taken lightly. She shocked him from the first words.

'I have proof that you and your parents have no right to the Cropton Estate and should not be living there.'

George was speechless in amazement. Had he heard correctly? 'What on earth are you talking about?'

'Precisely what I said. The Cropton Estate is not rightfully yours.'

'Don't talk nonsense! That's ridiculous.' With that challenge hostility entered the proceedings, heightened all the more because he had come here as a friend and now found that status undermined.

'I'm afraid I'm not,' Olivia countered.

'I think you are.'

'You came into the property as a very distant relation of Squire Hardy on his wife's side?'

'Correct. Though distant we were his relatives and his will left the estate to his nearest . . .'

'. . . real or illegitimate heirs,' she finished for him, emphasising 'illegitimate'.

'He had no one else. His son was killed in a fall from the cliffs near Whitby,' George began, then his eyes widened at what she was implying. 'You mean, there is someone else? He had another child?'

'Yes.'

'I don't believe you.' The words came automatically.

'I wouldn't have asked you here if I couldn't substantiate what I am saying. I have proof that there was another child.'

'Who?'

'A daughter called Ruth.'

'Where is she? Have you seen her?'

'She is dead.'

'If that is so, what is this all about? Why drag it up now? If she is dead it makes no difference to our position.'

'Ah, but it does. You see, Ruth had a child.'

'And that child is alive?'

274

'Yes, though a child no longer.'

'You can verify all this?'

'Would I be telling you if I couldn't?'

'Prove it!' he challenged. 'If Ruth is dead, how do you know who her child is? And how do you know this Ruth was Squire Hardy's illegitimate child?'

'I have met her mother.'

'What? Where?' George was astounded, the ground being cut away beneath his feet with every word she spoke, this woman he'd considered a friend, and once as more than that.

'In Hull.'

'Then I insist on seeing her for myself.'

'You can't, she's dead.'

'How very convenient,' he sneered.

'She was at death's door when I saw her and died that same night.'

'So where's your proof?'

'There.' Olivia flourished a piece of paper triumphantly. 'A statement made by her that Ruth was her daughter by Squire Hardy, signed and witnessed as you will see by Jeremy Halstead, a Hull attorney, and two other witnesses. Nothing could be more legal and binding than that.'

George took the piece of paper, read it and examined the signatures carefully. This looked genuine. His heart weighed heavy at the thought. A steely light came into his eyes. He would fight this, for his parents' sake. They would be devastated if they had to surrender their fortune and return to the shabby lifestyle they had thought to leave behind them forever. It could kill them. Certainly his father who was not in good health. He handed the paper back to Olivia. 'What do you intend to do?'

'See that the rightful owner gets what is his.' Her voice was full of cold determination.

'You know him?'

'I'm married to him.'

'I beg your pardon?'

'I'm married to him.' Olivia deliberately stressed her words this time.

'Kit . . . he is Ruth's son, Squire Hardy's grandson?'

'Yes. Kit's father, David Fernley, married Ruth Harwood, the Squire's illegitimate daughter.'

'Does Kit know this?'

'He knows his mother's name but that is all. He does not know that she was the daughter of the Squire. I only found that out through contacting her mother. Kit had expressed a desire to know more about his mother, something his family were reluctant to enlarge upon, so I decided to find out about her while he was away. I never expected this but now I know the truth, I . . .'

George curled his lip in derision.

'You want to exact your pound of flesh?'

He had always distrusted the easy way in which she seemed to have shrugged off his rejection of her. Now he saw how right he had been.

'If you had married me none of this would have happened!'

'But I didn't love you, Olivia,' he said gently.

'You did until you found someone else.'

'So that was your surmise? Oh, I won't say I couldn't have fallen in love with you, but now I'm very glad I didn't. I see it all now. That day I told you I'd found someone else you screamed that I loved you. Never once did you say you loved me. It wasn't me you wanted, not really, it was what would become mine – the Cropton Estate. You coveted the role of mistress there. You had to settle for Kit instead.'

'The man I really love,' she broke in. 'And I have done since I first saw him.'

George frowned in disbelief. 'Yet you were willing to sacrifice that love in order to become my wife so you could lord it among the gentry.' His disgust was plain and a part of Olivia cringed before it. But she did not give him the satisfaction of revealing that.

276

'And now, as it turns out, I shall have both.' The triumph in her voice was unmistakable.

George clenched his fists as he stood up. 'What about us?'

She shrugged her shoulders and stared coolly back at him.

'What about you?'

'Have you nothing to offer us in recompense?'

She remembered Giles's advice, but after the way George had openly scorned her she was damned if she'd pay him off.

'You are not entitled to a penny,' she said.

'But it will kill my mother and father.'

'Don't be so dramatic, George.'

'I'm not. You'll be condemning us to a life of poverty. The shock of returning to that after the life we've known here will be too much for them.'

'So be it.'

'Olivia, I beg you, consider this very carefully. The consequences will be on your head. You will have to live with your conscience.'

She ignored the inference. 'I want you out of the Hall before Kit returns,' she instructed coldly.

'Then God help you when he finds out what you have done to his friends!' Without another word George swung on his heel and hurried from the house.

Chapter Twenty-One

Excitement mounted in Ailsa when she caught her first glimpse of Whitby Abbey high on the cliffs. A new life would begin for her here. Soon she would be with George again and this time they would announce to their families that they wished to spend the rest of their lives together. The voyage from London had been smooth and she hoped the rest of her life at Cropton Hall would be the same.

'Will you be going straight home, Aunt?' she asked, hoping she sounded casual about it.

'Goodness me, no,' replied Betsy. 'I must be here to greet Kit after his first whaling voyage. The return of the whaleships is something special, and more so for the Fernleys on this occasion.' She gave a knowing smile. 'Just a little while longer and you'll be with George,' she added in a whisper.

Ailsa blushed and glanced sharply at her aunt. 'You've guessed?'

'I did when you were with me at Cropton.'

'And Mother?'

'She knows the signs of a woman in love.'

'She's said nothing.'

'She realised you were waiting for the right time to tell her and respected your wish.'

'I want to tell her and Father together.'

'Then you shall, so far better for you to wait in Whitby until he returns. It shouldn't be long now.'

The excitement of arriving in port was lost on Ailsa who had her thoughts on George, fervently wishing she was watching the arrival of the *Mary Jane* from the Arctic so that the announcement could be made and their future together secured.

Once they were ashore and their luggage handed to three young boys eager to carry it and make a penny or two, they made their way to Jenny's. Amid the effusive exchange of greetings Jenny said to Ailsa, 'There's a letter on the hall table for you. It was delivered by hand a few days ago.'

Curious, she retrieved the letter and, recognising George's writing, took it to her room. She dropped her bonnet and shawl on a chair, sat on the bed and slit the envelope open. Eagerly she drew out a sheet of paper and read:

My Dearest Ailsa,

It is with a heavy heart that I write this letter to tell you we have lost everything. My parents and I have been forced to leave Cropton Hall and give up all we thought was ours and would have been mine upon which to build a life with you. I cannot inflict my new circumstances, which verge upon poverty, on you. I beg you therefore to try and forget me and find happiness elsewhere in a marriage befitting your upbringing and gentle nature.

In due course you will, no doubt, hear of the events that have brought this evil fortune upon us. I do not wish to write about them here. Believe me, the loss has been painful for me and my parents, but even more painful is the thought of losing you and that you will be hurt by this letter.

Forget me, Ailsa. I cannot give you the life you are used to and deserve.

Love,

George

She stared disbelievingly at the words. They couldn't be true! But there they were, staring coldly back from the paper, imprinting themselves on her mind. The hateful words swam before her as her eyes filled with tears.

'Oh, no.' Her exclamation was drawn out in disbelief. Her life seemed to drain away. Though she read the words again to verify she had not been mistaken she was hardly aware of them through the tears that flowed. With them came the hammer blow of pain. She clutched the letter to her, collapsed on her pillow and sobbed.

What had happened? Why was George no longer at Cropton? Why couldn't he write about it? What was he hiding from her?

'Oh, George,' she cried out to herself, 'don't you know how much I love you? Wherever you are, whatever the circumstances, I would be happy just being with you. Where are you?' She uncreased the letter and cast her eyes anxiously over it again. Had she missed something? But there was no indication of where he had gone. 'Oh, George, why didn't you tell me where you are?'

The sobbing subsided but her misery remained.

With a knock on the door her mother came in, saying, 'Ailsa, there's a cup of ...' Her voice faded and her expression changed to one of deep concern. 'What's the matter?' Beth was across the floor quickly and hugging her daughter to her. She saw the empty envelope and the piece of paper still clutched in Ailsa's hand. 'Is it that letter?'

She nodded weakly and held it out so her mother could take it.

Still with one arm round her daughter, Beth read it. 'Oh, my love, I'm so sorry. What is it all about?'

'I don't know, Mother. I wish he'd told me.' Her voice choked. 'I wish I knew where he is.'

'You love him so much?'

'With all my heart.'

Beth glanced at the letter again. 'There's love for you in his words. Something bad has happened and he thinks to spare you the pain of association with him. If you wish, we will try and find him.'

'Oh, Mother, do you think we can?'

The cry of desperation tore at Beth's heart. 'We'll do our best but I must wait for your father, he will know what to do for the best. The *Mary Jane* shouldn't be long now.'

Ailsa wanted to cry out that she couldn't wait but she trusted her mother's understanding and wisdom and nodded as she fought down her tears.

'Now wipe your eyes and come downstairs.'

'I can't face the others.'

'You will have to sometime. Better sooner than later. It will be easier now. Aunt Betsy and Jenny will understand and keep this to themselves.'

'Whaleship! Whaleship!' The cry started on the top of the east cliff and swept through the town as if borne on a wind determined that everyone should know. Joiners left their saws, jetworkers laid down the pieces they were carving, clerks dropped their pens and closed their books, housewives threw down their cloths. Almost everywhere work stopped. Young and old alike hurried from their houses, their places of work or turned from their idle chatter to hurry to the staithes, piers and cliff tops. This was a special time. A whaleship had been sighted. There could be more. Whitby had to welcome them home from the hazards of the Arctic, had to know if her menfolk were safe, needed to see if there was bone at the masthead, a sign that the catch had been good and the ship was full for that meant prosperity for the town and a winter when there would be less want.

'Ailsa, did you hear?' Beth shouted from the bottom of the stairs.

'Yes, Ma.' Excitement drove out the despondency and impatience of the last five days. The ship might be the *Mary Jane*. Her father might be home. He might be able to find George. She grabbed her bonnet and shawl and raced down the stairs.

Beth had gone back into the front room where Jenny and Betsy were putting on their coats. Though the day was fine and sunny the wind could always chill on the cliff top. She hoped it was David's ship and that his homecoming would drive away the misery that stalked her daughter and bring back the sparkle to her eyes.

They left the house and were swept along by the crowds flowing down Church Street towards the Church Stairs, the hundred and ninety-nine steps that led to the parish church on the cliff top. They climbed them as fast as they could. Breathing heavily from the exertion, they hurried through the graveyard and found a place among the folk gathering on the cliff edge. Eyes strained to try to identify the ship.

'Is it the *Mary Jane*?' asked Beth of Jenny. 'Your eyes are used to this.'

'They are not as good as they used to be,' she lamented. Nevertheless she was the first to make an identification. 'The *Mary Jane*!' she announced, relief in her voice. She had recognised the set of a ship dear to her heart, her mind travelling back over the years to a time when she had stood here waiting to embrace her beloved Adam and the other man who had held a special place in her heart and was coming home to his own wife. How she wished Adam had been sharing the deck with David today. But she had lost him to the sea and even after all this time she missed him, especially when the whaleships returned to Whitby. She wiped a tear from her eyes. She had to be joyous for the sake of the people with her.

'There's bone at the head!' The shout went rapturously up from the crowd, and swelled even more when another two ships with bone hoisted high were sighted.

The *Mary Jane* slid gracefully between the two piers, her captain in total control. Sails were furled, ropes were thrown out and taken by the boats waiting to tow her to her berth beyond the bridge. Sailors crowded the rail and hung from the ratlines. Cheers of welcome and shouts of joy were audible across Whitby's river.

'There they are!' cried Beth, seeing father and son standing on the port side near the bow.

Jenny slipped the red shawl from her shoulders and waved it. There were more tears in her eyes when she saw David make the same special response as he had done so long ago. It was many years since she had waved a red shawl for a whaleman's return. The years fell away and she was young again. After a few moments in the past, she started. 'Let's get to the quay,' she said. 'We just have time to get there to see the *Mary Jane* tie up.'

They pushed out of the crowd and hurried across the churchyard, down the steps and along Church Street. By the time they reached the quay on the east bank of the river, ropes were being thrown out and wound round capstans to secure the ship against the quayside. Wives, some with a child in arms, others with children at their skirts, sweethearts, mothers and fathers were among those on the quay to greet the returning sailors, home after five months facing the hazards of the Arctic.

The gangway was run out and first ashore were David and Kit. In a moment David was in Beth's arms and Betsy was hugging Kit. Jenny stood apart with her memories.

'I missed you so, David.' Beth felt warm and safe again in his arms.

'And I you,' he returned. He held her gently and away from him and looked deep into her eyes with a love that had weathered the vicissitudes life had thrown at them. 'You are as beautiful as the first day I saw you.' He kissed her long and hard then turned to Ailsa and the others as Kit hugged his stepmother.

'Olivia not here?' he asked, his eyes searching the crowd for her.

'No,' replied Beth. 'I expect she wants her welcome to be at your own home, just the two of you.'

'Then I'm off.' He sprinted away, calling over his shoulder, 'See you all later.'

'Hasn't he still work to do on board?' asked Jenny, smiling at his sudden departure.

'No. Captain Timms said he was free as soon as we

docked.' replied David, a twitch of amusement at his lips. 'Sentimentalist. Probably regards Kit as a newlywed still.'

'Are you free too?' asked Beth.

'I'm one of the owners. The Captain let me off duty too, he's a sensible man.'

'Good,' said Beth and linked her arm with his as they started from the quay. She manoeuvred their position so that they were behind the other three. 'Did all go well?' she asked. 'Did Kit measure up?'

'Yes. The crew were a little rough on him at the start but as soon as they saw he was willing to do his full share of work alongside them and wanted no special privileges as my son, they took to him. He's had his eyes opened. It will have done him good. He's seen tragedy as well as success.'

'Tragedy?' Beth showed concern.

'Yes. A young man from Hull left his ship in Shetland, wanting to serve on a whaleship. He'd heard tales of the magic of the Arctic and wanted to see for himself. He died there saving a Whitby man.'

David seemed reluctant to say more, his jaw set firm.

'I'm so sorry. It will be hard for his relatives.' Compassion came into Beth's tone, for she knew how heart-rending such a loss could be to a family.

David shook his head, sadness in his eyes. 'No family will miss him. He had no relatives. He was completely alone but he will be remembered by all our crew.' He paused, then asked in a brighter voice, 'Has everything been all right here?'

'Ailsa and I went to London. I felt I should see how Dominic was.'

'And was he all right?'

'Yes. He's doing well and has taken to the responsibility you gave him. You should be proud of him.'

'Good. What about Ailsa? She doesn't look as well as when I left.'

'She's worried, and that worries me.' Beth told him

about their daughter. 'It's preying on her mind and that isn't good. We must do something about it.'

David's expression was grave. He had a deep affinity with his daughter, would do anything to ease her pain. But concern was mixed with admiration too at the way she had hidden it from him so as not to spoil his special moment of reunion with her mother.

'I was so anxious for your return, David. I didn't know what to do or where to start looking for George.'

He patted her hand comfortingly. 'We'll find him, love. Don't worry. In the meantime we must give Ailsa all the support we can.' He looked thoughtful as they walked a few steps in silence. 'The only person I can think of with any connection to the Chilton-Brookes is Olivia's father. He bought timber from them and with an eye to the future may have been in contact with the new owners or else have heard something from Olivia. A pity she wasn't here today, we could have asked her. I'll go and see Coulson as soon as I've seen you to Jenny's.'

David returned from that visit none the wiser. Edward was surprised to learn that the Chilton-Brookes had left Cropton Hall. He had had no word from them, nor from the new owners. He also informed David that he had not seen his daughter for about two months and on that occasion she had not mentioned any changes at Cropton Hall.

'What can we do?' cried a disappointed Ailsa when her father broke this news.

'If Kit hadn't left in such a hurry he would have known about this and could have made enquiries on reaching Cropton. Olivia, being at Howdale Manor, must have heard. But take heart, he will soon be back, he must be to be discharged from the ship and collect his pay.'

Kit raced off the quay and along Church Street oblivious to the curious glances his haste attracted. Reaching the White Horse, he expressed his desire to hire a horse immediately. The landlord informed his stableman to lose no time in getting the best horse available ready. He drew Kit a tankard of ale, cut him a slice of bread and a hunk of cheese. Kit thanked him and arranged to return the horse as soon as possible.

Once he had climbed the hill out of Whitby he put his mount into a fast gallop across the moors. He had known the pain of parting from the bride he loved far too soon after marriage. Now he would know the ecstasy of reunion. Though he loved the moors and the countryside hereabouts he had no eyes for them today. They made no impression on a mind full of thoughts of Olivia.

The sound of hooves pounding the turf brought Olivia to the window of her bedroom. One glance was sufficient. She would know Kit's command of a horse anywhere. A thrill surged through her. He was home! Even now she could sense his arms around her, feel the power of his body close to hers. She turned and ran from the room, raced down the stairs and flung open the front door. She ran on to the stone terrace and stopped at the top of the steps. Excitement gripped her. Kit raised an arm and she waved back. Then he was there, hauling his horse to a halt, jumping from the saddle, taking the steps two at a time to sweep her into his arms. His lips met hers in a kiss that claimed all the kisses he had missed in the five months of their parting. Not a word was spoken as he took her by the hand, led her inside and up the stairs.

'Kit, I've something to tell you.' Olivia spoke the words tentatively as she lay in his arms, her yearning for him over these past months only partially satisfied.

'Not yet, love.'

She heard the husky longing in his voice and knew like her he wanted more. She slid her body over his and kissed him hard and long before they satisfied themselves again and sated the appetite that had overwhelmed them on their reunion.

'You bought the land I told you about?' he asked, antici-pating her news as he stroked her arm with gentle fingers.

'I did more.'

'More?' His voice sharpened with curiosity.

'I bought some more land along with a stretch of water on the Seven.'

Kit twisted over to look down at her as she let her hair spill across the pillow. He saw the satisfaction in her eyes. 'Gurney's?'

'Yes. Jack thought it would be a useful addition so I consulted Jeremy and he helped to conclude the sale as he did with the land at the auction. And with his help I've already let some of the fishing rights.'

Kit smiled in admiration. 'You're a wonder. You've certainly taken to this life while I have been away. I was worried in case you missed Whitby and its social round.'

She laughed. 'That was becoming a bore. But then I met you and my life became exciting.' As she was speaking her arms came around his neck and she pulled him to her and kissed him in a way that was full of promise. 'There's more to tell,' she said as their lips reluctantly parted.

'More?'

'Yes. Get up, get dressed and then I'll show you and tell you all about it.'

'Tell me now?'

'No, you must see first.' To show that she meant it, she turned the bedclothes back and slid from under them. 'Come on,' she said over her shoulder as she stood up.

Half an hour later they were riding away from Howdale Manor with Olivia still refusing to tell him where they were going.

'Cropton Hall?' Kit was intrigued when they turned through the gates. 'What have you to show me here?'

'You'll see in a few minutes.'

'Does George know we are coming? He can't. He could-n't possibly know I was back.' He caught Olivia's smile, one which signalled her pleasure in knowing something he did not. He realised he would get no more information until she was ready to impart it.

They rode on until the Hall came into view. Olivia pulled her horse to a halt. Kit stopped alongside her. Puzzled, he looked around but saw nothing untoward. The landscape was as he remembered it. Why should it change during his absence?

He looked at his wife. 'What is this all about? Why are we here?'

'It's yours, Kit.'

'Mine? What on earth do you mean?'

She was smiling, delighted at surprising him. 'Exactly that. It is yours, my love. The Hall and all its land.'

He stared at her wide-eyed. He just could not believe what she was saying. She was making a joke, but why? 'You can't have bought it,' he said doubtfully. 'You couldn't. We haven't that sort of money.' His eyes widened in alarm. 'You haven't borrowed?'

A surge of relief passed through him when she said, 'No.' Her lips twitched. 'But it is yours.'

'How can it be?'

'Let's go in to the house.'

'We can't just walk in,' he protested. Her insistence that it was his had not sunk in. He still believed she was presenting some sort of conundrum.

'Come with me and find out.' She set her horse forward.

Puzzled, he stared after her for a moment and then drew alongside her to ride in silence until they reached the Hall.

There was no sign of anyone as they walked on to the terrace. Olivia tugged the bellpull and a few moments later Kit recognised the maid who opened the door.

'Hello, Jane,' said Olivia.

'Good day, ma'am. Good day, sir. I hope you had a successful voyage?'

'I did, thank you.' Though Kit's words were delivered pleasantly they did not disguise his bewilderment as he followed Olivia inside.

'Jane, will you ask Mrs Dawson to make us some tea and bring it to the drawing-room?'

'Yes, ma'am.' She hurried away.

'What's going on?' asked Kit, his voice tetchy. This charade was too prolonged. 'You're acting as if we own the place.'

'I told you, you do.' They reached the drawing-room. 'Now sit down and I'll tell you everything.'

He sat down in an armchair and she took one opposite him.

'You remember how you told me you knew practically nothing about your mother? How much do you really know?'

He looked at her strangely. 'What is this to do with her?'

'Just tell me,' Olivia insisted firmly.

'Very little. She was a Cropton girl Father married when he went to Whitby to sail on the whaleships. They did well, then Mother was drowned when the London packet went down. I was only a baby at the time. As Father was going to be at sea a lot he decided it was best for me to go to Grandmother and Grandfather at their farm in Cropton. They, Aunt Betsy and Uncle John brought me up. I was old enough to take over the farm when Uncle John died, he having taken it on after Granddad died.'

'The family never said any more about your mother?'

'No. By the time I was grown up Father had gone to London and married Lydia who died having Dominic. Father, trying to get over the loss, went on a whaling voyage from London to the Pacific. He saved some American sailors and put in to New Bedford in America. There he found Beth whom he had first met in Shetland. So, you see, Mother had become a distant memory to everyone then.'

'Did you ever make any enquiries about her family in Cropton?'

'I did once through Jeremy but all he found out was that they had left the area shortly after Mother went to Whitby. No one really remembered them. They'd lived in a dilapidated cottage way out of Cropton. They were a rough lot, I gathered, so that may be why my family did not want to talk about my mother's relations. Nobody knew where they had gone so I didn't bother asking any more.'

The tea had arrived and Olivia poured, telling Kit to help himself to scones and jam.

As the door closed behind Jane, he said, 'Where's George and his mother and father?'

'They've gone. Be patient and all will be clear.' She took a sip of her tea and said, 'Knowing you were interested in your mother, I decided to try and find out something about her and have the information as a surprise for you when you got back. But I found out a lot more than I expected.'

'This homecoming is presenting a lot of surprises.' Kit raised an eyebrow and waited for her to go on.

'I enlisted Jeremy's help. We were getting nowhere except that Jeremy discovered the name of her family was Cornforth. Then we had a stroke of luck. While he was negotiating for the land by the river Mr Gurney offered him some woodland to the north of your land and told him that there was a tumble-down cottage there. He thought it could be repaired and used by an employee whom you might appoint to look after the woodland. Jeremy quite casually asked him who had lived there. Mr Gurney said a no-good family named Cornforth.'

'What?' Kit almost shot out of his chair in surprise. 'Did he know anything about them?'

'A little. The wife's name was Rebecca, and he said that apart from the children by her husband there was another child, a girl, but he couldn't remember her name. With this slender information Jeremy made further enquiries and, to cut a long story short, they led him to one of the Cornforth boys in Scarborough. He told Jeremy that his mother, Rebecca, had had a daughter by another man before she married Cornforth. When they left Cropton she had gone to Hull but that was many, many years ago. Whether she was still there or even alive he did not know. Jeremy saw we

290

could not leave the matter there and said he would see if an attorney friend in Hull had any suggestions, so we went there.'

'You went with him?'

'Yes. Something told me we were getting close to learning the truth about your mother. Even though the prospect of finding Rebecca Cornforth seemed remote, I had this feeling. It was just as well I did go.'

'Why was that?'

'We found her. She was an old woman, as you might expect, and we immediately realised that she was dying. When she saw me a strange thing happened – she thought I was Ruth. I didn't disillusion her because it obviously brought her some happiness and I saw my opportunity to clear up the mystery. I asked who Ruth's father was.'

'What? Who was he?'

'Squire Hardy.'

'I don't believe it,' Kit gasped though he had no reason to disbelieve his wife.

'It's true. I realised you would want positive proof so I had Jeremy draw up a statement, got your grandmother to sign it and had it witnessed by Jeremy, his attorney friend and the two people who had led us to Rebecca. I made enquiries and found out that Squire Hardy's will stated his assets were to be divided equally between all his offspring, whether legitimate or illegitimate. His son, Jonathan, his only legitimate child, was killed in a fall from the cliffs at Whitby and so . . .' Olivia let the implication hang in the air as she saw the realisation of what she was about to say dawn on her husband.

'The estate and everything with it should have gone to my mother, and on her death . . .'

'To you,' she finished.

He was thunderstruck. This was almost too much to take in. Everything took on an air of unreality. He was sitting in a room in Cropton Hall drinking tea with his wife as if he had every right to be there. But wasn't that what she had just revealed to him? He was here by right. He met her smiling gaze and saw triumph there as if she had achieved a long-cherished desire. Was it the desire to find out about his mother or did it go further than that? Was there the triumph of having gained Cropton Hall?

Kit frowned as he realised she had kept something from him.

'What has happened to George and his parents?'

'The evidence I was able to present was irrefutable. They had to leave the house and estate. Oh, George didn't go down without a fight. He saw Squire Hardy's solicitors in Whitby. In spite of their confirmation of the justice of your claim he had another solicitor look for loopholes. There were none, as I was certain there would not be. Cropton Estate is definitely yours.'

Kit seemed less than delighted by her assurance, however.

'I know they counted themselves very lucky in getting this inheritance and that they came with very little. Were they provided for when they left?'

Olivia shrugged her shoulders. 'I don't know.'

'But surely you did not let them go with no more than they came with? Could you not have helped them?'

'Why should I? They were really no concern of mine. It was their misfortune I happened to discover the truth, I did not set out to claim the estate from them. How could I? I did not know who your mother's father was. But when I did, was I expected to do nothing and deprive you of your rightful heritage?' She frowned. She did not like the expression of concern that was clouding his face. She'd expected joy and heartfelt thanks, not this downcast reaction. 'Kit, you always wanted a large estate. Isn't that what you expressed to me? Wasn't that the idea behind buying more land?'

'Yes, but it bothers me that we have achieved it this way, at the expense of a friend's welfare.'

'I would have offered them some compensation but . . .' She hesitated and, deciding not to reveal the truth in her confrontation with George added, '... thought it was up to you to do that.'

Kit nodded his approval then said thoughtfully, 'I wonder if Father knew, and if so why he kept the secret from me?' He paused, his face a picture of concentration as he battled to discover an answer. When none was forthcoming the determination in his next five words was more than evident. 'I mean to find out!'

Chapter Twenty-Two

In spite of a restless night troubled by a wild mixture of thoughts on the implications of his wife's discovery, Kit was up early, determined to ask his father for the truth about his first wife.

He had insisted on returning to Howdale Manor for the night, the home he knew as his own. Much to Olivia's chagrin he could not fully comprehend that Cropton Hall was really his. It did not seem right to be spending the night there.

Olivia woke to find him almost dressed. When he saw her sit up in bed he said, 'I don't know when I will be back. Soon, I hope, we have been apart long enough, but it depends how things work out.'

'I'm coming with you.' She was swiftly out of bed.

'I want to see Father on my own.'

'Oh, no! I started this quest and wish to give the reasons why. Your father will not hear it second hand from you but from my own tongue,' she insisted. The firmness in her voice and the determination in her eyes told him that she would brook no argument.

When he came downstairs Kit hurried straight to the stables, casting an anxious eye towards the sky on his way. He was thankful that it looked to be heralding a fine day. A wet ride to Whitby would have worsened his mood. He told Jack to have the horse and trap ready by the time he and Olivia had had some breakfast.

Few words were spoken during the meal and it was not until they were driving away from the Manor that he mentioned his misgivings. 'Olivia, I am troubled by the whole situation. I've no doubt you did what you did with every good intention but I wish you had waited until I had returned before you took any action on what you had discovered.'

'I did it for you,' she emphasised.

'I know, love, I'm not being critical but I have a feeling there must be a lot more to this than we know. My father must have held something back, for whatever reason, and that could affect our whole outlook about the inheritance.'

'It can't alter the fact that the Cropton Estate is rightfully yours,' she insisted.

'I agree. The evidence is strong, but I wish you had not been so hasty about turning George and his parents out. They've been uprooted from a life of luxury, one to which they had become accustomed. To return to what I expect are humble circumstances could devastate them. Mr Chilton-Brookes is not a well man, the upset could be fatal.'

'Oh, don't be so dramatic, Kit. They'll be all right.' Not wanting to have this angle pursued any further she added quickly, 'Don't do anything silly. Get the truth. Stand up for your rights. One of the biggest estates in this part of the country is ours and we don't want to lose it. There's no reason why we should. We have the evidence. We have your grandmother's signature witnessed by reliable people. And we have the authority of Giles Bickerstaff's verification of Squire Hardy's will.'

Kit said nothing but he was disturbed by her tone. He could not mistake her determination to keep the Cropton Estate. It was as if this had been her dream all along and she had seized the chance to grasp it. Yet it appeared that they had right on their side and if that was so why shouldn't they take it as their own?

Kit drove straight to the Angel, hoping that his father had not gone out. He was relieved when the landlord told him that as far as he knew Captain Fernley was still in his room.

David raised his eyebrows on seeing Kit and Olivia when he answered their knock. 'Hello. I didn't expect to see you back in Whitby so soon. Come in. I'm sorry, Beth and Ailsa aren't here. They've gone to see Jenny.'

'It's really you we want to see. We didn't know when you would be leaving for London and there is something important I need to ask you about,' Kit told him.

David raised his eyes heavenwards. 'Not another of my children in trouble?' He had concluded something was amiss even before he put that question for he had noted Kit's strained expression. Olivia seemed ill at ease too though he realised that she was trying to hide it behind a show of confidence.

'Another? Why, what's the matter here?' Kit queried.

'Your sister Ailsa.'

'What's wrong with her?' Concern had entered Kit's voice for he thought a lot about his sister.

'She's suffered a terrible blow – well, she sees it that way. I must say I was alarmed when I saw her on our return, she did not look at all well. You probably did not notice, you were so eager to be away to Cropton.'

'No, I didn't. What's caused this?'

'A broken heart.'

Olivia felt a chill grip her. What had George said to Ailsa? Had he just walked away? She'd known that love was awakening between them and had never expected him to abandon the girl.

'You'll remember that Ailsa went to stay with Aunt Betsy when your mother sailed with me to Shetland?' Kit nodded. 'Well, it seems that while we were away she fell in love with George Chilton-Brookes. She and Aunt Betsy came to Whitby to visit your mother a little while after her return. Your mother wanted to go to London to see

296

Dominic. Aunt Betsy was going with her so Ailsa had to go too, against her wishes I'm told, but there was no one at Cropton for her to go to. When they returned to Whitby, to be here for our arrival from the Arctic, there was a letter waiting for her from George. In it he said he could not marry her.'

'Why?'

'He said his family had had to leave Cropton Hall and that, because of his changed circumstances, he could not hold her to their marriage plans. The girl is broken-hearted. She cannot understand what has happened for him to make such a decision. He seemed to have everything. The future looked bright for him and Ailsa. She is distraught. To see her like this is taking its toll on her mother even in this short time. I'm worried, son.'

'Did George say in the letter where he is now?'

'No. If he had we would have followed him at once.'

'Have you made any attempts to find him?'

'If only we knew where to start. You see, we know little about the Chilton-Brookes. I was going to come to Cropton to see you. After all, you know him better than any of us. That's why your mother and Ailsa are at Jenny's, to see if they could stay there while I was away, so it's fortuitous you have come to Whitby.'

Kit shot Olivia a querying glance. Receiving a slight nod in return he knew she had anticipated his desire to disclose what he knew, and approved.

'I know why George left and wrote as he did.'

His father stared at Kit in astonishment. 'You? How could you?'

'For the moment just take it that I do, and so does Olivia, but first I want some explanations from you.'

David frowned, looking puzzled. 'What can I explain that has any relevance to this?'

'You can tell me about my mother.'

'You know about her.' David was instantly on the defensive. 'What has this to do with Ailsa's loss anyway?' He tensed with irritation. His daughter's welfare was paramount at this moment. Kit and Olivia obviously knew something but now his son was sidetracking.

'Not everything, only what you chose to tell me,' Kit persisted.

'What more did you want?'

'The whole truth.'

'You've had it.'

Kit shook his head. 'I don't think so. Growing up, I saw so little of you, with you being away in Whitby and London. Whenever you visited Cropton, which was infrequently, and a curious young boy asked about his mother, you always fobbed him off. "She was drowned when you were a baby," you would say. "Grandma and Aunt Betsy have been more like mothers to you." Which told me nothing. Who was she? Where did she come from? What features of my mother's have I inherited? Am I more her descendant than I am yours?'

David looked grave, his face drawn, as if this reminder of the past was most unwelcome. His son had obviously found out more than he was letting on at the moment. David had to know what that was before he offered further explanations. 'You know something, don't you? Tell me what you have learned and how.' He sighed. 'I thought the past was buried forever.'

'I'm sorry, Father, if this is causing you pain. I don't want that but, believe me, my mother's past is linked with Ailsa's present trouble.'

'I don't see how it can be, but tell me what you know and I'll add to it what I can.'

Olivia read the resignation in his voice as a sign that he was prepared to talk. 'Mr Fernley, maybe I had better offer some explanation as I am responsible for what has happened. But let me say first that I do not regret what I have done. I think a grave injustice has been put right.'

David's look was searching. What did this girl know? How was she involved in something that only remotely

298

concerned her as Kit's wife? And what injustice was she referring to? 'Well?' His voice was sharp.

Olivia took a deep breath.

'Early in our relationship Kit and I talked about our families. It helped us to understand each other better. But there was one aspect of Kit's life which remained shrouded in mystery, and that was the character and background of his mother. He wished he knew more about her. I thought if he did it might make our relationship even stronger, so when you both went off to the Arctic I thought I would see what I could find out. Of course I had no idea if I would find out anything at all. I need not, at this stage, take you through every step I followed, that can come later. Sufficient to say now that I enlisted the aid of Jeremy Halstead, an attorney friend of Kit's, who practises out of Pickering. You may remember him from our wedding?' Posing the question gave her a pause in which she could draw breath and remarshal her thoughts to proceed.

David nodded. 'I do. A likeable young man.'

'He discovered that Kit's grandmother on his mother's side was still alive.'

'What?' David was staggered by the news that they had found a woman he had held in contempt for not resisting the brutality her husband had meted out to her illegitimate daughter.

'Yes, Rebecca Cornforth was still alive and living in Hull.'

The words penetrated his numbed mind. 'Was?' His question was tentative.

'Yes, the poor woman died shortly after I saw her.'

'You visited her?'

'Yes, I had to. She was the only person who could tell me something about her daughter, Kit's mother. Rebecca was dying in extreme poverty. Her circumstances horrified me. I left money with the two people who had led us to her and they promised to do what they could for her. I know they did, for after her death I had word from the Hull attorney whose help Jeremy enlisted.'

David looked relieved. This alleviated some of the guilt he was beginning to feel at not telling his son more about his mother, facts which might have led him to find the wretched old woman and do more to lift her out of the poverty into which she had sunk. He waited for Olivia to go on.

'Mrs Cornforth, in her parlous state, thought I was her daughter. She told me the truth about Ruth's birth. In order to have the evidence for Kit I got her to sign a statement to that effect. It was witnessed by Jeremy, his attorney friend and the two people who took us to Mrs Cornforth. I have it here.' She drew a sheet of paper from her bag and passed it to David.

He unfolded it and gave it a quick glance, confident that Olivia was telling the truth.

'I realised that Kit was the rightful heir to the Cropton Estate.'

David looked astonished.

'How could he be?'

'He was a nearer relation than the Chilton-Brookes.'

'But was he, in the eyes of the law? Did Squire Hardy's will provide for any illegitimate offspring? I think we will have to find that out.'

'I already have,' said Olivia. The cold certainty in her voice was unmistakable.

David was surprised. He had not realised Kit's wife was such a determined young woman. He found himself in the role of a judge. Did he detect a covetous pleasure in what she had found out? Had an insatiable desire for wealth and position led her to her discovery? Or had it always been there, dormant, just waiting for a spark to ignite it into devouring flame? His mind linked Olivia with Ruth and the way ambition had engulfed her and ruined the life and love they had once shared. He hoped against hope she would not ruin his son's life by such an obsession. 'What more have you to tell me?' he asked sharply.

300

'I found out who'd handled Squire Hardy's affairs – Giles Bickerstaff's uncle. Giles looked into them for me.' She went on to reveal what she had learned. 'So, you see, there is no doubt that Kit is the rightful owner of the Cropton Estate,' she concluded with a triumphant note in her voice.

David was silent, overwhelmed by this news. His mind was in turmoil. If this was true he would have to recognise Kit's rights, even though they could be at the expense of his daughter's happiness and the destitution of the young man she loved. Could his son be so cold-hearted as to let that happen? He shuddered. Would the thing he had tried to guard against all those years ago still come out? Would Kit's mother exert her baleful influence from beyond the grave? How much of her avarice and driving ambition had Kit inherited?

His thoughts were cut short by his son. 'I think there is more to my mother's story. And I think it would be as well if you told me everything now.'

David hesitated but only for an instant. He saw that there was no way he could escape from telling his son the truth. Had he in fact been wrong to have kept it from him all these years?

'Very well. As Olivia discovered, your mother was the illegitimate daughter of Rebecca Cornforth by Squire Hardy of Cropton Hall – Hardy never acknowledged her. I learned later that he paid the Cornforths to keep the secret. Your mother's stepfather was a brute. I befriended her out of pity at first and she and I fell in love. When I left for Whitby and the whaleships my mother took her in. Later Ruth came to Whitby and we married. I had ambitions to progress in the whaling trade. Your mother approved and gave me all her support. What I didn't realise for some time was that she had ambitions beyond mine and would do anything to further them. She had a ruthless streak in her that I trace back to Squire Hardy, who was a hard and unrelenting man. She got over-ambitious, used men not only to further those ambitions but for her personal gratification. She brought the firm we had built up almost to ruin and was leaving me with one of her lovers on the London packet when it was wrecked on Saltwick Nab. I witnessed it from the cliff top and made an attempt to save anyone I could but the task was hopeless. No one survived, or at least that's what everyone thought. Your mother's body was never found.'

David paused. Kit and Olivia did not speak or they realised the pause came as if one episode in Ruth's story had been completed but there was another one to come.

'Your mother had by some miracle survived, but for her own ends she kept that a secret. It was after my near-ruination that the Thoresbys, who had always been dear friends since my first coming to Whitby, offered an amalgamation of our businesses that saved me. But we had not reckoned on your mother. A man who worked for the Fernley-Thoresby firm was infatuated by her. It was he who saved her from the sea. She used him to seek revenge on me and the Thoresbys whom she had come to hate for no good reason but what she'd conjured up in her own depraved imagination. She thought Jenny and I were lovers which was not true. We were close, very dear friends.' He looked wistful. 'Maybe there was a time when I contemplated marriage to her – Adam had been lost in the Arctic, your mother had been drowned, or so I thought – but Jenny's love for Adam was too strong.'

His expression grew more resolute and his voice strengthened. 'Once again your mother worked to ruin the firm and almost did so but finally she and her lover left for New Bedford in America. I was in London, having left Whitby and joined Hartley Shipping. From there I made a voyage to the Pacific where I rescued some sailors who had survived their vessel's sinking. They were at death's door. Among them was the man Francis Chambers who had betrayed our firm at your mother's instigation. He had

302

served his purpose as far as she was concerned and she'd tried to get rid of him because he knew too much and she wanted him out of the way while she married a bigger fish. I got the whole sordid story from him before he died, and I learned that your mother might still be in New Bedford which was where I was taking the survivor sailors. It was there that I found Ruth. She was still legally married to me and I told her to get ready to leave for England with me in a week. I left her and that was the last I saw of her. I had not gone far when the house went up in flames. What caused it I do not know. I raced back but there was nothing I could do. Your mother and her housekeeper perished.'

For a moment a taut silence filled the room.

'Why have you not told me this before?' demanded Kit.

'I, your grandparents and Aunt Betsy thought it best that you did not know the full story.'

'But why?' Anger and pleading were mixed in Kit's voice. He felt Olivia's hand slip comfortingly into his.

Innocently she had opened a door, and once she saw that that door could lead to her achieving her ambition of becoming the mistress of Cropton Hall she had prised it open even further. She had not thought there could be evil consequences to her action, blinded by her determination to achieve her own desires, no matter what the cost to other people. She began to feel misgivings now but cast them from her mind. She had right on her side. She must not let anything dissuade her of that.

'You were a babe in arms. There was no need for you ever to know your mother's sordid past,' David maintained stoutly. 'If I'd told you, I feared the knowledge might influence your thinking and view of life. I thought it might prey on your mind and that any Hardy traits you had inherited from your mother might overpower the Fernley influence.'

Kit's face darkened. 'You didn't think I would be strong

303

enough to face the truth? You didn't trust me. And that hurts.'

'I did it for the best,' David sought to reassure his son.

Kit shrugged his shoulders. 'Be that as it may. Indirectly you deprived me of my rightful inheritance.'

'I did not know of Squire Hardy's will. How could I? I had no reason to think he would leave anything to an illegitimate child. He must have had a conscience after all.'

'Well, the estate is rightly mine. We've every proof. No one can dispute it. All these years I've watched George run an estate which should have been mine while I had to strive for every step forward.'

'And in striving, didn't you find more satisfaction from gaining what you wanted? Haven't you known happiness? Would you have had that if you had been given the land as a young lad?'

But Kit was furious at the deception that had been practised on him. He wanted no platitudes from his father. 'It should have been mine.'

'It is now, love.' Though Olivia's remark was intended to soothe Kit it also held a steely reminder to his father.

'Aye, that may be right,' replied David testily, 'but at what price?' His eyes were cold as he met Olivia's defiant gaze. 'Don't you destroy my son as his mother nearly destroyed me. Ambition is commendable, used rightly. Unwisely it can devastate not only you but others too. Believe me, I know.'

'Yes, Mr Fernley. I know to what you are referring, but you see unlike your wife, I do not take lovers. My only concern is for Kit, whom I love very much and who should have what is his by right.'

David's lips set in a tight line at this reminder of the past. How dare she throw that at him? His face clouded with anger. 'You are to be commended for your love and concern for my son. I hope that you will always feel those things – but in the right way. I'm just afraid that the wrong path is being taken now. But it is not too late to change it. Ruthless ambition, and this applies to you both, can destroy not only the love you share now but close friendships and the happiness of other people.'

'You've already indicated that in your account of Mother's history but that won't happen in our case,' said Kit with conviction.

'I hope you're right, son. But hasn't it already started?'

Kit frowned and gave an irritable shake of his head. 'What do you mean? Our love for each other is solid. Getting the Cropton Estate will not affect that.'

'But what about others? Haven't you already influenced the lives of the Chilton-Brookes for the worse? Shouldn't you have given them more consideration? I didn't know George until I came to your wedding but he must have been a special friend for you to choose him as best man. What have you done to him? And what of Ailsa? Would you destroy her happiness?'

Olivia stiffened. Mr Fernley was using every means to thwart their good fortune.

'Kit, I think we should leave. Mr Fernley, the Cropton Estate is Kit's. Nothing you say will alter that or change our mind about it.'

David looked concerned. 'Olivia, I liked you when I first met you. Thought my son was lucky to have found a suitable girl.'

'And now you've changed your mind?'

He shook his head. 'No, I still think you are that, but I don't want you to destroy yourself or Kit on the horns of ambition.'

She gave a half smile. 'I won't, Mr Fernley. I promise. Come, Kit.'

Without a word to his father he turned to follow her.

David was in despair. He could feel the blighted past crowding in on him, threatening all the happiness he had worked so hard to attain. If Kit and his wife walked away now the die would be cast. He must do something. 'Kit.'

His voice was soft but penetrating. It brought his son and Olivia to a halt. They turned to see the imploring expression on his face. 'Remember John Fawkes.'

Chapter Twenty-Three

Olivia glanced from David to Kit. She saw his face blanch though he met his father's gaze without faltering. He nodded his head then left the inn, still holding her hand. Neither of them spoke for a while. Outside Kit drew a deep breath as if it would help to drive out the unpleasantness of the scene with his father.

Olivia knew he was troubled so merely said, 'We'll stay with my parents tonight.'

He frowned as if battling with his thoughts.

'Should we go there now?' she asked tentatively.

'I would like to walk first,' he replied, his voice expressionless. Still holding her hand, he turned in the direction of Pier Road.

She was thankful he still wanted her with him at this critical time and did not want to be alone. She felt a tightening in her chest at the thought of the different directions this situation could take and what she would do if he chose the path she did not want to follow.

She broached the subject obliquely for she felt sure that Mr Fernley's last remark must be significant. 'What did your father mean by "Remember John Fawkes"?'

Kit did not reply immediately. Olivia, deeming it wisest, respected his silence. He would tell her when he was ready. He seemed oblivious to the activity along the quayside and to the hustle and bustle around them, though he guided her with uncanny ability. It was only when they started out along the west pier and moved from the protection of the cliff that they were aware of the wind. It was neither strong nor gentle, but sufficient to make itself felt and with its touch Kit's mind cleared. She saw the expression on his face change as if he had grappled with his confused thoughts, sorted them out and reached a decision.

'John Fawkes served aboard the *Mary Jane*. He was from Hull, had left his ship in Shetland because he had an intense desire to experience the magic of the Arctic.' He paused.

'Did it come up to his expectations?' asked Olivia.

Kit's wistful smile was touched with sadness. 'Oh, yes. Captain Timms put in to Harstad, a small fishing community on the Norwegian coast, in order to put a sick man ashore. It was evening when we left and I will never forget the scene. The evening light was suffused with a white glow to the north, as if reflecting the shimmering ice that we were yet to see. The breeze was soft. It caressed us, and I thought of your fingers touching my cheeks.'

Olivia felt love for him surge at this remark but did not interrupt his flow of words, merely pressed his fingers in response.

'The silence held a magical quality. It penetrated the creak of the timbers, the rub of the ropes, the crack of the sails and the swish of the sea. That silence held eternity. I was on deck with John, we'd struck up a special friendship. Maybe it was because we were both new to the whaleships and experiencing the Arctic for the first time. We certainly sensed the call of the north together that evening as we sailed out of Harstad. Not a word passed between us but we shared the same feelings, the same moments in time that will never be forgotten. Later John mentioned it and said he believed he had found his place on this earth. You see, Olivia, he had no one, no family, no relations whatsoever. He was all alone. At that moment he felt sure he would return to the Arctic time and again to feel the magic he had experienced that evening.' He paused.

Olivia saw sadness in his eyes intensify. Alarm shot through her. Was Kit regretting that he was not going back to the Arctic? Had it cast a spell on him which he too would be unable to resist? Was this what was troubling him?

'Will he be going back?' she asked cautiously.

Kit shook his head slowly. 'No. He had found the place he loved but sadly he was killed there while saving my life.'

For a moment the last four words did not penetrate her mind with any significance. Then they struck with searing force.

'Kit!' She swung round to face him, alarm twisting her features. 'I might have lost you!' Her eyes widened in fear. 'What happened?'

He gave a half smile. 'I'm here aren't I, love? I wasn't even hurt, apart from a soaking in the icy sea.' He stopped as if reluctant to go on.

'What happened to John?'

Kit drew a deep breath. 'I wasn't going to tell you any of this and swore my father to say nothing to you. He hasn't and I know he'll keep his word. We shared much on that voyage, came closer. I learned a great deal about him and my respect for him grew. I'm sorry about what happened just now but I'm sure he's as hurt as I am over our exchange of words.'

'But why did he mention John Fawkes?' Olivia pressed.

'To make me think. As I said, John saved my life. In a moment of danger he did not hesitate. We were flensing a whale – that is, stripping it of its blubber alongside the ship. John and I were standing on the creature intent on our job. Some tackle for hauling the strips of blubber on to the ship broke. It hit me and sent me spinning into the sea. A few moments in that icy water and you can be dead. John leaped into the sea after me without any thought for himself and grabbed me. I was unconscious. He hauled me over to two men who had jumped down on to the whale. They pulled me out of the water and passed me up to willing hands on the deck. It was all over in a matter of moments. Just as they turned to help John the swell swept him away. There was nothing anyone could do. Boats were launched but he was never found.' Kit's voice choked.

'Oh, Kit, I'm so sorry.' There was genuine compassion in Olivia's voice.

He grimaced. 'I lost a good friend, a man who'd wanted nothing more from life than he already had.'

The silence was broken by Olivia. 'What has this got to do with us and Cropton Hall?'

'John saved a life, put someone else's above his own. Should we destroy Ailsa's – and George's and his parents' too? What might we do to ourselves with their ruin on our conscience?'

'Aren't you being over-scrupulous?' she asked harshly, seeing where this was leading.

'Am I?'

'Of course you are. People suffer setbacks but combat them and get on with life. If they are strong they'll survive.'

'Will they? How do we know? John's action saved my life. What about our actions? Ailsa is already devastated by this, you heard my father say so.'

'She'll find someone else.'

'Will she? Won't she see what George has done as a sign of how much he loves her? He's willing to sacrifice his future with her so that she won't have to endure hardship. Might ours be destroyed by what we do now?'

'You are talking nonsense,' she snapped. 'You wanted to be a landowner and rival George. Well, now you've got what you want.'

'Rival him? I think not. We enjoyed a competitive friendship, it's true, but there was never anything stronger to it. I will miss George's presence in my life more than I can say.'

'Won't I make up for that?' she asked, her voice husky, her eyes full of tempting promise. She had to combat the course she feared Kit might take.

310

'That's different.'

'I can give you all the excitement you'll need and together we can run the Cropton Estate and share the thrill of developing it as we want. Kit, right is right. Cropton is yours.' She saw he was still troubled by his father's parting words. 'Let's return there now. Things will look different when we are home.'

He hesitated to reply.

'Please,' she said. 'Let's go home.'

'All right.'

They left Whitby without any further contact with the family. It was not until they were crossing the moors that Kit said, 'I wish I had seen Ailsa before we left.'

'She'll be all right. She has the family around her. I'm sorry for her too but she'll soon get over this disappointment.'

Kit did not reply, wondering how much guilt he would feel if his sister did not rediscover happiness and he had made no effort to relieve her pain. His mind drifted to John Fawkes.

He drove the trap straight to Howdale Manor. It was on the tip of Olivia's tongue to chastise him for not going to Cropton Hall but, sensing that he still had not come to terms with the situation, she thought it wiser to make no comment. Throughout the evening she tried to keep the conversation light but there was little response from her husband.

She tried to divert him when they went to bed but there was little passion in his loving.

'Kit, you've got to accept things as they are,' she said irritably as she lay back on her pillow. 'We've everything we want: land, a fine house, position. You will be someone in the community at last.'

'I know,' he replied 'But I don't want things handed to me that easily. I don't want to take on George's role, it doesn't feel right somehow.'

'Is that all you think to my efforts?' She rolled over and stared down at him, trying to will him to see the situation as she wanted him to. Annoyance flashed in her eyes.

311

'Of course not. You did well in buying the land and the water rights on the river. They added to Howdale, the place I've built up. As for the Cropton Estate, I only wish gaining it wasn't at the expense of George and his parents, and I certainly wish Ailsa hadn't suffered.'

Olivia sank back on her pillow with a long sigh. 'Be careful you don't ruin everything,' she warned.

The following morning the subject was not mentioned during breakfast. She knew this meant that Kit had not reached a decision. When he had he would inform her of it. Only then would she voice her own opinion, depending on what course he had decided to take.

As he finished his final cup of tea and replaced his cup in its saucer, he said, 'I shall be out riding all morning.'

'Very well.' Olivia made no offer to accompany him. There had been no invitation from him and she recognised that as a sign that he wanted to work things out on his own.

Every night since the shock of the letter Ailsa had cried in the silence of her bed until her body ached and she fell into a fitful sleep. Last night had been no exception and now she woke reluctantly to the early-morning light spilling across Whitby's silent buildings. She faced another day of sympathetic platitudes from her family. She knew they meant well and that her mother and father were deeply concerned for her. Her father's attempts to find George had come to nought, however, for there was little chance of finding a lead in Whitby and from the tone of George's letter it seemed unlikely he would have told anyone in Cropton of his destination. Ailsa was desperate. There was only one person she wanted – George. He was the only one who could pull her out of the mire of desolation that threatened her life. Her tormented mind cried out to her to escape from the misery of inaction that was threatening to overwhelm her. She must do something. Waiting would not help. But what did she know of George other than the fact that he lived, or rather had lived, at Cropton Hall. Where was he now? Could the answer lie at Cropton?

She dressed quickly and was soon downstairs, informing a sleepy landlord to have a horse made ready as quickly as possible. Within ten minutes she was riding out of Whitby, having sworn the landlord and the stableman to say nothing to her parents about her departure until they missed her and started making enquiries.

Reaching the heights above the town, she put the horse into a gallop. She pulled her cloak tightly to her, unfastened her bonnet and let the wind whisk it away. Her hair streamed out behind her. The freedom only emphasised the confines of her dilemma. She must find George! If she failed, being alive would mean nothing, a mere existence tortured by thoughts of what might have been, of a love lost. Life could not be lived with a broken heart.

She urged the horse faster as her raging mind convinced her the answer lay at Cropton Hall. The hoofbeats pounded the words 'George' and 'Cropton' into her mind with a regularity that became overpowering.

She was only jolted away from them when the Hall came in sight. She took charge of the horse's wild gallop and gradually slowed it until she approached the house at a walking pace.

Her eyes searched the building. The silence that enveloped it was heavy with no movement to break it. The implausibility of her venture sobered her. What could she hope to find here? George had gone. Would anyone here know anything of significance? She doubted it. He would keep his destination a secret, intending to spare her. But maybe he had let something slip in the presence of the staff ... so long as they remained here and had not been replaced by the new owners, whoever they were. Might they know? During the negotiations for the sale of the estate might George have had to impart his new address? She would clutch at any chance to find him. As she moved slowly forward the house seemed to mock her.

*

It was mid-morning when Kit returned to Howdale Manor. He purposely approached it from the front. It revived memories of the first time he had seen it and had sworn that some day he would purchase it and that it and its land would be the basis for expansion into a considerable estate. His efforts had been repaid, and further shrewd buying had given him great satisfaction. Because of this Howdale Manor meant a great deal to him. Now it would be swallowed up into the greater Cropton Estate, and the Manor and its significance would diminish. Did he want that?

He swung from the saddle in front of the house, walked slowly on to the terrace and sat down on one of the two chairs placed near the front door. He leaned his elbows on the arms of the chair and linked his fingers pensively in front of his lips. He never knew how long he sat there lost in his thoughts. Quietly spoken words interrupted him.

'Hello, love, I didn't know you were back.' Olivia's voice was soft and soothing. It stirred him and reminded him of the love they had sworn and celebrated in passion. It was precious. He did not want to lose it. And yet lose it he might if she heard what he felt certain she did not want to hear.

'Did you have a pleasant ride?' she went on as she sat down next to him.

'Yes. I viewed our estate.'

'Does that include the Cropton Estate? Did you view that too?'

'No.'

'Why not?'

'I wanted to decide how much Howdale meant to me.'

'And now it has the addition of the new estate to make it doubly meaningful.'

'I don't think the Cropton Estate will do that. It came too easily.'

'That's nonsense.' A note of irritation had crept into his wife's voice. 'It's a very negative attitude of mind.'

'And I'll always have a mind troubled by what happened

314

to George, his parents, and most of all to my beloved sister. Won't you?'

'Why should I? We have right on our side and that is all that matters.'

'Is it, when other people's lives are involved?'

'What do you propose to do then?' she sighed.

'Find George and come to some arrangement with him. I haven't worked out the details. Maybe bring him back to Cropton Hall, give him half the land. With that and the love I suspect he has for Ailsa and she for him, their future will be assured.'

'Kit!' gasped Olivia. 'You can't. You'll be giving away a fortune.' Her mind was reeling under the impact of his proposals. He had not indicated they were definite but if he carried them through she would never be the lady of Cropton Hall. She must purge this idea from his mind. Anger was not far from the surface but, realising that to expose it would only make matters worse, she quelled it.

'If I need to I will. Money, land, position – they're not everything in life.'

'And my love?'

'More precious to me than anything.'

'Then don't do this.'

'Would it destroy your love for me if I did?'

Olivia's lips tightened. 'How can I answer that? The situation hasn't arisen.'

Kit shrugged his shoulders, his acceptance that an answer to a theoretical question was no way to solve his problem. He had to find a way to keep her love and at the same time ease his conscience over George and Ailsa.

Olivia rose from her chair. 'Wait there until I come back.'

He looked questioningly at her but received no explanation as to what lay behind her words.

Ten minutes later she reappeared in her riding habit leading a horse she had ordered Jack to saddle for her while she changed.

315

'Where are you going?' Kit asked in surprise.

'More correctly, where are we going? Come, and you will see.'

Kit pushed himself from the chair, went to her horse and helped her into the saddle. Assured that she was comfortable, he swung on to his mount and matched the gentle trot she had adopted.

It soon became apparent where she was leading him. 'The Cropton Estate,' she said. 'I have every sympathy for George, his parents and Ailsa, but I want you to see what you would be losing if you take the drastic measures you are contemplating.'

Chapter Twenty-Four

Ailsa stopped her horse in front of the house. She sat in the saddle for a few moments, her mind dull, then slid from the saddle. She walked slowly up the steps on to the terrace, lingered there as her thoughts transported her to happier times spent with George. Their future had looked so bright with nothing to mar it. But now? That consideration jerked her back to the present. There was no room for sentimental recollections. She was here for a purpose, one she hoped would be fulfilled. She tugged the bellpull and waited nervously. Though she showed surprise when the door was opened by a familiar face she also experienced relief.

'Jane.'

'Why, it's Miss Fernley.'

'May I come in?'

'Certainly, miss.' Jane moved to one side, held the door wide and closed it after Ailsa had stepped inside.

A quick glance told her that, except for the absence of two pieces of furniture she remembered, nothing had changed. 'I believe the Chilton-Brookes have left?'

'Yes, miss.'

'Won't I be intruding on the new owners?'

Jane gave her a strange look. 'No, miss. They aren't here at the moment and I'm not sure when they will be coming, but I am certain they will raise no objection to your being here.'

Ailsa's surprise at this statement invoked the question, 'Who are they, Jane? Anyone I might know?'

Jane gave her an odd look. 'Miss, don't you know who they are?'

Puzzled by the maid's attitude, Ailsa shook her head. 'No, how could I?'

'Well, it's your brother and his wife.'

Bewildered, she stared disbelievingly at the maid. This couldn't be true! Jane must have got it all wrong. How could Kit possibly have purchased Cropton Hall? He had been on his whaling voyage when she had received the letter from George. Had he planned it with Olivia and left her to do the negotiating? And where had the money come from? Kit wouldn't have had it. From her father? Ailsa doubted that. The estate would cost an enormous sum. Thoughts of money revived her earlier suspicions of a mystery behind George's departure. If he had sold the estate he would not have written 'we have had to leave'. Nor would he have said, 'I cannot inflict my new circumstances upon you.' Both statements implied a devastating loss leading to a situation in which her happiness would be threatened. She felt her body weaken as if it had been dealt a physical blow. Her legs turned to water. Her face drained of colour.

'Are my brother and his wife living here?' she asked, her voice barely above a whisper.

'Not yet, miss.'

Ailsa nodded. Her eyes had lost their ability to focus, her mind to concentrate.

'Are you all right, miss?' Jane's face clouded with concern.

There was a pause that heightened her worry.

'I'll just go and sit down for a few minutes,' said Ailsa with a weak wave of her hand.

'Very well, miss. Ring if you want anything.' Jane headed towards the door that led to the domestic quarters.

Ailsa's steps were slow and heavy as she started to the

318

drawing-room. She stopped, turned and put the question feebly, as if she already knew what the answer would be, 'Do you know where Mr George is living now?'

'No, miss. Everything happened so quickly, he and his parents were gone almost before we realised it.'

Ailsa gave a nod and went on wearily. She slumped on to a chair, swamped by dejection. What had happened? Why had George had to leave in such a way that he could no longer offer her the life he thought she wanted? What role had Kit and Olivia played in this? Kit, her own brother, whom she thought so much of and whom she had felt sure reserved a special affection for her. And Olivia whom she had come to regard as a dear friend and with whom she had looked forward to sharing so much when she came to Cropton Hall as George's bride. Now all those hopes were dashed.

She felt betrayed but did not want to believe what Jane's disclosure meant. She tried to shut her mind to it but it would not be denied. It drummed and thundered in her head until its significance was overwhelming. George had left, unable to cope with whatever had been thrust upon him by people she had loved and admired. The shock of it all permeated her very soul. In her bewilderment she rose slowly from her chair. Unseeing, she wandered from the room and was drawn by impulse to the stairs. Each step was slow, her movement trance-like. She reached the landing, turned to the right and automatically went to the third door on the left. She turned the knob and the heavy oak door swung easily open on its large brass hinges. She moved slowly into the room. She knew nothing of the furniture or its layout but walked unerringly, each step taking her to the tall window at the south-west corner of the room. It was open wide and drew her to it. Below was the stone terrace.

Olivia pulled her horse to a halt on a small rise. Kit stopped alongside her.

'There! As far as you can see in every direction the land is yours,' she said with a triumphant note in her voice. 'Yours, Kit. Yours!'

'And something you dearly want,' he said, a touch of sadness in his voice. He looked at her hard. 'I'm right, aren't I?'

'And what is wrong with wanting what is good for us both?'

'Nothing. But it must not destroy us.'

'How can it?'

'I see troubling parallels in the life my parents led. My mother's ambition destroyed their love. I don't want ambition to destroy ours.'

'There were other circumstances in their lives, other men.'

'No doubt ambition led to those situations.' He looked earnestly at her. 'Our love is very precious, I'm not going to lose it.'

'Make no decisions until you have seen more.' She sent her horse forward before he could reply. She must prevent him from taking any rash step. The house was distant. She hoped, as it grew more distinct before them, he would begin to change his mind, especially when they walked through it together.

'There, Kit. There's our home.' She injected excitement in to her voice. 'Race you to it!'

Before he could react she was off, her laughter torn away by the wind.

He hesitated a few moments. Maybe she was right. Didn't he owe it to his mother to come here and so repay her for the suffering she had endured through the refusal of Squire Hardy to recognise his daughter? And didn't he owe Olivia for what she had done in discovering his rightful inheritance? But he wanted to do right by George and his parents, and he wanted most of all to obliterate the torment in Ailsa's mind. The only way he could do that was by finding George and dispelling his notion that he could not give Ailsa the life she deserved. Take the path he had determined and he could lose the thing he held dear: the love of the girl who rode like the wind ahead of him. Take another and he knew he could lose the respect and love of his family, especially Ailsa. There must be a way to satisfy everyone.

Olivia, her horse at a gallop, glanced over her shoulder. Kit was a considerable distance behind her but she was pleased to see he had put his spurs to his horse. She hoped the thrill of this ride across his land would help to drive away the drastic measures she feared he had in mind. She would use her charm, when they were in the house, to eliminate what was left of them.

Earth flew beneath cutting hooves. The house drew near. Even in the exuberance of the ride she admired it and thought what life here would be like. Her composure was jolted by the sight of a horse close to the terrace steps. Whose could it be? She slowed her mount as she neared the house. The unknown horse was sweating and was spattered with earth. It had been ridden hard. Why? By whom? Where was the rider?

Her gaze ran across the whole façade. At an open window on the first floor movement caught her eye. Someone stood near it. Who? And what were they doing? The figure turned. Ailsa! Olivia's surprise deepened. She'd thought the girl was in Whitby. Had she ridden from there this morning? Why ride the horse so hard?

She was about to call out and wave, but something in Ailsa's attitude warned her not to. Her sister-in-law stood trance-like close to the window. Ailsa must have seen her, yet there had been no sign of her having done so. Alarm gripped Olivia. She flung herself from the saddle, was on to the terrace and into the house almost before she realised what she was doing. Something drove her to get to that bedroom as quickly as possible. She was sure Ailsa intended to jump. She must stop her. She raced up the stairs and along the landing. Then caution asserted itself. Bursting in might startle Ailsa and provoke her into the final act. Olivia reached the door, gripped the knob, turned it firmly and pushed the door open smoothly. Ailsa had her back to her. She gave no sign that she was aware of Olivia's presence.

The sound of a galloping horse came through the open window. Tension heightened in Olivia. Kit! He was riding the horse hard. He must have seen Ailsa. She hoped he would not do anything to disturb his sister's hypnotic state. It could be fatal. She must move quickly. She glided across the room with soundless steps.

Ailsa gave a great sigh and leaned forward. Olivia reached out. Her fingers closed tight on Ailsa's shoulders, arresting the movement that had started. She tightened her grip and eased the girl away from the window. 'Don't!' Her voice was soft but firm.

Ailsa jerked at the intrusion. She tried to shake herself free of the hands that held her. Olivia twisted her so that they came face to face. Her sister-in-law struggled furiously but Olivia held firm.

Recognition came to Ailsa's eyes. 'You? You bitch! What did you do to get rid of George and destroy our lives? I may as well be dead, let me go!'

The hatred and anger made Olivia quail. 'Ailsa, jumping won't solve anything.'

'It will! It will!' she cried in desperation.

Olivia kept her grip on her. 'It won't. Didn't you think of what it would do to George?'

'He wouldn't know. He's gone – driven out by you. No one knows where he is so no one could tell him.'

'I can find him.' Olivia's words were sharp, each one driven home with conviction.

They had a sobering effect on Ailsa whose struggling stopped. There was disbelief in her query. 'You?'

'Yes.'

'You know where he is?' Her eyes widened hopefully.

'No, but I know someone who might do.' She saw some of the hope drain from Ailsa. 'Trust me,' she pressed. 'We'll go tomorrow.'

'Today! Please!'

'Too far today, but we'll start out early tomorrow.' Disappointment clouded Ailsa's face. 'I promise,' Olivia added and led her to the bed. As they sat down she'd taken the girl's hands in hers and looked into her eyes with all the sincerity she could muster. 'And I'll promise you something else. You remember saying how good it would be for you and me to be living near each other?' Ailsa nodded. 'Well, so we shall be.'

Ailsa looked mystified. 'But . . .?'

Olivia halted her. 'You and George will live here, in Cropton Hall as you'd both planned.'

'I don't know how you got this estate, but if it belongs to you and Kit, what will he say to what you have just promised me?'

'I know Kit's way of thinking and this is what he would want.'

'It certainly is.' They both turned on hearing the voice that came from the doorway. He came to sit beside them on the bed. He had seen Ailsa at the window and had raced to the room but as he'd neared it he had heard Olivia and knew that his sister was safe. He had stayed close to the door and listened. A surge of admiration and love for his wife almost overwhelmed him when he heard her promise regarding Cropton Hall. 'How we come to be here is a long story, Ailsa,' he went on as he put a comforting and reassuring arm around his sister's shoulders. 'You'll hear it all later. For now the most important thing is finding George. When we do that you and he will be married and live here and we'll come to some arrangement about the estate.' He looked at his wife. 'Where do we go tomorrow?'

'I remembered that at George's birthday party there were some friends of his mother and father who live near Beverley, Mr and Mrs Campion, their son and daughter, Archie and Sabina. Archie told me of their friendship when we were dancing. They befriended Mr and Mrs Chilton-Brookes when they lived in Hull, and Richard and Esther

323

never forgot their help and kindness and were generous to them when they came into this estate. I think George and his parents would make for Hull, the place they know best and I feel sure that in that case they would contact the Campions.'

'Then it's to Beverley we go tomorrow,' said Kit.

'And I'm coming with you,' cried Ailsa.

'I think it best if you stay here,' Kit suggested.

'But I want . . .'

'I know,' he cut in. The brotherly love in his voice could not be mistaken when he added, 'We do not know where our search will take us. You'd be better here.'

'Mrs Dawson and the rest of the staff will look after you. You'll have a chance to get to know them and Cropton Hall while we are away,' added Olivia. 'The beds are made up. Kit and I will stay here tonight and leave early in the morning.'

'You've had a traumatic time. The rest will do you good.'

The recent experiences exerted their pressure and weighed heavily on Ailsa. Tiredness sapped any resistance she might have put up and she accepted the wisdom of their suggestion.

'Do Mother and Father know you are here?' asked Kit.

She shook her head.

'You did not tell the landlord or the stableman of your destination?'

'No.'

'From the state of your horse, I thought not. It has every sign of having been ridden hard and to me that indicated a spur of the moment decision. I'll ride to Howdale and send Jack to Whitby to reassure our parents that all is well and you will return to Whitby in a few days time.'

While Kit was away Olivia acquainted Ailsa with the story of Cropton Hall and confessed to her part in it. 'I'm truly sorry for all the hurt I have caused and I hope you can forgive me.'

324

'Of course I can. Life is too short to bear grudges. I probably would have done the same myself if I had been in your shoes. Besides, we are sisters-in-law and are going to be near neighbours so we should not be enemies.' She came to Olivia and hugged her. 'And thank you for your generosity to George.'

When Kit returned Ailsa was resting. Olivia told him of what had taken place. They strolled on to the terrace.

'Where I first met you,' said Kit, his voice full of feeling. He turned her to him, looked deep into her eyes. 'I love you so very much.'

'And I you,' she whispered as their lips touched.

'Thank you for saving Ailsa. I was proud of what you did and what you said. And thank you for making the decision about the future of Cropton Hall. I know how much you wanted to come and live here. What made you change your mind?'

She gave a small wistful smile. 'Yes, I had my heart set, but with hindsight I was letting that blind me to the consequences. I'll not deny that when I entered that bedroom I was still determined to dissuade you from what I believed you would do. It was only when my hands were firmly on Ailsa's shoulders that I realised what I had done and that it meant I had saved a life. Your story about John Fawkes came vividly to me. He had saved your life but paid with his. Made the ultimate sacrifice. He was someone you would never forget and would always admire. I hadn't sacrificed anything. I would always be remembered as someone who had saved Ailsa but had been the cause of her near suicide. I had given nothing, sacrificed nothing, and unless I did people would be hurt, among them dear, dear friends and you, my love. I think you would have given way to my ambition to be lady of Cropton Hall. But I remembered what ambition had done to your mother and father. You thought more of Howdale Manor than you did of Cropton Hall because you had gained it by your own hard work. We'll take some of the Cropton land. It's only right that you should have something of your inheritance, only fair to your mother and grandmother. But we will be able to work together to make Howdale land even better. I never told you that after you had gone to the Arctic and I came to our home alone I viewed the buildings there, with an eye to developing them and enlarging the house before any question of Cropton Hall came up. Now that we are going to forsake the Hall we can think of that again.'

'Whatever you want, my love.'

'First we must find George and I must make my peace with him.'

Chapter Twenty-Five

Olivia and Kit had little trouble in finding the Campions when they reached Beverley, for the name was well known. But the next stage of their attempt to find George's whereabouts proved difficult. Mr and Mrs Campion who remembered both Olivia and Kit from George's birthday celebrations would not disclose his whereabouts. 'Admirable as your intentions may be and which you have taken care to emphasise, we are people who keep our promises. We made one to George to keep his whereabouts a secret. We feel bound by that promise.'

'But our intentions *are* honourable,' pleaded Olivia. 'We want to put things right with him.'

'That may be so, Mrs Fernley. George told us a little of what had happened but like the man he is he gave no details, mentioned no names, so for all we know there may be a special reason for his wanting to keep the place where he is living a secret.'

'The happiness of my sister is at stake,' pleaded Kit.

Mr Campion shrugged his shoulders and spread his hands in a gesture which said that he was sorry but there was nothing he could do about that. That was a personal matter for George and the lady concerned. He had no right to interfere in any way. His final 'I'm sorry', while being an apology for being unhelpful, was also a dismissal.

Olivia and Kit were gloomy as they returned to their horses. They were standing discussing their next move when they heard footsteps hurrying along the street.

'Miss Olivia!' The call was quiet but attention-catching.

'Archie!'

'Oh, I'm so glad I caught you,' he gasped, trying to catch his breath. 'I need to speak with you.' He acknowledged Kit with a nod, looked back at Olivia and gave a wistful smile. 'I often recall our dance at George's party. You danced so exquisitely.' He blushed as he paid the compliment.

'Nice of you to remember but you had to lead.' She added quickly, so that if he had any thoughts towards her they would be quelled, 'I'm not longer Miss, Archie.'

'Oh ... er ... yes ... naturally. Congratulations.' He stuck out his hand which Kit took and shook firmly. Archie looked back at Olivia. 'I overheard what passed between you and Mother and Father. They are sticklers for keeping promises even though they may agree with your good intentions. But I'm not bound by them. I made no promise to George and I know where he is.'

'You do?' said Olivia and Kit together, both their voices charged with excitement.

'I would not give you this information if I had not judged your intentions were good. George told me of his love for your sister so I'm happy to play a part in a romantic situation.' He gave a little chuckle of satisfaction.

'We and George will be ever grateful for this,' pressed Olivia.

Within a few minutes Olivia and Kit were riding away from Archie who touched his cheek where Olivia had kissed him.

The knock on the door of a terraced house on the outskirts of Hull was answered by George who stared aghast when he saw who stood on the step.

'You! What the devil are you two doing here? You're not

wanted.' He started to shut the door but found it impeded by Kit's foot.

'Hear us out, George,' rapped Kit firmly.

'I've nothing I want to hear from either of you, least of all her.' He gave Olivia a scathing look.

'If you won't listen for yourself, listen for Ailsa,' returned Olivia, ignoring his barb. She saw his eyes soften so pressed on with her persuasion. 'She is broken-hearted and wants only you.'

'I can't give her the life she deserves, thanks to you. And I won't take her into the poverty that faces me. I love her too much for that.'

'It's you she loves, George, not what you can give her. I understand your attitude, but you will be able to give her the life you want to and I hope when you hear what we have to say you will forgive me for what I did. Ailsa has.'

George hesitated a moment. What had been going on since he had left Cropton? 'I think you had better come in.'

Within half an hour he had been told the facts and the reasons for Olivia's actions. He pondered a few moments more when she had finished then he came to her and kissed her on the cheek.

She felt in the touch of his lips and the way he hugged her that he held no malice towards her.

He turned to Kit and held out his hand. A new bond was forged between two friends who would soon be more closely related. 'I'll not take Cropton Hall and some land as a charity,' he said.

Kit shook his head. 'It won't be that. It will be our wedding present to you and Ailsa.'

As the three riders approached Cropton Hall they saw a figure come on to the terrace.

'Ailsa!' George put his horse into a gallop.

Olivia drew rein and Kit stopped beside her. They watched for a few moments then Olivia started to turn her horse. 'We won't be wanted there,' she said with a knowing smile. 'I

329

think you and I should go home, to Howdale Manor.'

'Then you can describe your ideas to make the house and buildings as grand as Cropton.'

'Grand or not, it will be special to us.'